THE LORE OF

PROMETHEUS

GRAHAM
AUSTIN-KING

The Lore of Prometheus

At the going down of the sun and in the morning,
We shall remember them.
—*For the Fallen*, Robert Binyon

PART
I

CHAPTER ONE

"Eight," the blackjack dealer announced as he laid out the card onto the baize next to the eight of hearts I already had.

It was an easy decision. Sixteen wasn't likely to get me anywhere; not with the dealer already showing a seven.

I sighed as I pushed the chips forward. "Split them."

The card gave a crisp snap as the dealer flipped it. "Seven."

Shit.

Eight gave me a fifteen. A hard hand.

The odds of me improving it were about fifty-fifty, probably slightly less. A quick glance across the table gave me the rest of the bad news. A two and a three were showing, and there had already been more than enough low cards passed through since the last shuffle to ruin the odds. The chances of getting anything useful were about the same as the dealer not having a ten to go along with his seven, and if he didn't then he'd probably bust. If I was lucky. Not that luck had been anywhere to be found tonight. She clearly had better things to do.

"Stand," I muttered, waving a hand over the cards as I focused on the next set.

"Six." The dealer's voice was flat, professional, as he dealt out the card, but I couldn't help but feel there was some smug satisfaction in it. It was something I seemed to notice more with the male dealers, though I've had my share of female croupiers let a smile slip as my chips dwindled. Maybe it was a testosterone thing. The man was getting to me, working his way under my skin, and it wasn't like me to let that happen. Everything about him was beginning to irritate me: from the perfect croupier uniform, right down to his styled black hair; held in place with some kind of gel, or wax, or whatever shit they used these days.

"Fuck it, hit."

"Language, sir," the dealer chided as he dealt out a ten. "Bust." He flipped over his own card. "Dealer has seventeen."

I sat back in my seat and sipped at my water, taking a breath as the shiny-haired bastard gathered up the chips. The couple at the end of the table had won on a pair of kings and were making the kind of noise you'd expect if they had won thousands, and not just a couple of quid. Other than them, the casino was quiet, though at this time of night it ought to be. The drunks and the partying idiots had left long ago, and now it was just the desperate, the lonely, and the addicts.

My time of night.

I never used to play to win, not normally anyway. I played for the game, for the thrill of it, and the challenge of beating the house. Blackjack has some of the best odds of any casino game and, provided I was paying attention, I could make thirty or forty quid last all night and leave with a profit, or with most of it, still in my pocket. These days I needed the money. Luck is a fickle bitch, and she'd been avoiding me for too long. If she didn't come back to visit soon, I was going to run into some serious problems.

"Well that was shit, Carver."

The voice drew my gaze over to the wall where the man in uniform slouched.

"Probably the worst few hands I've seen played in a while. Why don't you just throw your money at the dealer and have done? Oh, but it's not your money, is it?"

I ignored him, or tried to. Blood had soaked through the man's combat jacket, staining the webbing and painting half his side and leg dark, as it dripped down onto the garish red and gold patterned carpet.

It had been a while since I'd seen Johnson. He was easily the most vocal of my visitors, and definitely the most annoying.

"Oh, would you look at that," Johnson muttered, in a voice loud enough to carry, as he noted the puddle of blood beside his foot and the lurid red streak he'd left on the white wall. "I'm making a right mess of the place."

Johnson always was a prick. I closed my eyes and took a deep breath. The smell was coming back. It usually did when I have visitors.

Dust and hot plastic.

The dust had been everywhere, every day, no matter where you went. It was part of the air, working its way under your clothes, in-between your teeth, under your eyelids; until there was no escaping the feel of it. The plastic smell came from the cars sat in the sun; the frames of the windows melting in the unrelenting heat. There were other smells of course: sweat and my own kit; food and coffee coupled with spices; but it was the dust and hot plastic that sticks with me.

The smell of Kabul.

I shoved myself up out of the seat. I'd been sitting for a few hours and my legs weren't the steadiest, but that's only the half of it, if I was being honest. It took all the control I had just to snatch up the handful of chips I had left and lurch away from the table into the maze of slot machines.

The smell followed me, clinging to my nostrils until the taste of the dust seemed to coat my tongue. The yelling would come next, I knew that. Along with the gunshots and the screams.

I doubt I was a pretty sight as I stumbled down the line of slot machines, leaning on the chairs as my balance left me. A couple stood talking in the middle of the row, but I barely slowed as I shoved my way past.

"Drunk bastard!" One of them called after me.

The toilet was empty, which was something at least. I leaned heavily on the counter as one hand worked the tap. The cold water didn't help, but I'd known it wouldn't. There was a cycle to this. A pattern. I was a hostage to this once it began. I was a prisoner to the visions that would follow.

3

I closed my eyes as the first gunshots rang out, as the blood flowed, the screaming began, and the scene played on. The pleading filled the casino bathroom. The shouts echoing off tiles that hadn't even been there at the time, and making the shouting all the louder for it.

The hand landed heavy on my shoulder, which is never a good idea. I've had too much training to just turn it off. I was moving before I'd thought.

"I think you've had enough, mate. Time—" the security guard cut off as I grabbed his wrist, ducking under his arm and twisting smoothly into the lock as my thumbs drove into the pressure point on the back of the man's hand.

"Fuck me!" He was a big man; security guards in these places usually were, but he sank to his knees instantly as I held the pressure.

Choices. It would be simple enough to kick to the face here, with a fair chance of putting the guy out. An elbow strike would break his arm easily; a quick wrench would dislocate his shoulder.

Neutralise the threat. Disarm. Move on.

The thought brought me back to myself. There was no threat here.

I stepped back, dropping his hand. "Sorry, mate. You surprised me, is all. I moved before I thought."

"Bastard," the man muttered, shaking out his wrist. "Time you pissed off, while you've still got some teeth."

Who are you kidding, mate? I raised an eyebrow as I looked the man over. He was a big guy; far too big for his suit, really. It was a stupid thing for a bouncer, or any kind of guard, to wear. Too restrictive; but then he wasn't here to lay hands on people, he was here to look big and intimidating. A paid bully. His toughest job was probably herding the drunks and hookers to the door.

"I'm going," I muttered, backing away from the guy as he reached for his phone.

*

4

The night was windy as I made my way out of the Stratford West-field complex. Whoever thought it was a good idea to put a casino on top of a shopping centre in east London probably needed help. The place was a mess of shadows and dark corners—a mugger's delight. The transport links weren't much better. Easy to get to in the daytime, but leaving in the middle of the night required a ten-minute trek through dark streets to reach the nearest tube station.

Muggers were the last thing on my mind though. My liquid cash was running low and I'd made bugger all on the tables tonight. Things were getting tight.

I hunched down into my thin leather jacket and tried to coax more warmth from a garment already poorly equipped to cope with the temperature. The chips tumbled over and over in my pocket as I flicked and flipped them. It's a habit that got on my own nerves. I should have cashed them in before I left, though Captain Security would probably have objected.

The thought brought a laugh at the memory of the big man's face. Shock and pain had given way to fear fast enough to show that the guy had probably never had to deal with anyone who knew what they were doing in a fight. It's true what they say; bullies are usually cowards, and Captain Security hadn't liked finding that out. He'd probably have had another go at me if I hadn't left so quickly. His anger had been clear enough; shining through the fear and the shame.

A blast of wind that was far colder than it ought to be in June sent me ducking into a side street. This casino was good enough, and closer to me than any other in London, but Jesus this place was miserable at night.

A shadow detached itself from the wall ahead of me and I froze, cursing. I should have been paying more attention than this.

"You Carver?" It was a young man's voice, thick with a street accent that was supposed to make him sound tough.

"Never heard of him," I said with a shrug. More figures emerged from the shadows and I made a show of looking around at them. It would be better for me to look nervous here. "I don't have any money on me, just a couple of casino chips."

"We don't want your money, Carver," the shadow said, stepping into the faint streetlight. "Mr Cresswell wants to talk to you."

Fucking Cresswell, that was all I needed. "What does that bastard want?"

The figure wasn't much more than a kid. Dressed up in street clothes and trying to look dangerous. Christ, he'd even gone as far as wearing a bandana. Probably trying to make a name for himself.

He ignored my question, glanced around at the other shadowy figures, and pulled a gun from his jeans.

The gun looked like it was probably a converted blank-firing Baikal or something similar. It was easy enough to convert the barrel to a rifled one capable of firing a bullet, but they weren't cheap.

"Mr Cresswell reckoned you was something special. Something to be careful around. You don't look like much to me. Just a sad old git."

Old? The cheeky fucker. I probably looked a little weathered for thirty-eight, but fifteen years in the army will do that to anyone.

I stayed quiet, letting him rant and ramble as I glanced around. There were easily five of them, but it was hard to tell without being too obvious. They were all kids—probably hadn't even reached their twenties yet. Five would be manageable, but it was more than likely they were all carrying knives. The damned gun complicated things. You can run from a knife but there isn't much point running from a gun, not at this range anyway.

"Nice gun," I noted. "What did that set you back, a thousand? Fifteen hundred?"

The kid shrugged.

"Oh, Cresswell gave it to you?" I guessed. "Have you fired it yet? You've still got all your fingers by the looks of things, so I'm guessing not."

The frown told me enough all by itself; the kid had no idea what he was holding. I smirked. "You can't just buy a gun in this country mate, not normally. That's been converted from a blank-firer or a tear-gas gun. They're not made to shoot bullets. Sometimes they have to drill the barrel out. If they don't do it properly and you fire it, you'll be picking up your fingers for a good long while."

"It'll put a fucking hole in you," the kid snarled, stepping close and jamming the gun into my side. "I should pop a cap in your ass right now!"

That was too much, and a snort escaped me before I could stop myself.

"Think this is fucking funny, old man?"

"Pop a cap in my arse?" I didn't bother trying to hide the laughter, or the scorn. "What do you think this is, L.A? You sound like you just finished playing *Grand Theft Auto.*"

The blow was easy to see coming, his fist still wrapped around the gun. I blocked easily, smashing a palm into the kid's elbow to twist his torso to one side, before I jabbed a fist into the side of his face. Another strike down to his wrist sent the gun off into the darkness, and then I unloaded a full punch, turning my hip into it and dropping the kid like a stone. All in all, it had taken less than three seconds.

There was moment of silence before the side-street exploded into violence.

I moved quickly, working my way in the darkest of the shadows to give me an advantage. Where the gang members had to search to find me, everyone in front of me was a target. Five to one. No time to muck about. You've got to be efficient and brutal in something like this; work to disable as quickly as possible whilst still keeping moving. Standing in one place in this kind of fight is an invitation to house someone's knife in your guts.

I ducked under a wild swing and came back up with an elbow strike, driving it into a nose hard enough to break it. A knife glinted in the faint glow of the streetlamps and I twisted, kicking out at the side of a knee. The grisly crunch and howling scream were enough to tell me the job was done.

Two left.

I moved into the centre of the small street to give myself space to move; a stupid idea against four or five, but worth it for the two that remained. I stood, trying to look calm, like my pulse wasn't racing as I watched them. A fight like this is more psychological than anything else, and it was important that they saw me as holding all the cards. In truth, I already ached like a bastard. I hadn't moved nearly fast enough and half a dozen glancing blows had struck my ribs and face already.

"I'm gonna cut your fucking face up!" A dark-haired kid growled, pulling a kitchen knife from his jacket. He'd caught a blow to the face at some point and his cheek was red and swollen already. He was scared enough to piss himself, his anger was just a convenient place to hide it.

"Smiffy," the other, younger, of the two hissed. "Smiffy, look at Jenks an' Addie. Fuckin' look at 'em, mate."

Smiffy shot him a warning look but his gaze darted to the slumped forms on the ground and the kid moaning and writhing, clutching at his leg.

I considered running for half a second. Even going so far as having to stop myself glancing behind to see if the way was clear. It would be a stupid move, I knew. They were younger, in better shape, and probably faster. The fight had turned us all around and the street lay just beyond the two thugs, invitingly close.

It was the flicker of the kid's eye that warned me. Another second and I could have avoided it. As it was, I half-turned, just in time for the brick to slam into the side of my head.

CHAPTER TWO

I woke to the stench of ammonia burning my nostrils. It was a lousy way to come around, and I don't recommend it. I spent a few minutes coughing and trying to pull myself upright in the chair, before my brain caught up and noticed the plastic cable ties binding my wrists. The stinging in my cheek reached me moments later. Smelling salts had worked where the slap to the face hadn't, I supposed.

"Hello, Jonathan." The voice was cultured, amused, and really not one I've ever wanted to wake up to. Cresswell was not what you might call small. He looked like his suit had been built around him to act as scaffolding as his bulk threatened to overflow the chair and pool out onto the floor. I pitied the seams straining to hold all that flab in.

"Cresswell," I had to force the smile onto my face and it wasn't fun. Clearly, they'd put the boot into me a couple of times after I went down. I probed at a tooth with my tongue. Was that loose? "You know, most people simply phone when they want to catch up."

Cresswell shifted his bulk in the leather swivel-chair and leaned forward on the desk. "You don't own a phone, Carver."

I shrugged. "There is that, I suppose. Still, sending a toddler group to fetch me seems a bit foolish."

It wasn't much. Cresswell was never one to let his emotions play on his face, but the muscles down by his jaw flexed momentarily as his eyes narrowed.

"Yes, you were especially mean there, I felt," the fat man replied. "I believe you broke young Alexander's leg quite badly."

"He shouldn't play in the street then," I grunted, and glanced around the small office. Not much had changed; the same collection of battered filing cabinets crowded up against one wall, and Cresswell's odd collection of aged and antique furniture filled the rest.

"Are these really necessary?" I asked, tugging at one wrist.

"Merely a precaution, Jonathan," Cresswell murmured with a small smile. "You never can tell how someone is going to wake up." He gave a nod to someone behind me, and large hands reached to cut the ties free.

The mountain of meat that loomed over me was everything that Cresswell wasn't. I doubted if there was more than an ounce or two of fat on him.

"You kept Lurch!" I beamed up at the minder. "I hoped you would. I think he brings a certain lumbering elegance to the place."

Lurch, for his part, ignored me as he cut the ties free and stepped back to stand at the door.

"I think that's about enough banter, Carver," Cresswell cut in. "Where's my money?"

"It's only the third, Cresswell," I said with a shrug. "Payment isn't due until the fourteenth."

"Don't give me that shit," Cresswell snapped. "You're bloody broke. You owe me four grand in less than two weeks, and that's mostly interest."

Cresswell sucked a deep breath in through his nose, and pulled a drawer open to take out a packet of cigarettes. Where most of the country seemed to have switched to the electronic variety that filled the streets with clouds of vapour, Cresswell had stuck to his beloved Marlboros.

He flipped the lighter and shook his head as he sucked the cigarette into life. "You're going to be the fucking death of me, Carver. Too much bloody stress. I didn't get into this game for the stress."

"Why did you, then?" My mouth asked before my brain gave it permission.

"It wasn't for fucking altruism, that's for sure." Cresswell hauled himself out of his chair and made his way out from behind the desk to prop himself up on the front of it. He glowered down at me for a minute as he sucked on the smoke and puffed like some kind of human volcano. "I'm not a bloody charity, Carver. What the hell are you doing in a bloody casino pissing away my money?"

"It's not your money until—"

"Bullshit!" Cresswell roared, spraying spit into the air and dropping his cigarette. "Fuck," he muttered, grunting as he reached down to retrieve it.

This wasn't going well. Cresswell's moods were mercurial; though so far, I'd never seen them drift even close to cheerful. This wasn't one of his better ones.

The cigarette was too much, filling the room with the harsh stink of it. I've been in some foul-smelling places, smelled things far worse than unwanted cigarette smoke, but it had been a rough night and the ammonia they used to wake me up wasn't helping. Fifteen years ago, I was smoking along with everyone else—now the smell was almost enough to make me throw up the dinner I hadn't had.

Cresswell finished dusting off the cigarette with his fingertips and sucked it back to life. "You're in for fifteen grand, Carver. Fifty percent interest monthly until you clear it. You've already missed payments and given me incomplete amounts. This isn't how I do business. You make this payment in full or I take the car to pay your interest. You miss a payment after that, I'll have some boys visit you and put a hammer to your legs."

I closed my eyes. It was better to look defeated right now. The car was nothing special. A Mercedes from when I'd been feeling flush and stupid. These days I'd be lucky to get more than seven thousand for it; less than half my debt.

"I'll make the payment," I said, though God knows how I was going to.

"And don't let me catch you in another casino until you have."

I frowned at that. How had he known where I was? My brain was still catching up with the situation. Being clubbed in the head with a brick will do that to you.

"The security guard," I said, as realisation dawned. Captain Security, in the casino. He'd been reaching for his phone as I left. At the time, I thought he was phoning the police.

Cresswell gave me a smug little smile that made me want to smash my fist into the middle of his fat face. "I like to keep an eye on my investments, Carver. You more than most."

He gave a nod to Lurch, who dragged me out of my seat, marched me down the back stairs, and shoved me out into the street. It was growing light already, a shitty start to the day but at least I was mostly intact.

Eleven days. Not even two weeks to get four thousand pounds together.

I was fucked.

Cresswell's office, if you could call it that, was in a grotty area of London just five minutes from Canary Wharf. His own little financial district just outside the actual financial district. I'd probably been bundled into the back of a car to get here but getting home meant a long, cold walk.

Ten minutes later I was on a train headed back towards Bow and home. I hadn't paid. It was a stupid thing to do but I was in a foul mood and stupidity often goes hand-in-hand with that. The Docklands Light Railway (or DLR) trains in London are driverless; something that takes a bit of getting used to, but which does make it possible to not buy a ticket. Most people use contactless payment, just touching their bank card to a sensor—which makes 'contactless' a stupid name for it I suppose. It's faster, and on the DLR at least, there are often gates that only open once you've paid. There are ways past those if you're really determined, spot checks, and the fines are hefty if you get caught, but I really didn't care.

I grabbed a coffee from a little place outside the station with a crumpled up five pound note I'd found lurking in a pocket of my jacket. I took this as proof that God wasn't a complete arsehole. Small mercies like random fivers discovered in pockets are the things that keep us going.

Home was a little flat in Bow, in the east end of London; a gorgeous place in what was once a Victorian match factory. If you've ever heard of Swan Vestas matches, this is where they first got started. There's a little plaque telling the story of the place just inside the gates, though I've never read it.

The flat was a one-bedroom place that I had nothing to do with picking out. Susan found it. She'd made the appointments with the agents, organised the viewing I vaguely remembered going to, and paid the rent. A year's worth in advance. It was somewhere to take the pressure off, a place to decompress and adjust back to civilian life. At least, that was what she'd said.

She'd left, of course. Who wouldn't? It had taken a while, and a bit of effort—or a lack of, on my part—but I'd managed to fuck that up, too. The flat looked like nobody lived there, which was true: nobody did. I haven't lived in a long time; existing doesn't count.

Pearson sat in the corner, watching me. He was hunched down into his usual position, arms gripping his knees as he looked up with that ever-present terrified expression. The hole in his head was a new development. He normally had his combat helmet on and a stream of blood running down his face.

I could have lived without seeing the hole, to be honest. I sank down into a chair and cradled the coffee cup to my chest. What the hell was I going to do now?

"Well, you're pretty well fucked, mate," I said to myself.

Most people talk to themselves but it's usually just rehashing old conversations, or planning future ones. I've been known to have full conversations with myself; even to the point of winning, and losing, arguments. It wasn't a good sign and I knew it. But talking to myself was better than talking to any of the visitors... although I suppose, in a way, it amounts to the same thing. I'd done a pretty good job of lying to myself and avoiding the truth of my condition, up until now, and I didn't plan to change that anytime soon.

I needed money, that much was obvious. My living costs were more or less covered. The rent wasn't an issue for another few months. I had enough set aside from my last run of luck at the casino to cover food and minor bills, but that wouldn't stretch to four grand. And given Cresswell's mood, I wasn't about to try and give him a partial payment. My luck at the casino seemed to have worked itself dry, and I didn't have the time or the resources to try and win what I needed.

What I needed was a job. An actual job, not this half-arsed card sharp routine I'd been running. The obvious solution drifted through my mind like a dead fish in a pond; an unpleasant, unwanted, but undeniable reality.

I railed against it as I sat in the chair, my coffee passing from lukewarm to cold, my mind running through scenarios that ranged from the unlikely to the absurd, knowing all the while I only had one choice.

CHAPTER THREE

It was light when I woke. I checked my watch and grunted. I'd gone the rest of the day, and then the whole night, in the chair. I suppose it shouldn't have been a surprise, I hadn't had any sleep the night before—being unconscious doesn't really count.

I'm always the same when I wake up anywhere but my bed. There's a process, a system. I listen first, for absences as much as for sounds. Sometimes a silence can say more than any shout. My eyes move before my head, checking the surroundings for visible threats before I commit to moving. My arms and legs shift ever so slightly, checking for restraints.

Then, and only then, do I move my head; checking the corners first, and the exits second. It's not a conscious decision, it's something my body has decided to do on its own. To be fair, it's probably tired of having the shit beaten out of it.

I was still holding the remains of the coffee. It's very rare for me to spill a drink, even when I fall asleep holding it. Spilt coffee would be bad. Spilt whisky would be a bloody travesty.

I groaned as I hauled myself out of the chair, bruises combining with the aches of stiff muscles to make every movement a slow agony. I must have looked about ninety as I staggered into the shower. God knows I felt like it.

Twenty minutes under hot water did some good but not enough, and I huddled under a towel as I searched through the cabinets for painkillers. Ibuprofen 600s—little capsules of joy. You can't buy them in this country, but I'd brought them back from Spain where they are more sensible about these things. I stood and admired my bruises in the mirror for a minute. My face was a mess, but my ribs were spectacular. The left side of my torso was turning a lovely shade of purple. I probed at it gently with one hand and took an experimental deep breath. None of the ribs seemed broken, which was something at least.

The flat wasn't really cold. It didn't ever get truly cold. The ones above, below, and to either side worked to heat it, but it was too cold to wander around in just a towel, especially in the condition I was in. I threw some clothes on that smelt like I could get away with wearing them again, and stood for a minute considering the kitchen. I needed coffee, and the ibuprofen would work better with something inside me. I spent a pointless couple of minutes opening and closing cupboards and looking into the fridge. A can of beer, some bacon that really needed throwing out, and a bottle of milk that I wouldn't even consider opening. I glanced at my watch. It was almost half-past seven

"Get moving, Carver," I muttered. "Before you talk yourself out of this."

I threw on my jacket and left, my feet doing all the thinking for me. There was only one other solution to Cresswell, one I'd avoided thinking about yesterday. I needed money, and realistically that meant either a job or something shady. I wasn't quite desperate enough for something shady. Not yet, anyway.

I'm not really designed for the real world—for the civilian world. Fifteen years in the army changes a man in more ways than one. I carry my scars well enough, some of them are even visible. It's more than just the scars, though. I have skills that most people wouldn't even think about. Being able to assess a situation for threats and hostiles in a glance; knowing a variety of ways to disarm and neutralise a man in moments; or assemble a weapon in thirty seconds, aren't the most transferable of skills unless you want to work in security. And I didn't.

The sun hadn't done much of a job of heating London up yet and I shrugged myself deeper into my jacket. A homeless guy in a doorway glanced up at me as I passed, watching me from where he'd bundled down into his sleeping bag. He was an older man, with long hair poking out from under his hat. I looked away, avoiding eye contact. Avoiding the thoughts seeing the homeless gave me.

I'd done better than some people who come out of the forces. I had a roof over my head, though admittedly I didn't pay for it. I had a bit of money, though that came with more debts than I cared to admit. And I hadn't fallen apart, although seeing dead people and talking to myself probably meant I was well on my way.

So, yeah, okay; maybe I wasn't doing that well.

If you talk to the homeless in London you might be surprised at how many are ex-forces. Look under Southwark Bridge on any given day and you'll find at least one in amongst the other homeless and lost. I've met a few people who claim this is just laziness. Sleeping rough is what we're trained for, after all. They say choosing that life once you're out of the forces is just a refusal to adapt, to get on with it. I generally ignore people who come out with shit like that, though I've punched one or two.

I try to avoid the homeless, if I'm honest. I don't like facing the truth about my life unless I absolutely have to. It's a simple philosophy but it's served me well enough for the past few years. Learn to lie to yourself and life is infinitely more bearable.

Ten minutes walking through cold streets got me to the underground. Another thirty minutes crammed onto a tube train, listening to a recorded voice announce the stations whilst I was pressed closer to sweaty men in suits than I'm really comfortable with, and I was in Westminster. London is a strange place. In most parts of it you can go from abject poverty to grandeur in a few minutes walk. In Westminster they try to keep the abject poverty hidden away under bridges or on the back streets.

Westminster is the heart of government. Parliament, Whitehall, the Supreme Court, and even the Queen herself, are all within a mile of each other. It's also home to more consultants than anyone would expect. There's nothing like the government to hire in external experts at five times the price it would cost them to do things themselves.

Paragon was just one of two dozen or more consultancies that worked closely with the Ministry of Defence. It was also the only one I had a contact in, and the one place I promised myself I'd never step foot in.

The building was nondescript; just another featureless concrete and glass block. I made my way through the glass door and scanned the list on the wall. I don't know why I looked, really. I knew where Paragon was. The lift was crowded, men and women in expensive suits giving me odd looks as if I were a stray dog that had wandered in from the street.

Paragon had its offices on the fourth floor. A stunning receptionist glanced up at me as I made my way in from the lift. Dark brown hair and a tight black dress contrasted with her scarlet lips. She looked like she'd escaped from a Robert Palmer video. Her eyes flicked to the side and behind me for the briefest moment, and I caught the minute nod before a false smile spread over her lips.

"Good morning, sir. Can I help you?"

I didn't need to turn to know that the security guard was watching me.

"I need to talk to McCourt. James McCourt." My voice came out as a rasp, like I'd spent the night in a gutter sucking the last drips out of a whisky bottle. Her smile didn't falter, like it was some kind of mask she could hide behind. "Do you have an appointment, mister…?"

"Carver," I told her. "And no, I don't, but he'll see me. I'm an old friend."

Her frown was the single flaw on her perfectly made-up face. Faintly disapproving, like I should be ashamed for coming in here and disturbing her. She tapped away at her computer for a moment and shook her head. "I'm sorry, Mr Carver. I don't think it's going to be possible today. Mr McCourt is very busy."

I sighed. Somehow, I'd known it was going to be one of those days. "Just give him a call and tell him I'm here, please?"

She gave me a long look, weighing things while she ran her eyes up and down the length of me. She wore a faintly disgusted expression, like a bad smell had just reached her. Maybe it had. "I'm sorry, he's very busy. You'd need to make an appointment."

I took a deep breath and sighed again, tapping my fingers against my thumb inside my pocket. It was better than screaming at her, but I've never had the patience for things like this. "Fine. When is he free?"

"If I could just ask what this is concerning?"

"No."

"I'm sorry?" Her shock at my rudeness broke the perfect mask for a moment, putting her on the back foot.

"You don't need to know what it's about. You've got my name."

She tapped at the keyboard again. "The earliest he might be free is Friday next week."

A week on Friday? Jesus. Cresswell would be kicking down my door by then. The panic was there, building inside me, but for now it was trapped beneath a rising tide of irritation.

"Can you give me a direct number for him, at least?"

Another frown. "I thought you were a friend?"

This was getting old. My patience was slipping, and it was showing on my face. Susan had called it 'the danger sign'. When my jaw began to clench and the furrows around my eyebrows deepened as I frowned, she'd known the stress was getting to me. She'd make fun of me, calling me 'stress-head' and poking me until she made me laugh.

Susan. Shit. What had made me think of her, now of all times?

The receptionist shook her head, her own disapproving frown firmly in place. "I'm sorry, sir. I can't simply hand out contact information, and if you won't tell me what the meeting is regarding, then I'm afraid I won't be able to make an appointment for you."

"Oh, for fuck's—"

I cut off as the security guard made a noise between a cough and a grunt. He stood a few feet behind me. A smart distance, out of punching range unless I really lunged, and far enough to give him time to react to any move I made.

"I think it's time you left, sir," he said, in a tone which almost made it an apology.

I sighed, giving myself time to size him up. A big guy, but a careful one. He knew enough not to just rely on his bulk, which is more than the idiot in the casino had. Shaved head, though the stubble showing said he wasn't bald. Probably a professional choice. Any man who faces the threat of a fight every working day will either cut his hair so it's too short to grab, or shave it off. He was calm too, taking his time, probably doing the same thing I was.

I shook my head. "I'm not leaving without speaking to Jim. I don't want any trouble, but I don't think it's asking too much for you to call him." I threw the last over my shoulder at the receptionist who wore an affronted expression as if I'd walked in here naked.

"You need to go, sir," the guard grated through clenched teeth. "I don't want to have to hurt you."

What was it with me and security guards lately?

I smiled and shook my head again. "Make me," I told him, glancing up at the CCTV camera.

The grab was clever. A low, jujitsu-style lunge, rather than a tentative one-handed reach. It was easy enough to avoid, and I shifted to one side, bringing an elbow down into his back as he passed me. It was a light blow; a warning shot rather than a real strike.

The receptionist had moved back out of range of anything that might be coming her way, as her hand stabbed frantically at something under the desk. A panic button most likely. I didn't have time to watch her as the bald guard recovered and squared up to me.

"This is only going to end in the police being called, sir."

"Not if she learns how to use a bloody phone, and gets McCourt out here!" I shot back.

He bulled in while I was still talking. Another grapple attempt. I slapped the grasping hands away, jabbed at his face and shifted to the side, slamming another fist in under his ribs. He hadn't tensed and my fist sunk into his flesh, sending him gasping to the floor.

I turned back to the receptionist in time to hear the door open.

"Jesus, Carver. You didn't have to beat the shit out of him." McCourt hadn't changed much since the army, despite the offices, the expensive suit and the years since I'd seen him last. It was the same cheesy grin working to distract you from the same calculating eyes.

"Well, I couldn't get an appointment," I shrugged, working to catch my breath.

Jim looked past me to the hired heavy pulling himself upright on the reception desk. "You all right, Tom?"

Tom nodded, still bent over, avoiding looking at us.

Jim looked back and forth between us and shook his head before waving me through the door. "Come on, then."

I followed him through a succession of hallways until we reached his office.

"Have a seat," he said, as he settled himself down behind the desk. It was a smoked-glass and chrome monstrosity, and far too big for the single laptop and phone that sat upon it.

I made a show of looking around the place. "Christ, Jim. Looks like you've landed on your feet."

He shrugged but couldn't help the small smile showing. He'd always been a vain bastard and a bit of flattery doesn't hurt when you come cap in hand.

"We've done well the last couple of years," he said. "It was touch and go for a while though. Do you want a drink? Coffee or anything?"

I shook my head and he scratched at his cheek as he looked at me in silence.

"Bloody hell, John," he said finally. "You look like shit. What happened to your face?"

Fuck, I'd forgotten about the bruises. I was suddenly aware of just how bad I must look. I hadn't shaved, I had a face full of bruises, a swollen lip, and I was still in last night's clothes.

"I got jumped outside a pub last night," I lied. "No big deal."

Jim grunted, obviously not believing a word of it. "So, what can I do for you, mate? It's good to see you, but you've caught me on a crap day. You should have phoned."

"I don't own a phone."

"Still?" He snorted a laugh. "Any plans to join the twenty-first century at all?"

I managed a half-smile as I shook my head. "I wanted to know if your offer still stands?"

He blinked, sitting back in his chair. "Of course. I didn't think you'd ever take me up on it. I'll have a chat with Simon and Tom, and see what we can get together for you. Can you give me a couple of weeks?"

I winced, suddenly aware I was picking away at the seam of my jeans with one hand and forcing myself to stop. "Not really. Any chance of something quick?"

He looked at me for a long moment before he spoke again. "How bad is it?"

"Bad enough," I admitted.

"How much are you in for?"

I grimaced, looking away and out of the floor-to-ceiling window. The office was high enough to see the spires of Westminster Abbey above the rooftops. "Does it matter?"

"It matters if it's something that's going to follow you here."

Cresswell bothered me more than I wanted to let on, but he knew the rules London functioned by. The police would leave him alone so long as he stayed within certain limits. He wasn't about to show up at Paragon no matter what I did. I've dealt with bigger problems than loan-sharks in my time. He was just persistent.

"It isn't," I said flatly.

He chewed on his lip for a minute.

"I might have something," he said slowly, gauging the impact of his words. "It would mean going back though, to Kabul. Most of our work is out there at the moment. A bit in Iraq still, but mostly Afghanistan."

I stared at him as the smell hit.

Dust, always the dust.

McCourt was saying something but I couldn't make it out over the sound of the rotor blades and shouted orders.

I closed my eyes, biting at the inside of my cheek.

Not now. Please not now.

"John?" McCourt frowned at me as I stared at the wall below the window. "You all right?"

I nodded, swallowing hard as a thin line of blood began to run from the bullet-hole in Pearson's head. He sat beside the end of the desk. Curled up as always, with his terrified eyes locked on me.

"Of course," I managed. "Yeah, Kabul. That's fine. When?"

"Soon as you can, really," McCourt said, as he stood and made his way to the window. "It's a babysitting job," he told me over one shoulder. "Security training for one of the Afghan government compounds. Shouldn't last more than six months or so."

I nodded. It wasn't anything I couldn't handle, if I could keep my shit together. "How much are you paying these days."

Jim grinned. "Going rate is about seven hundred, sometimes more. It depends on the job, and on the man." He paused, considering. "I could go as high as eight fifty for you. How does that sound?"

Eight hundred and fifty a day, plus being out of the country for six months. It would solve all of my problems in one go, provided I was still alive at the end of it. I wasn't scared of Kabul, or anyone I might find there. I was more worried about the baggage I was bringing with me, in every sense. I gave him a smile and hoped the battle between relief and terror wasn't showing on my face. "That sounds good, McCourt. Thank you."

Jim nodded and looked out the window for a moment. "Is there… anything I need to know about? Drugs?"

I shook my head. "No, I'm clean. Never touched them, you know that."

He glanced at me and went back to his desk, tapping at the laptop, embarrassed. "I have to ask. You know how it is."

I had no idea how it was. Drugs had never appealed to me. Except for alcohol and caffeine, of course, and they don't count. It's okay to drink your drug. They should be the least of his worries anyway. You can overcome a drug addiction. What's the cure for seeing dead people? Apart from joining them?

"You'll need to use a different name," McCourt said, as if it were an afterthought. "Use your own passport, but once you're there, better to be someone else."

"Still?" That surprised me. It had been years. Surely people had forgotten, or dismissed all the stories as bullshit by now.

McCourt nodded. "It's not a story that's going to go away anytime soon. John Carver, the Miracle of Kabul."

"It's bollocks, is what it is."

"I saw it, John," McCourt said. He spoke in a low voice, looking down at his desk as he toyed with a pen. "I saw the bullet. I don't think Yates could, not as well as I did anyway."

"You're wrong, Jim," I muttered. I didn't want to go through this again. Right now, I just wanted to leave.

McCourt shook his head. "I'm not, John. I saw him pull the trigger. I saw the muzzle flash. And then I saw the bullet. I saw it just hanging there in the air, halfway to you. I'll never forget it, or the look on your face. Pearson died scared, but you, you had this look… I don't even know how to describe it. It was like you were taking a test or something. Like you were concentrating, but furious at the same time. So angry, I've never seen anyone so angry. And your hand, held out, like you were warding the gunshot off…"

I pulled at my collar and ran a hand over the stubble on my face. The place was like a damned furnace, I didn't know how he put up with it. A wave of nausea uncoiled from my stomach and lurched up towards my throat. I had to get out of there. Leaving before I threw up or collapsed on the floor would probably be best. "When will you have the travel details for me?"

McCourt shook his head and sighed before meeting my eyes. "I'll have a pack put together for you—should be ready by this afternoon. Do you need any time to sort things out here?"

"No," I said, shaking my head. "I just need to pack a few things. I'm ready whenever."

"Fine," McCourt nodded, heading to a cabinet set against the wall behind his desk and reaching into a drawer. "Take this, I'll text you the travel details and email you the job packet."

I looked down at the phone in his hand.

He snorted out a laugh. "It's not going to fucking bite you, John. Just take the damned thing."

I couldn't explain my distaste for mobile phones. It's something about always being reachable, always being on the grid, like being on the end of a leash. I grimaced, mostly for comic effect as McCourt laughed again, and tucked it into an inside pocket.

"Go and pack," McCourt told me. "Sort your shit out. I'll see if we can get you on a flight tomorrow or the next day."

CHAPTER FOUR

She was thirsty.

That was the first thought that made it through the fog. That she was thirsty, and that her wrists hurt.

It was dark, too. She blinked, reassuring herself that her eyes were actually open. It wasn't the darkness of a bedroom in the night, but a total, utter darkness—the kind of blackness you might find in a cave or a cellar. She licked her lips, tasting something sour as she tried to sit up, and failed. Something held her arms. The noise was slight but the silence around her made it all the more pronounced; metal on metal, as the links on the fabric cuffs around her wrists caught at the chains.

She turned her head in confusion, trying to peer at her wrist, but the darkness was absolute. Her thoughts were slow, fumbling things, fighting their way through the groggy mess inside her head. Her skin rubbed over whatever it was she lay on and, with a start, she realised she was naked. That discovery almost overrode the shock she felt at being tied up. But not just tied—actually bound—wrist and ankle.

Panic found her as realisation caught hold and she pulled at the cuff; first tugging, and then throwing herself against the restraints until she was thrashing like a caged animal.

"Help!" Her cry was a small thing, like a young child in the night, wanting her mother but too afraid to leave her bed and face the darkness. She tried again, until her screams were loud and hard enough to tear at her throat. Until they faded into a muted sob. She cried for a time, her tears going unanswered in the blackness as they ran down the sides of her face.

She was alone.

There would be no help or comfort. She was lost. She took a deep, ragged breath that sounded too loud, even to herself, but it worked to calm her. She needed to think rationally. She'd always been a problem solver; this was just a bigger problem.

"No shit," she muttered, snorting a laugh that drifted all too close to hysteria. She took another deep breath.

"Okay, think Mackenzie. What do we know?"

The noises she made sounded odd in the darkness. The room wasn't large, at least not large enough for the sound of her screams to distort or echo. She was bound to what felt like a padded wooden frame with some kind of fabric cuffs at her wrists and ankles, but reclined enough to take the weight off her feet.

She sank back against the frame. She felt sick, like she'd had too much to drink. The room felt like it was spinning in that awful, unpredictable way that she found when she'd first experimented with alcohol, dipping as it spun, until her stomach lurched. She gagged, turning her head as her stomach heaved. Vomit spattered over a floor she couldn't see, and she spat, the acid burning at her throat. Tears streamed down her cheeks and she reached to wipe them away, only to be stopped by the cuffs.

God, she couldn't even wipe the sick from her lips.

Where was she? Was she even in Kabul? The darkness somehow made everything worse. She could have been here for days for all she knew.

Okay, she told herself. *You're smart, Mackenzie. You can get out of this.*

"Sure," she muttered out loud. "So smart you got yourself chained up naked in this shithole."

She shook her head, taking a deep breath.

Fine, it's dark. So, focus on what you know.

The room was small; either that or there were other things in here that stopped any echo. She wasn't hot or cold either. She'd shivered after she threw up but that was due to shock, not cold. That meant the room had its temperature regulated. She wasn't outside in a cargo container or anything. If she'd been locked up in a tin box, the June sun would have roasted her alive by now.

"So, what does this all add up to?" she muttered. Her voice was loud in the darkness, but it was better than the silence. "You're fucked, that's what it adds up to."

She sighed, taking another couple of deep breaths to stave off the panic that was building again. The regulated temperature meant heaters and air-conditioning. It meant she wasn't out in the middle of nowhere. And that meant there was some chance of being heard, of being found.

She screamed again, shouting for help until her voice cracked and her throat burned. She screamed until her voice failed, until her screams became whispers, and she lapsed into first silence, and then sleep.

*

Light, blinding and harsh, blazed into life above her as three spot-lights clicked on. Mackenzie gasped, swearing as she closed her eyes against the brightness, and turned her head away. The light seared at her, burning her eyes even after she'd closed them. Water blasted at her from every direction, high-pressure hoses sluicing away the vomit that encrusted her arm and the frame holding her.

The water was cold, and she gasped as it dripped off her, shaking her head to try and clear it from her eyes.

"Fuck!"

She looked around quickly, taking in what she could while the light lasted. The room was larger than she'd imagined, though not much more than seven metres lay between her and a dark glass wall. A grate set into the concrete floor beneath her drained the water and mess away.

Two thin, clear hoses were positioned to either side of her head, extending out from larger pipes that ran down from the ceiling, hanging just within reach. A clear droplet clung to the end of one of the hoses and she reached to touch it with her tongue.

Water.

She sucked on the tube and drank, drawing deep before she thought to worry about what might be in it. Fuck it. If whoever had tied her up wanted her drugged they wouldn't need to hide it in the water, they could just walk in and stick a needle into her. It wasn't as if she could do anything about it.

The water helped. She could feel the fuzziness in her head begin to clear. Despite the sluicing, she'd woken groggy and nauseous, and drinking had helped with both. She examined the other tube. It was wider than the one that held the water. She took it between her teeth, drawing on it slowly, until she was rewarded with a thick paste. She screwed her face up at the taste and grainy texture. It was like humus, but without the garlic. Some kind of ground pea or grain, mixed with an oil or water.

And it was vile.

She spat the mouthful down at the grate on one side of her. It would probably keep her alive, but she'd need to be a lot more desperate before she started eating it.

How the hell had she got here? She remembered leaving the clinic, the walk-in centre they'd worked so hard to keep open after the Red Cross cut back on numbers. She wasn't some naïve nineteen-year-old. She knew how dangerous Kabul could be.

She took the proper precautions; covered her head in public, respected local culture and tradition. You heard stories of people being arrested in Dubai and other Islamic nations; but they were idiots getting drunk, and having sex on the beach, and then wondering why they'd been thrown in jail for public indecency or blasphemy. She'd known what she was coming into. These days, Afghanistan was nothing like it had been at the height of Taliban rule, but it was still an Islamic country, and still very conservative.

Her mother would almost be pleased about this. She'd lectured her for weeks about how Mackenzie was going to be kidnapped, or raped in some back alley. Even when it became obvious that Mackenzie wouldn't change her mind, she'd persisted. She very nearly hadn't come to Brisbane International to see her off. Stubbornness was a trait that ran in the Cartwright family, and Mackenzie had it just as bad as the rest of them. The only difference was that she recognised it for what it was. Her mother was always right, even when she was wrong. There had only ever been one way of doing things: her way. Anything else was either wrong, or simply inadequate. Sometimes she wondered how her father put up with it for as long as he had.

She blinked. She could remember the car!

The thought had drifted out of nowhere as she lay thinking about her mother. She remembered leaving work with Sayeed and Sarah, and going to the car. They'd taken the short walk together, around the corner to where they hid the car in a backstreet.

It was never a good idea to park outside of the clinic. No westerner was truly welcome in Afghanistan. The goal of removing the Taliban and crushing Al-Qaeda might have been the reason, or the excuse—depending on who you asked—but the country had been devastated by a fight that showed no sign of ending. The uniforms and the men holding the guns might change, the factions involved waxed and waned; but the fight was always the same, and the result always seemed to be injured children. Westerners were always going to be resented by some, and the fact she was Australian, not American or European, would be of no help.

Parking outside the clinic just advertised which car was theirs and she'd seen far too many burned-out wrecks to fall into that trap. They'd made their way home the same as many other nights, Sayeed driving and Mackenzie in the front next to him. Sarah was always dropped off first, her place was closer—an ex-embassy property that she shared with four other aid-workers.

"Oh my God!" It wasn't much more than a whisper, but the silence took it and amplified it.

She remembered the water. Sayeed had offered her a bottle of water as they set off after dropping Sarah. She'd only taken a couple of sips.

"It tasted funny." She mouthed the words, barely giving voice to them.

Sayeed was an Afghan who had been brought in to work as both a translator and a driver. He'd been hired in Kabul but wasn't local to the city. Like so many, he'd drifted in to Kabul as the fighting wore on, then never quite managed to leave. Working for the Red Cross was easy money. He translated when necessary, did some light carrying and fetching, and drove some of the workers home at the end of the day.

Had he drugged her?

The more she thought about it, the more plausible it became. The bottle had been in a zipped up cool-bag, nestled between the two front seats, but the car had been a furnace when they first got in. Hours in the Kabul sun had superheated the air inside the vehicle and they'd had to open the doors and wait a few minutes before they could climb in. Even after waiting, they were both sweating within seconds. Saving the water until after they dropped Sarah off seemed odd now.

He *had* drugged her!

She was suddenly sure of it. She remembered going to the car with Sarah clearly. She remembered dropping her off. It was only after that when her memory grew blurry. All she could recall with any clarity was sipping the water, and making a face at the taste. That, and Sayeed urging her to drink more. To stay hydrated in the heat, he told her.

"Bastard!" she spat.

That son of a bitch had drugged her.

"Sayeed!" she screamed, hurling her fury at the black glass windows across the room. "You son of a bitch, let me out of here! Let me *out*!"

Her only answer was a single red light which blinked into life on the other side of the glass. She frowned as she peered at it. She'd assumed that the glass was tinted, but maybe it was just dark on the other side of it. The light was small, no bigger than the blunt end of a pencil. A power light, she thought. Or a recording light. The slimy bastard was filming her.

"Sayeed, you little shit. You let me out of here *right now!*"

There was no answer. She hadn't really expected one.

She sagged back against the frame and her anger slipped away like quicksilver. The temper was her mother's, too. Her father had always been the calm one. He had to be, she supposed. He was the calm, rational one, thinking a way through a problem whilst her mother raged at it.

She frowned. This couldn't be Sayeed, she realised. The room she was in was constructed of poured concrete. The sluice and the drainage grate below her were well-made, probably custom fitted. He didn't have the money for anything like this.

"But the water…" she muttered, trailing off into silence. The answer was obvious. So apparent that it defied any argument, and the truth of it left her cold. He couldn't possibly afford this place. This wasn't a kidnapping; he'd drugged her and then passed her on.

He'd sold her.

She'd been bought and sold like a piece of meat.

CHAPTER FIVE

It didn't take me long to pack. I didn't own a lot, and most of what I did have wouldn't be of much use in Afghanistan. I was done in twenty minutes, an entire life bundled into one duffel bag. I'm used to spending most of the day asleep, a life spent in casinos tends to do that to you, so I wasn't really equipped for killing daylight hours. I passed the time watching daytime television and waiting for the phone I didn't want to bleep at me. I don't really recommend either one of them.

McCourt's phone call naturally waited until I'd been exposed to the full range of low-budget quiz shows and pregnant women hurling abuse at their unfaithful ex-lovers. Jim was good to his word—my flight was booked for Eleven the next morning. Kabul via Istanbul.

I spent the rest of the time cleaning out the flat. If I was going to be gone for six months I'd rather come back to something that didn't stink. That was assuming I made it back alive, of course. You can only spend so long cleaning, and I lived a pretty spartan life, so it didn't take long. Once I'd beaten the bacon-based life-form in the fridge into submission, and removed the toxic milk, it was largely a matter of tidying up; which left entirely too much time for thinking.

I admired the bruises on my face a few times in the bathroom mirror. The swelling was coming down on my lip, but the bruise on my cheek was coming up nicely. I'd look great by the time I got to Kabul.

I've become pretty good at lying to myself over the years. I suspect that it's a skill that anyone in a high-stress situation develops. Yes, you can convince your wife that working late is necessary, and it won't develop into a screaming row. No, the bank isn't going to repossess your house if you miss another mortgage payment. Of course that isn't an IED tucked underneath the front of that car and your squad isn't about to be blown to bits. It's something that goes with the territory, and I'd got pretty good at putting my worries about Cresswell and my debts onto a shelf in the back of my mind. With the flat tidy, and nothing else to do, they came back with full force.

The weather beyond the flat's windows was miserable—grey and wet and unappealing. Definitely a day best spent inside... except I wanted to be out. I've never been good at being cooped up. I had a day to kill, and I would have preferred to be outside. I hate nothing more than the feeling of being caged.

Worrying about Cresswell didn't help. By midmorning I'd caught myself twice, checking the street outside for suspicious cars, or men who might be watching the flat. Both times I managed to give myself a kick and laugh at myself. Cresswell wasn't watching the flat, and if he was, I wasn't going to spot him by twitching the curtains.

I forced myself to relax, which was almost as successful as it sounds. I spent a fruitless ten minutes looking for a book I hadn't read five times or more, then switched the television back on, only to turn it off five minutes later. I even sank so low as to mess around on McCourt's phone, sending him a couple of texts to arrange for payment of my bills, and to deal with Cresswell when the time came.

I left early the next morning, too early if I'm honest, but I wanted to be gone. I wanted to be out from under Cresswell's boot. I needed breathing space, even if that meant Kabul. I took the underground to Heathrow and checked in without issue. From there it was just a matter of passing through security and killing more time. At least if any of Cresswell's thugs had followed me to the airport, they wouldn't be able to get through security. Once through there, I could relax a bit.

I fed my bag through the x-ray machine, stepped through the scanners whilst ignoring the stares the security staff levelled at my battered face, and set off to find some breakfast. Food at Heathrow is expensive. It is in most airports. There's really nowhere to go, nothing to do, and until you board the plane, there's nowhere to eat but the over-priced restaurants. Despite this, I always went for the biggest breakfast I could find. I knew, I was a captive audience and I was going to pay through the nose for it, but for some reason I didn't care.

I ate in a bar that doubled as a restaurant. I ordered coffee and sipped at it while I waited for the food to be ready. The place was busy, but then Heathrow doesn't ever really get quiet. I amused myself by people-watching for a while, noting the three or four groups who were already drinking beer. They were either on connecting flights, or starting their holidays before they reached the beach, or even the plane.

The food was good; a full English breakfast that I was putting away at speed until the figure sank into the chair opposite me. I stiffened until I realised who it was.

"Fuck, I miss bacon," Johnson moaned, looking down at my plate as he bled all over the chair.

"Piss off, Johnson," I muttered around another mouthful. I closed my eyes and sighed as I realised what I'd done. I only have three basic rules in civilian life: don't drink in the daytime, don't stay at the table when your luck's run out, and don't talk to the visitors.

"Bit rude, mate," Johnson chided. "Your buddy Cresswell getting to you? You want to relax a bit more. Try meditation, or yoga." He put his palms together and took a deep breath as he closed his eyes.

I swore under my breath and crammed one last mouthful in before I stood and walked out, leaving Johnson to meditate in peace. The plate was still more than half-full, but no rule is complete unless it comes with a punishment.

I found an empty row of seats at the boarding gate and sat down with my book, glaring at anyone who thought to sit too close or try to start a conversation. My cock-up with Johnson had put me in a foul mood and I sat staring at the pages of the book, chewing over how badly I'd bungled things, until it came time to board.

The plane was almost full, and I slid into my window seat quickly, plugging the headphones in straight away. I liked to fly, but I wasn't in the mood to get trapped into hours of conversation. The headphones would serve as a visible "piss off" sign to anyone seated next to me. As it turned out, I needn't have worried. That seat was one of the few left empty.

I pulled out my book again and ignored the safety briefing. I've flown a lot, and on planes a damned sight more dangerous than this. I looked out the window and watched take off. For some reason I've always been fascinated by it. There's something profoundly unnatural about the way a plane throws itself into the air.

It was about an hour into the flight that I felt a kicking into the back of my seat. Every few minutes; kick, kick, kick. A glance between the seats showed a frazzled-looking mother in her early forties trying to calm a young man, maybe fourteen or fifteen years old.

He stared back at me and then loudly asked his mother about my bruises.

"I'm sorry," she told me. "Flying always upsets him."

I gave her a smile to tell her not to worry about it. The kid very obviously had some kind of mental disability.

"Fuck off, Jasmine!" the boy said, looking at me with a smile.

"He doesn't mean anything by it. It's Tourette's," the mother said, wincing her apology. I smiled again. This was going to be a long flight.

I managed to lose myself in an in-flight film for a while. An action movie with a giant ape and some overly-pretty English actor. At least Hollywood seemed to have learned how people hold guns now. I grew up watching the A-Team on Saturday evenings, watching Hannibal fire off fifty rounds from a clip that only holds thirty at best, and managing to be a crack shot despite firing from the hip. I've learned differently since then; it's not that easy to knock someone unconscious with a single blow, you can't blow a car up by shooting into the back of it, explosions aren't always a giant ball of fire. Frankly, the A-Team has a lot to answer for.

"Fuck off, Jasmine!" the kid behind me bellowed. Maybe he was yelling at the giant ape.

Yeah, I thought. *Fuck off, Jasmine.*

I joined the army as young as they'd let me in, learned the basics and did my time until I'd worked out which end of the gun was the dangerous one, then I ended up doing something I would never have predicted.

Most people have heard of the SAS, Britain's elite special forces. These are the guys you call in to get the job done. Soldiers who appear out of nowhere, zip-lining down from a helicopter. We didn't even admit they existed until after that business with the Iranian embassy in 1980. The SAS walk softly and carry a big stick, going behind enemy lines to take out vital targets on ops that will never really be admitted to.

I ended up in the SRR, the Special Reconnaissance Regiment, and that's something different entirely. The SRR are ghosts. We're smoke on the wind. We pass through without leaving a trace, and leave you thinking our footprints are your own—or dead.

I must have fallen asleep at some point. I dream often, though I rarely remember them, and I woke as we were on final approach into Istanbul with the taste of dust in my mouth, and the imprints of my fingernails in my palms. I blinked myself awake as we landed and taxied to the terminal. I stayed in my seat while everyone else rushed to stand up and queue for the door. I'll never understand why people do this, it's not as if there was anywhere to go until the doors opened.

Istanbul Ataturk Airport is a decompression point. For many, it's the first time they step outside their comfort zone and realise that not everyone in the world speaks English and eats at Burger King. The ubiquitous Starbucks and Cafe Nero were still there, along with the standard western fast-food places; but intermingled with them were Turkish cafes and restaurants selling everything from elaborate pastries, to menemen and kofti. I grabbed a sandwich and a Coke, fully embracing the culture, and made my way to my next gate.

It was another four-hour flight to Kabul. This plane was quieter and I got some more sleep before we touched down on the sun-blasted runway. The heat hit me as I made my way down the steps and followed the other passengers into the terminal. Hot, loud, and dirty sums up my lasting memories of Hamid Karzai airport. I doubted the place had changed much and I wasn't wrong. Baggage collection was fast today for some reason, so that was something, and I grabbed my pack and headed to immigration.

Passport control was a mess. It usually was. The lines were long and slow-moving. Bored soldiers from the Afghan National Security Forces wandered aimlessly in pairs, hands on their weapons. I scanned the hall and spotted the man I wanted, holding a card with "Thompson" written on it. I wove through the lines towards him, nodding a greeting as I approached.

"Mr Thompson?" he asked as I drew closer.

I nodded again.

"My name is Mujib. I am Mr Gharfour's head of security." His greeting was friendly enough, but his eyes were calculating as he took my measure. To his credit they passed over my bruises without pause. I was almost impressed.

I smiled and reached to shake his hand. He was a shorter man, slightly over-weight, and dressed in a strange semblance of a uniform; plain trousers and a shirt, with combat boots and a cap. Take the boots and cap away and he would have looked like everyone else. Apparently boots and a cap were all it took. Put a gun in his hand and that made him private security.

"Nice to meet you, Mujib. Have you made arrangements?" I asked with a look at the immigration officers.

Mujib followed my gaze. "It will not be a problem, sir. This way, please."

Immigration in Afghanistan can be a nightmare. Most foreigners need to register their presence in the country, a requirement that goes over and above the need for a visa. Mujib led me past the lines of frustrated travellers, to the officials in their kiosks. A nod and a smile were all that my immigration process involved. I looked across to the other lines as we passed through, where a German reporter was arguing at another kiosk in thickly accented English. My passport never even left my bag. I smiled at the reporter and held my hand up, rubbing my thumb and fingers together. He'd know better for next time I guess. Kabul works on a system of bribes. It's not so much the grease that keeps the cogs turning, but rather the grime that stops the machine falling apart entirely.

Mujib escorted me out of the airport and into the heat. I knew from the pilot's announcement that it was going to be hot. Thirty degrees Celsius is about eighty-six in Fahrenheit. It's silly but I've always used Fahrenheit for the higher temperatures, I have done since I was a kid. It's probably because it sounds more extreme at either end of the spectrum. Some things we never grow out of, I suppose.

The car sat baking in the steady heat. Already the dust was getting to me. It was like walking into a dream, or a nightmare. The smells of dust and hot plastic had followed me home. They'd haunted me, accompanying every hallucinated visitor, every flashback. Now I'd walked willingly into that smell. It was like I was welcoming a nightmare with open arms. I paused for a moment beside the car as Mujib climbed in. It would be all too easy to just go back into the airport, book myself a flight and go home. In hindsight, maybe it would have been better for everyone if I had.

Mujib drove a white Toyota Corolla, like just about everyone else in Afghanistan. About eight out of every ten cars in this place were Corollas. It's like they came here to die. Except the Afghans don't let them die. Servicing and repairing them was a cottage industry here. They kept going until they fell apart. Or until they were blown up, of course.

I stared at a crack on the windscreen as Mujib drove. It gave me something to focus on without having to look outside, or show Mujib that his driving scared the living shit out of me.

It had been five years since I was in Afghanistan last, and I'd almost forgotten about the roads. Traffic signs were almost non-existent, and nobody followed the few that were around. There are two rules for driving in Kabul; do it fast, and always assume you have the right of way.

The place hadn't improved much since I'd left, but then Kabul isn't anything like most people think. The majority of the city isn't in ruins; at least, not in the same way as Damascus, Raqqa or Aleppo in Syria. The war had turned into an insurgency long before coalition troops ever reached the city. In many ways it was similar to the Troubles in Northern Ireland. You can live here and never encounter anything more worrying than the occasional set of old bullet holes in the walls, or a distant explosion and plume of smoke.

The one thing that does stand out here is the poverty. The Taliban hit Afghanistan hard in terms of trade. Then the war, the occupation, and the mess that's been here ever since, fucked up what was left. It's pretty damned hard to find work in Kabul that isn't, in some way, connected to the coalition; and if the western powers ever left this place it would probably fall right to pieces all over again.

The beggars were pretty hard to miss, too. We slowed down to pass through a check-point and I realised I was counting them. They were mostly children with lost, hopeless eyes that didn't even bother to look at the people passing them. Some leaned on crutches, poor replacements for missing legs, while others simply looked neglected and malnourished. I turned away.

"Selfish bastard," Johnson whispered at me from the back seat.

Mujib barely spoke as he drove, throwing me the occasional critical glare that told me enough all on its own. He was Gharfour's head of security, and here was I, at least a decade younger, a foreigner, and a kafir at that, hired in over his head.

CHAPTER SIX

The car slowed for a more involved check when we entered Waj'zir Akhbar Khan. This was the most affluent part of Kabul, hosting the diplomatic quarter, and it showed in everything from the size and condition of the buildings, to the security presence. ANSF soldiers manned the checkpoints and patrolled the streets. This was where the money was. This was where the foreign powers were. The rest of the city could clearly go to hell so long as this part was patrolled and protected.

I glanced at Mujib as we slowed again outside the entrance to a secure compound, and received a nod in return. A large house was just visible over high walls that were topped with razor wire. Mujib stopped at the security barrier and leaned out of the window to speak to the guard. The barrier was just a painted wooden boom, less effective than the barriers you'd find at the entrance to a car park. I snorted a laugh to myself as I watched the men standing behind it smile and wave a greeting to Mujib. Not one of them held their weapon in any kind of ready position. Not one of them stood to the side of the boom. If we'd been going at any speed, we would have taken out the red and white barrier, and probably at least two of the guards.

Christ, what have I signed up for?

The compound itself was utilitarian. A number of small buildings ran along the inside of the surrounding wall—stores, I guessed, or possibly homes for the staff. The main residence itself was drab, covered in the same dust that eventually swallowed everything in Kabul. The real luxury and grandeur would be inside, locked away from the eyes of the masses as if they might soil it.

Mujib drove up to the front of the building and climbed out, opening the boot of the car to hand me my bag. The heat was even worse now that the sun had had a chance to bake the concrete. It would get a lot worse by mid-afternoon.

"This way, sir," Mujib waved me onward with a smile that didn't reach his eyes, and led me into the residence.

The renovations can't have been finished long; the faint smell of paint and sealant was still hanging in the air. The air-conditioning was a relief, but with the tiled floors and high, white ceilings, it was almost enough to make the place cold.

I looked around as we walked, noting the CCTV cameras and the locations of the few guards we encountered. They didn't look to be ANSF, which I thought was odd given Gharfour's government position. Instead, Gharfour seemed to have opted for a private security force that, so far at least, looked to be both older and in worse shape than any of the ANSF troops I'd seen. There had to be a good reason for that, but I was damned if I could think of one.

Mujib knocked at a door and then led me into a small side-office. An older man stood as we entered, making his way out from behind a desk. Dressed in a grey perahan tunban, and wearing an elegant long beard and a keffiyeh, this man was a traditionalist.

"Mr Shabib, please allow me to introduce Mr Thompson?" Mujib asked.

Shabib placed his hand over his heart and nodded at me, a formal greeting given to someone who might be unaccustomed to being touched. A more traditional greeting would have involved a handshake and alternating kisses on both cheeks. I nodded my own formal greeting, impressed at the sensitivity despite myself.

"Mr Thompson," Shabib said, with a slight pause before my adopted name that was enough to make me wonder just how much he actually knew. "You must be tired after such a long journey."

I smiled. "It was a long flight."

"I am sure," Shabib said with an odd little smile. He considered me for a moment before glancing at Mujib. "Mujib here will have someone escort you to your room. Take some rest and I will introduce you to Mr Gharfour later, or in the morning, if you prefer? I'm sure there is much to discuss."

I watched Mujib slip out and let a sigh escape my lips. It was a relief, to be honest. It might be mid-morning here, but it was still about six in the morning as far as my body was concerned; I'd been up all night, and I was still carrying the bruises left on me by Cresswell's men.

"I'm sure this afternoon will be fine," I told him. "If Mr Gharfour has the time, of course. I'd like to look over the existing security arrangements tomorrow, then get started on a few things."

"As you say," Shabib said with another nod, glancing at the door as Mujib returned with a shorter, vaguely south-east Asian looking man.

Shabib dismissed me with vague pleasantries, and I followed the servant through the halls. The man's features told me he was a Hazara, one of the minority ethnic Shi'ites; the traditional servant underclass. There's an Afghan saying that when God made the donkey the Hazaras wept because they knew their role had been stolen from them. Things had supposedly changed under President Karzai, with the Hazara having equal legal status to everyone else in the country, but apparently things hadn't changed all that much.

My rooms were better than I'd expected, with a good-sized bedroom, bathroom, and even a small kitchen area. I sank down on the bed as soon as the servant left, taking a minute to let my eyes close before dragging myself up and over to the duffel bags piled against one wall.

Paragon had arranged to have my equipment delivered from a local supplier. Just about anything is for sale in Afghanistan if you know where to look, and they had produced pretty much the same black-bag of kit that the army does, right down to the anti-microbial underwear. They're designed to be worn for days at a time. Hopefully this job wouldn't come to that.

I pulled open the first bag and began inspecting the kit. I carry my own personal protective equipment, or PPE. Boots, gloves, knee-pads; they're all better if they're worn in. McCourt had provided everything else. I checked over the body armour, and field-stripped the M4 and the Glock 17, checking each piece was in good condition and free of any dirt that might cause it to jam. I paid particular attention to the Glock, even though I'm not a big fan of handguns. There aren't many situations when I'd rather have one over a good rifle, but close protection doesn't often work like that and, although I was here to train Gharfour's security team, I had no illusions about what I'd be doing for the first few weeks.

I was idly checking the combat webbing when I found the phone. The pouches should have been empty, but it's always best to check them for holes. The phone was an old Nokia 3310. They used to call them bricks. The things are practically indestructible compared to a modern smartphone and just about every country had them at some point. I fished it out and scowled at it, turning it over in my hand.

It wasn't on the equipment list, and it shouldn't have been there. I almost turned it on before I stopped myself and popped the back cover off. It wasn't all that hard to pack one of these things with explosives, and death by mobile phone was not the way I planned to leave this world. Whoever had hidden it in the webbing had somehow known I was coming.

As it turned out, the Nokia was exactly what it looked like. An old, sturdy, and almost untraceable phone, provided it was used correctly. I seriously doubted Gharfour would have provided it, which just left me with unanswered questions. The phone was too old to help anyone pinpoint my location with any great accuracy, no matter how good whoever supplied it was. At best it would show them Gharfour's compound, and they obviously already knew I was here.

I set the alarm on my watch for five hours—I'd been up all night but I knew better than to sleep on my own schedule. I've always found it's best to force yourself into a new time-zone as quickly as possible. Five hours would be enough that I wasn't yawning into Gharfour's face, and should still let me sleep tonight.

I glanced at the phone again.

"Screw it," I shrugged and held down the power button. The phone flashed and went through its start-up sequence; I don't know what else I'd expected really. I stared at it for a few minutes before tossing it aside. Whoever had put it in there had clearly wanted to contact me. The ball was in their court now.

The phone bleeped just as I was dropping off, naturally. I fumbled for where I'd left it on the nightstand. A text message.

Secure the phone. Power off and remove SIM.
Further instructions at 9pm local.

What the hell? I'd just flown for nine hours, survived the demolition derby that was the streets of Kabul, and now some mystery idiot wanted to play games with me? I was in no mood for this crap. I did, however, crack the back of the phone off and pull out both battery and SIM card. If nothing else, it would stop the bloody thing waking me up again.

*

The tap at the door was tentative, but it was enough to pull me from sleep. I blinked myself awake, reaching for the handgun on the nightstand, before I thought better of it.

"Yes?" I called. I glanced at my watch and saw it had just passed two in the afternoon.

The door opened slowly to reveal the same Hazara servant who had brought me to the room earlier.

"Excuse me, sir. Mr Gharfour will see you now." He had an odd manner of speech that managed to make the sentence both statement and question.

"Good enough," I nodded. "Give me a few minutes." I pulled on the combat dress, webbing and PPE. Might as well look the part. When you're paying eight hundred and fifty pounds a day for a British soldier, there are some expectations.

Gharfour's office was on the top floor. I followed the servant up the stairs, taken at my request, noting the cameras and the absence of any guards. I still didn't know the servant's name. He was deferential to the point of obsequiousness, avoiding eye contact and ushering me along with softly spoken directions.

Shabib was waiting for me in the outer office. "You are well rested, I hope, Mr Thompson?"

"Thank you, yes," I lied through my teeth. Something about the man bothered me. He didn't seem particularly interested in my responses, but this was more than just small-talk. He watched me as I spoke, gauging my reactions as if he was looking for something, and it set me on edge.

I followed Shabib into the inner office to where an elegant man, who I assumed to be Gharfour, sat behind a huge mahogany desk. The thing must have weighed more than three big men, and God only knew how they'd managed to get it up the stairs. There was no way it would ever have fit into the lift.

Unlike the desk, Gharfour was slight; a thin man in a pale grey suit with a close-cropped, black beard.

"Mr Thompson, sir," Shabib introduced me.

His smile was unexpected; a warm and genuine smile that lit his face as he came around from behind the desk to grasp my hand.

"Mr Thompson! I am Hassan Gharfour. It is a pleasure to meet you." He glanced at Shabib and the servant hovering near the door. "That will be all."

He made a point of waiting for the door to close before he spoke again. "I know who you are really, of course. I think it probably best if you remain Thompson, rather than Carver, outside this room."

I gave him a genuine smile of my own. "I appreciate that, sir."

"It is a curious rumour that you carry around with you," Gharfour mused. "How on earth did you come by it?"

I shrugged to cover my shock. He knew? Of course he knew. He would have done his homework as soon as McCourt assigned me to the job. I've told this lie more than a few times, by now it even sounded like the truth to me. "Who knows how these things get started?" I said. "Soldiers gossip, and they can be as superstitious as anyone else."

Gharfour nodded with a small smile, letting the topic drop as he made his way to his seat and motioned me into an empty chair.

"Please, sit. I am sure your superiors provided you with a brief on my requirements, but I'd like to go over them again." He paused long enough to elicit a nod from me. "I am not new to this position, but there have been developments of late that will require an increase in security. Mujib, whilst he is a good man, I am not convinced that he has the skills or training necessary."

"What developments?" I asked, then checked myself. "If you consider it relevant, sir."

Gharfour smiled. "You need not worry about being overly deferential, Mr Carver. There might come a time when you do not have time for 'sir'. I am the Director of Drug Demand Reduction, part of the Ministry of Public Health. In most other countries this would be an administrative post, working closely with social workers and support networks. But this is Afghanistan, and it is not like any other country."

He fell silent for a moment, turning to gaze out of the window. "They say that when Allah made the world, all of the pieces that were left over he put into Afghanistan. We have such a diverse country. Mountains; deserts; rangelands; and fertile plains; all in one small nation. But some days it feels that we have more of the *teryakk*, the opium poppy, than anything else. Did you know that before this war began, only four percent of our farmlands were used to grow opium? After twelve years there are more poppy farmers than ever. In the last two years alone, production has soared because of a new, hardier poppy plant brought in from China. This country is drowning in a sea of opium, Mr Carver, and it is my job to try and reduce the demand for it. To do that, I need to give the people of this nation an alternative to growing this cursed flower. You can imagine how popular this makes me."

I snorted a laugh at that. "Not overly, I imagine."

"No," Gharfour replied with a smile. "This country has grown to depend on the poppy as much as any addict. You could not simply stop production; the economy would collapse entirely. It must be done slowly, it must be negotiated. And, in the middle of all of this, it is your job to keep me safe, and allow me to do my job."

"Yes, sir." I mentally shook myself awake. The man was a rambler but was finally getting to the point. "Is there a particular area you'd like me to focus on?"

Gharfour spread his hands and shrugged. "Security is not my field, Mr Carver. This is why you are here. So long as I am alive, I can only assume you are doing your job. I suggest you begin with Mujib. He can give you my schedule."

I nodded. The man would be good to work with, I suspected. I've heard horror stories about jobs where the principal thinks he knows what he needs, and interferes or pushes back every step of the way. Gharfour seemed willing to just let me get on with it; but then if what he said about the opium was true, he had his hands full already. The mobile phone sprang back into my thoughts. Was it something to do with the drug barons? I shook myself, covering it with a cough as I realised Gharfour was looking at me expectantly.

"I'd also like to do a complete review to start," I told him. "There are some things at your compound that need changing immediately. There may be others that aren't so obvious."

Gharfour nodded, absorbing that. "Such as? Immediate changes, I mean."

"The gate, for one," I told him. "Your guards are on the wrong side of it. They should be stopping the cars before they even get close. At the end of the day, the gate is just a wooden pole. It's not going to stop anyone who really wants to get in. Nor will it stop any cars with an IED in it."

I didn't bother explaining what an IED was. Anyone who lived in Kabul knew the acronym for an improvised bomb.

"I see," Gharfour murmured, reaching into his pocket for a packet of cigarettes, lighting one with a polished zippo lighter, and drawing deeply. "Smoke?"

I shook my head. I'd almost forgotten how many people smoked here.

"And so, what would you suggest?"

"I'd need to take a closer look at the gate to give you a real recommendation, sir." Hell, if the gate was anything to go by, I'd need to have a bloody close look at everything. "I'm basing this on my arrival last night. I'll conduct a full security review and come back to you with my report."

"You mean, your arrival this morning?" Gharfour said with a laugh.

I laughed with him. The first rule in any job: always let the boss think he's funny. "Yes, sir. This morning."

"Very well then," Gharfour said, rising to his feet. "Conduct your review. I will be back at the office tomorrow. I assume you will be accompanying me?"

I nodded. Hopefully I'd get some real sleep between now and then, or it promised to be a bloody long day.

Gharfour grunted and fell silent for a moment. "Are your rooms to your liking?"

"They're excellent, sir," I said, standing up. It was true. I've bunked down in places far worse than this.

Gharfour nodded, obviously pleased. "Good. I have a very talented team of cooks on the staff who will be happy to make any dish you desire. Or, if you prefer, you have a small kitchen in your own rooms. The staff will procure any supplies you wish, though I would appreciate it if you kept your alcohol order to a minimum. This is still an Islamic nation and alcohol is illegal, as I'm sure you know."

I did know. I also knew it was a law that only seemed to apply to those that weren't rich or in government.

"Of course," Gharfour continued, "I'm sure you'd always be welcome to eat with Mujib and the rest of your men."

My men? Something about that didn't sound right to me. It had been a long time since I'd had men, or led any kind of team.

"That's a good one, isn't it, Carver? *Your men*?" The voice was Scottish. I didn't need to turn my head to know it was Turner, he had been the only Scot in my squad. I ignored him. Gharfour was still speaking, and I'd missed most of it, but his meaning was clear enough. I nodded my acceptance of the dismissal, as Turner continued his rant, and made my way to the door.

"Because when you're in a *team*," Turner carried on, his voice rising to a hoarse shout as I walked away. "When you've got *men*, you look after them, don't you Carver? You don't fucking sit there and watch them get shot, do you?"

I closed the door behind me, taking a deep breath as I walked.

"I've got a fucking hole in my head, Carver!" Turner screamed after me. "A hole. In my head!"

CHAPTER SEVEN

I'm not crazy.

I am a little fucked up, but I'm reasonably sure that I'm not actually insane.

What I have is some kind of PTSD. Hallucinations brought on by trauma and survivor's guilt. I've done enough research on my own, whilst avoiding support groups and therapy, to know that much. I know avoiding the help is a bad idea. Maybe I'm hoping it will burn itself out. Maybe I'm an idiot.

Blame it on testosterone. Blame it on stupidity. Hell, you could even blame it on the squaddie mentality—the stubbornness beaten into us in training. Blame it on whatever you want, but I'd spent the past few years hoping it would go away on its own, and knowing it wouldn't.

But the visitors weren't going away. They were loud. Louder than they'd been in a long time, drawn out by the mention of a team and my memories of what happened to the last squad I led.

The thing is, I've had my visitors for a couple of years now and, in terms of the guilt, I'm really starting to just not give a shit anymore. I did what I had to do. I don't feel a lot of guilt about it. Because of that, I could really do with the lot of them fucking off.

I moved away from Gharfour's office slowly, forcing myself to relax. Turner let me go, which was a rare blessing. More than once he'd followed me around for an entire day, screaming at me and bleeding over everything he could find.

I glanced down at my watch, though I didn't know why I bothered. The sun alone could have told me it was mid-afternoon. Time enough to have a look around the place. I stopped back at my rooms for the rest of my kit. PPE and body armour are bloody annoying, right up to the point that you need them. I checked the M4 and the Glock and brought both. It might be overkill, but I'd rather have them and not need them than the other way around.

The main residence was larger than it looked from the outside. Lavish hallways lined with luxurious suites gave way to a ballroom, a cinema, and even a well-stocked library. The lower floors held a servant's wing, disused drawing rooms, and a dining room large enough to host a state banquet, though I doubted it got used too often. I found the servant stairs, along with fire escapes and half a dozen different ways into the building. Most importantly, though I passed four or five servants, I only found a single guard; a bored man, who I was almost on top of before he even looked at me.

Gharfour, apparently, lived alone. There was no evidence anywhere in the house of a wife or children. That was a good thing so far as my job went—less people to guard. That said, it also made for an empty house with fewer eyes to spot things out of place.

I took the servant's lift down to the basement and the main kitchen. The opulent paintings and statues vanished immediately, replaced with plain concrete blocks, painted a functional white. I followed the hallway through to the kitchen. Three men in chef's whites glanced at me as I entered, but made no move to stop me as I made my way past the stainless-steel surfaces and stoves.

Three doors led off from the kitchen, one of which was clearly a freezer or cold-store of some kind. I picked one of the others at random, and found myself in a store-room with large double doors leading out to a loading dock. I stepped out into the delivery bay and swore. No guards here, either.

I spent the better part of an hour wandering through the compound. The mid-afternoon sun in Kabul is relentless, but it's the dust that makes the difference. If I'm really honest it doesn't actually get that hot in Kabul. It's no worse than a really hot summer day in London; it just feels like it. The dust tends to cake your skin and lips, leeching the moisture out of you. Wearing full kit didn't help.

I made a slow circuit of the compound, stopping once to fill a water bottle in the kitchen. Mujib was nowhere to be seen, though the three men at the gate pointed me in the direction of a low building close to the wall. 'Pointed' was the operative word here. None of them spoke much English and my Pashto was very rusty. I would need to brush up on it. A misunderstood instruction could easily be the difference between a safe client and a dead one.

I found Mujib sitting at a table at the end of a long bunkhouse, watching a small television and smoking. He glanced at me as I came in and muttered something to himself as he swung his feet down from the desk. He sucked a final drag out of his cigarette and reached for an ashtray, looking up at me as he stubbed it out.

"Mr Thompson. What can I do for you, sir?" There was a tone to his voice. Nothing so blatant as contempt or sullenness, just a flavour—an undercurrent that it would have taken an idiot to miss. It wasn't anything I haven't seen before. Nobody likes to be replaced, or have someone brought in over their head. It all comes down to how you handle it.

"I was hoping you could walk me through your procedures?" I asked him. "Mr Gharfour's schedule, transport arrangements, the guard's shift rotations; that sort of thing. It'll probably take me a while to get up to speed with your arrangements, and I thought it would make sense to talk to you. I imagine you set up most of them."

A bit of flattery never hurt in a situation like this.

He didn't quite hide the smile as he scratched at his beard. "Of course."

I spent the next few hours going over Mujib's arrangements, walking the compound and poring over maps of Kabul. To be honest, I've seen a lot worse. Most of the problems were based on over-confidence and an over-reliance on physical barriers. It's all very well to rely on a blast-wall to protect you, but you can't really test them. Discovering that it's faulty and that a mobile IED would blow right through it, is something that usually happens when it's too late to do much about it.

Mujib hadn't planned for an actual attack. His security strategy revolved around guards standing at the gates with guns, looking intimidating. I managed to talk the men at the gate into standing in front of it, though Mujib had to translate, and I suspect he threw in a few choice words about me as he did. I volunteered for the early shift and left them to it. I needed something to eat.

The kitchen staff were great. The head chef spoke excellent English, and was more than happy to throw some food together for me. I have fairly simply tastes; whatever I wanted he'd have to cook from scratch anyway, so I had my pick. I took the pasta up to my rooms and ate as I worked with a pad of paper.

The main issue was the men. They might be capable of holding a gun and standing at a gate, but it didn't look like they were trained to do much more than that. I was here to bring the security arrangements up to a decent standard, not to put these guys through basic training. I was going to have to talk to Gharfour and see what his budget was for security. It would be easier to just replace the lot.

I flicked on the television after a while, background noise filling the room as a welcome distraction to the Nokia sitting on the night stand. It should have been easy to ignore it. I probably should have. I ought to have mentioned it to Gharfour as well. Whoever left it in my kit knew who and what I was, and they wanted to talk to me without Gharfour knowing about it. Those two things were never going to add up to anything good.

The text had said 9pm. I looked at my watch. It was 8.45pm.

Curiosity killed the cat, or so they say. I repeated that to myself three times before I gave in, stalked across the room and put the battery and SIM card back into the phone. It began its glacial start up process as I went to my small kitchen and made coffee.

I checked my watch again. Three minutes to nine.

I hadn't deleted the old text.

Secure the phone. Power off and remove SIM. Further instructions at 9pm local.

Instructions. That was an odd choice of word. Not *contact.* Not *details.* Just *instructions.* Whoever sent this thing clearly intended me to do their bidding. The phone buzzed at 9pm exactly. A new text flashed on the screen.

Is area secure for coms? Y/N

I stared at the phone and sipped my coffee for a few minutes. The area was as secure as I could make it. There was nothing more I could do. I was waiting just to wind them up, really. I thumbed a one letter response and waited.

The phone buzzed a few seconds later, ringing this time.

"Mr Carver?" A female voice. Soft, young, and American.

"Who is this?" I demanded. Might as well start off on the right foot. I was in control of this conversation, not her.

"Let's not play games, Mr Carver. We don't have time for that. You're an intelligent man, you know who this must be."

I paused, taking a deep breath before I spoke again. So much for my being in control of the conversation. At the very least I could stay in control of myself. My heart was already pounding. I hadn't signed up for this, and I certainly hadn't expected it. This was supposed to be a glorified babysitting gig. "What do you want?"

"I'd like to meet with you. There are some things we should discuss."

"I'm a bit busy, Miss…?"

"Call me Artemis."

A Greek goddess, and The Huntress at that? I rolled my eyes. Bloody Americans and their egos. I put a patronising edge on my voice. "Fine, Artemis it is. I'm a bit busy, darling. New job and all that."

"You're here for the money, Mr Carver, let's not pretend otherwise. I'll make it worth your while."

She had a point. It takes a while to adjust to that new reality when you make the shift from being enlisted to being a security consultant. You're not there for your country, for your squad, or, a lot of the time, even for your own career. You're there purely for the cash. I might be a whore with a gun, but I'm an honest whore. Once I'm bought, I like to stay bought.

"I don't need the money that badly, Artemis. You're going to have to do a bit better than that."

She sighed, impatience carrying through the phone. "I have credible intelligence that will impact your client."

I pulled the phone away from my mouth to cover my sigh. She was probably full of it, but it wasn't something I could just ignore. "Fine. When and where?"

"The Bird Market. Tomorrow at 3pm."

I gnawed on my lip. "How will I find you?"

"I'll find you, Carver. Just don't make life too difficult for me."

"Fine. I'll be there for three, Artemis, but this better be worth it."

I killed the phone, pulling the battery and SIM out. She had been pretty specific about making the phone unable to trace. The thing was, the Nokia was basically a dinosaur. It didn't have GPS capability. It wasn't a smartphone. The only way to trace or track this phone would be to triangulate through the signal towers. In another country that would require a level of government involvement. Here, it just meant someone with a lot of money.

*

My alarm woke me at 3am and I rolled out of bed and stumbled into the shower. I used to be able to wake and be up and moving in moments, sometimes your life can depend on it. It's something that I lost when I left the army; something I need to get back.

Ten minutes later, I was sucking down the last of my coffee and checking my webbing. I gave my weapons a brief inspection and made my way out. The early morning air was cool on my face, probably only about ten degrees or so, but I was still waking up and it felt colder. I shrugged down into my gear and made my way over to the compound gate, waving a hello to the two men on watch. I frowned as I drew closer. One of them was Mujib.

"I thought you were on later?" I asked.

"I changed the rota," he said with a shrug. "I thought it would make sense to take you in to the office myself so I can answer any questions."

I nodded. It did make sense, but helpfulness and initiative weren't something I'd had from him so far, and it seemed at odds with the disdain he'd shown me. I couldn't blame him for it. People like me were the reason his country was circling the drain. People like me had come here, guns blazing, and blown the place to hell in an effort to flatten the Taliban and get bin Laden. Then, after we'd fucked it up, we left without so much as a goodnight kiss.

I pushed away the creeping guilt and put a friendly tone into my voice. "Quiet night?"

"So far," Mujib replied. "It usually is."

I grunted, looking around. "When was the last patrol?"

Mujib looked at me blankly. "What?"

"The last patrol of the compound?" I repeated.

Jesus Christ, someone tell me they're doing patrols...

It was probably the only thing I hadn't already asked about, maybe because I'd assumed he at least had a basic understanding of securing and defending a position. Apparently, I was wrong.

Mujib shrugged. "We don't do that. What would be the point? This gate is the only way in."

I took a slow breath before I spoke. "What about the walls, Mujib?"

He gave me a look. The same look you'd give an irritating child. "The walls are twelve feet high and covered in razor wire, sir."

"I could clear those walls and be inside the building in less than five minutes." His expression told me he didn't believe me. "Mujib, the razor wire isn't live. There are no sensors on it, so you have no idea if or when it's been cut. All it would take is a man who knew what he was doing, and some bolt cutters, and he'd be inside in no time."

"Fine," he snapped. "Then we patrol."

"No." I shook my head. "One man on the gate at all times. I'll patrol with…?"

"Samir," Mujib supplied, glaring at me.

"Samir," I repeated. "Tell him to work his way around the left, I'll go right. Tell him to take his time."

I waited while Mujib relayed the orders. I didn't catch everything he said, my Pashto wasn't good enough and he was speaking quickly, but I did hear one phrase; *da khar zoya*. Loosely translated, it means 'son of a donkey'.

I waited until he looked at me and sketched a smile. "I only got two things from my father, Mujib. One was being stubborn, and the other…" I paused and grabbed my crotch.

His laughter was slow to come as he grasped both my meaning and that I'd caught his insult.

"Now do your bloody job," I growled, and left to patrol.

CHAPTER EIGHT

Mackenzie sucked hard on the water tube, swilling it around in her mouth before she swallowed. The grainy paste clung to the inside of her mouth, sticking to the back of her teeth. She might have to eat the stuff to stay alive but, dear God, it would take a lot longer for her to actually enjoy it.

She'd lasted almost two days before she gave in and swallowed it down. For most of that time, she'd been too nauseous to feel hungry anyway. Eating had cleared away the last remnants of whatever drug she'd been fed, and the water had done the rest.

She figured she'd been in the room for about four days, but it was hard to tell with no windows to give her any reference. The lights came on right before she was blasted with water. She suspected they were on some sort of daily timer. It was impossible to know for sure, though. It could have been every eight hours for all she knew.

Sometime between the first water blast and the second, she'd given up screaming and started listening. Anyone within ear shot would have answered already if they were going to. Listening though; that had told her something new entirely.

The faint whine of electronics was just about audible through the walls, though she had to hold her breath to hear it. Once, she thought she caught the sound of footsteps, but the most important sounds didn't come until the second day: the faint sounds of shouting.

The shouts were like hers to begin with, the words indistinct, but the tone was clear. Whoever it was passed back and forth between outrage and fear, alternating between screams of fury then, later, a quieter begging.

She'd shouted back until her throat burned, not realising the futility of it at first. She'd only heard them when she was holding her breath and utterly silent, and even then, she'd just caught the barest hint of their shouts. Whoever it was had no chance of hearing her unless they were as silent as she was. She needed them to adjust to their situation. To accept where they were for the time being. To stop yelling and start listening.

The voice, when it came, was soft—almost tentative, and from a completely different direction.

"Are you real?" it asked.

"Yes!" she shouted her answer, her heart suddenly pounding in her chest. "Yes, I'm real. I'm here."

There was no answer.

She fell silent, concentrating on not making any sound that might drown the voice out. It had been louder than the distant shouting, loud enough that it could have been from the next room. Maybe it was.

Her patience ran out. "Are you there?"

No answer.

"Hey!"

Silence.

"Hey, arsehole. Answer me!"

"I thought I was dreaming again."

Was it a man's voice? It was hard to tell through the thickness of the walls. He, if it was a he, sounded either delirious or stoned, or maybe he'd just lost his grip on reality. Any of these were equally plausible in a place like this. She was barely keeping it together as it was.

"What's your name?" she asked carefully, keeping her tone soft and level, as if speaking to a spooked horse.

There was a long pause before he answered. As if he had to wrack his brain for the answer.

"Armond. My name is Armond."

French then. Or maybe German? It didn't really matter. "I'm Mackenzie. Do you know where we are?"

He laughed then, the sound high and hysterical as it came through the concrete. "We're in hell, Mackenzie. Hell on Earth."

Probably better to just ignore that one, she decided. "Are we still in Kabul?"

"Where? No, but this room is dark most of the day, Mackenzie. I have no windows. I have no idea where we are."

"Were you in Kabul, too?"

"Afghanistan? No. No, I was in Syria. In Damascus."

Damascus? Syria was the other side of Iraq. It was thousands of miles away from Kabul. Where the hell was she?

He had a tone to his voice, an edge, like he was broken. It didn't matter, it was enough that there was someone to talk to. Enough that she wasn't alone. They spoke tentatively; like young lovers touching for the first time, each both excited and afraid of the other, but unable to stop themselves.

He'd been in Syria, with Oxfam, when he was taken; an administrator for one of their regional projects.

"How long were you there?" she asked.

"Eight months," he replied, before his voice drifted into silence. "Before. You know, before *this*."

"What did you do before that?"

"Iraq. *Medecin sans Frontières* for a couple of years. I don't like going home so much these days. This job gets to you, and everyone at home just seems so blind to what they have."

She nodded, despite the fact nobody could see her. He was right. The last time she'd gone home to Brisbane for Christmas it had been almost painful. The food left on the table was more than the street children in Kabul saw in a month.

Talking to Armond was hard work. He tended to fall silent for long periods, ignoring her when she called him, and she wondered if he was passing out. Or maybe he was being fed drugs. It wasn't just that though. He was maddeningly guarded and refused to answer many of her questions about himself or what had happened to him.

It was another two days before she thought to ask the most obvious questions. "How long have you been here, Armond? Have you seen anyone?"

He'd fallen silent again and she forced herself to count to two hundred before she called out again. He was damaged, that much was obvious from his voice. Yelling at him would only make things worse.

"They still come for me sometimes," he said, when she'd just about given up on getting an answer. "Not so much as they used to. Sometimes I think they forget I'm here."

"What do they want?"

He laughed; a bitter, splintered sound that barely made it through the wall. "They want miracles, Mackenzie."

"What do you mean?" she asked, but Armond had fallen silent again.

*

By the end of what she thought was the first week, she was fatigued and listless. She blamed the diet. The gruel was enough to keep her alive, but it likely lacked a lot of essential nutrients. She slept often, though how much of that was down to boredom was anyone's guess.

Armond hadn't spoken to her in days and in her weaker moments she wondered if he was still alive. She'd wondered more than once if he'd ever really been there in the first place. She marked the passing of time by the lights. Each time the spotlights blazed on, it was the beginning of another day. By her reckoning, she'd been in this prison for nine days.

The door was built into the glass wall, fitted so closely that it was invisible in the shadows that wreathed that end of the room. She gaped at it as it opened, an impossible thing that made her bolt up against the restraints. The figures that emerged were dressed in white medical garb. A man and a woman. They did not look at her, busying themselves with erecting a small stand a few meters from her. It was some manner of clamp, designed to hold something in place.

For the briefest moment she was bothered by her nakedness, a fleeting hangover from when she'd had a normal life.

"Hey!" she managed, her voice croaking. "Let me out. Please?"

The man glanced at her once. A plain, Middle Eastern man who could have come from anywhere. His eyes flickered over her bound form and then he turned back to the clamp, setting a large candle into it and lighting it before heading for the door.

"Let me go!" she screamed after him.

The door gave a pneumatic hiss, slid shut, and thunked back into place.

"Mackenzie?" A voice broke into the room through unseen speakers. "You are well?"

The question called for an answer, but it brought with it a realisation. They could hear her. The room must have a microphone in it somewhere. The thought that they had been able to hear her screaming for days on end, and just ignored it, passed quickly, smothered by the knowledge that they had probably heard every word she had shared with Armond. Somehow that was worse, and a spark of rage ignited in her chest.

"I'm tied up, you sick fuck! How the fuck do you think I'm doing?"

"Tell me about the fire, Mackenzie."

"What?" She frowned at the glass wall across the room. "What fire?"

"You were nine years old, I believe?"

She stiffened against the frame, biting down the gorge that rose in her throat. "Fuck you."

The voice ignored her, continuing in a calm voice. "The fire burned out your apartment complex in Brisbane. It completely destroyed everything above the third floor. What floor were you on, Mackenzie?"

"Go to hell!" She'd worked long and hard to bury that memory. It was why she'd left home in the first place. Tears pooled in her eyes despite herself, and she swore she'd cut the bastard if she ever got out of these restraints.

"But your apartment was different, wasn't it? In the living room was a clear area. A circle untouched by the heat and the flames. That is where they found you, isn't it, Mackenzie? But it was only you, wasn't it? Your mother and father were killed, even your sister, died in those flames. How long did you spend in care homes, Mackenzie? How long was it before you were finally adopted? Was it until every child worth having had already gone?"

She bit down on her shaking lip, tasting blood. She'd be damned if she would answer him. The story had spread throughout the local news. It had followed her through counselling and into foster care, and then to two different schools when the bullying and name-calling had driven her out. They'd called her a freak. They'd thrown lit matches at her, and set her hair on fire, laughing as they told her to put them out.

"I believe it was *you* who held back those flames, Mackenzie." The voice was relentless, droning on despite her tears and clenched fists.

"What do you want from me?" she grated from between clenched teeth. Maybe if she offered them something, they would leave her alone.

"Show me how you did it. Put out the candle."

"*What?*"

"Put out the candle, Mackenzie."

She stared blankly at the glass. What was this? "How? I can't reach it, you idiot."

The voice turned hard. "Do not play with me, Mackenzie. Put out the candle and you will be treated well."

The threat hung in the air, unspoken, but she heard it anyway.

She tried blowing, though she was easily three meters away from it. The best she managed was to make it flicker.

"I can't," she said, sagging back against the frame.

"Put out the candle, Mackenzie. Don't blow it. Put it out."

"I don't know how," she admitted.

"You do. You have tamed fire before. Put out the candle."

She was going to die. The knowledge came slowly, creeping in like fog over a field. They wanted the impossible from her. Armond was right. They wanted miracles, and she had nothing to give them.

64

"I don't know how I did it," she called out again, pleading and hating herself for the weakness in her voice. "I don't even know if it was me."

"Put out the candle."

The voice nagged and demanded for what felt like hours, repeating the order as the candle burned down, and wax dripped onto the floor. Eventually it fell silent, ignoring her protests as they turned to begging pleas.

She remembered so little of it. She'd been so young and what she could recall had a vague, dream-like quality to it. Sensations were all she could really remember.

The heat on her skin, and the roar of the flames in her ears.

She remembered the fear, so strong that it overrode everything else as she'd curled into a ball and pressed her eyes to her knees. Beyond that, it was just memories of the aftermath. The feel of the fireman's jacket as she was carried out; rough and yet smooth on the hi-vis stripes. The smell of the smoke, and the way everyone looked at her— wonder mingling with a sympathy so sharp it cut into her.

"I can't," she whispered. "I don't know..."

She let her voice trail off. They weren't listening. They were going to kill her. It might take months, but eventually, when they grew tired of her failure, they would kill her. She let the thought grow, the certainty growing with it, until it overwhelmed her and the tears began again.

"Give them what they want."

She looked up, tossing her head to throw her dark hair back from her face. "Armond?"

"It's better to just give them what they want, Mackenzie," he repeated. He sounded calmer than usual, more lucid.

"I can't," she said. "They want a miracle and I didn't bring any with me."

She snorted a laugh then, tears still fresh on her face. It started as a giggle and built until she couldn't stop even if she'd wanted to. She laughed until her stomach hurt and it left her gasping. She'd been drugged and abducted, chained up in this room by mad men, and told to perform wonders or die. The whole situation was so absurd that it seemed like there was nothing else to do but laugh.

CHAPTER NINE

Patrolling has more functions than most people think. It's not just about spotting someone climbing over a wall. To be honest, it's more about deterrence. They're far more likely to spot you, than you are them—they are the ones hiding, after all.

Not only that, patrolling keeps you moving, keeps you alert. Standing guard in one place, especially at night or in the early morning, doesn't give you much to look at. Standing leads to leaning, leaning leads to dozing; and then you might as well not be there.

I walked the perimeter, taking my time to learn where the shadows fell most deeply, and the best places to try and breach the razor-wire. I seriously doubted anyone would actually bother. If you were going to attack this compound, the best way would be right through the ridiculous front gate. Or just blow a hole in the wall.

I passed the other guard, Samir, at the back of the compound, and gave him a nod and a thumbs up. He wasn't much more than a kid—twenty-something at best, but he was following instructions, taking his time. Him, I could work with, and probably make something of. I wasn't so sure about the others.

We stood at the front gate, speaking softly as the dawn approached. I sent Mujib and Samir on the next patrol, and stood at the gate alone. I didn't like it, but there was only the three of us to manage the whole compound. That was another thing that needed changing. Three men weren't enough. Eventually it led to someone being on their own, and that would lead to trouble one way or another.

I wasn't stupid enough to stand in the middle of the entry way. Instead, I kept to the shadows by the wall. Anyone trying to come in at this time of night wasn't likely be here on friendly business and I had no desire to end up with any more holes in me than I already had.

Four men came to relieve us at 6am, leaving us to get the car ready for Gharfour. Government offices in Kabul were open from 7:30am to 4:30pm, Wednesday to Saturday. It takes a bit of getting used to.

I went into the residence to escort Gharfour to the vehicle. The car surprised me; a fully armoured Toyota Land Cruiser—I'd been expecting a Mercedes or something. I rode in the front beside Mujib, with Gharfour in the back. I was relaxing already; this was a quality car, and the door had that heavy thunk that you only got with a fully armoured vehicle.

I reviewed Gharfour's schedule as Mujib drove; a day of meetings and various appointments. Easy enough in terms of work for me, but it meant a day of standing outside his door. Today didn't promise to be a bundle of laughs but then, that's one of the reasons why the pay was so good.

The day dragged. I was out of practice at standing around doing nothing. Mujib made a few attempts at conversation but I wasn't in the mood for small-talk. Talking on a job distracts you. It's not a good idea.

I glanced at my watch more than I should have, aware that my meeting with Artemis was creeping closer. At two o'clock I made my excuses, telling Mujib to escort Gharfour home if I wasn't back in time. He wasn't happy about it, and Gharfour wouldn't be either, but I needed to find out what Artemis wanted. Her line about credible threats was probably bullshit—a carrot to entice me to meet her. But an excuse like that works both ways, and I could feed Gharfour the same carrot if need be.

The Bird Market was actually quite close to the Ministry of Public Health, but twelve minutes by car in Kabul was easily forty-five minutes on foot. I did it in thirty. Making sure I knew the back-alleys of Waj'zir Akhbar Khan was one of the first things I'd done when I started working here with the SRR. Learning how to blend in was something I'd been trained in before I ever stepped foot in this place. Walking around alone in combat gear in Kabul is just about as clever as it once was in Belfast—you just don't do it.

Kabul goes to the dogs the second you step out of the diplomatic district, where the security is tightest and where most of the money is. The second you step beyond this, the extravagant compounds become crumbling homes, pockmarked with bullets and shrapnel, pressed tight together in an effort to stay upright.

I'd grabbed a loose thobe and a pakol from the Ministry, which went over my other clothes easily enough. Clearly this wasn't the first time someone had needed to be inconspicuous. The slit I discovered inside one pocket that allowed easy access to my handgun if I needed it raised an eyebrow though.

The streets were busy and the heat reflected back from the concrete, doing its best to cook me inside my clothes and make me miserable. I moved at an easy pace, fitting in with the crowds as I made my way south towards the river. It felt good to be doing this again. Like climbing into an old pair of jeans. This is what I'd trained for, what I knew and loved. It sounds crazy, but I felt more relaxed than I had in weeks.

The Ka Froshi Bird Market was nestled in a long alleyway and a few adjacent small streets tucked away behind one of the larger mosques. Mud-walled shops and market stalls were clustered close together, pressed against the walls, their brightly coloured canopies yellowed and muted by dust.

Afghans take a great delight in birds, and the alleyway was filled with the sound of finches, larks, and canaries, somehow managing to be heard over the squawk of the fighting cocks and partridges. It was impossible to move with any speed through the Market. Stacked straw cages and small aviaries crowded the pathway, surrounded by groups of haggling men. Despite all of this, the street had a relaxed atmosphere—as if the tensions of this wearied nation were forbidden to set foot in the Bird Market.

I picked my way through the throng, all but invisible in my pakol and thobe. I hadn't shaved since I left London, and my stubble was long enough to cover my cheeks. Clean-shaven men are rare in Afghanistan, and the last thing I needed was to stand out.

I moved casually, just another man enjoying the sights of the Market. My eyes scanned the crowd, never settling on any one thing for too long, trusting my instincts to pick up anything out of the ordinary.

She'd find me, Artemis had said. Perverse though it was, I didn't want to make it too easy for her. That said, I didn't particularly fancy spending all afternoon in the Bird Market either. It might be a haven for the locals but after eight hours or more in the heat, the place was choking on its own dust and the smell of the birds; which, oddly, smelled an awful lot like their own shit.

I made my way along the narrow street and stood near a circle of men watching a kowk-fight. I glanced around, trusting the clamour of the crowd to hide the fact that I wasn't watching. They were making more than enough noise as they threw down money, betting on the partridges. Wherever Artemis was, she was late.

Nearby, a woman in a blue burqa haggled with an old market-trader over the price of birdfeed. I watched her for a moment with a tight smile, before turning back to the street. I resisted the urge to check my watch. The woman paid the shopkeeper and made her way along the alley. I joined the flow of people and followed her. It didn't take me long to catch up.

"Follow me," I told her as I passed. I moved quickly, but not so fast that she would lose me in the crowd. I made my way from the market and ducked into another side street—this one empty and quiet.

I didn't have to wait long, and reached out to grab the woman and pull her into a doorway as she entered the alley. "Hello Artemis."

She jerked back from me with a muffled curse. "How did you know it was me?"

"Your skin is too pale," I told her.

"That's it?" she snorted. "I could have been anyone."

I shrugged. "It took you too long to pay for the seed. You couldn't find your money, and you look uncomfortable in the burqa."

She swore again. "I have a car around the corner, we can talk there. I can't breathe in this thing."

The car turned out to be a massive white Land Cruiser. Not exactly subtle, and rather similar to Gharfour's, but not unknown around here either. I scanned the empty front seats before I climbed into the back beside her. Meeting her was one thing, but I wasn't stupid enough to let myself be driven off.

"Christ, I hate these things," Artemis muttered, pulling the burqa back over her shoulders. She was blonde, and about thirty years old, if I had to guess. Attractive enough, though the heat had left her red in the face, and strands of her hair plastered to her cheek.

"So, you're what? CIA?" I asked as I pulled off the pakol, relishing the air-conditioning as I scraped my fingers through my hair.

She shrugged, brushing her hair from her face. "Something like that. Suffice it to say the United States government would like to hire your services."

My eyebrows rose and I leaned away from her a little. I'd run across my fair share of spooks, both MI5 and MI6, during my stints in Northern Ireland, Iraq, and Afghanistan, and I couldn't say that I cared all that much for their type. They had a different view of the world than I did, thinking in terms of agents and assets, and generally considered information to be far more valuable than a life.

Don't get me wrong. I've killed plenty of people. More than I really want to think about, if I'm honest, and usually it was in the process of retrieving some kind of intel. The difference was: I went in to get it, I risked my own arse. Five and Six? They take a handler approach. They manipulate, bribe, and extort to get what they need and if that puts the asset at risk, then so be it. I know it wasn't much of a distinction, and it probably made me a hypocrite, but I count it as the least of my flaws.

I eyed her and tried to ignore the increasing dryness in my mouth. I didn't like these people, and I didn't want to get caught up in whatever shit Artemis or her government had going on. "I'm already on a job. I told you that on the phone."

She gave me a thin, dismissive smile, reaching into a briefcase for a folder. "And I told you that we both know you're only here for the money. Well, this is money." She waved the folder at me.

She was right. I wasn't in this sweltering dustbowl working for Gharfour out of some sort of loyalty to him. I was here for the money. I *needed* the money. I sighed. "What's the job?"

She smiled again, a warm smile this time, her brown eyes dancing, as she dropped the folder back into the case.

"Not much more than you're doing already," she told me. "We need someone on the inside to keep an eye on Gharfour. We want you to be that eye."

I paused long enough to make her fidget. "What are you looking for?"

"Gharfour has contacts with most of the drug-barons in Afghanistan," she said. "We've known that for some time. The way the economy works, they wouldn't stop the drug trade right away, even if they could. To a point, we're fine with that; but we suspect Gharfour is crossing the line. We've reason to believe he's in the process of negotiating long-term contracts with these people, facilitating their exports into the United States. We're less happy with that, as I'm sure you can see why."

She smiled at me. It was a good smile, and her brown eyes were just as devastating. The woman could probably flirt her way into a bank vault. I'd been in this game long enough to know when I was being manipulated. Two could play at this.

"What's your name?" I asked with a smile of my own, lowering my voice and leaning a little closer.

"My name?" she blinked rapidly, the question taking her off guard.

"Well, I'm not calling you Artemis. It's like something out of a bad spy novel."

She laughed then, a genuine laugh—or a damn good fake. "Joanne. My friends call me Jo."

"And what should I call you?"

Those flirty eyes again. "I think you could use Jo."

I gave her a flat look and held it long enough to make her smile falter, long enough for her to know I was onto the game she thought she was winning. "What exactly is it you want from me, Joanne?"

Her eyes hardened, and her lips pressed into a line as she leaned away and shifted uncomfortably on the leather-bound backseat of the Cruiser. Her expression could have meant any number of things, and all of them unpleasant. "Gharfour is going to be hosting a meeting with some of these drug-barons. We want you to let us know when this is."

"What makes you think I'll know?"

"Let's not play games, Carver. You were hired in to ramp up the man's security. Of course you'll know."

I managed to keep a straight face. She might be American, but she wasn't an idiot. "And what do I get out of this?"

"For sending the text? Twenty."

I nodded, chewing on that. Twenty thousand was a decent amount. The phone was a burner so that wouldn't be traced, and I could easily ditch it once I had the money. "Pounds not dollars," I countered.

She paused for a long moment before she agreed again.

"Any idea when this meeting is going to happen?"

She shook her head. "That's your job to find out. We know he's held three or four of them already this year, but they're not on any kind of regular schedule. It could be tomorrow, a few weeks from now, or a few months."

"That's helpful," I grunted. "You're monitoring the burner phone all the time?"

"Yes," she nodded, scratching at the back of her hand. She seemed more edgy and easily flustered than I'd come to expect from her type. "The number you have goes direct to the embassy. It will be flagged as soon as you send something."

"And payment?"

"A direct wire transfer to your UK account. We already have the details."

I blinked. "You have done your homework."

She smiled that crooked half-smile again. It was more effective than I really wanted to admit.

"Of course I have, John. I like to know who I'm getting into bed with," she let that hang for a second, "so to speak."

I laughed. "You're a dangerous lady, Jo." I reached for the door as she shot me another smile. "I'll be in touch."

*

I made my way back to the compound and my rooms. Mujib had his instructions and was probably on the way back already. I needed some time to chew over Jo's information. I also really needed a long shower to wash away the grime of the Bird Market.

I stopped before I made it to the shower. I'm very much a creature of habit, almost compulsively so, and something wasn't right with my room. I'm not the tidiest of people but I do tend to follow a pattern. If I toss a shirt on a chair, you can bet your last penny that it will be there tomorrow, and probably the next day too. It took me a few long minutes of circling the room to realise what was bothering me.

My bags weren't all the way under the bed. I'd shoved them under there as soon as I unpacked. There was nothing in them I'd need for a while, and the rooms weren't so big that I wanted them out in the way. Now my travel bag poked out slightly, causing the blanket on my bed to bulge out.

I did a quick circuit of the rest of the apartment, checking the bathroom and the kitchen. Finally, I had a good look at the door and the lock, but nothing seemed out of the ordinary. Just the bag.

I flipped the blanket back and crouched down beside the bed. The bag had definitely been moved, but why would anyone bother? I pulled it out and went through the pockets and compartments. Some spare clothing, and a couple of books. Nothing anyone should be interested in.

I unzipped the end pocket and pulled out a paperback.

"Son of a bitch!"

73

My passport was the only thing in here, tucked in between the pages. I'd put the passport *inside* the book soon after landing, using it as a bookmark. It probably wasn't the safest or smartest idea in the world, but it's what I do. The thing was, I hadn't needed my passport at customs, Mujib had met me and walked me through. My passport had been wedged between the pages of the book. Now it was just inside the cover.

It had been moved.

Stolen passports, especially British or U.S. passports, can go for a fairly high price. I'd heard of them fetching upwards of three thousand U.S. dollars. But mine hadn't been stolen. It had been left in the bag. It wasn't the item they were interested in, it was the contents.

And that meant someone knew who I was.

And not just who I was, but *what* I was.

If I'd been anywhere else in the world, this wouldn't have bothered me so much. Anywhere else in the world, I didn't carry a legend around with me. Anywhere else in the world, I wasn't the Miracle of Kabul.

CHAPTER TEN

I was in the shower when it came to me. The first day I could put down to tiredness; the flight was long and I'd basically been up all night. The second day, I suppose I could say I was getting to grips with the processes and Mujib's way of doing things. Today was the third day though, and I had to face the fact that I was being a bloody idiot.

I was expecting Mujib and his men to know what they were doing. That was stupid enough all on its own, but I was in danger of falling into their routines. The fact was, I had been brought in to bring Gharfour's security up to scratch, not to be their boss. This wasn't a permanent job. This was a training consultancy.

I dressed quickly and made my way down to the main kitchen. I ate at a prepping station, surrounded by stainless steel. None of the kitchen staff spoke English, other than the head chef, but they were friendly enough. I shovelled down a bowl of some kind of porridge and muddled through my thoughts.

The first thing to do was get Mujib on side—this was his team after all. If I had to work around him, then not only would the job be twice as hard, but any changes I brought in would probably fall by the wayside the moment I left.

I rinsed my bowl and left it to dry beside a sink, earning me a smile from one of the kitchen staff, and made my way out to the gate. I could spot Mujib from the doorway, his ever-present cigarette glowing in the early morning darkness.

Three other guards were arrayed around the gate, looking tired and bored. If I could tell that just by their posture, then so could anyone else who might be watching. Something else to take care of.

"Mujib," I greeted him as I drew close.

"Mr Thompson, sir. Good morning." The hostility was still there, though more sullen than it had been before.

I ignored it and ploughed on. "I want to go over a few things with you this afternoon, once the client is back at the residence."

He didn't work especially hard to keep his face straight and the slight grimace shone through. "What sort of things, sir?"

"Some of the changes I want to bring in, and the new equipment."

Mujib frowned. "Equipment?"

I nodded. "Some secure coms equipment."

He gave me a blank look, as if the term was new to him.

"Better radios," I clarified. "A uniform, and higher quality weapons."

"What is wrong with our weapons?" Mujib hefted his rifle.

I couldn't help sighing. "The AK-47s are okay I suppose, but they're just okay, Mujib, and there are better weapons for this job."

He didn't look convinced.

"Look, it's just not well designed." I pointed at the weapon in his hand. "The ammunition is too big and powerful for the gun, which is why it pulls up so much on recoil. They tend to fire high and to the right of your target anyway, and some of the damned things will jam if you fart with the safety off."

Mujib grunted, throwing a dark look at Samir who had sidled close enough to listen in and was busily agreeing with me.

"Here," I handed my rifle to him. "Try this."

Mujib took the M4 gingerly, turning it over in his hands like a child with a new toy. He tucked it into his shoulder, pulling it in tight, and looked along the sights.

"That's an American M4. It's a bit lighter and a damned sight more accurate than what you're using." I smiled at his expression. "Let's talk this afternoon, and then I can talk to Gharfour about his budget."

"Yes, this is a good idea." Mujib handed back the weapon with obvious reluctance as I cast an eye over the others at the gate.

"I want you to put two men on the gate today. We'll take two cars and bring everyone else with us for the transport—treat it like we know there's a security alert."

Mujib nodded, eyes still on the gun.

"You've run two cars before?" I asked.

He didn't answer.

"Mujib!"

His head snapped up.

"Have you run a two-car detail before?"

"Yes, sir. Many times." He spoke too quickly and, inwardly, I grimaced. This was not going to be fun.

*

The streets were already crowded as the cars eased out through the gates. I rode with Gharfour and Samir, leaving Mujib to follow in the chase car. Samir was a good driver, as far as that went. I normally tried to avoid driving there. Actually, no; that's not true. I try to close my eyes and go to a warm, safe, place until we've arrived. Transporting Gharfour didn't give me that luxury, but I'd still rather be scanning for threats than driving the car.

The traffic was busy, even by Kabul standards, and Mujib was driving close—almost climbing into our back seat until we hit the junction. A red Corolla barged in front of him, forcing him to brake or crash. It sounds worse than it was, this was pretty much the norm when it came to driving there; but the Corolla had split us up, and by the time we hit the intersection outside of the British Embassy I couldn't even see Mujib.

They call this type of junction a roundabout in the U.K. They call them 'traffic circles' in the U.S. I have no idea what they called them in Kabul, but they weren't supposed to work like this. It was an absolute mess. Cars ignored lanes, other drivers, and the laws of physics, as they flew around in what looked like an attempt at mass suicide. A glance at Samir showed he wasn't even slightly concerned, which just goes to show why he was the driver, not me.

The blast-wave from the bomb reached out across the road ahead of us, flipping over the cars it could reach, and smashing the windows of the ones it couldn't. The ground beneath the Cruiser shook and Samir slammed on the brakes. A car rammed into us from behind and we crashed forward, ploughing into the back of a handful of smaller vehicles in front of us.

There was no fireball. No blast of flame reaching out to engulf the road. Just an expanding circular wall of dust and debris. I checked myself over quickly and found nothing amiss. The sheer bulk of the armoured Cruiser had taken the impact in its stride, and I silently thanked God for seat-belts.

"You all right?" I asked Samir. The air bag had gone off in the steering wheel, splitting his lip where it had slammed into his face. He looked pale and shaken but otherwise unharmed.

"Sir?" I called back to Gharfour. "Sir, are you hurt?"

He'd climbed down, or been thrown down, into the footwell behind my seat. Not a bad idea if he'd done it on purpose. A bit embarrassing if he hadn't.

"No," Gharfour managed, clambering out with a shamefaced expression. "A little bruised but I am okay. Can you get us out of here?"

It was a good question. The car was armoured, and whilst it wasn't exactly a tank it had fared better than most of the others caught in the blast. We could probably drive away if it wasn't for the fact that the road around us was chaos. At least two cars had been flipped completely over, and half a dozen more had collided, or been forced into each other, by the blast. Our vehicle wasn't going anywhere.

I pulled a radio from my pocket. It was old and worn, and frankly I didn't hold out much hope that it would reach anyone, but it was worth a shot. "Mujib, come in."

I glanced over at Samir and nodded back at Gharfour.

"Mujib?" I tried the radio again. The thing hissed at me in response, which wasn't what I'd been hoping for.

"Get him into a vest," I muttered over the sound of static from the radio. The bullet-proof vest was bulky and uncomfortable, and if the radio was anything to go by, then I doubted it would do much more than make Gharfour feel better. That said, putting it on would keep them both busy for a minute.

I tried the radio again. The adrenaline was starting to hit and I watched my hand shake as I pressed the button to talk. "Mujib, where the hell are you? We need an extract."

People began to clamber out of vehicles, staggering aimlessly across the road. I couldn't see much more than that. The dust-cloud was still climbing. In another minute or two the screaming would begin.

I stowed the radio and flipped open a map from the compartment in the door, though I already had a decent idea where we were. We were in the heart of Waj'zir Akhbar Khan. The checkpoints would be closing already, and ANSF troops were likely only moments away. Getting out of the area would be nigh on impossible. For now, at least, the safest place was probably in the car.

I changed my mind the minute the first of the shots rang out. The AK-47 has a distinctive sound, and I've spent more than enough time listening to it to recognise it.

"Get down!" I barked at Gharfour. Manners could wait. The car might be armoured but that didn't count for an awful lot. Any armour can be breached and I wanted him out of sight.

I pulled the Glock, nodding at a more lucid Samir to do the same. Our rifles were useless until we got out of the car.

Smoke and dust obscured much of the view. The real irony was the British embassy was about fifty yards away from us. The place was a veritable fortress, but it would be on lock-down by now, and we were on the wrong side of the gates.

A bullet pinged off the side of the car and I swore. I glanced up, making out a handful of murky figures heading towards us through the dust and smoke. If Gharfour was the target, then this car had just become more of a trap than a shelter.

I leaned around the seat towards Gharfour, who was crouched in the footwell again, and spoke in a low, calm voice. "We need to get out of the car, sir. I can get you out of here, but we need to move quickly, quietly, and without asking questions. Do you understand?"

Gharfour lifted his head and nodded. He glanced out the front and side windows in quick succession, then back at me.

"I'll go first," I told him. "Samir, you follow out my door. We stay low and move fast. Sir, put your hand on my back and don't take it off. I need to know where you are without looking. Ready?"

Neither one of them looked happy about it, but then, neither was I.

I eased the door open and slipped out of the car, keeping low and using the door for what little cover it gave me. I holstered the Glock whilst I waited and readied the M4. Range mattered and if we were spotted on the move then the time for quick and quiet would be over. I heard rather than saw Samir and Gharfour tumble out of the vehicle, and felt Gharfour's hand land on my back.

Then we were moving. I stayed low, sighting along the rifle through the swirling dust as we ran. Shots rang out again ahead of us, and then more as someone returned fire from behind our position. I crouched by a car, the others scrambling in behind me. ANSF soldiers would be setting up positions behind us. If we didn't move soon, we'd be stuck in the middle of this mess.

A figure emerged from the dust. Any civilians had picked up those they could carry and run by now. This was not somebody looking to make friends. I tucked the M4 into my shoulder and aimed for the chest, but the figure looked to have already been shot. Blood had soaked through one side of his torso, darkening the uniform with a stain that looked black from this distance.

More shots rang out, the distant muzzle flashes half blocked by the figure staggering towards me.

"Mr Thompson," Samir hissed urgently. "We should be moving."

I ignored him, eyes fixed on the lumbering figure in combat dress.

"Look at me!" the figure yelled out in English. "Look at the bloody mess I'm in, Carver. Will you look at the state of this?" Johnson picked at the front of his uniform, tutting over the blood. "Look at that. That's going to stain, I'll never get it out."

I squeezed my eyes shut against it all.

Fuck!

A fucking hallucination? Now? How much of what I was seeing was real?

"Fucking Johnson," I growled, blinking rapidly and drawing odd looks from both Samir and Gharfour.

I looked back up and into a different scene. The dust was clearing and the forms of the dead and wounded littered the street. Three ANSF soldiers lay dead close to our car, the bloodied bodies of militants, probably ISIL fighters, could be seen not far in front of us. I took a deep breath and gripped the gun tight.

"Let's go," I ordered, and took off between the cars, squatting down behind any cover I could find.

This was shit. Gharfour was on the edge of all-out panic, and Samir wasn't far behind him. We had to get off this street. Fighting militants like ISIL is an orgy of confusion at best, and this situation was getting worse by the second. We were caught between a force with no uniforms, and the approaching ANSF soldiers; my gun and combat gear were fast becoming a liability. I might as well have painted a target on my back.

I peered up over the bonnet of another car, plotted a route, then we were running again. Gharfour was as good as his word—his hand never left my back. The rush across the road lasted only seconds, but then combat is so often like that; each moment stretched out thin until it's a wonder they can hold all of the panic and pain. The real battle of times like this has nothing to do with your opponent. It's about trusting yourself, and trusting the training you've been through.

I saw the first bullet, saw the dust thrown up as it struck the road. And then all I heard was gunshots, coming from both directions. There was no time to do anything else—there was nothing to do but run.

Gharfour was sandwiched between us, with Samir behind him. I felt the tug before we'd gone ten paces. Gharfour's grip on my back changed. His fingers bit, a desperate grab against my jacket, pulling downwards as Samir collapsed.

I whirled around and saw Samir on the dust-covered asphalt. My gaze darted across his body, searching for the reason he'd fallen, until my eyes settled on the ragged mess above his boot. The bullet had hit Samir in the ankle—probably one of the worst places to get hit. There's almost no chance for the bullet to pass through tissue. It's practically guaranteed to hit bone, and when a bullet hits your ankle, most of the time the bones don't break—they shatter. The pain hadn't hit him yet and he'd collapsed onto the road clutching his leg. He had that look on his face. I've seen it too many times before. It's an odd mixture of shock and anguish that only comes from being really badly hurt. He couldn't even see what kind of state his ankle was in yet.

"Shit!" I grabbed Samir's arm and hoisted him up, throwing him over my shoulder. "Keep moving!" I barked at Gharfour.

The pain found Samir before we reached the edge of the road and hurried into an alley, his screams drowning out the gunshots for a moment. The alley was packed. Those that could flee already had, but the ground was littered with wounded and the frantic few that cared for them. I forced my way through, ignoring Samir's screaming and Gharfour's protests until we came out onto another street. The traffic was still moving here, there was a surreal normality to it considering the fire-fight taking place only minutes away. I dumped Samir on the pavement and stepped out into the traffic, levelling the M4 at the first car that came close.

"Get out!" I'm not sure if the driver even spoke English, but a gun in your face and a jerked thumb are easy enough to understand no matter where you're from.

I don't remember driving to the hospital. I do remember Gharfour's face though; the utter helplessness and panic carved into his features—that and Samir's screams.

CHAPTER ELEVEN

I don't enjoy my own company after a combat situation, especially one where somebody has been injured. It's too easy to start second-guessing yourself, to fall into the trap of blaming yourself for what happened and overthinking it. That's only natural, I suppose, but my situation was a little different. I was never really alone.

"Well that was a right fuck-up, wasn't it, Carver?" Johnson said again, calling over from where he leaned against the sink in the apartment's kitchen. "You should have stayed in the car."

I ignored him.

Rule Three: Don't talk to the visitors.

The thing was, he was right; and I knew it. The bomb had been a lure to draw as many emergency services and Afghan security forces into the area before the militants started shooting. Gharfour had never been the target. I don't think they even knew he was there. But he easily could have been their target. There was no way of knowing at the time. I took a chance, and made a choice, and that choice may well have cost Samir his foot.

I rolled off the bed and grabbed a beer from the small fridge. I wasn't back on duty until tomorrow, and right now I needed a drink. I hadn't even opened the bottle when the pounding began—a fist, thumping hard on the door.

"What?" I barked into Mujib's face as I wrenched the door open.

"You!" he snarled, pushing past me into the room. "You are dangerous. You should have stayed in the car. You put Mr Gharfour in danger, you put *everyone* in danger. You come in here, the so-called security expert, and you have turned everything upside down. I have been with this man for five years with no serious incidents, you have been here three days and already we have a man in the hospital! Allah only knows—"

"How is he?" I asked, cutting Mujib off mid-flow.

The man deflated. "I don't know. The doctors were still working on him when I left. His family are with him."

I nodded. I felt for Samir, but I wasn't going to take sole responsibility for this. I fixed Mujib with a hard stare. "Where the hell were you, Mujib? What's the point in a chase car if you're not behind us?"

He glared at me. "We got separated. This was your fault. You should not have been going so fast. We did not need two cars." He paused, meeting my eyes. "We do not need *you*."

"I wasn't the one driving, Mujib," I reminded him. "Look, everything went to shit pretty quick once the IED went off. Where was your radio? That's my point right now. We didn't know what was going on, or who the target was. In circumstances like that, you extract. Christ, you always extract. Clients get panicky, they do stupid things. When it goes to shit, you get out. You should know this."

"The radios do not always work well." The admission was quiet as Mujib's gaze slid off my face to skulk down by my feet.

"And you didn't think—" I bit off my retort, sighing explosively as I turned away. Johnson watched Mujib with interest, jerking his fist up and down in an obscene gesture. I scowled at Johnson, which just brought a grin to his face. Diplomacy was never his strong point, but right at that moment I agreed with him.

"Fine, look," I said, turning back to Mujib. "I'll talk to Gharfour in the morning about getting new equipment. In the meantime, I want to go over everything again—all the procedures, the lot. If it isn't good enough then it goes, and we're not going to argue about it. This went to hell today because of an IED, but there's always going to be something. That's why we need the right gear. That's why we plan for everything. I can make your team better, Mujib, and that will make everyone safer, but you've got to trust me. This just isn't going to work if I have to fight you every step of the way."

Mujib's face was impassive as he looked back at me. "You are not from here, Thompson. This is not your world. You westerners come in here thinking you can change everything and that everyone will just jump into line and follow you. It is not as simple as that."

I let another sigh escape. I couldn't really disagree with him. It didn't help that the country was crawling with western security contractors making a small fortune, while many ordinary Afghans remained poverty-stricken and jobless. "I don't want your job, Mujib. I want to help you do your job *better*. Get me all your procedures, and we'll sort this out. Gharfour will have to stay here tomorrow while we go through everything."

Mujib nodded. "Mr Gharfour wasn't going into the office tomorrow anyway. He is hosting the banquet."

I closed my eyes for a moment while I bit back something vile. "What banquet?"

"A private meeting," Mujib told me with a shrug and a ghost of a smile as he caught my expression. "He does it every few months. There is often little warning."

My sympathy vanished. I hadn't had much to begin with and this wasn't helping. "I can't keep him safe if he's going to spring things like this," I grated. "How long have you known?"

Mujib shrugged again. "No more than an hour. Mr Gharfour asked me to inform you."

I reached for the beer and twisted the cap off. I had been going to wait until the security chief had left; some people here can be touchy about alcohol. I needed a drink though, and right now, as far as I was concerned, Mujib could get fucked.

I took a long drink, and then a deep breath, before I spoke again. "So, who's coming to this meeting?"

"Local businessmen…farmers."

There was something in the way he'd said it that gave me pause. "What kind of farmers?"

Mujib sighed. "What kind do you think? You know what it is that Mr Gharfour does. Who do you think he is meeting with?"

"Drug-lords?" I burst out. "Jesus Christ, Mujib. And you're telling me this *now*?"

He spread his hands with a smile. "As I said, Thompson, I have not known long. This is how the director does things. I suspect the farmers insist upon it."

It made sense. How better to ensure your safety than to hold meetings at the drop of a hat? It prevented anyone planning anything. It prevented me from planning anything too.

"What time is this thing happening? We'll need to arrange things."

Mujib shook his head. "It is in hand. Mr Gharfour, he does not want you involved."

I frowned. "What?"

The smile was slow to make its way across his face—a slow and insulting thing that made me want to put my fist into it. "That was Mr Gharfour's instruction."

"Get out, Mujib."

He looked at me blankly for a moment, as if he hadn't understood me until I said it again. "Just, get out."

I watched him leave through the open door and called after him. "And get me your damned procedures. And a map!"

What the hell was the man thinking? What was the point in hiring in an expert and then keeping things from him? I glanced over to the bed, to where I'd stashed the phone under the mattress.

This was the information Artemis wanted. This was the intel that would earn me twenty grand, if I just picked up the phone. On one hand this felt like a betrayal. On the other, I really was just here for the money and I owed Gharfour nothing.

I took a long drink of the beer, still staring at the bed as I did, before I started moving. "Fuck him, then."

The phone snapped back together and I thumbed out a text.

Meeting scheduled for tomorrow night at the residence. Local 'farmers' attending.

The response was fast, less than two minutes.

Understood.

And that was that. From thinking about it, to actual betrayal, in less than five minutes. Was it really betrayal though? I hadn't done anything to compromise Gharfour's safety, or his men. Or had I?

"This is probably how it always starts," I muttered to myself.

"I bet you're right," Johnson said, coming over to squat down in front of me as I perched on the edge of the bed. "I bet this is how Six get their agents. CIA too, for that matter."

I drank the beer, looking away. He'd vanish soon enough. They always did.

"Thing is though," Johnson went on. "How do you actually know she's actually with the CIA or whoever?"

I stopped, mid-swallow.

"I mean, you found this phone in your kit, you agreed to meet this woman… Sure she was American, or she sounded like it, but that doesn't mean shit does it? Not really."

I lowered the bottle and looked at him, breaking the rules again. Fucking Rule Three, as if the first two weren't hard enough.

"She could be anyone, couldn't she, Carver?" Johnson dipped his finger into the blood pooling at his feet from the hole in his side, and used it to paint a rough circle on the clean floor beside him. "Hell, maybe you just tipped off ISIL? Wouldn't that be a laugh?" He dabbed two dots and an arc into the circle and stood up, nodding down at the happy face he'd drawn. "Still, chin up eh?"

I swore to myself as I finished the beer and grabbed another one from the fridge. The bastard might be right, but that didn't mean I was going to admit it. The bigger issue was what Artemis was going to do with the information I'd just delivered on a silver platter. If she wasn't from American Intelligence, then who the hell was she, and how big of a problem had I just created for myself? I avoided thinking about just how stupid I might have been. When someone has pulled the pin on the grenade they're juggling, it doesn't really help to tell them it was a bad idea.

*

I spent most of the next day hunched over a desk down in the bunk-house, as I sketched out replacements for the shambles that Mujib called procedures. The most important thing was new and functional equipment, but that would be the easiest fix.

The work was easy enough and, to some extent, I've always enjoyed it. It gave me time to think, and took my mind off the fact that Gharfour had locked me out of preparations for the banquet. Planning and working out contingencies lets you keep things at an abstract level. It's when a bomb blows your car over and you're picking glass out of your face while trying to find your gun that life gets complicated.

The men I had to work with were one thing, but the equipment was another matter. Gharfour's budget wasn't limitless, but the whole episode after the IED could have been avoided if we'd had proper kit. Requesting equipment on a private job isn't that different to doing it in the forces. I drew up a wish-list, knowing I'd only get half of it, and made my way through the residence towards Gharfour's office.

Shabib intercepted me before I got halfway, stopping me with a smile. "Mr Thompson, please accept my thanks for your actions yesterday. I suspect that Samir owes you his life, and certainly Mr Gharfour."

I've never taken compliments well, and I cringed a little.

"It's not a problem," I said with an awkward shrug. "I'm sure Mujib would have done the same if we hadn't been separated."

Shabib's smile faded a little. "I'm sure he would have tried, but there is a reason you are here, Mr Thompson."

He was diplomatic at least. I managed a tight nod and let it drop. "I need to see Mr Gharfour, if you think that could be arranged?"

Shabib shook his head. "Not at the moment, I'm afraid. Is it something I could help with?"

Gharfour probably was busy; though what getting ready for a dinner with a selection of drug-lords entailed, I had no idea. I wondered briefly if Shabib was under instructions to keep me away.

I handed him the papers. "I've drawn up some new procedures that I want to implement with Mujib and his team, including four different routes to get Mr Gharfour to the ministry. We also need new equipment for the detail; newer firearms, protection, and secure coms equipment especially."

Shabib glanced over the top sheet with the equipment request. "I will see to this personally, Mr Thompson. It will not be an issue. I can arrange for you to see Mr Gharfour tomorrow morning to go over your plans, if that suits?"

I frowned. "Tomorrow? I'd assumed he would be back at the ministry?"

Shabib shook his head with another small smile. "No, I do not believe he is required in person for the next few days. Sometimes it is easier to work from here."

I cleared my throat. "Listen, Shabib, about tonight—"

The older man cut me off with a shake of his head. "There is nothing happening today that you need to be concerned about, Mr Thompson."

"I think we both know that's not true, Shabib. I can help. Tell me what's going on."

He gave a helpless sort of shrug and spread his hands. "The people meeting here tonight have rules. They take their security very seriously. You are not part of what is agreed and acceptable."

"That's fine," I said. "But we need to look to our *own* security. That's what I'm here for."

Shabib shook his head again. "It is in hand, Mr Thompson."

I sighed. "Fine. I'll make myself scarce."

I didn't understand what his game was, but I wasn't about to fight him over it. I nodded down at the papers. "If you could pass those on to

Gharfour, I'll make myself available whenever he can meet me? to discuss them."

Shabib smiled with a small bow. I know a dismissal when I see one, and frankly the man was beginning to irritate me.

Mujib was talking with a man I didn't recognise when I got back to the bunkhouse. I raised an eyebrow as they broke off, looking at me.

"This is Khalid," Mujib said by way of introduction. "He will be standing in for Samir."

Standing in—literally, I supposed.

I winced at the thought and forced a smile onto my face. "Nice to meet you, Khalid. Ever shoot an M4?"

The man was slight, and shorter than either Samir or Mujib and neither were big men. He was probably one of their relatives, a younger brother or a nephew, but to be honest, I didn't care. I had bigger shit to deal with right now. Coming back to Afghanistan was beginning to feel more and more like a mistake.

"I have not, sir," Khalid replied in American accented English, probably a product of one of the language schools that had sprung up across Kabul since the coalition set up shop.

"Well, let's go and try it out then." I looked over at Mujib. "You come too. If we're lucky, Gharfour will have an order in for some before long."

Khalid, as it turned out, wasn't a bad shot. A bit over-eager, but nothing that couldn't be worked out with a bit of training. Mujib, however, I wouldn't trust with a gun unless I was stood directly behind him. And maybe not even then.

CHAPTER TWELVE

The door opened, pivoting out to one side with a soft pneumatic hiss. The sound called to Mackenzie, and she lifted her head from where it lolled back against her shoulder. She blinked and scrunched her eyelids together, trying to clear the sleep from her eyes as she glared at a man in white surgical scrubs. He looked her up and down, then glanced at his notes.

"What do you want?" she asked. Her voice was a weak croak and she turned her head to sip water from the hose.

When had she stopped caring that she was naked? She was strapped to a frame in the middle of a room, stark naked, and she couldn't care less about it. For a fleeting moment she realised that wasn't normal, but the thought vanished almost as soon as it arrived. Was that a sign she was giving up?

"Just some tests," he said in a soft voice. She looked at him as he stepped into the light. Another Middle Eastern man with a short, dark beard and excellent English. Just like all the others who came in here wearing scrubs and carrying clipboards, he could have been from anywhere. He pulled an ear thermometer from his bag and reached for her head with one gloved hand.

"Don't touch me," she hissed, twisting her head away from him.

"Easy," he said, speaking to her like she was a spooked horse. "I will not hurt you. Just let me take your temperature to start with."

It wasn't as if she had much choice. She could make it difficult for him, but in the end, he would get what he wanted, and all her struggles would get her was a sore ear.

"Fine," she said, sighing and relaxing her neck.

She stared at a point on the featureless wall as he took her temperature and worked a cuff around her arm to test her blood pressure. She flinched as he took hold of her chin but forced herself to relax again as he examined her eyes with an ophthalmoscope.

"Why are you doing this?" she asked, blinking at the light from the scope.

He ignored her, walking around the frame to examine her other eye and making a notation on his clipboard.

"You're a doctor, or a nurse at least," she carried on. If he didn't want to talk, he could damn well listen. "Aren't you supposed to help people? How can you be a part of this?"

He glanced at her then, meeting her eyes for the briefest moment before looking away. "I need to take some blood. Are you going to cooperate?"

She glared at him in silence until he parted his lips to speak again.

"Do I have a choice?" she growled.

He shrugged and tightened a strap around her upper arm, going through the process of drawing blood that she'd done so many times herself at the clinic in Kabul.

"What's your name?" she asked, knowing he wouldn't answer. She was a lab rat, you don't talk to your lab rats. The thought brought a small smile to her lips.

"My name's Mackenzie," she told him, enjoying the wince her words brought to his face. "Mackenzie Cartwright, from Brisbane. A person, with a mum and dad, friends. People who miss me."

Their eyes met again for a moment and she felt a small surge of pleasure in the minute grimace that had shown behind his circular glasses. You don't name your lab rats either. It's much easier to hurt something when it doesn't have a name, or a life beyond its cage. But she had a name now, and he knew there were people who would notice she was gone. He might not be responsible for her abduction, but he was responsible for himself; and if she could make him suffer, then she would. He didn't speak again, taping to cotton wool swab on the inside of her elbow and leaving quickly.

She sank back against the frame with a sigh. Calling him out like that might have been cruel, but she didn't have time to be nice. She needed answers. "Fuck it," she muttered. "Maybe it's time to be cruel."

"Armond?" she shouted.

He didn't answer for a time. It had been days since he'd begun any conversations himself and his responses to her shouted questions had been brief and confused.

"Mackenzie?" He sounded alert and concerned, rather than dulled and exhausted. What had changed? It didn't matter. He was alert, that was something at least.

"I need to know what's coming for me, Armond," she told him. "I need some answers."

He didn't respond, but then she hadn't really expected him to.

"How long have you been here?" she asked, wondering if his lucidity had faded already.

"I don't know…" His admission was a quiet thing. Small and uncertain, as if he feared to give voice to it.

"Weeks? Months?" Mackenzie persisted. "You must have some idea?"

"I think maybe six months. It might be longer. It's so hard to tell."

Six months?

Shit.

What would being penned up like this do to you after six months? It was no wonder Armond drifted in and out. The body needs to be up and moving to keep muscles from atrophy, and the mind is little different. Six months with nothing to look at but these four walls would be enough to drive anyone crazy.

She bit back a response and took a deep shuddering breath before she spoke. "How many others do you think there are?"

"I'm not sure," he replied, his voice curious, as if he wasn't sure where she was going with this. "At least two others. There hasn't been anyone else I could actually speak to for a long time. I could hear them sometimes, though."

"You spoke to someone else, someone before me?"

"Yes," he admitted. "A Dutch woman, Femke. She had two daughters. Do you have children?"

She ignored that. The mention of children and family somehow made this all so much worse and, for a moment, she was grateful she didn't have the kids she'd always wanted. What was happening to her was bad enough without her becoming the mother who simply vanished one day.

"What happened to her?" She hadn't meant to ask the question. She certainly didn't want to hear the answer.

He paused again, long enough that she wondered if she'd lost him.

"She went quiet," he said. "She stopped answering me."

There was no need to query what that meant. She knew as much as he did. Death wouldn't come with screaming and blood in this place. Death lived in the silences between their conversations, waiting to reach out and claim another victim.

"Do you think anyone ever gets out of here?" Her voice was hesitant, laced with her fear of his answer.

Armond's reply was quiet, just on the edges of her hearing. "I don't think so, Mackenzie, no."

"They're crazy, Armond. They think I can do some kind of magic."

"I know," he replied, and she shivered, shocked that the mention of magic hadn't even given him pause.

"I told you they are looking for miracles," he said. "What do they want you to do?"

She swallowed a lump from her throat. "Put out a candle, so far. They think I can control fire."

"Can you?"

She stared at the wall for a moment before she trusted herself to speak again, raking her teeth across her lip. There had been no incredulity or surprise in his voice, as if controlling fire were perfectly normal. She cleared her throat and hoped she sounded more certain than she felt. "No, of course not. What do they think you can do?"

"I heal," Armond told her. "I heal much faster than other people. They wanted to know how far they could take it."

She fell silent as she thought about that. How would they test that? There is only one way to see how fast someone can heal. "Dear God, Armond. What... what have they done to you?"

"They cut me, Mackenzie. They cut me and then record how long it takes to get better. It started small in the beginning..." He trailed off, and for a few minutes there was silence.

She waited, hoping he would come back on his own.

"Armond?" she called, her patience gone.

"There is no stopping them," he spoke suddenly, as if unaware he'd fallen quiet. "No begging or bargaining will help. Just give them what they want."

"And what if I can't?"

It was his turn to be shocked into silence. "I don't know," he admitted finally. "I don't know what you do then."

"You sound like you've given up."

"Perhaps I have."

"You can't give up, Armond. You have to fight. You have to believe you're going to get out of here somehow. That *we're* going to get out."

There was an odd noise and for a moment she thought he might be crying. "I can't leave, Mackenzie. I can never leave. Not now..."

She frowned. What sense did that make? "Why not?"

When he spoke again there was an edge to his voice. Hard, and brittle as broken glass, but no less able to wound. "They discovered I can heal, Mackenzie, so they cut me. Small cuts to start with, to test how long it took the wound to close. After time, the cuts got bigger, deeper. And then they took a finger."

She grimaced as he carried on, ignoring her gasp.

"The wound healed, and in time, the finger even grew back a little. So, they took more. They took my foot, and then my lower leg. They've carved me up, Mackenzie. Chopped me into pieces like meat on a slab. There's nothing left of me. Don't you understand? I barely have arms or legs now. They're going to keep taking until there's nothing left of me to scream."

The whisper of the door mechanism cut off her next question, and the same mute technicians she had seen before entered.

"I can't do it," she called out, prompting a glance and a whispered conversation between the two of them.

She froze when she saw the needle. A simple hypodermic, something she'd used countless times at the clinic; but then she'd been doing simple inoculations or administering pain relief. Somehow, she doubted this contained anything so innocent. In a sci-fi film it would have been some kind of lurid green liquid. As it was, it was just a clear fluid. But you can hide any number of horrors in a clear liquid: Ebola, HIV, Cancer… the options are almost endless.

She flinched back as far as the straps would let her as they drew closer, faces half-hidden behind the surgical masks they wore today. "What is that? What are you doing?"

"A mild sedative, do not worry. It will simply help to relax you."

"No," she pleaded as the nurse took hold of her arm, and then there was that peculiar sensation that comes with an injection—part pain, and partly the odd feel of the needle inside her flesh. They fiddled with the candle as she watched through half-lidded eyes and then withdrew quickly, as if she were some kind of caged animal that might bite if they lingered too long.

Whatever it was they had given her was already starting to take effect. Her arms hung limp from the restraints and her head sank back against the frame as she viewed the world through a detached haze.

"Put out the candle," the voice commanded her through the speakers. She looked around, searching for whoever had spoken until she caught herself. The technicians had gone, the door was already closed. How had they left without her noticing?

"Put out the candle."

The candle was suddenly lit, burning bright, not three meters from her face. When had they moved it closer? She watched the flame for a time, fascinated by the colour until she shook herself.

Christ, what was in that needle?

It was a little like being very drunk.

"Put out the candle, Mackenzie."

Did the voice speak again? Or was she just remembering it? All at once the words made sense to her, like an image coming into focus, and she turned her head from where it had lolled back against her shoulder.

"Put out the candle."

She puffed at it, giggling away to herself as she sang. "Happy Birthday, dear Mackenzie…"

"Not like that. Use your mind, your power."

A small crease grew on her forehead as she puzzled over that. The words made sense in isolation but—

"Put out the candle."

God, anything to shut him up!

She reached out, almost lazily, and touched the flame with her awareness. It guttered, and then froze as she grasped it, strangling it. She shrank it down to a pinprick, not pausing to consider how she was doing it, and then lifted it higher, turning the tiny fleck of flame into a raging torrent that consumed the candle in moments.

"There," she muttered in a slurred voice, rolling her head back towards the window. "Happy now?"

CHAPTER THIRTEEN

I'm not a very social person. I never have been. I'm at home in my own company and I don't especially care what other people think. I suspect I miss a lot of the silent cues and social niceties that other people pick up on. It doesn't help that the people I see most often have already been dead five years, and I've worked hard to train myself to ignore them.

I'm not completely blind though, and Gharfour's kitchen staff were making it pretty clear I wasn't welcome.

A short man chopping vegetables glowered at me from his station; I gave him a smile as I shovelled another forkful of food into my face. The complications and irritations of this job aside, the food was excellent.

I wasn't in the kitchen just to irritate the staff, though I'll admit, I was enjoying it a little bit. The dinner for Gharfour and his tame drug-barons was taking place this evening. Mujib and Shabib had made it abundantly clear that not only were my services not required, but they'd rather I was out of the way. I worked in the SRR. I'd spent years training in reconnaissance and sneaking into places where I had no business being. I'd basically had my nosiness honed to a razor's edge. There was no way on Earth that I wasn't going to at least peek at these people.

The main reason for my setting up camp in the kitchen was opportunity. The kitchens had their own loading area that led out into the residence, which made for an easy way to get in and out. Not only that, but professional kitchens have a very obvious tempo. You can instantly tell when dinner guests have arrived from the inside of a professional kitchen. The joking and talking stops, the chef barks orders, and everyone hunkers down and gets on with the job.

I've seen it happen a dozen times before over the years, and it was easy to spot. I pushed the rest of my meal aside and made my way to the back of the kitchen. The other great thing about kitchens is that they are messy places. I've never yet been in one that doesn't have spare sets of whites lying around. I grabbed a jacket and threw it on, snatching up a clipboard from a hook inside the door as I climbed up the steps and emerged out into the heat.

The sun was just beginning to think about going down, and the white stones of the building threw back the heat as I made my way up the steps. The loading area was around the side of the building— nowhere a guest would be headed. I didn't even attempt to hide, there wasn't much point. Most people make this mistake when they don't want to be seen. There is nothing in this world that stands out more than someone trying to sneak with little to no cover. Instead, I picked up one of the empty plastic crates standing beside the loading dock, walked confidently to the corner of the building, and began restacking them. I was just another part of the scenery.

Three cars were lined up outside the main doors, with another four already parked to one side. Anywhere else I would have expected limousines or something similar, but there is a premium on safety here, and these people probably trusted each other less than anyone else. They arrived in oversized Range Rovers and Jeeps, all of them as armoured as you can make a vehicle without actually turning it into a tank. The heavy thud of the car doors was testament to the thick metal plates buried inside them. I stood at the corner and consulted my clipboard, watching the proceedings out of the corner of my eye.

Gharfour's guests were dressed as if they were heading to Cannes rather than a dinner with a government lackey. I don't know much about suits, but I know what I can't afford, and the men emerging from the cars were probably wearing at least a year's worth of my normal earnings in clothing and watches. They had other ornaments that probably cost twice as much. Social mores tend to go out the window with these kinds of people, and it makes sense when you think about it. If you're making millions supplying the world with illegal drugs, then what does it matter if your wife or mistress isn't wearing a hijab or a burqa. I'm no expert on fashion, but I was willing to bet that the dresses cost a lot more than the suits.

The security detail was huge. Bigger than it needed to be. From my position, I counted four arrivals, and each of them came with between ten and fifteen men. Gharfour's house was big, but this was just stupid.

Security usually comes down to two things; line of sight and distance. If your client can be kept at a distance from the threat then it can be easily neutralised, or simply left. Guns complicate the issue, which is where the other factor comes into play. There were too many men in these escorts for anyone to really assess a threat, and too many unfamiliar faces to manage them all.

It was an assassin's delight.

Even if they left half the men outside, I could probably take out any one of the drug-barons using a knife, and probably all of them with a handgun. By the time the hired goons had figured out what was going on, I'd be long gone.

I glanced up from the clipboard in time to see the latest cars arrive; three white Toyota Land Cruisers—these guys were nothing if not original. I fussed with the non-existent contents of the top crate as I watched the security detail climb out and scan the area. They were good, professional, and far better than the others had been. I watched them checking the rooftops and securing the path into the building before reaching for the car door.

The man who emerged was nothing I hadn't already seen four times, a little shorter and fatter than some of the others, but still sporting the expensive suit and gold watch. I was more surprised by the lady he had on his arm than the watch on his wrist.

The dress was stunning, crimson, and flowing in a way that would make a dead stick sit up and take notice. But it was her face that stopped me cold.

Artemis looked up and ran a casual eye over the compound. There was no way she hadn't seen me, but her gaze passed over me without slowing.

"Mr Thompson?" The voice was soft, almost apologetic, and I jumped. I spun around to see Shabib frowning at me.

"Shabib," I said. It wasn't much of a greeting, but I couldn't think of anything else to say.

He nodded an acceptance. "You are aware that Mr Gharfour had asked you remove yourself from any security duties during this event?"

I nodded with a grimace.

"He and I have revisited this decision," Shabib went on. "It does not seem prudent. Perhaps you could provide some supervision to our newest security employee?"

Khalid? I frowned for a moment. Was I being asked to go and babysit the new guy at the gate? I'd been brought in as a consultant to bring Gharfour's security up to scratch. While I needed to know was how each aspect of the security measures worked, I wasn't really supposed to be making sure the gate didn't get stolen. That said, they were the ones paying the bill.

I shrugged. "Of course."

It didn't take me long to ditch the chef's whites, grab my gear and get to the gate. Khalid was a nice enough guy and standing post can be miserable work. Mujib left as soon as I arrived, giving me a smile as he headed into the house. The man was beginning to really get on my nerves. As far as Khalid went, he seemed glad for the company.

It was past midnight by the time the first of the cars began to roll out through the gates. The line of vehicles made their way out onto the street, a parade of criminals that I suspected ran most of the drug-trade across Afghanistan. I watched as they passed and wondered briefly what impact on the global heroin supply a few well-placed bullets would have.

The last group of cars slowed as they passed us, and a window wound down. I tensed as the man inside looked at me. It was far more than a casual glance. His eyes narrowed as he toyed with the sunglasses in his hands, taking my measure. I frowned, about to say something—though I have no idea what—but he muttered something to the driver and they moved off.

"What the hell was that about?" I asked Khalid. His shrug matched his face, as confused as my own.

CHAPTER FOURTEEN

I waited until morning, but that was as long as I was going to give anyone. It's quite surprising how fast you can put an old Nokia together when you really need to. The phone was supposed to be a burner. Unregistered on a prepaid sim card. The idea was not to use it unless you really had to, and then it was best to stick to texts—short bursts of data that nobody would think to intercept or trace. Calling was a bad idea. It broke a whole pile of operational protocols and procedures. Which was exactly why I did it. They weren't *my* procedures, and if they got violated then it wasn't my problem.

The first five calls rang out, going to a voicemail service that hung up without taking a message. About what I'd expected really. I gave up on calls and tapped out a text message.

We need to talk about last night.

Any other time, I probably would have laughed at how the text read. Right at that moment I wasn't laughing. I didn't have to wait long for a reply, either.

Our business is concluded. Do not attempt further contact.

That, on the other hand, did make me laugh and I snorted as I thumbed out my reply.

I can keep calling for as long as it takes. Hell, I can even give the phone to Gharfour if need be.

It took a moment for the message to send, and the reply buzzed in a few seconds later.

Meet at the Bush Bazaar. 3pm.

*

The Bush Bazaar was essentially an outlet for Kabul's black-market. It's a market for western goods that were largely stolen, or sold with a wink and a nudge, from the NATO military bases around the country. The Bazaar wasn't a single shop, though. It was a collection of stalls and stores clustered together in what was once the busiest market in the city. American rations—M.R.E. packs, or Meal Ready to Eat—sat on shelves next to cakes, protein powders, combat boots, and everything else in between.

At its height, the Bazaar was the driving force behind what was left of the Kabul economy. Now it was a broken ruin. The US withdrew most of their forces around 2014, dropping from about 130,000 to less than a tenth of that. The Bush Bazaar began to die the day the withdrawal was announced.

Somebody told me once that the Bazaar was nothing new. It wasn't born from the American, or even the NATO, presence. During the Russian occupation in the 1980s the Bazaar was known as the Brezhnev Bazaar, although I suppose we called them Soviets back then. The place is a tick, clinging to the arse of whatever military complex sets up shop. For all I know the place was around during the British invasion in the 1800s.

These days it's a quieter place. The troops were still in Kabul, but the numbers had dropped. Fewer bases meant fewer supplies, which in turn meant fewer thefts, and therefore fewer black-market goods. The

Taliban and Al-Qaeda might have celebrated the withdrawal, but in the Bush Bazaar, the news was met with fury and dismay.

It was quiet when I arrived. A handful of shopkeepers chatted beside half-forgotten stalls as stray dogs sniffed about for scraps. Charred beams and scorched shelves attested to the fire that had ripped through the place just a year ago.

Unlike in the Bird Market, I was attracting attention and I knew it. It wasn't a pleasant feeling, my borrowed thobe and pakol could only do so much to disguise my western features. My beard was still closer to stubble with delusions of grandeur, and I've always been pale. When it came right down to it, there simply wasn't enough people here for me to be able to fade into the crowd.

I made my way along the alleyways, stopping occasionally to look over the goods on display. A stack of M.R.E packs were piled beside old tins of Campbell's baked beans. I looked closer at the American ration packs.

Menu 16.

I nodded to myself, suddenly understanding why they were still there. Menu 16 was pork. Looking closer at the beans I saw they had pork in them too. I buried my laugh inside a cough and glanced at the shopkeeper.

"You want?" he asked in English. So much for my blending in.

"No." I shook my head. "Thank you."

"It's good. Lamb and rice."

I looked down at the pork M.R.E with a half-smile, shaking my head. Did he know? Probably, I decided. Times were hard these days in the Bazaar. The stall-owner still had to eat, and he couldn't eat this.

"Not hungry, Carver?"

I turned and flashed a grin at Jo. "Not for this. God, I don't know how your lot survive on it."

She cocked her head inside the burqa. She was probably raising an eyebrow but it was impossible to tell. "We've had M.R.E. packs since the early '80s. I'm sure they're fine."

"Yeah, judging by the way your boys will trade just about anything for a British rat pack, I'd say they're excellent."

"Shall we?" she edged away from the stall and turned, making her way out of the market.

The same car waited, parked in a quiet backstreet. Jo climbed in, pulling the burqa off the second the door was closed.

"So, Carver," she said with a smile. "What's got your panties in a bunch?"

She looked at me with a bright smile while I scratched my cheek. "Did you send someone into Gharfour's place a few days ago?"

She shrugged. "You know I'm not going to give you operational info, Carver. Please tell me you didn't drag me out here just for this?"

"Someone went through my stuff when we met at the Bird Market," I told her. "It's a bit of a coincidence, wouldn't you say?"

She frowned for a moment. "And you think we did it? What do you have that's so valuable that you think we'd be interested? What was taken?"

"Nothing, but my passport was moved. What were you doing there?"

She grimaced, then shrugged. "You can't think we had anything to do with that? I already know everything I need to know about you. As for my role in the operation last night? That's really none of your business."

It was my turn to grimace. She was right. I'd been reacting and not thinking this through. Seeing her at the party had thrown me. Regardless of whether she was CIA or not, she already knew my name. Why would they bother getting a look at my passport?

I pushed on. "Do you have anyone on his staff?"

She shook her head. "No. You've seen how small his staff is. Getting anyone in has always been more trouble than it's worth. We're reasonably sure that Afridi has his hooks into someone, though."

I raised an eyebrow "Afridi? As in Haji Ayub Afridi? The drug-lord? I thought he was dead?"

Jo nodded. "He is. This is Ehsan Ilyas Afridi."

"A son?"

Jo shrugged. "He could be, I suppose. I don't know, to be honest. I suspect it's more likely Ehsan is just from the same tribe and letting people assume a closer connection. Afridi was a bit of a legend after all."

I nodded. Afridi had been known as the founder of the Afghan heroin trade and had built himself an empire before he died. "So, this Ehsan has someone on the inside. What for?"

Jo shrugged. "Probably an insurance policy. Gharfour is playing ball with the Afghan/Pakistan cartel right now, but his ultimate aim is to bring down the drug-trade altogether. At least, that's his public goal. I would imagine Ehsan's man is just keeping an eye on things."

"Until Gharfour steps out of line and Ehsan wants some fingers broken."

"You're a big boy, Carver," Jo said with a smile. "You know how the game works."

I looked out of the window, staring blankly at a doorway. It had been painted blue once. Now the colour was faded and peeling. Whoever had looked at my passport had to be either on Gharfour's staff, or someone who'd been let into the compound by them.

The memory of the car slowing down at Gharfour's gates came back vividly. The passenger in the back seat had looked at me with more than just a casual glance. There had been more to that look than idle curiosity. And she had been there too. This game was more complex than I'd imagined, and I wasn't sure of my part in any of it anymore.

"Shit!"

"Problem?" Jo asked.

I'd been sent to the gate by Shabib. It had seemed odd at the time but was there another reason for it? Had he sent me there to be seen? He didn't seem the type really, but the way he'd used my alias had made me question whether he knew who I was. Gharfour certainly did, so what was to say Shabib wasn't in on the secret.

I muttered something dark and vile and glanced at Jo, meeting her gaze. "Nothing I can't handle."

She gave me a cold smile. "I really wasn't that interested, Carver. Not unless your problem is likely to become my problem?"

I gave her a tight smile of my own and shook my head.

"Then I can't see us needing to be in contact again. It was nice doing business with you."

I grunted my agreement and reached for the door handle.

"Oh, and Carver?"

I paused, one foot hanging out of the door.

"Don't bother me like this again. I'm sure it's a problem that needs addressing, but, and I really can't stress this enough Carver: it is *your* problem."

The things I called her as I made my way back through the Bush Bazaar could have had me arrested and, depending where I was, possibly stoned to death.

Mujib met me with Khalid at the gate as I arrived back at Gharfour's compound. I wasn't sure to what level he was involved in this business with the passport, if he was at all, but I wasn't expecting the smile.

"Mr Thompson, the new equipment has arrived."

I wasn't expecting that, either. Urgency and quick deliveries aren't things you tend to come across in Kabul, and certainly not within the Afghan government or military sector.

I nodded with a smile. "Let's see it then. Where is it?"

"Most of it is in the bunkhouse," Khalid said.

"Though there is something special in your rooms, according to Mr Shabib," Mujib added.

I frowned at him. That didn't sound right.

He spread his hands at my expression. "I have no idea, sir."

I hadn't ordered anything particularly special. The M4s and coms equipment could easily have gone to the bunkhouse. I made my way into the residence and up the stairs. I'd made it more than halfway before I registered that Mujib was still with me. My confused look was met with a broad grin. I suppose everyone likes new toys.

The package was in a long wooden crate, about the size I'd have expected the M4's to arrive in. I grabbed the crowbar that rested on top and worked at one end as Mujib stood and fidgeted behind me.

I didn't feel the prongs as they hit me, but then apparently you rarely do. My back arched as over fifty-thousand volts tore through me and I did my best to drown out the clicking of the taser as I screamed.

"Sshhhit!"

The crate was kind enough to break my fall and I rolled, screaming as my muscles convulsed. Mujib stepped around me, into my field of vision, as he held the trigger of the damned thing. Tasers don't actually knock you out. Instead they overwhelm your nervous system to the point that your muscles barely know your brain is screaming at them to move.

"Bastard!" I hissed out between clenched teeth.

"Goodbye, Mr Carver," Mujib said, abandoning my alias with a smile. He dropped the taser and took a hypodermic needle from a leather wallet. "I don't think we'll see each other again."

He flicked the body of the syringe and depressed the plunger long enough to push a bead of fluid out the end and send it sliding down the needle's length. Nice of the bastard not to give me an air embolism.

He took his time finding a good vein in my arm, and I watched him with horrified fascination as my body continued to ignore my brain. I had long enough to get a last good look at his face, long enough to plan to put a bullet into it one day, and then the darkness took me.

CHAPTER FIFTEEN

Kabul, Afghanistan, early 2013

The radio clicked twice, short bursts of static, and then we were moving. Boots thumped hard on the packed dirt, sounding too loud in the dark. The door was just thin, sun-baked, boards. SAS or SEALs would have kicked it in and entered like a hurricane. We weren't the SAS. That's not how we worked.

The door was eased open and we drifted in like smoke on the breeze, checking corners and exits, whispered voices calling "clear" through the comlink. I saw the hand signs in the lurid green of my night-vision gear.

Team Two were heading to the left and up the stairs, we would carry straight on.

The target was a man known as The Gatherer, though we knew his real name to be Azzat bin Shah. Somewhere, a room full of men in dark suits had decided he was a person of interest, which made this job a smash-and-grab. If he had the documents we'd been sent for with him, then so much the better. Mossad are more widely known for this sort of thing, but that doesn't mean we don't do it. We just do it more quietly.

We were down to two teams of four. Two men left outside with sniper rifles sighted on the front of the building, and then four of us in each team. Ten men, eight if nothing happened outside, up against however many were in here.

The first shots fired were ours. Subsonic rounds fired from an MP5-SD. You can forget anything you might have seen on television, suppressed rounds don't sound like that. If anything, it's more of a tinny, metallic clack. Most of the boom of the bullet is gone—that's dealt with by the suppressor, and the fact that the bullets don't break the sound barrier. As for that high-pitched sound, like a chipmunk sneezing, that you hear in the movies? No, that's just bollocks.

I followed Johnson to the slumped forms of the men he'd shot, checking the second as he crouched over the first. Neither would be much of a threat to us now, but silence was a commodity we hoarded. A moan, or a call for help at the wrong time, would have changed that night into something very different in moments.

I gave him a thumbs-up in the darkness, then followed him deeper into the house, moving along the hallway. The rooms to either side of us were empty, devoid of both occupants and contents. Already the place was bigger than it should have been—bigger than the plans we'd been shown in the briefing. Two of the rooms had walls that had been knocked through into adjacent buildings. If they'd done the same in those buildings too, then this place had changed from a small house into a rabbit warren.

A tunnel had been dug down through the floor of a room that might have once been a kitchen. Lights were strung along the length of its ceiling, bright enough to make our night-vision gear useless. I grimaced as I pulled the goggles clear. Night-vision wasn't perfect by any means, but the lights in the tunnel would level the playing-field between me and whoever might be pointing a gun at me down there. I've never seen the point in playing fair if I don't have to.

"What do you think, Roasties?" Johnson's words were a whisper that barely made it through the throat-mic and ear-piece. Roasties was his latest ridiculous nickname for me. My name had taken him to roast dinner, and from there to roast potatoes. So 'Roasties' it was. The names never lasted long though, which was something, I suppose.

I scowled at the tunnel. If bin Shah was anywhere, then chances were he'd be down there. Climbing down into a tunnel with a team this small sounded like a stupid idea to me, but then so did searching the ground floor of this maze in a team of four. I nodded and motioned for Turner to take the rear.

"Two, be advised there's a tunnel network down here. We're going in."

The coms clicked twice in my earpiece in acknowledgement.

The tunnel wound like a snake. If it had been intentional then it was genius—every fifty feet was a potential ambush point. I doubt that it had been, though. More likely, it was just built by men who couldn't dig in a straight line.

I spotted the man a fraction of a second before he saw me. My gun was already up and he didn't stand a chance. What I didn't see was the second man further around the curve of the tunnel. He could have shouted, I suppose, but there isn't much that carries better than the sound of gunfire. An AK-47 is loud at the best of times; inside the tunnel it sounded like a cannon was shattering the silence.

"Fuck!" Johnson always managed to break silence first, I guess it was just too hard for him to keep that big mouth shut. Not that it mattered now.

We took the shooter together, one high and one low. I think it was Johnson's shot that took him. He was running anyway but that didn't matter at this point. This was damage limitation, and it would mean one less gun to face.

"One? Report," the voice sounded in my earpiece. I could hear the gunshots over the coms clearer than the distant reports that reached my other ear. They were obviously having as much fun upstairs as we were down here.

"Going to shit down here, Two," I replied. "No sign of the asset."

Shots rang out as I was saying the last word. The man must have been firing before he even rounded the corner. An AK-47 firing on fully automatic is a bloody horrible thing to try and hold on to, let alone aim, but somehow this guy managed it.

Pearson took him out. He was dead before his age really registered. He couldn't have been more than fourteen.

I grimaced. "Fuck."

My mutter came at the same time as Turner's, but pain filled his voice, lending an urgency to it. He was halfway to the ground before I turned. The bullet had caught him in the thigh, passing through but making a bloody mess of it.

Turner was already seeing to himself before any of us managed to get there, jabbing a morphine shot into his leg. He wadded gauze into the wound while Johnson and Pearson kept watch and I dropped back to help tape him up. It must have hurt like hell. The morphine shots they give us work like an EpiPen—fast acting and pretty much idiot-proof. They don't work miracles though, and Turner's thigh was a mess. The morphine dose has to be low enough that the soldier doesn't drift off to play with the fairies.

We should have bugged out at that point, or pulled back until Team Two finished their search. I knew it, Johnson and Pearson knew it. Turner didn't know much right about then, but he would have agreed if he could. We didn't. We pushed on.

Pearson guarded the rear while Turner moved in a pained hobble that wasn't quiet or fast. Johnson stayed with him as I moved ahead, working my way around the curves of the tunnel.

We heard the footsteps first—rushing feet, and then calls in Pashto that told all four of us that there were more men coming than we were really equipped to handle.

I glanced back at Turner and grimaced before I dropped down to a crouch. We weren't in any position to be running anywhere.

My gun fired in quick, controlled bursts, and the first three fell before they even knew what happened, but we didn't have more than a breath before the tunnel filled with the roar of gunfire.

They issue you with ear protection for missions, but nobody uses it. It turned out to be a good thing none of us had, as we could barely hear each other over the damned AKs as it was. The coms were full of chatter from Team Two, and they clearly had their own problems. We ended up resorting to a mix of hand signals and shouting at each other as we fought a retreat. The tunnel had turned into a screaming mess of pain, blood and bullets. I'm making it sound more controlled and disciplined than it really was. The truth is that, when it came down to it, we tossed a flash-bang and a smoke grenade and then legged it.

Pearson had another man dead in the corridor by the time I made it out of the tunnel, and the building seemed as loud as the tunnel.

"One, where the fuck are you?" The voice in my earpiece demanded, the first hints of panic edging in. It was Richards, by the sounds of it.

"Coming out of the tunnel. Time to get out of here."

"Understood."

"Fuck this," Turner spat. "Let's move before I grow any more holes."

I wasn't about to argue with him, not when he was making sense.

We made it as far as the first rooms before things completely fell apart. A round tore into the wall by my face, missing me by inches. My weapon followed my head as I whipped around. Men were swarming out from a hole in the wall that led through to the adjacent house. I dropped one, grabbed Turner, and ran.

"One, this is Gabriel," the sniper said through my earpiece. "Be advised your exit is compromised. There are trucks pulling up."

"Fuck!" I screamed into the chaos of the hallway. "This just keeps getting *better!*"

There was no time to talk this through. If there was no way out the front then I'd rather be in a group of eight than two groups of four. We charged up the stairs as fast as Turner could go, tossing another smoke grenade and a flashbang as we went.

The place was as confusing upstairs as it had been below. Team Two had been as busy as we had and the enemy body count was up to five already as we moved toward the sound of their gunfire.

"Two, we're coming to you," I said.

"Understood."

114

Team Two were holed up in a small room at the end of a narrow hallway. I didn't stop to count the bodies, the fact we had to climb over them was enough.

"Nice place you've got here," I said as I put a wall between my skin and any bullets that might come down the hallway.

"We like it," Richards grinned.

I'd like to claim the forced calm was a British thing, but really, it's a kind of institutional stupidity, something you'll run into just about anywhere in the armed forces. When things go to shit, we act like it's nothing and make jokes about it. The Americans are more or less the same. Our jokes are better, of course. And we're better looking too.

I glanced at the corridor. Johnson had taken up a position with Pearson and McCourt, one of Richard's team, while Yates and Wilson saw to Turner's leg.

I looked out of the small window. There was a twenty-foot drop to the ground, onto what looked like broken stone and rubble. Not anything I wanted to jump out onto if I had a choice. "Gabriel, what's it looking like out there?"

"Like shit, Roasties," Gabriel replied. "There are four trucks out here and more coming in. Shall we thin the herd for you?"

I thought about it for a minute. Two men with sniper rifles can make a sorry mess out of just about anyone. That said, it was dark, and the muzzle-flash would give away their position quickly. Snipers are for individual targets, not truck-loads of militants.

"No, hold off for now. Get on the horn and report back just how well things are going here though." I glanced over at Richards. I was about to ask him about ammunition but Pearson was already firing. Johnson and McCourt joined in, and then we were back to it.

The hallway was long enough that we weren't going to be mobbed unless they were really eager to die, but it was going to be a long, messy, stand-off unless something changed quickly. Right up until the point where one of the bastards brought an RPG up here and really ruined our day.

I peered around the corner long enough to judge the distance and tossed a grenade. I'd never been the greatest with those bloody things and it caught the wall at the end of the corridor before bouncing out of sight. The sound of the blast was almost as bad as the moaning and the high-pitched screaming that followed. You don't forget noises like that. The moaning was worse for some reason.

I grimaced and cast my eye over the team. "Turner, how are you holding up, mate?"

"Got a hole in my leg, Roasties. I'm bloody marvellous."

I grinned at that. "Yeah well, time to lose some weight then, you fat fucker. You're too good a target." I smiled along with the laughs—I wasn't feeling it. I jerked my head toward the window. "Have another look outside for me, sunshine?"

His response was lost as more gunfire came down the corridor. And then the floor was gone, lost in a roar that made the gunfire seem like a sneeze in a hurricane.

CHAPTER SIXTEEN

Kabul, Afghanistan, early 2013

I came to when a boot caught me in the ribs, adding to all the fun I'd had falling through the floor. I'm not sure what language my new friend was barking at me in, but he managed to make himself understood. An AK-47 barrel jabbed in the side and a pointed finger is usually enough for most people to understand that they're expected to move.

My hands were already bound behind my back. Cable ties by the feel of it. I scrambled up and made my way over to the others. Pearson, Johnson, and the rest of the team were on their knees, lined up against a wall, with three Afghan men guarding them. I did a quick head count and looked around the room.

Wilson was missing.

It took me a minute to spot his body in amongst the rubble. I grimaced and looked away. There are worse ways to go. At least his had been quick.

A glance up at the remnants of the floor we'd been standing on revealed what had happened. Unable to get to us along the upstairs corridor, they'd simply blown down the ceiling of the room below us. If I'd been anywhere but here, I might have had some grudging respect for the idea. As it was, I'd just fallen twelve feet onto broken stone, wood, and plaster. It was a miracle I could still walk.

A man in a chequered shemagh and sunglasses crouched in front of Pearson, barking questions at him as he jabbed the muzzle of his AK into his chest. All of our captors wore the Arab headscarf, pulled up over their faces so only their eyes were visible. I don't know why they bothered, it wasn't as if we would recognise any of them, or even if it would matter if we did.

I was going to die. I realised this even before I came around fully. What struck me was how calm I was about it. It's kind of an accepted practice to save the last round for yourself in these situations. Even before the beheading videos started showing up on the internet, it was common knowledge that if you were captured, then you were in for torture and a bloody end.

Of course, using that last round required access to your gun, and whoever these guys were—Taliban, Al-Qaeda, drug-lords, or just pissed off locals—they had confiscated all our weapons. I didn't know who these people were. They certainly weren't the handful of guards we'd expected escorting bin Shah. They'd been thorough, too. Looking at the others, I saw that they were all bound and that our captors had taken our throat-mics. For now, at least, we were on our own.

There are a lot of things that go through your mind at times like this. Girlfriends I'd been less than nice to, friends I'd fallen out of touch with—lost opportunities. Rather than make me sad, or scared, it simply pissed me off. I don't know what end I'd expected my life to have, but it bloody well wasn't this.

Sunglasses made his way slowly along the line until he came to me.

"American?" he demanded in thickly accented English.

"British," I told him.

He grunted with a nod. "Bush, Blair—very bad men. This is *our* country. You should not be here."

I shrugged. He was out of date on his presidents and prime ministers, but I couldn't really disagree with him.

"Why did you come here?"

"We were looking for someone," I told him. "We were told Al-Fayed would be here." I made the name up on the spur of the moment, and it was only days later that I realised I'd given the name of the old *Harrods* owner.

The days of only giving your name, rank, and serial number were long gone. These days we're more likely to be fighting insurgents, or states who couldn't care less about the Geneva Convention. The official line was, if captured, avoid giving away secrets, but cooperate, to a point, if it will help. The level to which we cooperated was down to individual discretion. There's a lot of leeway in that. I wasn't stupid enough to think that anything I said was going to help us. The best we could hope for would be to keep these guys talking until the cavalry arrived.

The cavalry could be anyone from the SAS, to the SBS, or even regular forces. Most likely it would be the SAS. They'd just love the chance to save a sorry squad of SRR boys and lord it over us until the end of time. There's a level of rivalry between SAS, SBS, and SRR, but if something like this happens then the whole bloody regiment goes pounding on doors to try and get you out. Whether we would still be alive when they got there was another matter.

Giving them Al-Fayed's name bought us some time, and the four of them argued back and forth in Pashto, far more quickly than I could follow.

Sunglasses was disagreeing with a shorter man, stabbing his finger at him. Any in-fighting or arguments could only be a good thing for us, I decided, and I took the chance to glance over at the others.

Turner was in a bad way. His leg was bleeding through the bandage, he'd lost his combat helmet, and his face had taken a battering on the way down. Either that, or they'd knocked him about before I came to. He had the beginnings of a lovely black eye and his lips were split and bleeding. I caught his eye, giving the briefest of nods as I tried to force a sentence into that one gesture.

"You all right?" asked that nod.

His answering nod was just as slight. "Yeah, fine. Fuck 'em."

To be fair, Turner was about as mad as they came. When you run across the stereotype of the practically feral Scot, it's Turner they're talking about. I'd heard rumours, more than once, that the only reason he joined up was because of some nasty business with the police in Glasgow after a night out.

He turned away from me and glared at Sunglasses and his mates. He probably would have taken on the lot of them if I'd given him the nod. Bound hands and a bullet wound wouldn't have stopped him either. They call the headbutt a *Glaswegian Kiss* for good reason, and I reckoned Turner would have happily snogged the lot of them.

Sunglasses was done arguing. He crouched down in front of me again. "You lie. There is no Al-Fayed. Nobody is supposed to know about this place. You are looking for The Doctor. How did you know he is going to be here? Who told you?"

That shut me up.

The Doctor, or The Teacher, was a name that made anyone in this job sit up and take notice. Ayman al Zawahiri, The Doctor. One-time teacher and confidante of Osama Bin Laden, and now leader of Al-Qaeda. My thoughts tumbled over each other as I tried to make sense of it all.

Jesus Christ, what have we wandered into here?

Were these men Al-Qaeda? Or were they Taliban? What the fuck was going on?

"*Who?*" Sunglasses yelled the question into my face.

I've been through interrogation training. I've been yelled at by the best of them. But training, no matter how good it is, never really matches the real thing. There's always a line you know won't be crossed. In the back of your mind, you always know that you can stop the exercise with a word. Real life doesn't work like that. There's no safe-word with Al-Qaeda.

Focus, John, I told myself. *It doesn't matter who these guys are, just get through it.*

"Nobody," I replied. "We had no idea he was here, we were looking for someone else."

Sunglasses shook his head and muttered something over one shoulder at the other three, and made his way down to where McCourt knelt in the rubble.

"Where did you get your information?" he barked down at McCourt.

McCourt didn't look good. I don't know if he'd been hurt in the fall, or if he was just shitting himself. Whatever it was, I think if he'd had anything to tell, he'd have spilled his guts to the guy at that point.

"Satellites," he muttered.

Sunglasses reached down and grabbed him, holding him by the hair at the base of his neck as he jammed the barrel of his weapon into his face. "Do not lie to me, kafir."

He glanced over at me as he shoved McCourt down to the ground. Turner never had a chance. The AK-47 swept around and sent a round through his head. Turner dropped, toppling sideways into the rubble as the red mess dripped off the wall.

For a few moments everything was chaos. The sound of the gunshot still felt like it filled my ears. Johnson was screaming something at Sunglasses while Richards and Yates were shouting at him, trying to get him to shut up. Only Pearson, McCourt, and I were quiet and somehow that drew us together, pulling our eyes until our gazes met.

You can say a lot with a look. McCourt was a broken man, resigned to his fate. Pearson was on the edge of panic, his eyes begging, pleading with me to do something, *anything*. And I had nothing to give him.

"Who told you?" Sunglasses was looking at me again. "We know how to avoid your satellites and your spies. Someone must have told you we would be here."

"We weren't looking for him," Johnson blurted. "We were looking for The Gatherer. For Azzat bin Shah."

Sunglasses spun around to face him, barking something to the men behind him. The shortest of the four of them stepped forward again, speaking to Sunglasses in a low voice. Sunglasses, by the looks of things, was having none of it. He shook his head and snapped something that sounded suspiciously like "shut the hell up," in Pashto.

He held his weapon ready as he walked the five steps to Johnson.

"Do you think I am stupid?" he demanded. "bin Shah is nothing. He is a supplier, nothing more. Why would you send eight men for a merchant?"

He spun on his heel, stalking back to me and ripping his sunglasses off as he grabbed hold of my face with the other hand. He bent close, close enough that I would have been tempted to headbutt him if the other three hadn't had guns on us.

"Do I look like I want to play games?" he hissed at me.

The shot was one-handed, the kind of cowboy bullshit that you see on television. It's a miracle he managed to hit anything. If Johnson had been turned even slightly towards me the round would have hit the front-plate of his body armour. Instead it managed to find a gap between the plates, burying itself in his side. He managed to clap a hand over the wound, but the blood was already spilling out between his fingers. He coughed, an ugly tearing sound that sent a bloody froth out between his lips, and then sank back against the wall, sliding down with a confused look on his face

Pearson went next, a bullet to the head before anyone could even react. It went straight through his helmet, blood streaming down his face as he fell.

I was a dead man.

I knew it then. The next bullet was mine and Sunglasses was already turning to face me. The bastard grinned as he levelled the gun at me and I was suddenly furious.

This was bullshit.

We weren't even here for these guys. My anger passed through rage and into something I couldn't even put a name to; a white-hot fury that burned all other thought from my mind.

And then he pulled the trigger. I stared at the barrel of the gun, as the bullet erupted from it, carving a path through the air towards my flesh.

It was the gasps and the utter silence that brought me back to myself. The bullet had stopped midway between the gun and my head. It hung in the air, flattened out as if it had struck a metal plate and somehow forgotten how to fall.

I realised then that my hands were free, as blood dripped from my wrists.

I don't know what happened to the plastic ties, but I was crouched, one hand on the floor and the other outstretched towards the bullet, as if warding it away.

Sunglasses gaped, lifting his gaze from the bullet and up to my face. A gun clattered to the ground and the first of his men fled.

He glanced back as another man muttered. "Sehr! Jahdoo!"

The bullet fell as I rose to my feet, and they ran. The words echoing along the hallway.

Sehr. Jahdoo.

Witchcraft. Sorcery.

CHAPTER SEVENTEEN

The drugs were wearing off again. She knew the stages by now. First, the pain would drift in; little slivers that stabbed at her through the fog like tiny needles of hate. Then, the nausea would begin. It had been the same for days, as she'd woken first whimpering, and then crying out, until she vomited.

She blinked hard against the light, twisting her head to reach for the water tube.

"Here, let me help you." Mackenzie's head shot around as the man came closer. He wasn't dressed like the others in their surgical scrubs or lab coats; instead he wore a suit and tie that fit him too well to have been anything other than tailored.

"Who are you?" she croaked at him.

He smiled. "I'm the man with the water, Mackenzie."

He reached out and held the tube closer to her mouth so she could drink. He smelled of something she recognized, a scent. A deodorant? An aftershave? It was familiar, but she couldn't place it.

There was an IV pole standing behind her arm, the line running down to a cannula taped in place on the back of her hand. When had they hooked her up to an IV?

She swallowed and moved her head back, letting the water tube drop. "Who are you?" she repeated.

The man ignored her question, pacing across the room as he spoke. "Do you believe in magic, Mackenzie?"

She shook her head, trying to make sense of words that had no relevance. "What?"

He carried on, as if she hadn't spoken. "Did you know, Mackenzie, that there is not a single country or people in this world that doesn't have some legend involving magic or witchcraft?"

His eyes shone as he spoke, like a child counting down the days to Christmas. "It's true. Every country on the planet has their tale, from witches to sorcerers, shamans to wizards—every one of them has its legend of people with powers that cannot be explained."

"Why are you telling me this?"

"Because, Mackenzie, all of these tales take place in the distant past. There is this assumption that they are just stories, or myths or fables—superstitious nonsense. Yet, if you look at the news there are so often stories with fantastical elements. Men and women performing acts of superhuman strength, lifting cars off the injured, surviving falls with no explanation. I do not believe the powers of these ancient sorcerers ever left us, we simply stopped taking notice—or we dismissed it. And now you, Mackenzie. You are living proof I was right."

The man was insane, she realised. "What are you talking about. I've never done anything like that."

He laughed—a delighted, child-like sound. "But you have, don't you see? The fire in your home when you were a child? And then just yesterday, when you put out the candle. You reached out to the flame and it danced to your tune. I watched you raise it to a raging torrent with your mind before you extinguished it. You simply need to learn how to *control* it, how to summon the power without the need for the Cocktail."

"What are you talking about?"

He frowned. "Do you really not remember? You had a mild sedative, and another combination of drugs in your system as well—the Cocktail, but surely you must remember some of it?"

Mackenzie closed her eyes, shaking her head. "I don't know. I don't think so."

He shook his head with a small smile as he fished out a phone, swiping through images on the screen. "Look."

She frowned at the small screen as the images played across it, saw herself bound naked to the frame, and then gasped as the flame of the candle in front of her shot skyward, surging up in a column of fire that licked at the white tiles of the ceiling.

She looked past him, eyes searching for, and then finding, the blackened section of ceiling tiles.

"You see?" the man in the suit said with a broad grin, pointing at the screen. "You see what you did? This power is in you, Mackenzie. With our help you have unlocked it. It is simply a matter of learning to control it now."

"Please?" Her plea was barely a whisper, but it was enough to give him pause. "Please, just let me go?"

He froze, looking at her curiously. "You want to leave? Even now that I have shown you this?"

Her voice cracked as she spoke. "I don't remember it, any of it. I just want to go home."

His smile fell, the child-like enthusiasm fading away, and for a moment there was a look of genuine sorrow on his face before it drifted into something cold and jagged, and his eyes turned hard.

"I'm sorry, Mackenzie. I can't let you go just yet. Not until I have discovered how you do this." He turned towards the door and waved the technicians into the room. "Show me how you put out the candle, Mackenzie."

"I can't. I don't know how."

He looked at her again and even the memory of the smile had faded from his face. "There is a long way between 'cannot' and 'will not', Mackenzie. Do not test me on this."

They put the candle closer this time and fixed a clear screen between her and the flame. Some kind of tempered glass or plastic, she couldn't tell, but it would be enough to keep her from blowing it out.

She watched as the door swung back into place, pneumatics hissing. She waited until there were no human eyes to see her before she let the tears fall. They were never going to let her go. She would die in this cage as surely as a lab rat in a cancer research trial.

"Put out the candle, Mackenzie." That same voice through the speakers. A different man to the one she'd just spoken to. This voice held none of his passion. It was cold and clinical.

She'd taken to giving names to the people she'd seen. The Man in the Suit, the Technician Twins, Bored Microphone Man. It was something to anchor her. She had no windows, no idea if it was day or night, or even if the time-cycle of the lights meant a day had passed. She needed something, so names and silly stories about the people she saw was what she worked with.

She blocked out the sound of the nagging voice and sucked the grainy sludge from the food tube, forcing it down. She leant forward, straining against the restraints. She could just see the bruise on her hand where the IV had been inserted. It had already faded to a greenish yellow. How long had she been unconscious?

"Armond?" her voice sounded weak and feeble even to herself. She tried again, it was easier the second time but there was no response. That didn't mean anything, she'd grown accustomed to him going silent for days at a time.

She looked at the candle burning in its stand. Had she really controlled the flame? Her memory of it was brittle, made hazy by whatever drugs they'd had her on. The Cocktail, The Man in the Suit had called it. God only knows what they'd been pumping her full of, or what damage it was doing to her brain or her organs.

"Put out the candle, Mackenzie."

Christ, didn't he ever get sick of saying that? It wasn't even as if it were a recording; the inflection changed occasionally. He was probably torturing himself far more with it than he was her by now.

She took a deep breath and sighed as she looked at the candle. Maybe it was time to try. She'd spent so long telling them she couldn't do it, that she'd never actually stopped to wonder if she could. The laughter bubbled out of her, high and nervous as it flirted with hysteria.

The candle flame sat in front of her, calling her. Taunting her. She looked at it, concentrating on the colour, on the minute movements of the flame. She willed it to move. Nothing. She stared at it, straining with her eyes until she felt a pushing sensation in her forehead. Slowly she began to develop a headache.

*

They brought fresh candles in over what she thought were the next four days, scraping away the wax that built up in a little stalagmite beneath the stand.

"What's your name?" she asked a technician on the fifth day. She didn't recognize him. Was he new? Or was her memory just failing her? He jumped, staring at her as if she'd spat or shrieked at him, then gave the door a nervous glance as worry lurked in his dark eyes.

"I am not really supposed to speak with you."

"But you just did, didn't you?" Mackenzie smiled into his worried expression. "So, you might as well tell me your name now."

"Kareem," he said, with another quick look at the door.

"There are others here, aren't there?" she asked him. "Like me, I mean."

Kareem nodded, tightening something on the candle's stand.

"Can any of them do things like this? Miracles?"

Kareem looked up at the glass wall, to where she'd so often seen the red light of the camera and shrugged. "Some have, yes. But not like you."

She frowned. What did that mean?

"What do you—" but he was already headed for the door.

He paused in the doorway. "I should not have spoken to you."

*

The candle came along with a syringe the next day. Mackenzie watched without comment as the technician injected the contents into the IV line.

"You do not need this drug, Mackenzie." The voice came through the speakers as the technician left. "This Cocktail, it is a catalyst. A beginning. You have already moved beyond where this drug can take you. At this point it is little more than a sedative, it just allows you to forget what is and isn't possible. Now, put out the candle."

They left the wax this time, perhaps as a reminder of what she'd done. It had pooled out in a misshapen circle beneath the stand, an undeniable reminder. She'd melted it so quickly that it hadn't had the chance to build up into a mound but instead had ran out over the floor in a shallow puddle until the concrete leeched the heat out and it solidified.

Mackenzie stared at the white pool. She had done that. Somehow, God only knew how, but somehow, she had done that. Unless they were lying to her, then the drug didn't do much. This power, this ability, was in her—not in the syringe. And yet each day they brought a fresh candle, and each day she failed to make it do more than burn down slowly.

Over the days she began to realise something was changing in this place. There was a tension growing in the bored voice when he instructed her to put out the candle. The technicians cast nervous glances over their shoulders at the camera and the door as they worked. It was nothing more than that, nothing overt, and yet she could feel it, a tension building, like the charge in the air before a storm.

*

The Man in the Suit came the next time the lights flicked on. She'd decided that the hours of light and darkness couldn't be a full day. If that were true, then she must have been here for months already and that was something she wasn't prepared to accept.

She hadn't had a period. The thought came out of nowhere and she gasped aloud. Were they feeding her a contraceptive somehow? Or was her body so traumatised that her cycles had simply stopped? She'd always been as regular as clockwork, but this was the only time in her life she'd ever found herself wanting one.

Her eyes opened slowly as the door hissed open; it was so easy to slip into a doze without really realising. The Man in the Suit stood in the doorway, watching her as she roused herself. He stepped into the cell, making his way over to the pool of wax and crouching to inspect it.

He didn't look up at her as he spoke. "You understand what it is that is expected of you, do you not? There is no confusion over this?"

She shook her head. "No."

He stood, adjusting his suit as he turned to look at her. For the first time in ages she felt her nakedness. His gaze passed over her body like a stranger's caress—cold and unwelcome, as he moved closer. "I am not a man who enjoys being toyed with, Mackenzie. You do not need the sedative. Put out the candle."

"I can't—" she cut off as he grabbed her face, squeezing her cheeks together between thumb and fingers.

"Do not tell me what it is you *cannot* do," he told her in a low voice. "I am not interested in what you think you *cannot* do. The Cocktail that was given to you tells me that you have no idea what you can or *cannot* do. You do not need it now."

He let go of her face, shoving her head roughly back against the padding on the frame as he began to pace.

"Perhaps what you need is more of an incentive." He made his way back to the stand that held the candle and looked down at his feet, stepping heel to toe as he paced out the distance to her hand.

"Excellent!" he glanced at her with that same look of child-like exuberance. "Ten feet, literally." He broke off in a delighted laugh. "Every hour we will move the candle a foot closer. If you have not put it out by the time it reaches your skin, then you will have your incentive as your flesh burns along with the candle."

"No, please!" Her begging became a piteous wail as he lit the candle and withdrew.

She stared at the flame for the first hour solid, willing it to go out, to change, or even just to flicker, anything to acknowledge her existence.

The Technicians ignored her as they moved the stand closer and withdrew as swiftly as the Man in the Suit had.

"Come on, you bastard. Go out!" she hissed from between clenched teeth. The candle ignored her, burning down slowly as the wax began to drip onto the floor.

By the eighth hour she was pleading with it, as if the flame might somehow hear her and obey. The clear screen fixed in front of it worked to block her attempts to blow it out.

She was crying before the door eventually opened. Instead of the expected technicians in their surgical scrubs, the Man in the Suit came in slowly, dressed as immaculately as the first time she'd seen him.

He sighed, looking over the trail of wax that charted the progress of the candle across the room. "I have to say, I really didn't think it would come to this."

"No, please. Give me more time. I can do this."

She pulled at her arm as he picked up the candle stand, wrenching backwards against the restraints as she tried to force her wrist through the cuff.

"That isn't going to work, Mackenzie," he told her, holding the stand in front of her. "Put out the flame. That's all I'm asking, something you've done twice already. I really don't want to have to hurt you." He set the candle into position beneath her wrist and stepped back to watch, a slight smile on his lips.

The heat was a gentle warmth for half a breath and then it changed, almost instantly, becoming a blistering heat that had her screaming as she twisted and wrenched at the unyielding cuffs. The Man in the Suit watched her, unmoved by her screams, as the skin on her hand and wrist scorched and blistered.

"Damn you!" he cursed and snatched the candle away. "You can do this, girl. I have watched you do this. I had thought this would be enough incentive, perhaps I was wrong."

He looked towards the smoked glass at the end of the room.

"Bring him in."

The technicians brought in a metal chair first, setting it in a corner of the room over a small grate. She watched them leave again, confusion battling with the searing agony of her wrist and forearm.

She waited, frowning at the open door until they emerged. The man was emaciated, so thin the hospital robe hung from him like a sheet on a washing line. He looked at her as they carried him through the door, his eyes calm despite the gag buckled around his face. She would have known him even without the amputated limbs.

"Armond," she said, it was barely more than a whisper.

"Yes, I thought perhaps if you didn't care about yourself, then maybe you'd care about your little friend here." The Man in the Suit smiled fondly as he watched the technicians strap Armond to the chair, fastening broad leather belts around his torso and what remained of his arms and legs.

The Man in the Suit grimaced and turned to her with a shrug. "It's not quite as good as the frame we have you in, but we had to improvise."

Was he apologising? Mackenzie shook her head. "What are you doing to him? Why is he gagged?"

"Well, you and he have been speaking for quite some time now. It was beginning to become a distraction for you. As for what we're doing to him, well that rather depends on you." He picked up the stand, the candle still burning on top, and crossed the room to Armond.

"I would say this won't hurt, old friend. But I think we both know better than that, don't we?"

Armond shook his head violently and looked up as the man lowered the stand and put the candle in place, burning beneath the stump of one leg. The gag muffled the screams, but the agony still managed to find a way past it as he thrashed against the restraints. The Man in the Suit turned to Mackenzie with a broad smile.

"There you are," he said, sweeping an arm towards the screaming Armond. "Incentive."

"Leave him alone, you sick bastard!"

"Such language." The Man in the Suit shook his head in disapproval. "If it bothers you so much, put out the candle."

Armond's skin was blistering already, smoke or soot turning the skin around the burn into a dirty grey colour.

"Let him go!" Mackenzie screamed.

The man shook his head with a small smile. "It hurts, there's no doubt of that, but it won't cause him any lasting damage."

She glared at him, face twisted with disbelief.

"Look." The man pointed.

He was right. Where the blisters should have been rupturing and the burn deepening, fresh skin was already fighting to close over the burn. The wound was in flux, fighting to heal even as the candle flame gnawed at the flesh.

"His healing truly is quite remarkable," the Man in the Suit told her, making his way past the technicians to the doorway. "Sadly, it's not anything that could be replicated. The testing has been interesting but, honestly, I think I've run my course with it."

"So, what?" Mackenzie spat, not even bothering to hide the contempt in her voice. "You're bored with him?"

The man laughed, waving a finger at her. "Be careful with that tone."

He went out through the door. All the while Armond screamed into the heavy gag strapped to his head and beneath the muffled sound of his screams, the faint sizzling of the candle cooking his flesh.

She closed her eyes against the horror of it all, trying to block out the screams, until her nose betrayed her. The smell of scorched flesh wasn't all that close to cooking meat, but it was close enough. Dear Christ, was she salivating?

The Man in the Suit returned within moments with a red jerry can. "You haven't put that candle out yet, Mackenzie? Poor Armond really is counting on it."

She froze, staring at the plastic jerry can in his hand. She knew what those were for. "Please, don't do this."

He smiled at her, spreading his arms and spinning in a slow circle as he walked over to where Armond screamed. "Let's see just how quickly he can heal, shall we? Unless you want to put the candle out? I really don't think you'll be able to manage it in a moment."

"I can't, you son of a bitch! You sick bastard, you know I can't!"

The smile fell from his face and he worked the top free of the jerry can. "That was the wrong answer, Mackenzie." He kicked at the candle, sending the stand clattering across the floor as the candle went out.

"You can't say I didn't give you your opportunity," he shot back at her, and then sloshed the can over Armond, sending the fuel splashing over his body. Armond's moans of pain turned to panicked shrieks as the Man in the Suit pulled out a zippo lighter and stepped back away from Armond.

"I always liked fire," he told her with a little smile. "There's something so magical about it."

And then the lighter was burning and flying through the air towards Armond.

The fuel caught with that odd *whump* you so often hear on television, and Armond's shrieks were lost in the sound of the flames and the Man in the Suit's laughter.

She focused on the flames until her head pounded. Until Armond's screams had turned to silence and the only sound was the extractor fans in the ceiling. Until her own screams had faded to whimpers and sobs, and the horror of it all claimed her.

CHAPTER EIGHTEEN

I woke in darkness. Not the murky gloom of early morning, but an inky blackness that made me wonder if my eyes were actually open. For a few moments I was still caught in the memory of Kabul. Call it a dream, call it a flashback, it fucks me up every time I suffer through it. It had been months since the last time I was dragged through it all, but every time it was just as sharp.

I could almost smell the dust of that place. I woke with the feeling of it coating my tongue and lining the inside of my throat, and behind it all was the smell of the blood—that faintly metallic scent that forced me to remember the red mist that drifted down through the air after Sunglasses shot Turner.

And then the taste filters through, past the dust and the dirt on my tongue. I try to avoid thinking about whether that taste was real. Whether we'd been forced to breathe in tiny droplets of his blood that were still hanging in the air. Sometimes it's better not to know the truth of things.

It wasn't the bodies that bothered me; the dead are just that. We all knew what we'd signed up for. We knew the risks of the job. No, the looks from the men still living were far worse than the blank stares of the dead. The questions and accusations came later, but the looks from McCourt and Yates said everything they would put into words afterwards.

How did you do that?

Why did you wait?

You could have saved them. How could you let everyone die?

I've always hated being drugged. I had four teeth taken out when I was eleven so the dentist could fit me with braces. I must have been one of the last kids they knocked out with gas instead of just using an injection for local anaesthetic.

I can remember breathing in through the mask and the man counting backwards with me from ten. I remember the room spinning, and my vision sinking down into darkness as if I were being sucked down into a whirlpool.

It's the 'coming to' that I remember the most. The feeling of being roused, pulled from a deep sleep that shifted far too quickly to nausea, and then leaning over the edge of the chair, stomach heaving as I threw up onto the floor whilst the dentist swore at me. I remember the feeling of the wads of cotton wool, or gauze, or whatever it was that they'd put in my mouth to help stem the bleeding. More than anything I remember the drive home. I sat in the back of the car as I probed at the new holes inside my mouth with the tip of my tongue, and prayed for my head to stop spinning.

This felt worse. The darkness wasn't helping. My head was spinning and lurching in that awful way it does when you're really drunk and haven't quite managed to pass out yet. When you lay flat on the bed and cling to the edges with both hands and feet to keep from being thrown off. If I'd had something to look at, I might have been able to focus on it. As it was, I lay there and squeezed my eyes shut against the darkness, using the feeling of my eyelids pressing together to convince myself I wasn't dead.

I don't know how long it was before I noticed the restraints. The passing moments could have been minutes or hours, and the after-effects of the drugs weren't enhancing my ability to think straight. I reached to run my hand over my face, to pinch at the bridge of my nose and scrape the sleep from my eyes. The cuff stopped me before my hand moved more than an inch, the metallic clink of the chain reinforcing what my wrist was already telling me.

I took stock of things slowly, facts fighting their way through the fog inside my head as I became aware of my situation. I was naked for one, the skin on my back was sticking to the cushioned padding of whatever it was I was bound to. It pulled free with a sucking, tearing, sound as I shifted. I was bound, wrist and ankle, with a wide band pressed against my chest and stomach.

"Fuck." My voice sounded strange in the darkness. The drugs had left my throat dry and my voice was a hoarse, rasping thing.

"I'd say that's about right, yes." Johnson's voice was loud enough to make me jump, coming from somewhere over to my right.

"Oh Christ." This was all I needed.

"Not me, mate. Don't think I'm really cut out to be anyone's messiah."

I didn't need this. I needed to focus, to work out where I was, and if I could get out. Being captured and confined is all about control. The only way to really survive it is to hold on to something—to find something that you yourself can control no matter what they do to you. At least, that's what they told us in training. It's a bit like the prisoners who go on hunger strikes. When everything else has been taken from you, one of the last things you can control is your willingness to eat. I needed to find something like that. Something I could cling to. Having a hallucination muttering in my ear wasn't going to help.

"Fuck off, Johnson," I muttered.

And that was Rule Three broken again. I looked over towards where I'd heard his voice. It was odd how I couldn't see him in the darkness. How was it that I needed light to see something that was only in my head anyway? The mind is a strange thing.

"Focus, Carver, for God's sake." I shook my head and forced myself to concentrate. The room was heated, which was something at least, and that simple fact had a host of implications. If Mujib, or whoever had me now, were going to bother to heat this place then they wanted me in reasonable condition. It also implied that whatever it was they wanted me for would require my cooperation. I took some comfort from that.

I slept for a time. With nothing else to do, and my mind still fuddled, it was probably the best idea, and when I woke for the second time it was with a clearer head. Thirsty and aching, but clearer.

I debated with myself for a while about whether I should call out or not. The only cards I had to play against my captors were psychological ones, and given that I spend quite a lot of my time seeing people who aren't real, then that deck was suspect. In the end, I decided water was more important than games, and called out.

They didn't answer.

The cuffs were leather, I decided. Worn enough to have some give to them, but new enough to still be smooth and free of any cracks that I could feel on my wrists. I spent a bit of time pulling on them, testing whether my hands would slide through if I lost enough weight. Possibly, I decided. But if I lost that much weight then I'd probably be too weak to get out of the torso restraint, and almost certainly too weak to get out of wherever it was they were holding me.

I took naps, sleeping whenever I could in an effort to save energy. It didn't work well. I've always had a tendency to sleep with my mouth open and it was dehydrating me faster than staying awake would have. The human body is about two thirds water. You can last weeks without food. Water is another story. The most an average person can last is about a hundred hours.

By what I thought might be the third day, I'd broken.

I called out. I screamed.

Sometime after that, I begged.

The lights woke me, blasting down at me like a desert sun. After so long in total darkness the lights were so bright that I couldn't bear to open my eyes and had to let them adjust to the red glare that came through my eyelids.

I was utterly unprepared for the water. The cradle I was strapped to had a system of sprinklers surrounding it that blasted my naked body with cold water as it rotated around and below me. The cradle was shaped like a rough X with my arms and legs stretched out but held at an angle so I was slightly reclined. A hole was cut between the base of my back and upper thighs, I'm sure you can figure out why. Even so the stench of my own waste and filth was enough to make me gag as the water sluiced it away.

I licked water from my lips as the sprinklers shut off and I looked up. A plastic tube hung down on either side of my face and a droplet clinging to the end of the one to my left was all the invitation I needed.

Water.

Bloody hell, I swear I've never had anything as sweet as that first drink. Drinking pints of water after being dehydrated is a great way to make yourself throw up, and I forced myself to stop after a couple of mouthfuls. God, I didn't want to though. I wanted to draw on that tube until it ran dry.

The other tube held some kind of gruel. It was almost tasteless, with a grainy texture, but it was food. I've survived on a lot worse in the past, and this was calories. Not eating or drinking for so long had taken a toll on my body, and I suspected I would need all the strength I could get.

The door opened before I'd finished eating. A glass panel pivoted to one side on metal struts letting in a man in a pale suit.

"You're awake, Mr Carver. That's good."

I didn't really have a response to that, so I used the opportunity to study him as he drew closer. He was Middle Eastern, with a close-cropped dark beard. The suit looked tailored, though I've never been an expert on these things. He stopped well out of my reach, pacing back and forth as he ran his gaze over me; admiring his catch, I supposed.

He smiled suddenly, an exuberant grin that somehow managed to make him look like a child, despite the beard.

"You have no idea how long I've wanted to meet you. John Carver, *The Miracle of Kabul*. That's what they call you, you know?"

He ignored my scowl, his grin growing even wider. "Finding you was no easy task. The people I've had looking for you..." He fell silent, the smile fading as he looked me over again, concern touching his face as his brow furrowed. "But you must be tired. You'll need your strength for what's coming."

I shook my head. He wasn't making much sense and I'd already heard enough. "Who the hell are you? What do you want from me?"

He tutted, wagging a chiding finger at me.

"That's two questions, John, and you haven't let me ask you anything yet. Hardly fair is it?" He laughed at the incredulous expression that crossed my face. "My name wouldn't mean anything to you. I've worked hard to keep my identity secret. I have a number of names; so many that I've forgotten most of them. You can call me Afridi if you wish, though my connection to that tribe is a bit tenuous these days."

"Afridi? As in Ehsan Afridi? You're a drug dealer?"

"Oh Carver," Afridi shook his head. "I thought you knew more about this part of the world than that. There are millions of Afridis. The tribe stretches throughout Pakistan and across half of Afghanistan. As for the 'drug dealer' title," he pulled a face. "That's a little insulting. It's correct, or at least it was for a time, but I always thought of myself as more of a businessman than simply a peddler of narcotics."

The man was nuts, and clearly in love with the sound of his own voice.

"What the fuck am I doing here?" I snapped.

Afridi pursed his lips and ran his tongue over his teeth, looking every inch the disappointed parent as he sighed. "You're here to teach me, Carver."

I closed my eyes tight for a moment, blocking out the insanity of the situation. "Teach you? Teach you what?"

Afridi laughed, a surprised and delighted sound. "You stopped a bullet, Carver. You stopped a bullet with your power. Your name is still whispered across Kabul and half of Afghanistan. You're here to teach me how to do it."

Oh God, not this. Anything but this.

"I didn't...' I began, scrambling for the words. "I mean, I don't know what you've heard, but it wasn't like that."

Afridi laughed, shaking his head at my protests. "No, none of that here. I know you did it. I've met people who *saw* you do it. Shall we see

140

if you can do it now?" He reached into his suit jacket and pulled a gun from a shoulder holster.

"No!" My cuffs clanked against the restraints as I tried to move. "No, I can't. I don't know how I did it!"

Afridi looked up at the ceiling with a sigh. "Why do they always say this?"

He cocked the gun, pulling back on the slide to chamber a round.

"Now, hold still. I'd rather you stopped this, but if you do fail then let's keep this to a flesh-wound at least."

"No!" I threw myself against the cuffs, but even if the torso restraint hadn't been there, I had no leverage. Afridi watched me in silence, gun held by his side while I thrashed. "Have you about finished?"

"Fuck you!"

He shook his head. "Now, that's just rude. This is going to happen, Carver. If you don't want to get shot, then stop the bullet."

He raised the gun as he spoke, levelling it at my thigh.

Shit, he was actually going to do this. I'd lost weight in the last four days. Dehydration and lack of food had wasted away my fat reserves and torn my muscles down. I couldn't see my own legs well enough to judge, but I could feel the weakness in them. If he hit bone, he could cripple me. If he hit an artery, he could kill me.

I looked up at him. "Don't do this. I'm no good to you dead."

Afridi shrugged. "Stop the bullet then."

And he shot me.

PART
II

CHAPTER NINETEEN

"Mackenzie?" The voice was nagging, persistent. She rolled over, or tried to, but her arms and legs were held by something.

"Mackenzie, you need to eat." The hand was soft on her face, stroking her hair away from her cheek. She cracked her eyes open and peered between lids that felt dry and crusted with something that scratched her eyes.

"I don't want to." Her voice wasn't much more than a whisper, but she saw him give her a sad nod. The Man in the Suit was older than she'd first thought. Up close, where she could see past the suit and the exuberant personality, he was just a thin man with sad eyes and deep lines on his face.

"How about some soup?"

"Soup?" The word didn't make sense for a moment, as if the notion of food other than the gruel in the tube was now an alien concept. "How?"

"I'm sure I could arrange something; would you like that?"

Soup sounded good. Since she'd been small it had always been her comfort food. She nodded absently but it was so hard to stay awake. Her eyes drifted closed again and distantly she heard the hiss of the door.

The smell tugged at her, bringing her back to consciousness and she opened her eyes to his eager smile. "Look what I brought you."

He stood beside her with a steaming bowl, eyes dancing with a childish glee at her expression.

"Careful, it's still hot," he said, and brought a spoon to her lips.

She swallowed before she thought about what she was doing. It was good, tomatoes with pulses and some kind of spice. The second spoonful went down as easily as the first and soon she was bringing her face to the spoon, eager for more.

The Man in the Suit set the empty bowl down by his feet and looked at her. "Why did you stop eating, Mackenzie?"

"I wanted to die." The admission pained her, and she looked away, trying to hide her face with her hair.

"And now?"

"I don't know." She met his gaze with hesitant glances, like a scolded child.

He smiled at her. "You don't realise what you are becoming, do you? You're special, Mackenzie. You're like a diamond lost in amongst a thousand chips of glass. With my help you can become something amazing."

"I just want to go home."

"Really? Even now? Now that you've felt your power? I know the Cocktail can make things confusing, and that you've already been through so much, but you must have felt something?"

She opened her mouth to answer him but as she did, she realised he was right—she had felt something. There was something new within her, something had changed. She reached out towards it, feeling for the small place within her with a tentative thought.

It felt... *wrong*, somehow splintered and fractured as she probed at it, like a tongue in the hole of a missing tooth, and she shied away in an instant. It reeked of power, of some force that she couldn't explain, but which felt utterly alien. It cut and tore at her, at the substance of who she was, drawing her in. There were questions inside her that needed answers. They nagged at her in the silence of her prison. Each time she drifted off to sleep, they burned. Despite everything, she wasn't ready to leave yet.

"Can you let me out of these?" she shook the restraints at her wrists.

The Man in the Suit smiled. "Soon. Just a few more steps. Trust is a two-way street, Mackenzie. If you will trust me to help you, I will trust you enough to let you out of those."

"Can you at least tell me your name?"

"My name?" He seemed surprised, almost amused by the request.

"I have nothing to call you. I can't keep thinking of you as 'The Man in the Suit.'"

"That's what you call me?" He laughed. "Call me Janan."

The soup was helping—calories bringing strength to mind and muscle that she'd abused with her attempt at starvation. Already, she felt more alert than she had in days. Already, things were coming back to her. She closed her eyes for a moment, taking a deep breath, as tears pricked at her eyes.

"You burned Armond." A statement that brushed only lightly against accusation.

"I did," Janan said without remorse, his voice oddly gentle, in a way that stood at odds with his admission. "He was very ill. Did you know he had cancer?"

Mackenzie frowned but the man was already carrying on.

"His healing abilities could cope with so much, but the cancer was insidious. It was as if his body had accepted that the cancer was a natural part of him, and did nothing to combat it. We tried, of course. He was remarkably resistant to drugs, and the normal kinds of treatments like chemotherapy. His abilities worked to preserve his body in what it thought was a healthy state." He gave a bitter little laugh. "It was the worst kind of irony really. Armond had an incredible gift. Were it not for the cancer, he might have lived forever. As it was, his gift worked to kill him, defeating us at every turn. We even went so far as amputation, you know? The cancer had begun as an osteosarcoma of the proximal femur. You're a nurse, aren't you?"

Mackenzie nodded mutely. Armond said they cut him for tests, not to remove cancer. Her mind was spinning, questioning what she thought was the truth against this awful revelation.

"Then you probably know more about cancer than most. This kind of malignant tumour should have spread to bones in his skull or torso, if it was going to spread anywhere." He grimaced. "Spread is the wrong word. My English is usually good, but this word just escapes me."

"Metastasise," Mackenzie muttered.

Janan smiled. "Thank you. Yes, a malignant cancer like this should have metastasised to the torso, his ribs, or maybe even as far as his skull; but with Armond it seems his abili*ties were s*ufficient to protect his core. Or perhaps he was simply unlucky. We tried surgery to begin with, removing a section of bone in his femur. His recovery was remarkable. Within two days you couldn't even tell he'd had the surgery. But then the tumour was back within a week and just as aggressive. Poor Armond was in constant pain. We had no choice in the end but to try an amputation."

Mackenzie shook her head, refusing to swallow Janan's version of events. "That isn't what he said happened."

"I know," the Man in the Suit sighed. "The cancer spread to both of his legs in turn. In the end, we amputated all of his limbs in an effort to arrest it. Not that it worked, of course. I don't know if we had somehow weakened his abilities, or if Armond had simply reached his limits. Cancer is itself a mutation. Perhaps it was connected to Armond's abilities—perhaps it caused it? We will never know now. The cancer reached his brain in the end, twisting his memories and perceptions. Some days he was lucid; other times he'd go days without saying a word, just staring at the walls."

"So why burn him?"

He shrugged, and for a moment a glimpse of his former persona shone through. "Because I could. I'm no saint, Mackenzie. I never pretended to be. I burned Armond to see if you would put out the fire. It was a mercy to Armond as well, I suppose. An end to his pain. Not the quickest of ends I'll admit, but we all must play the cards we are dealt, mustn't we?"

"You didn't have to do it like that. It was cruel."

Janan gave her a strange look, cocking his head on one side. "Was it? He was half out of his mind with pain, and there was nothing we could do for him. But then, Armond knew what was coming. He suggested it."

"What?" Mackenzie gasped. "No, he didn't. That's ridiculous. Why would anybody want that?"

Janan shrugged. "He wanted to die. He was in constant pain and the cancer was only going to get worse. Pain medication had little to no effect on him, he metabolised them too quickly."

"But why fire? If he wanted to die that badly, why not just shoot him? Anything but burning him alive!"

Janan looked at her for a long moment. "I could say that I wasn't sure a bullet would even be able to kill him, but honestly? I needed to see if you could put the fire out. Your power, this affinity with fire, it's almost as if it is somehow suppressed at the moment. You can use your power if we alter your consciousness with drugs, but you don't seem to be able to any other time. Since it first manifested under a situation of extreme stress, I wanted to see if we could replicate that."

"So, you *burned him*?"

"I did what I needed to do," Janan said in a flat voice. "I will bring the fire out in you, Mackenzie. You will learn to control this power."

He sighed and crouched to retrieve the bowl. He looked back at her once on the way to the door and seemed on the verge of saying something, then he shook his head once and was gone.

The technicians brought the candle in not long after he left, setting it into the clamp and lighting it, before leaving without a word. She stared at it, watching the flame eat away at the wick as it sent rivulets of wax down the candle's length.

He had burned Armond alive. That inescapable fact circled her thoughts, bursting in upon them like a wolf among sheep.

*

He didn't come the next day, or even the day after, and with each opening of the door, her excitement mounted until her hopes were dashed. It wasn't him that she missed; rather, it was the human contact. The technicians arrived each day in silence, avoiding her gaze as they went through the process of replacing and lighting the candle, checking the water and feeding tubes to be sure they hadn't become blocked. They ignored her attempts to speak to them, not even glancing her way as they worked. She wasn't human as far as they were concerned. She wasn't a person.

She was meat on a slab.

A culture in a petri dish.

A lab experiment.

She ate steadily, replacing the weight that she'd lost during her self-imposed starvation. But her body had changed, the muscles of her arms and legs had wasted even without the stress of starvation. With nothing more than staring at a candle to fill her days, she took to performing what exercises she could—lifting her bodyweight against the cuffs to work her arms, legs and abs. Curling and uncurling her fingers and toes. Tensing every muscle she could, from her feet up. The simple act of exercising felt good. Sweating felt good. But still Janan did not come back.

*

The candle taunted her. Burning merrily behind the perspex screen that blocked her breath. Even if the screen hadn't been there, it was too far away to blow out. The most she would be able to do would be to make it flicker with her breath, but yet, she had managed to control that flame. The cracked remains of the waxy evidence were still present on the floor.

Janan returned the next day. She glared at him, ignoring his ridiculous child-like smile until he drew close enough for her to see the bowl he carried. Not soup, but some kind of curried dish. Her nostrils identified tomatoes, turmeric, garlic, and her mouth filled with saliva before he even got close.

"For me?" she didn't even care about the pathetic begging tone of her voice. Real food! It was almost beyond reckoning.

"A little." Janan nodded with a smile. "Your stomach will not be used to it. Just a small taste this time."

This time? Did that mean there would be more times? She nodded eagerly, shifting her weight on the wooden frame as he scooped rice and chicken onto the naan bread. She moaned as she ate. A tongue so long deprived of stimulation was now drenched in flavours. Her teeth and jaw ached, unused to the work, but God it was worth it.

He set the bowl down after just two mouthfuls, shaking his head. "That's enough. Your stomach isn't used to it."

She sipped water from the tube, knowing he was right but hating him for it anyway.

"Have you made any progress with the candle?"

She frowned. Didn't he know? "No."

"It will come, Mackenzie. The ability is in you, we just need to find a way to bring it out."

She frowned at him. What was this? Was this some kind of joint effort now? Was he toying with her?

"Tell me, Mackenzie. Do you read?"

"I… I suppose."

He nodded. "Your western classical literature is not so very different from ours. I don't care much for the modern works. Tell me, have you ever read Homer?"

"Homer?"

"The *Iliad? The Odyssey? The fall of Troy?*"

"Oh." She shook her head. "No, not really. I know the story of Helen, but I didn't ever read it."

He pulled a paperback from the pocket of his suit. "*Moby Dick?*"

She shook her head.

"The great American classic, they call it. Everyone should read it before they die, or so they say. Would you like me to read some to you?"

What was his game here? She fought to keep her face straight, to keep suspicion from her eyes as she nodded.

He paced as he read, marking his place with one finger. He was a gifted orator and she enjoyed the sound of his voice, but the days of not eating had left her weak. The book was stilted, written in a language that was unfamiliar, and she found it hard to follow. Before long she was drifting, her eyes heavy as she let the sound of his voice lull her.

CHAPTER TWENTY

Hunger clawed at her. When she'd been trying to starve herself, she had found a way to block it out. She had pushed past it, and on into a listless weakness that allowed her to sleep and doze through the days.

Janan had changed all of that.

She'd been almost delirious when he'd fed her the soup. By the time she realised what she was doing she'd finished the bowl and her body was demanding more. The gruel was a poor substitute, and her stomach had become a force that would no longer be denied.

It was more than just the soup, or even the curry. Janan's explanation of Armond's death had robbed her of purpose. Despite her situation, despite the cuffs and the frame she was bound to, she had never truly wanted to die. Armond's death had taken everything from her. Though he'd often fallen silent, just knowing there was someone else out there had been a comfort. His death had magnified everything about her captivity, and killing herself had seemed the only means of escape.

Janan, with his damned soup, and this sudden kindness, had changed that. More than that, he'd forced her to confront the realities of her power. Her memories of the fire in her home as a child were clouded. Despite the drugs that had been dulling her senses, there was no denying what was happening with the candle.

She could almost remember the sensation as she grasped hold of the flame with her power. The raging column of fire that she'd sent roaring towards the ceiling before the candle burned out. It had happened. She knew it, but she needed to know how.

And then there was this thing within her. The broken, fractured place that hurt just to explore with her thoughts. It was related to the power somehow, she could sense that much. But what was it? What had they done to her?

The feeding tube had been adjusted, or perhaps it had always had a limit and she'd just never reached it before. Now that she was regaining weight, and with the increased exercise her routine was giving her, the tube didn't seem able to keep up with her. She glared at the candle burning merrily in front of her as her stomach growled again.

"You always seem to get enough fuel, don't you?" Her words sounded too loud in the silence and she laughed at herself.

She watched the candle burn down slowly. In the silence of the small room, every sound seemed magnified and she fancied that she could hear the candle itself—the faint hiss and crackle of the wax as the flame ate away at it.

*

The hours stretched out into days. Her exercises helped in some small way. Her calves and arms ached from the effort, but this was a pain that she controlled—a good pain. She had caused it and somehow that made it better.

The silence was so complete it was smothering her. The technicians came and went with a quiet efficiency, their ignoring of her so total that they may as well not have existed. She craved contact. Simple human contact. Even the shouted and confused conversations with Armond had been better than this.

"Please," she begged the technicians as they entered. "Please, won't you help me?" There was no response. She had known there wouldn't be.

You shouldn't have asked for help, she told herself. *Should have just asked them to talk to you.*

"Put out the candle, Mackenzie." The voice came through the speakers. The first time it had spoken in weeks and she jumped.

"I'm fucking trying!" she screamed back at him. "You can see I'm trying!"

She glared at the candle, pouring out her anger and frustration. If she could just get the flame to move. Just to acknowledge her that would be—

"Fuck me!" she gasped.

Had it moved? Had the flame just flickered?

"Did you see that?" she called out to the unseen listeners. "Please tell me you saw that?"

The voice didn't answer but she was already looking back at the flame. Could she do it again? It had been an odd, reaching, sensation. There had been heat there but no pain. She stared at the candle again, reaching, straining. The flame burned in silence, ignoring her.

She tried until her head began to hurt again and she wondered if it had ever moved at all. The door hissed open as she was beginning to drift again and Janan burst into the room with a grin that struggled to fit on his face. He rushed to her, consumed with an excitement that seemed larger than himself.

"I came as soon as I heard!" He said, his words fighting past the grin. "I knew you would do it. I knew it!"

He reached to embrace her, oblivious, as always to her nakedness. He tried to worm his arms under her back but the frame defeated him and he muttered in frustration.

"Wait here," he told her, as if she had any other option. "I'll be back."

He was back in minutes, pushing a wheelchair through the doorway and accompanied by two men in black uniforms.

"You've done it, Mackenzie," Janan told her. "You touched your power, without drugs, without stimulation! This first stage was always going to be the hardest part. It's impossible for some, and they find themselves broken instead, but you've pushed through. We can move you on from here now."

She nodded but bit down on the inside of her cheek as the fear rose.

The prospect didn't excite her. Instead, the idea of leaving the room, even leaving her frame, filled her with dread, like a phobia.

She'd always had a fear of heights. As a child her family had gone on a trip to Kosciuszko National Park where her parents had dragged her onto a ski-lift that took passengers up the mountainside. It was like being strapped to a park bench, swinging in the wind, with her legs hanging free in the air beneath her. The journey had been the most terrifying thing she'd ever experienced. It was probably completely safe, but the lift and the journey filled her with unreasoning panic. Her mother had to stop her from lifting the safety bar as she'd fought and screamed out that she needed to get off. The reality of the fifty metre drop below her couldn't make it through the terror that had blinded her. All she knew was she needed to be away from there.

The very same fear struck her as the men undid her restraints, every bit as powerful and mindless as it had been on the Kosciuszko chairlift. She sank down as soon as the cuffs were free, clasping her hands around her knees as she curled into a foetal position.

It wasn't until the first tear hit her knee that she realised she was crying.

They had broken her. The shards of herself lay shattered against the base of her prison. The sobs tore from her, ripping free of her body until she was a trembling mess.

Janan waved the guards off and knelt down in front of her, working the ankle cuffs free. He caught her as she fell from the frame, taking her into his arms and making gentle shushing noises as he stroked her hair.

This was the man responsible for her abduction, and all of the torment she had experienced since. She ought to be ripping his throat out with her bare teeth, but instead all she wanted was for him to hold her and not let go.

In time, they managed to wrap her up in a thick robe and ease her into the wheelchair. She clung to the armrests, fingers clenched, clawing into the padded plastic as Janan wheeled her towards the door.

She glanced back at the wooden frame she'd been chained to. She'd spent so many hours straining against those cuffs, and yet now she was scared to leave. The realisation wasn't a pleasant one.

Janan squeezed her shoulder through the thick bathrobe and she reached for his hand, taking strength from it. Her feelings were a tangled mess. She ought to hate this man. He was the architect of her misery, the cause of her ruin.

The truth lurked at the centre of the fear and self-loathing that filled her; he had brought her within a hair's-breadth of truly touching this power, this thing that she'd spent every moment since childhood convincing herself wasn't real. As much as she despised everything about him for the things he'd done to her, he was a figure of wonder. He was a man from a faerie tale, handing her magic, and how could she truly hate someone like that? How could anyone?

The door led out through a small observation room and then on to a nondescript hallway. Plain white walls and florescent lights set in panels in the ceiling gave the place a sterile quality. It reminded her of the hospitals she'd worked in back in Australia. The clinics in Kabul and Helmand Province had been nothing like this. Corridors were a luxury that went along with dedicated rooms. Too often the Red Cross clinics in Afghanistan were in temporary shelters, or warehouse-like structures.

She looked at the other doorways as they passed. Armond had been in one of those rooms. Were there more people like her? From what Armond had said, it sounded like there were, or had been. The hallway ended at a lift and Janan touched a key-card to the sensor before backing her in carefully and selecting a floor.

Her preconceptions had been shattered. Within the confines of her room she'd known nothing of the rest of this complex, or even that there was a complex. Bound to the frame, she could have just as easily been chained up in a cellar somewhere. This was nothing that she might have imagined.

"A lift?" she managed, glancing around at Janan.

His smile was like a child on Christmas morning, barely able to contain the excitement.

"I'll take you the long way around and show you something of what we've done here. We began building almost ten years ago now," he told her as the lift continued to rise. "Most of the complex has to be underground. Satellites are irritating things at times, and we didn't want to attract unwanted attention."

"We?" She murmured.

"We," Janan nodded. "The others working in what we've come to call the Prometheus Project."

Prometheus, the titan who stole fire from the gods. Was that what they were doing here? Seizing powers that were never meant for mankind? The thought brought a thrill, and dread, in equal measure.

The lift came to a stop and he wheeled her out into a broad hallway. The white walls were hung with the same bland paintings and photographic art that infests offices the world over. The mediocrity was broken only by broad windows revealing laboratories where men and women in white coats worked away at microscopes, computers, and other lab equipment.

"There is a staff of almost a hundred here now, not counting the guards and support roles," Janan told her.

"But why?" Mackenzie asked with a twisted frown. "What for?"

"For you, Mackenzie. And people like you," Janan said, wheeling her around a corner and through another set of double doors. "In a day or two we can answer all of your questions. For now, you need to rest and recover. Passing through the first barrier takes an incredible toll, but it is only the beginning. You'll need your strength for what's coming."

He pushed her through a maze of corridors and down several levels in another lift, before he stopped beside a door, touching the key-card to another sensor and wheeling her in to what looked oddly like a hotel room.

"These will be your living quarters for now," Janan explained. "There is a small gym in the next room and all the facilities you should need. Use the phone to call for food if you get hungry, but your meals will be provided on a normal schedule. For now, we simply want you to rest."

She frowned, bemused as the black-clad men helped her out of the wheelchair and onto the bed.

"Use the wheelchair if you feel you need it," Janan told her. "Your legs will be weaker than you think for a week or two."

And with that he left, walking through the door without a backward glance.

She sat on the bed and tried to process it all. She hadn't given much thought to what might lie beyond the room with the frame she'd been strapped to. It had been her cell, but it had never occurred to her that it was part of a complex; least of all a complex this massive and well populated. The door to the new room made a heavy thunk as it closed, and she heard the locks engage. For all its outward appearances of luxury and comfort, this was every bit as much a prison as the frame had been.

CHAPTER TWENTY-ONE

The bed felt strange. Months of being chained to a thinly padded wooden frame made the mattress feel too soft and giving. After tossing and turning for the best part of an hour, she threw the blankets and pillows onto the floor and slept there.

She woke hungry and sore. Her legs ached with a deep, bitter pain that had her curling up against it. Her stomach growled, and she found herself turning her head and craning for a feeding tube that wasn't there. The phone turned out to be a closed system and began ringing the moment she picked it up.

"Yes?"

Mackenzie froze for a moment, unsure what to say. "I... I need some food."

"Very well," the voice was brusque. Not rude or abrupt, just clearly not interested in speaking. "Something will be brought to you. Is there anything else?"

"My legs hurt. Could I have a painkiller? Something like ibuprofen?" There was a pause on the other end of the phone and a muffled conversation before the man came back onto the phone. "Something will be added to your food. We cannot give you the pills."

"Okay, thank you," she said, but the phone had already gone dead. The food arrived quickly, and the sensor beeped as the key-card tapped against it outside her door.

"Stand back from the door, please," the voice was low and guarded as the door nudged open. Mackenzie sat on the bed and watched as a tray holding a steaming bowl slid over the floor and into the room, before the door was pulled shut. It was like someone feeding a caged dog, or an animal in a zoo. Whoever had brought the food was clearly scared of her reaction. She looked down at herself, at the pitiful state of her body, and almost laughed. She was no threat to anyone. Just getting to the tray would be challenge enough.

The bowl contained a thick porridge. It was bland and would have benefited from both more cream and sugar but, compared to the cold gruel, it was glorious. She ate half of it before forcing herself to slow down and enjoy the sensation. Just feeling hot food go down was wonderful. The ibuprofen, if it was in there, was buried beneath the taste of the porridge and she finished it far too soon. She sat for a while, scraping the remnants of her breakfast from the edge of the bowl. It was made from a kind of rubberised plastic, like the spoon. The tray was thicker, more rigid, but still rubberised and unlikely to shatter.

Mackenzie pushed herself to the edge of the bed and levered herself to her feet, leaning heavily on the wheelchair. She explored the room with slow, shuffling, steps.

It hadn't been as apparent when Janan had brought her in yesterday, but the place had an odd design. There were no sharp corners on anything. The small bedside table had rounded edges, as did the desk. The television was bolted to the wall, and the room had no window. A quick trip to the bathroom confirmed that, whilst there was a shower, there was no bath, and the mirror looked to be polished aluminium set into the wall. The room had been built to be suicide-proof. The notion almost made her laugh; but then, she hadn't been far from wanting to die herself not so long ago, had she?

With no windows or clocks it was hard to tell what time it was. That was nothing new, but when she'd been tied to her frame things had felt different. It was as if now that she had the freedom to move, or at least as much as her legs would let her, her time belonged to her.

The gym was a small room on the other side of the bathroom. A range of resistance machines awaited her, built into the walls with touch-screens. No free-weights, naturally. She laughed again at the level of paranoia and made her way onto a treadmill. The touchscreen gave her a range of options as the machine itself weighed her. She blinked, staring at the screen.

"That can't be right," she muttered, looking at her weight.

The machine weighed in pounds, but a quick touch of a button converted it to kilos for her. Ninety pounds, barely over forty kilos. She'd always been slim, but that was insane. She looked down at her legs, at the pale skin and wasted muscle that had once been firm and toned.

Five minutes walking on the treadmill had her sweating and gasping as she clung to the bars set on either side of the track. Legs that had taken her through ten-kilometre races and one poorly-thought-out marathon, now would have struggled to take her the length of a shop. Her shock and dismay faded quickly, smothered by an anger that then faded into a grim determination.

She leant heavily on the wheelchair as she took herself into the shower. The water felt good, and just the simple act of washing herself was incredible. The wardrobes held simple clothes and she flopped down onto the bed, revelling in the feeling of having her skin covered.

The television had western channels. There were no news channels, which somehow didn't come as a surprise, but she managed to lose herself in the mindlessness of sitcoms for a while. Lunch came and went. The same nervous voice asking her to back away from the door before sliding a tray in. Dinner was much the same, and the hours ticked slowly away.

By the third day she was climbing the walls. It was as if her mind had been freed as much as her body, and it craved stimulation. The gym helped to calm her a little, and she spent long hours working every neglected muscle group she could identify. But you can only work-out for so long.

She was slumped on the bed in a half-doze when the key-card sensor beeped and the door clicked open.

"Mackenzie?" Janan's voice called as he knocked. "May I come in?"

She fought down a laugh. He'd had her abducted and chained up in a cell, before locking her away in this pseudo-hotel room, but still he knocked and asked permission to enter.

"Yes," she called back.

He entered slowly behind a black-clad guard.

"You look better," he told her with a smile. "Rested."

"What do you want?" she blurted out, then cringed inwardly. She hadn't meant to be so blunt.

If Janan was offended he gave no sign. "I'd like you to meet someone actually. If you're feeling up to it?"

Up to leaving the room and the delights of talking to herself? "Of course!"

He stood back as the guard helped her into the wheelchair. She stiffened as he produced a set of Velcro cuffs.

"Merely a precaution, Mackenzie," Janan said, with an apologetic smile that chased away his wince at her reaction.

She clenched her teeth tight together as her wrists and ankles were bound to the chair. Janan waved the guard away and took the chair himself. Apparently, all it took were wrist and ankle cuffs for him to find his courage.

He babbled away as they passed along the hallway and back towards the lifts. She made noncommittal grunts in response, or simply ignored him, but it didn't seem to matter. The man seemed perfectly happy to carry both sides of the conversation as they went up several levels and passed through a maze of corridors.

He stopped outside a door and knocked, smiling at her with a wink as if they were somehow friends. Despite everything, she wasn't sure how she felt about him, or what to make of him. She had to keep reminding herself to hate him, and a small, traitorous part of herself whispered that she was being foolish.

Janan pushed the door open at the summons and wheeled her into an office, leaving the guards in the hallway. The room was sparse, furnished in black leather and chrome, and dominated by a large desk. An older, black man sat at the desk, stabbing away at a computer keyboard with fingers far too large to be suited to the task.

"Doctor Elias, there is someone I'd like you to meet," Janan said.

Elias looked up from the screen with visible irritation that melted away as he saw Mackenzie. "Is this the one? Is this her?"

"It is," Janan said with a smile that was almost paternal.

Elias stood and worked his way out from behind the desk. The man was enormous, taller than Janan by a head or more and easily double his weight. For all that, he moved with a simple grace. He dropped to one knee in front of the wheelchair and offered his hand for her to shake.

"Toby Elias," he said. "It's a pleasure to meet you."

Mackenzie blinked, bemused. "Mackenzie Cartwright," she managed, taking his hand.

"Dr Elias is our lead parapsychologist," Janan explained.

"Parapsychologist?" Mackenzie said with a frown. "What, like Ghostbusters?"

Elias winced. "And this is why I wish you wouldn't call me that," he muttered up at Janan. "Parapsychology is largely dismissed as a pseudoscience. Foolish tests with flash cards and EEG monitors."

Janan gave him an amused look. "What would you have me call it then?"

"Extra-normative psychology is one term that springs to mind. It allows us to go beyond the restrictive boundaries without all of the negative connotations of abnormal psychology."

"Elias here is our lead psychologist." Janan said, straight-faced.

Elias gave Janan a hard look and then barked out a laugh.

"I imagine this is all a bit surreal," he said, standing and moving back to lean on the edge of the desk. "One minute you're a captive, the next it feels a bit like you're a hospital patient."

Mackenzie nodded. "Yes, that's it exactly!"

Elias glanced at Janan. "Maybe leave her with me for a little while to chat?"

Janan raised an eyebrow. "Are you sure?"

Elias looked from Janan to Mackenzie and back again. "We'll both be fine."

Janan didn't look convinced as he left, and the sound of him speaking to the guard in a rush of Pashto carried easily through the door.

"I'm sorry about that," Elias said, with an awkward glance at the door. "It rather goes with the environment."

Mackenzie nodded, looking around the sparse room as she wound her fingers through each other. "What do you want with me?"

Elias smiled at that. "To begin with, I wanted to see if you were all right. Beyond that, I have a more professional curiosity."

"All right? How could I be all right? You do know what happens in this place, don't you?"

"I do," Elias said, in a flat tone. "You might not believe this, but it is all necessary to a degree."

"It's necessary to kidnap people and chain them up like animals?" Her tone was scathing and, she knew, ill-advised, but right now she didn't care. She was done pretending this was all okay, no matter how they tried to justify it to themselves.

Elias sighed and made his way around the desk to sink into his chair. He looked at her for a moment, steepling his fingers under his nose.

"Do you know how the vaccine for Hepatitis B was first developed?" he asked finally.

Mackenzie frowned at the non-sequitur. "I'm not sure what—"

"The Willowbrook experiments," Elias answered for her. "It was a state school in Staten Island in the United States, a home for children with mental disabilities. A researcher named Krugman intentionally let the children there become infected with Hepatitis."

Mackenzie gasped. "Oh my God! Why would anyone do that?" she demanded, speaking through the hand she'd clapped over her mouth.

Elias nodded. "It's abhorrent. But it can't be denied that the research from it resulted in the discovery of both the Hepatitis A and B strains, and that led to the Hepatitis B vaccine.

The Nazis did awful things, but through their experiments, they developed the rapid active rewarming technique that is still used for hypothermia today. Ethics are a wonderful, and very necessary part of medical research, Mackenzie, but they can be a stumbling block. Modern science rejects even the possibility of powers like yours. Our experiments, our programme, could never exist if we worked within a fully ethical framework. Look how far you have come already in just a few short months. This couldn't have happened any other way. I know it has been hard, Mackenzie, but your abilities will never be fully realised, and certainly will never be understood, if we allow medical ethics to control what we can learn."

"But you're supposed to be a *doctor*? How can you do this?"

"It's a bit of a cliché, but I suppose the ends justify the means," Elias said with a shrug. "This research could herald in a new era of human evolution."

Bile rose in her throat and she swallowed hard as she recoiled in the wheelchair. "Even if it means burning people alive?"

Elias blinked. "What?"

"Janan. He burned Armond alive," Mackenzie told him. "In front of me, just to see if I could put the fire out."

"No." Elias shook his head. "We're not monsters, Mackenzie. We'd never do anything like that."

"I saw him, Elias. I was there."

Elias frowned for a moment. "You've been on some pretty heavy medication, Mackenzie. The Cocktail contains drugs that can cause hallucinations that might seem very real."

"It *wasn't* a hallucination," she grated, the anger building underneath her disgust.

Elias gave her an understanding but patronising smile. She'd seen it a thousand times. She'd worn it herself. It was the compassionate, condescending, look you gave someone when they were delusional, or on drugs.

"Let it pass for now," he told her. "There are more important things I want to discuss with you."

She ground her teeth and looked away. There was no point fighting him. She wasn't going to convince him of anything.

He nodded, taking her silence as acceptance. "Your powers, Mackenzie. The abilities of everyone we have discovered so far, have one thing in common. They all stem from a moment of great psychological trauma. For you it was the fire you were trapped in as a child. The fear you experienced, cut off from your parents and surrounded by flames, was something that few will encounter in their lifetime, and one that, I believe, led to a perceptual and conceptual break."

"I'm not sure I recognise the term," Mackenzie said, narrowing her eyes at Elias.

Elias nodded. "No, it's something I've coined myself. I'm still not sure I'm happy with it, to tell the truth. What I mean is that your fear and trauma at the time of the fire led to a psychological break from your understanding of reality."

"I went mad?"

"No, nothing so extreme," Elias laughed. "No, what I believe happened is you broke free of the shackles we place upon ourselves, the limits of what we believe is normally possible. It probably helped that you were a child, and that your understanding of the world, of what is possible and what isn't, was more fluid, and that enabled you to access this power."

"I decided it was possible, so it was?" Mackenzie wasn't convinced and the look she gave him was less than subtle.

Elias smiled. "I suspect it's a little more involved than that. There is almost certainly a biological element to this as well, though we've yet to isolate anything in all the tests we've done. One thing is certain—it is this psychological break, this ability to affect a disconnect from what most people believe to be the rules of physics and possibility, that drives these abilities. What matters most is learning to control both the power and the extent of the disconnect. That's what the Cocktail was for, to remind you of your ability, to push past the physical laws of this world, to reach through the disconnect and seize your power again."

There was more to this than he was saying, that much was obvious, but screaming for the details wasn't going to get her anywhere.

"That sounds fascinating," she said, giving him her best smile. There was more than one way to skin a cat. "So, where do we go next with this?"

CHAPTER TWENTY-TWO

I've never been shot. Shot at? Yes, sure, more times than I could count. But I've never actually been hit. It sounds a bit stupid to say after over ten years in the forces, almost like I really ought to have been shot at some point. But I suppose there's a first time for everything.

It didn't feel anything like I'd expected. The impact itself was like a baseball bat had smacked me in the leg, and for what seemed like ages, that's all I felt as I gaped down at the bloody hole in my thigh. That and an immense pressure, as if something were still forced down against my flesh.

Afridi was cursing, and medics rushed in to inspect the wound and sort me out. The heat came next, like a hot poker had been driven through one side of my thigh and out the other. The wound felt hot, and wet, and just wrong somehow. That's the thing that stood out to me most, just how odd and wrong and really fucking painful it was. Don't get shot, kids. It doesn't feel nice.

They pumped me full of drugs despite me begging them not to. The pain was bad, don't get me wrong. I'm not superman, and the pain was one of the most intense I've ever felt. But I don't get on well with opiates.

I broke my ribs when I was in my early twenties. Stupid boys racing go-carts on an indoor course in London. I spun out on a corner and another car slammed into the side of me. The impact smashed me into the side of the moulded seat, which helpfully popped a rib for me. Just breathing in felt like being stabbed slowly with a blunt knife.

They put me on codeine, but I stopped taking them after the third day. It stopped the pain, but it felt like I had ants crawling under my skin. After two nights without much sleep I binned the lot and dealt with the pain instead.

I've no idea what they pumped me full of after Afridi shot me, but it hit hard and held me for hours before I came to again. They had me hooked up to an IV, a saline drip by the looks of things, that hung on a stand beside the frame I was cuffed to.

There was something on my head too, some kind of rubber cap with wires attached to it that ran to a machine against the wall. If I craned my neck forwards, I could just see the bandages they'd bound around my leg. They'd taken care to wash the blood off me too, which probably meant they'd cleaned the wound and I was unlikely to die of infection. Maybe.

They left me alone for most of the day. A silent man in scrubs came in to check the IV bag at one point, and inject something into the drip line. It wasn't a pain-killer, or if it was then it didn't bloody work. I stared at him long enough to make him uncomfortable before he left.

This became the pattern for what I guessed to be about three days. Doze, eat the grainy slop in the feeding tube, and glare at the unlucky sod sent in to check my bandages. I did notice that nobody other than Afridi tried to talk to me, which I took to mean they weren't allowed to.

By the fourth day the bullet wound had healed enough that the pain had ebbed and I was able to consider my situation. I sucked a mouthful of cold, grainy goop from the feeding tube and forced it down.

"So, what the hell do I do now?"

Talking to yourself isn't actually all that uncommon. Getting answers, however? That's a little different.

"I'd say you're fucked," Johnson advised me with a cheery grin.

I shook my head and ignored him as the door hissed open.

"What the hell is that for?" I asked the two men as they wheeled in a machine. I make a point of trying to avoid Wimbledon when it infests the television each year. I have no real objection to tennis, but the grunts and groans get on my nerves. Despite my efforts, I've been subjected to enough of it to know this machine was a tennis ball launcher.

I watched the two of them set the thing up and load tennis balls into the hopper. It had some manner of laser pointer attached to the front of it, and the small red dot settled on the centre of my chest, just above the restraining band than ran over my stomach.

"I'm afraid my backhand's a bit rusty," I called over to them.

The taller of the two glanced at me, and fought down a smile. He spoke English by the looks of things, so at least that was something.

"So, what's the plan here, boys?"

They exchanged glances and one plugged the power cord into a socket in the wall. The machine came to life with a faint electric whine.

"Hey!" I shouted at them as they made to leave. "Answer me, you bastards."

"Please don't abuse the staff, Mr Carver." A voice came through speakers set above the door. "They are simply doing their job."

I didn't recognise the voice. It wasn't Afridi, I knew that much.

"Oh well, I'm terribly sorry to cause offence," I snapped back at the speaker. "Maybe being chained up is fraying my nerves? Or maybe it's the way you shot me in the fucking leg."

"You are The Miracle of Kabul, Mr Carver. If you object to being shot, then perhaps you should have stopped the bullet."

"Right. And for my next trick, I'll wish these cuffs away and fly home on my shiny new fairy wings."

There was no response to that, and when the man did speak again his voice was flat and hard. "The machine will launch every three minutes."

"Jesus Christ," I muttered, closing my eyes against the insanity of it all.

I looked at the launcher. It was a small black cube with a hopper on top, thankfully not that similar to the professional launchers you occasionally see on sports interviews. Those things can hurl a ball at over a hundred miles an hour. If a tennis ball hit me at that speed, I'd be blue for weeks.

The launcher shuddered and sent a ball slamming into my chest.

"Son of a bitch!" It didn't hurt as much as I'd expected it to, but it wasn't what I'd call a fun experience. At least it wasn't launching cricket balls, I decided.

The second ball caught me as unprepared as the first and I swore and yelled as if that might make a difference. By the fourth ball I'd started counting down the time to the next one. By the sixth I was trying to shift myself to the side so it wouldn't strike in the same place as the others. It didn't work.

I had no idea how many balls they'd tipped into the launcher, but the hopper was big enough to hold at least a hundred. My maths has never been that great, but it was good enough for me to know that the next couple of hours weren't going to be any fun *at all*.

A tennis ball isn't the hardest thing in the world, it's designed to bounce after all, and that requires a certain amount of give. The launcher wasn't going at full-power either, or at least I doubted it was. Add into the mix the fact that I'd just been shot a few days ago, so the pain was all relative. All these things combined to mean precisely fuck all after the first half an hour.

I'd been hit by ten tennis balls by then, three minutes apart and travelling at about fifty miles per hour by my best guess, onto exactly the same spot. It hurt. It hurt like a bastard, and even when the hopper ran out, that didn't help as much as you'd think. The repeated impacts numbed my flesh for the first little while, but that only lasted so long and when the numbness faded, the pain crawled out to claim me.

They refilled the hopper the next day, and again the next. Then on the fourth day they brought in something truly evil: a clock. Someone had even marked a little red dot above the number two, so I could tell just how many hours I had until they started on this again. Torture is an odd thing. People often make the mistake of confusing torture with pain, and they're not always the same thing. I won't say that the tennis balls didn't hurt, but the pain was nothing compared to the slowly ticking clock, marking out the time until the door would open, the hopper would be refilled, and it all began all over again.

By the end of the week, I'd lost myself in the pain. Every impact radiated agony across my chest, and it seemed to reach out to the dull, throbbing, ache in my wounded leg. My chest was a bruised and inflamed mess. A red welt lay over blue and purple bruised flesh and the skin was split and bleeding. Each tennis ball struck now with a wet slap and I'd stopped screaming or even crying out.

My body was a prison that I was eager to flee.

The visitors filtered in slowly, watching me suffer.

Johnson walked in through a wall, giving me a wink and a cheery wave. Pearson was suddenly just there, appearing between moments as he curled up in a corner, staring at me over the top of his knees with a look of horror.

One by one they all appeared; Johnson, Turner, Pearson—all my failures.

Every death, my fault.

Johnson made his way over to me, inspecting the shackles and the torso restraint. He looked on with interest as another tennis ball slammed into my bloody chest with a wet thud.

"So, as fun as this looks, Roasties," he said. "Why are you doing this exactly?"

"It's not exactly by choice, you prick." I was breaking Rule Three, but at this point I really didn't care. To be honest, I wasn't even sure I was fully conscious.

Johnson shrugged and looked at Pearson for a moment. "Looks like a choice to me, mate. I can't see why you'd let tennis balls mash you to a pulp when you could just stop them."

"You know, nice as this is, I'm not sure a hallucination is what I need right now."

Johnson smiled at me with a sideways look and snorted a laugh. "Did you ever stop to consider that maybe I'm not a hallucination?"

"What, so you're a ghost or something?"

"Perhaps." Johnson shrugged. "Who knows?"

"Ghosts aren't real, Johnson. People don't talk to the dead."

"People don't stop bullets with magic or their bloody minds, either, Carver."

I sighed. "I didn't either, Johnson. I don't know how it happened."

Pearson shook his head violently at that, as Turner muttered something that didn't carry.

"You know, Roasties, for a supposedly intelligent man, you're remarkably stupid sometimes."

"What the hell is—" I broke off as another tennis ball hit and I grunted away the pain that flared. "What does that mean?"

"He still doesn't get it, does he?" Johnson said over one shoulder to Turner. "Look, mate. You're missing the point. It doesn't matter that you don't know how you did it. Just that you *did*."

"Even if that were true, what good does it do me?" My voice was a pained rasp, pushed out through a chest that felt like it was simultaneously on fire, and about to collapse in on itself.

"I'd have thought that were bloody obvious..." Johnson paused as the launcher rumbled into life again, preparing to launch another ball. The ball flew towards my chest and then stopped dead, hanging in the air two feet from my bruised and bleeding flesh.

"Sorry," Johnson told me with a shrug. "Those things were really getting on my tits."

"How...?" I gaped at the ball.

Johnson shrugged. "Haven't a clue, mate. But then, I'm supposed to be dead, right? Maybe I'm not even here. And if I'm a hallucination, then who do you think just stopped that ball?"

The tennis ball wobbled in the air as the visitors vanished, and then dropped to the ground, bouncing into a corner as if it were the most natural thing in the world.

CHAPTER TWENTY-THREE

Mackenzie touched the orange key-card to the reader and pulled the heavy door open. The guard nodded a greeting and watched her as she made her way along the corridor. What was his name again? Saj?

The transition still took her by surprise whenever she took the time to think about it. Over a period of weeks her escorts to visit the various doctors, undergo tests, and to and from Elias' sessions had dropped; first from three guards down to one, and then to her finally being given her own key-card and a schedule. But then her own development made this almost insignificant in comparison.

Her time bound to the wooden frame was already becoming a hazy memory, eclipsed by the growth in her power since. Elias had replaced the Cocktail of sedatives and hallucinogenic drugs with deep hypnosis to try and encourage the development of greater control. She could no longer deny the existence of her power, and she no longer wanted to. In many ways she was even willing to forgive Janan for her abduction. Leaving all of this behind now was almost inconceivable.

She turned the orange card over in her hands as she walked, finger-nails tapping at the plastic. It was limited, of course. It allowed her out of her room if she needed to leave for a session with Elias, or if it was close to meal times it would give her passage to the cafeteria, but other than that it was inert—useless. It was probably running on some kind of time-lock, keyed to her schedule.

She sniffed, scrubbing at her itching nose with the back of one hand as she rounded the corner. Her steps were still slow at times, and she tired easily, but her muscles and mobility were returning with remarkable speed.

The sessions with Elias were an odd mixture of therapy, hypnosis, and scientific testing. Sometimes they simply talked, conversations that could have been nothing more than a casual chat were it not for Elias' note-taking. At other times they experimented with fire, using the candle to try to hone her skills when in an alert state.

She pushed through another set of doors and knocked at Elias' office, pushing the door open at his summons. The lights were low, and a single bright lamp was focused on the black leather recliner—a hypnosis session then.

"Have a seat, Mackenzie," Elias' deep voice came from the shadows. "Make yourself comfortable, I'll just be a moment."

She hopped up onto the recliner, laying back and closing her eyes against the light as she fought down the surge of anxiety. Her nerves were the same every time. Loss of control of any kind was always something that had made her uncomfortable, and the fact that the black leather recliner reminded her of a dentist's chair probably didn't help matters.

"And how are we today?" Elias asked, reinforcing the image of a dental surgery as he stepped into the circle of light.

"Fine," she said in a soft voice. "A little tired."

Elias smiled down at her. "Well, this won't be too taxing today. Just do the same as normal, try and focus on the lights." He set the circle of lenses spinning slowly. Reds, blues and greens rotating through a cycle as they played over her face.

"Now, try and relax. Relax and listen to my voice," he began. His voice droned on, and as always, she found her attention drifting, lulled by the soft tones.

Mackenzie swallowed hard and wrinkled her nose at the harsh smell of smoke.

*

"That was better," Elias told her with a broad smile as she blinked at the lights.

She licked at dry lips, frowning at the sour taste in her mouth. "How long was I under?"

Elias shrugged as he went to a side table and poured her a glass of water from the pitcher. "Not as long as you might think. A little more than two hours."

She took the glass from him and sipped at it, letting the water soak into her dry tongue before she swallowed. "It feels longer."

Elias nodded with a smile. "It always seems to with you. Remember I told you how different people react to hypnosis in very different ways? You have a strong mind, Mackenzie, a strong sense of self. It takes some effort to take you into a trance but once there, you seem to sink deeper than many others. In any event, I'm pleased to say you're responding extremely well to the programme."

She fought down the urge to grin at his praise and pushed herself up from the recliner, swinging her legs over the side. She sipped at the drink again and looked at the remains of the candle. The wick was barely visible in the solidifying pool of red wax that all but filled the metal tray. "I did that?"

Elias nodded but his smile faded as a frown grew. "You still don't remember?"

Mackenzie shook her head as she stood and made her way across to the table. "No, I don't remember anything after I lay down. It feels like I've just been to sleep."

"Odd," Elias mused, jotting something down in his notes. "I would have expected that to pass. It's unusual but not unheard of. Most people have at least a hazy recollection of what happens once they are in the trance. We can look at this next session, there are a few things I'd like to try."

Mackenzie nodded, not really paying attention. Her inability to remember the sessions had never really concerned her.

"This was a big candle." She pressed a fingertip into the wax, toying with the texture of it. "It wouldn't have burnt down to this in just two hours."

Elias snorted as she looked over to him. "Look up."

The ceiling was high in the office, easily twelve feet above the floor, but still the tiles were scorched and blackened above the candle.

"I'll admit, I panicked for a minute," Elias laughed. "I even started to run to fetch the fire extinguisher, before I realised I could just ask you to control the fire."

"And I did?" Mackenzie asked. "That quickly?"

It didn't seem possible.

Elias nodded. "Would you like to see the video?"

She nodded, and Elias motioned her over to the desk and the laptop. The recording was crisp and zoomed in on her from where the security camera was positioned above the door. Elias skipped through the process of inducing the hypnotic state; the droning voice and slowly cycling lights, until the candle burst into flame.

She watched as Elias had her raise the height of the flame until it raged in a meter-high column, and then gasped as the flame somehow left the candle altogether, burning in blissful ignorance of this impossibility as it hung in the air, away from the wick. Elias had her increase the height of the flame again; she snorted a laugh at his panic as the fire licked at the ceiling and he dashed towards the fire extinguisher, before instructing her to control it.

She met his gaze as he closed the laptop.

"You're a very special person, Mackenzie," he told her. He ignored her as she shook her head, and spoke over her attempts to talk. "You have an amazing gift, more powerful than anything I've seen in this complex, yet you seem determined not to embrace it."

"I'm not," Mackenzie protested. "I just…"

"You still cannot move past your abduction," Elias finished for her. "I've explained this to you, haven't I? How it was necessary?"

"Yes, but…"

Elias shook his head. "But nothing. The first stage of releasing your power, of releasing any power, is to confront it. This can only be done in a situation of great stress, when the body is weak enough that the mind is free to move beyond the normal constraints."

"I know," Mackenzie said in a low voice. "And I have tried. I'm still trying. Most of the time it doesn't even bother me anymore. I think it's just one thing to know it, to have it explained to you, but it's something quite different to live through it."

Elias nodded. "It's no easy thing to go through, I know that. It was never supposed to be."

His calm response suddenly irritated her.

"How do you know?" she burst out. "From videos? From books?"

He seemed content to let her rage at him, looking on with infuriating calm and a slight smile that just served to irritate her even more, as if he were humouring her.

"Tell me, Elias? Just how the fuck would you know?"

"Are you finished?" he asked, slipping in the question as she paused to suck in a ragged breath. "I know because I designed the process. And more than that, I know because I tested it. I went through it myself."

"You…" she fell silent. There were no words for this.

"Of course I did," he told her in his gentle voice. "I would never subject someone to a programme I hadn't experienced myself."

Her eyes narrowed for a moment. "But you knew it wasn't real."

"How wasn't it real? I was bound and naked the same as you. I was starved of distraction, of interaction, the same as you."

"Because you knew you could get out," Mackenzie muttered.

Elias nodded, scratching at his short beard for a moment. "That's true, I suppose. The staff all had instructions not to let me out, even if I begged, but I suspect you're probably right. It's human nature," he shrugged. "We respect the authority figure even when we're told not to."

"You could have got out," Mackenzie said in a flat voice. "Whenever it became too much, whenever you'd had enough, you could have been free as soon as you said the word. And now you're laying the blame at my feet because, *apparently*, despite how much I've forgiven everything you had done to me, deep down I can't fully trust you?"

"A level of trust is required for this to work," Elias told her, breaking his silence.

"Why are you doing all of this?" she asked then, as if the question had never occurred to her before.

He frowned for a moment with a bemused smile, before he burst into laughter.

"Why? You might as well ask why someone would search for the secret of flight, or eternal youth! I could say something noble, like it's for the advancement of human knowledge, for the betterment of mankind. The truth is that I just want to know. I've always been fascinated with magic—both the act of sleight of hand and also the myths and legends of wizards and sorcery. Western science is so dismissive of anything it cannot immediately categorise and label. Acupuncture, meditation, even the peculiar effects of aromatherapy or crystals. We dismiss most of it as superstition and nonsense. Even hypnosis is side-lined and often dismissed. But abilities like yours? Most scientists would reject even the possibility of it."

Mackenzie fell silent for a minute, digesting that. It did nothing to excuse the things she'd been put through, but at least her suffering had some sort of meaning to it now. Did that make it any better? She couldn't decide just yet.

She looked at the doctor. "What about Janan?"

Elias shifted in his seat, looking uncomfortable for a second as he sat back. "What about him?"

"What's his goal? You say that you're studying for your own curiosity but also for the betterment of man?" She paused long enough for Elias to nod. "Presumably, you'd like to publish your findings at some stage, if you could get results strong enough to overshadow the backlash? But what does Janan get from all this?"

"Janan wants the key, Mackenzie." Elias spoke softly, suddenly too still in his seat, almost as if confessing. "He wants to find the root of these abilities and replicate it. He wants the power for himself."

She nodded. "Not so very different from your goal on the surface. I suppose the real question is whether he would share the knowledge if he had control over it."

"I think you probably know the answer to that," Elias grunted. "It's irrelevant anyway. We have an arrangement, and Afridi isn't directly involved in the research."

"So, what happens to me, in the end? What happens to me?"

He looked confused by that, as if the question had never occurred to him, and she interrupted as he stammered his way to a response. "You can't think that I'm just going to be free to leave here once you have your results? I was brought here against my will. I've been abused and half-starved."

She held up a hand to stop him. "Yes, I know your reasons, but it doesn't stop the fact that it happened. I saw Armond murdered in front of me. I know you don't believe that happened, that it was just a hallucination brought on by the Cocktail, but I *know* it was real, Elias. I can't explain how, but I know it was. You were willing to push some ethical boundaries aside to get your results, but Janan pushed them much further than you would have done, and he's still pushing. So, I'll ask you again; where does it end? What happens to me?"

CHAPTER TWENTY-FOUR

Mackenzie pushed through the double doors and out of the cafeteria. Meal times were always a struggle for her. She could have eaten in her room but that meant isolating herself, and she'd spent enough time alone in this place. She usually managed to force herself to eat in the canteen at least once a day, but it wasn't a pleasant experience. She felt the eyes of the technicians and scientists on her as she ate. In a way, she supposed she couldn't blame them. It must be a bit like having a lab rat walk in and order lunch with the research staff.

She made her way along the corridor, fingering the key-card as she made vague plans to use the small gym in her rooms. Elias' words circled in her mind, like vultures waiting for their prey to falter and fall beneath the hot sun.

It was his silence that had been the most telling. His inability to answer her question—what would happen to her? That silence was violent. A brutal intruder into a mind that had shifted from abductee and prisoner, to willing collaborator. That simple fact, that Elias had been unable to tell her how far Janan might go, tore through her desire to learn more about this power and in the space of twelve short hours she had come face-to-face with what she had become.

She froze as she turned the corner.

The card was at the very edge of the carpet, close to a cylindrical metal bin that might have hidden it from anyone who wasn't walking along with their eyes downcast. She glanced around quickly, despite knowing already that the hallway was empty. There were no security cameras in this hallway; there was no need for them. The doors at either end of the hall were controlled by maglocks that would only release for enabled key-cards.

She stooped quickly and snatched up the card. Unlike her orange key-card, this was solid black with a retractable line that ran into a belt-clip. The clasp on the back of the clip had snapped, and she wrapped her hand around the card to conceal it against her leg.

The journey back to her room was a panicked scurry that would have stood out on any cameras that were being monitored. Despite the fact she passed nobody, and held the card palmed between her hand and leg, she rushed; convinced that she would be stopped and searched at any moment.

The door closed behind her and she pressed her back to it, breathing hard.

"Shit!" She looked down at the card. It was plain black with no other markings on it. There was no telling who it might belong to or what kind of access it might give her, but it would be more than she had right now.

Her heart pounded as she turned the card over in her hands. Was she actually considering doing this? Staying meant she might learn more about her fledgling powers, and leaving risked losing all of that. She deliberately didn't think about what might happen if she was caught.

"Come on, Mackenzie, you dozy bitch," she muttered. "You bloody well know what will happen if you stay here. It's just a matter of when."

She swore under her breath again and touched the orange card to the reader. It was now or never. If she let herself think this over any more than this, she'd never do it at all.

The door clicked open, maglocks releasing at the touch of the card on the reader. She was still within the lunch schedule. Leaving her rooms again would probably register on a log somewhere, but it wouldn't look as strange as if she used the black key-card, rather than her own, to open her door. She paused on the threshold, swore again, and made her way along the corridor, turning left and taking the route she would normally use to go to see Elias.

The lifts ran for six levels. Elias' office was two floors above where she was now, but the lift also had a camera mounted near the ceiling. She noticed it every time she stepped in there, its little red light glaring at her. The camera made the lift nothing more than the fastest way to be captured. Instead, her hopes were pinned on the door standing beside it.

She paused at the door, holding the black card in her fist.

This was it.

This was the moment.

As soon as she touched the card to the reader a line would be crossed. From this point it would be a matter of escaping entirely, or facing the consequences of failure. The image of Armond's screaming death as the flames consumed him filled her mind for a moment, and she shuddered at the memory.

Janan had been utterly unconcerned at the pain he had inflicted. Armond had been a means to an end, nothing more. How could she ever have imagined that he thought of her any differently? And yet she had. In the weeks since she'd been released from her cell she'd participated willingly, even eagerly. She'd lapped up every scrap of approval and praise from both Elias and Janan like she was some kind of scolded puppy. It went far beyond her own curiosity about her powers and the project. She'd come to accept the goals of this place as her own, she'd even begun to accept that not only was her abduction justified, but that her time chained to the frame in the cell had been necessary.

There was a name for people like her.

The French would have called her a *collaborateur* and that was probably the truth of it. She could claim she was suffering a level of Stockholm Syndrome to herself if she liked, but the problem with lying to yourself is that somewhere, deep down, you always know the lie for what it is. And now, faced with the truth of things, the disgust and self-loathing were so thick it was all she could do to keep herself moving.

The reader beeped as she touched the card to it and, as she pushed the door open a crack, she realised she'd been holding her breath.

What had she been expecting? Sirens?

She pushed the door open slowly, braced for a challenge or a room full of people, but it held only the stone stairs she'd hoped for. The cooler air felt slightly damp, and she shivered through the thin, blue, jumpsuit she wore, hugging herself against the chill.

Her progress up the first two flights was slow, an agony of fear and anticipation as she expected to find guards around every turn of the stairwell. She stopped at the top of the second flight, massaging the tension in her neck and shoulders.

This was ridiculous. She was just as likely to get caught creeping along as she was sprinting, and she may as well cover more ground.

"You've rolled the dice, girl. Go with it."

The jumpsuit had come with soft tennis shoes that barely made a noise as she raced up the stairs. She ran like a frightened mouse, scurrying upwards and then freezing, hunching low as she listened for any sound.

The camera was positioned above the door at the top of the stairwell. Mackenzie crouched down behind the railings at the bottom of the final flight, swearing under her breath. The stairwell was locked out to her orange key-card, which meant only those with the correct authorisation could get in here. This was both blessing and curse. Blessing because it meant that the camera was unlikely to be closely monitored, and curse because she would stick out like a sore thumb on the footage.

The sensible thing would be to walk slowly and calmly towards the door. The eye is drawn to movement, she knew, and a mad dash for the door would only increase the chances that a bored guard sitting in front of a bank of monitors somewhere would spot her. Of course, it also meant she'd be on the screen for less time.

"Fuck it," she muttered.

She was done being a mouse. She was stronger than this. She threw herself around the corner and sprinted up towards the door. The beep from the card reader seemed impossibly loud as the lock clicked and she eased the door open.

The woman wore a white lab coat. She turned at the sound of the door and froze, staring wide-eyed at Mackenzie. The two of them stood, rigid with indecision in some kind of ridiculous Mexican stand-off, until the woman jerked her head to the side, gesturing towards a line of metal cabinets that stood against the wall in the narrow hallway that opened out into the room.

She glanced over her shoulder and said something that Mackenzie didn't catch. It wasn't a language she recognised, but the tone seemed casual enough. Her hands clasped a clipboard in front of her and she jabbed her finger again, pointing to her left.

Shaking herself, Mackenzie finally moved, pressing herself down against the wall beside the row of metal cabinets. Her view was blocked as she pulled her legs in tight, hugging her knees, but she could still see the woman's legs.

Christ, what am I doing?

She had no reason to trust this woman. The guards could be coming for her right now; but then why would she tell her to hide? She bit down on her lip, hating the feeling of helplessness. The woman was clearly speaking with a man on the other side of the room. Her tone was light, and she laughed at something the unseen man said.

Footsteps receded across the room and a door closed a moment later. The woman turned and rushed to her, urging her up and ushering her across the room, speaking urgently. It was Pashto, Mackenzie realised, though not a dialect she recognised. Her meaning was clear enough despite this, and Mackenzie rushed through the lab, past white and clinical counters and desks filled with computers, microscopes and scientific equipment, to another door.

"Where does this go?" she asked.

The woman grimaced. "Up. My English, not well. Go! Go!"

Mackenzie reached for the woman's hands, clasping them tight as she smiled and whispered a thank you.

The woman touched her key-card to the door and pulled it open, pushing at her to move. The message was clear enough and Mackenzie went. Whatever the woman's motives for helping her, she was putting herself at risk. Somehow, Mackenzie doubted she knew just how much of a risk she'd taken.

The door led through to a poorly lit hallway. A faulty fluorescent strip-light flickered behind the plastic panel in the ceiling, lending an odd feel to the place. Wherever the woman had sent her, it didn't seem to be in as regular use as the rest of the complex.

The doors here had no maglocks. A quick peek behind the first three showed them to be storerooms. The corridor turned twice, and her steps slowed as the realisation struck.

She had no real idea how big this place was. Other than the vague goal of heading up through the levels, she had no idea of where to go. Would she even know when she hit the ground floor? If the complex above-ground was big enough to have interior corridors and rooms with no windows, then how would she know she'd reached the ground floor?

She stopped, resting her hands against the wall as the panic rose and threatened to overwhelm her completely.

"Just keep moving," she whispered.

The corridor ended at a lift, and another door with a key-card reader. As always, the doors had no windows and no indication of what might lie beyond. She leaned in, pressing her ear to it and listening for any moment.

A siren blared and she bit down on a shriek.

The siren was a piercing, cycling wail that could mean only a handful of things, and somehow, she doubted it was a fire alarm. They knew. They were looking for her now. The clock was ticking, time was against her, and she still had no idea of where to go, or how she might cope if she did manage to get outside.

She pushed through the door and found another stairwell, plain concrete steps starkly lit with more fluorescent strips set into the ceiling. Mackenzie ran until she heard the voices—loud and laughing, heading up towards her.

She froze for a moment before cursing herself for the stupidity of the action, and began to run. Her tennis shoes were light, but they weren't silent, and she moved as quickly as she dared. The door opened in front of her just as she was rounding the turn in the stairwell, and the guard that appeared seemed as shocked as she was. He froze for a moment before reaching for the gun as his hip.

Mackenzie backed away as he barked orders at her. The words made no sense to her. Panic overrode any chance she might have had at translating and understanding. She was a primal creature now, a wild animal hemmed in and cornered.

"Don't do this," she begged, holding a hand out to the guard as he came closer. "Please, just let me go."

She watched as his other hand reached around for a pair of handcuffs. Panic gave way to anger. She'd come so far, risked so much. To be stopped now, this close to escape, seemed almost cruel. Her anger mounted as he reached for her, and gave way to blind fury.

Her first blows were feeble scratching things. He swatted her hands away, grabbing her arms and pushing her down against the wall. Her fury raged and she smiled as the first few sparks danced from her fingertips.

The guard fell back as the flames touched him, crying out as he clasped his hand to his chest. His skin there was scorched, already turning to an angry red. He raised the gun again as he backed up the steps. Mackenzie barely noticed it, it was his eyes that held her gaze. He looked at her with a mixture of fear and disgust, horror twisting his features as the gun shook in his hands.

The fire surged within her as the gun went off, the sound loud enough to strike like a physical blow, and she flinched away from the stone chips exploding from the wall beside her. Flames flew from her hands, washing over the guard's body as he screamed, and the gun clattered down the steps, the weapon lost in his pain. Mackenzie watched on, and the tears coursed down her cheeks at what she was doing, at what she would continue to do, at what she had become.

She could feel the flames roaring within her, begging to be released. They wanted to burn, to destroy, and she would let them. Janan would have what he'd wanted now. He had created a monster, and unleashed, she would turn this world to ash.

"Do not move!" The order made her jump and she turned despite herself.

She barely had time to register the two guards before the needles hit, twin probes with wires trailing after them. She didn't scream—there was no time to draw breath before the pain hit. Instead, a low, hissing, moan escaped from between her clenched teeth as the taser clicked over and over. Her back arched as the electricity coursed through her.

And then she was down, her body a mass of spasms as her muscles convulsed.

She didn't pass out. On some level she had expected to. Instead she lay there, her body still wracked with pain, surging through muscles that were no longer her own.

The guards approached warily, the taser held ready as they argued over who should bind her. This was what she was now; an escaped animal to be feared and hunted.

She lay on the cold stone, unable to fight as they bound her and left her face-down on the concrete. She stopped listening to the voices, lost in her misery until she felt fresh hands on her. Medical gloves touched her skin, followed by the prick of a needle, and then they retreated, waiting until the drugs took her hand and led her into the darkness.

CHAPTER TWENTY-FIVE

Mackenzie licked at her lips in the darkness. Her tongue felt dry and hard, as if caked by something, and a dull ache throbbed behind her eyes. Overlaying it all was a vague fuzziness, as if she was experiencing everything through a fog.

She'd been drugged again. The thought was slow to come, and even when it hit it took long moments for her to process it.

She hung in the darkness, the familiar cuffs taking the weight of her arms as she dropped back into a half-doze, waiting for the drug-induced haze to clear.

Water.

She craned her neck, reaching for the tube but there was nothing. They wouldn't chain her up with no water, would they? Panic found her and she thrashed back and forth, casting about with her face as she felt for the tube.

The plastic tube spattered droplets over her face as she made contact, and she flinched back before searching for it again, and then drinking hungrily. Water helped, as she knew it would, and she felt the effects of the drugs clearing as she lay back against the inclined wooden frame.

"Hello?" she called out. The darkness took her words and swallowed them, leaving only silence.

"I know you can hear me," she shouted. "Answer me!"

There was no response. She was back in the cell again. Alone in the darkness with only her thoughts and her fear for company.

She hadn't expected this. The attempt at escape had been an act of desperation. She hadn't given any real thought to what might happen if she failed, but she hadn't expected to live through it.

Her worry grew. Would dying have been better?

The thought evolved slowly, an insidious whisper that spoke from the darkest corner of her mind. What if she had never actually left the room? What if everything she thought she'd experienced outside the cell was only a series of delusions from the drugs? What if she was simply losing her mind?

No, she shook her head. It had been real, too real to be a figment of her drug-addled imagination. The memory of the last moments of her escape danced in her head, of the fire surging up within her, and the ease with which she had become the monster.

She was a nurse. She'd spent years at university and in hospitals learning how to heal. Even once she'd qualified, she'd worked in warzones and relief camps trying to help the injured and sick. Taking a life should have been an alien concept to her, but she'd done it. She had killed without giving it much of a thought.

Bile rose in her throat. Not only had she done it, she had enjoyed it. Not just the surge of fire, but the power she'd held over that man. The ease with which she'd forced him back. The fear on his face. *That* was the true monster within her. Not the woman who controlled fire, but the creature who enjoyed inflicting it on those around her.

She shuddered and pushed the thought away, but the memory of the fire refused to go. She had called it. Always before, during all of the experiments, she'd either controlled a lit flame, or ignited something simple like a candle.

The fire during her escape had been nothing like that. Instead, she'd produced flame in its purest form—a fire without source or fuel. As if responding to her thoughts she felt the flame stir within her, straining against her efforts to control it, like a rabid dog pulling on its chain.

There was something on her arm. She could feel a dull ache and a pressure, but in the darkness, it was impossible to tell what it was. The ache felt somehow sharp as well. An IV line she decided, probably held in place with some kind of brace.

Her stomach growled, making her jump in the silence and she snorted a laugh at herself as she reached for the feeding tube with her mouth. It was harder than finding the water tube and she cast about in the darkness for long minutes until she realised the truth—it wasn't that she couldn't find it, it wasn't there.

Somehow the feeding tube was the catalyst, and she snapped. She'd come so far. She'd risked everything in the escape attempt, and now she was bound to this ridiculous frame, naked in the darkness, like something out of a bad erotica novel.

"Let me go!" she shouted, tears spilling down her cheeks. "Just let me out of here…"

The sprinklers sprang to life and she broke off into a shriek as they rotated around her. Last time she'd been bound to the frame, the lights had snapped on at this point, now she simply dripped and shivered in the darkness.

The room was warm enough for her to drip-dry and she fell into her old habit of dozing as much as possible. Always before she'd had the lights going on and off to help her mark out the days. Now, she would only have the spray of icy water from the sprinklers. Her stomach growled at her and a throbbing headache grew as the hours passed.

By the third day, her stomach had stopped growling. She no longer even felt especially hungry. The room felt colder, and the icy water that blasted over her each morning was enough to leave her teeth chattering for over an hour. Her body had given up, she knew. It had entered a starvation mode, and would be busily eating any surplus fat she had left before it moved on to protein and her muscle mass.

She was going to die.

The thought was a small one that took hold in a quiet corner of her mind and put down roots. It wasn't fear exactly, or even a worry; instead the thought was a certain knowledge—that it was not a matter of if, but when, her body would begin to fail, and she would die.

How far would they take it? That was the real question. Was this all some form of punishment that would end once they decided she'd learnt her lesson? Or would they keep her locked up until she starved to death? It wasn't as if Janan had any compunction about letting people die. Armond had taught her that.

The memory of Armond's death brought the fire back to her mind. She had controlled it. It had taken a raging fury for her to do it, but she had; the fire had come when she called, followed her whim. Could she do it again now?

She strained, trying to reach within herself to where she had felt the flames stir. She felt nothing. Had she really done it? The hunger was beginning to make her doubt herself. How long had she really been here? She shook her head in the darkness.

"No," she muttered. "No, the fire was real. It was all real."

The wound in her mind couldn't be denied. The jagged edges of it pressed on her like a migraine with teeth; fangs clamped down onto the edges of the tear in her consciousness and digging deep enough that she'd never get free without ripping herself apart.

She bit down on the inside of her lip, hard enough to hurt. Somewhere there was a camera watching her, recording everything. She would be damned if she was going to put on a display for them.

She froze as she felt the shift within her. It was a small thing, almost feather-light, but she had felt it. The fire moved sluggishly, like a great beast shifting in its sleep, but it had moved.

It was still within her.

Anger, she realised. Anger was the key—it always had been.

Think about Janan, she told herself with a grim smile.

She forced the image back into her mind—Janan smiling as Armond burned to death. His stupid, childish laugh as the poor man screamed. The fire in her stirred, shifted, and surged, straining at her to let it free, to burn and to rage.

Control, that was the key. If she was to be more than the monster Janan had created then she would need control.

193

She let the fire slip through her body, sending it along her arm until it reached her fingertips. Her hunger was gone now, the aches and pains of her body were nothing compared to the feeling this power brought her. More powerful than any ecstasy, the fire was better than sex. It was her drug and she knew then that the final battle would be against the flame before it consumed her.

But right now, none of that mattered. She needed the flame. She needed its strength, its heat, and its chaos. She would deal with the consequences later, if she lived through what was coming.

The spark was minute, but in the pitch black of the room, it flared like a tiny sun. It drifted from her fingertip until it hung in the air before her, and she wondered at it as she let the fire grow. She nurtured it, coaxing it until it was the size of a candle's flame, burning without wax or wick as it hovered in the air. Her anger faded, forgotten in the presence of this strange magic. The fire flickered, guttering and failing. Mackenzie forced the image of Janan back into her mind and the flame flared anew.

Her eyes swept over the room, lit by the glow of the hanging flame. It was only slightly different to the first cell she'd been held in. The sprinklers were set in a different configuration. The water tube was set slightly differently. The food tube was tied back, out of her reach and empty besides.

She sent the flame in a small circuit of the room, using the view of her prison to fuel her anger. The small room was as bare as the first prison she'd been kept in. The same black glass wall reflected the light of the fire back at her, and as she ran her eyes over it, the same tiny red light as the video camera behind it winked into life.

The tiny red light stoked her rage, goading her like a bull under the stick. They had thrown her into the darkness, chaining her like some kind of animal, and someone on the other side of the glass had watched her—yawning though her screams and panic until she did something worthy of hitting the button to record it.

"Bastards!" She fed her fury to the flame and forced it against the smoked glass. The laughter bubbled out of her as she pictured the technician panicking as the camera recorded nothing but flame.

Her laughter became a shriek as the sprinklers spurted into life around her, icy water hosing over her in an effort to break her hold on the power. The flame guttered and shrank down to a pinprick.

"I don't think so, you fuckers," she snarled, spitting water and shaking droplets from her face. Where before she had been consumed with fury, now a cold determination filled her and she stared at the tiny ball of fire, eyes narrowing as she bore down. The flame did not increase in size, instead the colour shifted from the comforting yellow-orange of an open fire, through a pale blue, to a blazing white.

The smoked glass had never been designed to withstand anything like this, and it distorted and sagged as glowing orange rivulets ran down the panel. Panicked shouts reached her as the flame burned through and the hole grew.

Mackenzie could no longer see the red light of the camera, and it no longer mattered. She was beyond thinking, beyond rage. She had become vengeance, and vengeance knows no mercy. She released the fire, relaxing all curbs and restraint, and with a muffled *whump* the fireball exploded, engulfing the small observation room in flames.

Mackenzie listened to the howling screams and smiled until the smile turned to a shrill and brittle laughter, that fractured into tears.

CHAPTER TWENTY-SIX

I was an experiment. I was a specimen in a fucking petri dish.

It took a few hours for this thought to really take hold. The flood of men and women in white coats began about two minutes after Johnson stopped the tennis ball in mid-air. I suppose they must have had some kind of CCTV hooked up. I lay there, glaring at them all as technicians and nurses drew blood, hooked up more electrodes and scanners, and fiddled with the rubber cap on my head.

I collapsed back against the frame, too tired and hurt to protest as they clamoured around me. I was their prize lab rat, but I hadn't just made it through the maze to my reward; I'd nibbled through the bloody walls, set up a little camp, and built a fire to roast the cheese. Technicians clustered around me like ants surrounding a dropped ice-cream. They spoke in Pashto, but not a dialect I knew enough of, and they were all talking too quickly for me to have a hope of following it anyway.

I suppose most lab experiments didn't talk much, and any attempts I made to ask questions were studiously ignored. Eventually I gave up and just let them get on with it. At least the damned tennis balls had stopped for the time being.

They left as quickly as they'd arrived, a line of white coats trickling out through the door until I was left alone in the silence. Pain rushed in to fill the void, as if it had been waiting for them to leave. My chest throbbed in time with my pulse. Already the red was deepening to a blueish purple, the pain enough to rival the dull ache in my leg.

The silence was a blessing at first. I drank from the tube and sucked down some of the grainy goop as I tried to relax and take stock.

Johnson had stopped the ball.

I might have passed the whole thing off as a hallucination if it weren't for the crowd of lab-techs that had rushed in. I suppose they could have been a hallucination as well, but I've never had that before. My madness is confined to the members of my squad that visit. The men I failed. The men I let die before I saved myself, however I did it.

I don't know when Pearson arrived. He's rarely spoken to me and this time was no different. I turned my head and he was there—the same horrified, terror-struck expression etched into his features, as he looked up at me over the balled fists he pressed to his face.

I jerked back in the restraints and spat out the mouthful of grainy goop as I jumped. "Fuck me, Pearson! Can't you make some kind of noise or something? You scared the shit out of me."

"Leave him alone, Carver, you grumpy bastard," Turner grinned as he came around from behind me. "Poor sod's scared enough already, I reckon."

I shook my head as I tried to work out what he'd said. I'd never done well with Turner's accent. Some Scots have a soft accent that isn't much more than a slight burr. Turner was Glaswegian to the core and there have been times when I've wondered if he's even speaking the same language as me.

"Fuck that," I muttered as I worked it out. "He's dead, I'm the one tied up in here with you lot wandering around at will."

Turner shrugged, coming closer to look over the frame.

"You're pretty well screwed I'd say, yeah." He crouched slightly to look at the steel band over my torso. A rivulet of fresh blood ran down over his face, tracing a path from the hole in his forehead to where it dripped from his chin. The blood splashed down onto the floor, and then the frame, as he moved over to examine the manacles on my wrists.

The blood wasn't real. Hell, neither of them were real; but the prospect of Turner's blood dripping onto my skin bothered me more than I could explain.

"God, Turner. Can't you piss off? You're bleeding everywhere."

"Oh, I am sorry," Turner told me, dripping sarcasm. "Maybe it's from the hole in my head. I wouldnae want to get your pretty skin all messed up, now would I?"

I didn't have the patience for this. I'd pissed all over Rule Three pretty thoroughly by now and I'd just had enough.

"Bugger off, Turner. Get the hell out of here, and take that bastard with you too!" I growled, jerking my head at Pearson.

They vanished almost before I finished speaking and I let my head drop back against the frame. I was losing my mind. PTSD is one thing, but this was taking things to the next level. I was slowly going insane, and there was nobody to notice who would care. God only knows what the people on the other side of the smoked glass were thinking. The speed with which they'd rushed in after Johnson stopped the tennis ball made it pretty clear there was always somebody watching.

The door hissed open as I lay there. I've never really been one for wallowing in my own misery, but now seemed like a good time to try it.

"Mr Carver, that was quite the display."

I didn't look up. I was pretty sure I recognised the voice, but there was nobody there I wanted to talk to. I closed my eyes as footsteps brought the speaker closer.

"Tell me, when you stop the ball like that, do you feel it?"

That was enough to make me open my eyes, and I gave Afridi an incredulous look. I'd just been ranting away at Turner and Pearson, which must have looked like I was screaming at thin air, and he didn't seem to have noticed.

"Carver," Afridi repeated. "Do you feel it?"

I shook my head. "No. It's not like that."

"What is it like then? Walk me through the process."

I sighed, giving Afridi a weary look. "It isn't like that because I'm not the one doing it."

It was Afridi's turn to give an incredulous look, but he opted for one of mild disgust instead. "Do not mock me, Carver. Tell me how you stopped the ball."

"Would you believe that I just asked the voices in my head?"

Afridi's eyes went flat as his lips tightened.

"I did not come here to be toyed with, Carver." He spun in place and strode to the launcher. "Perhaps some more practice will make you more inclined to explain the process."

The machine rumbled to life as he adjusted the settings and my heart thumped in my chest, as if it were trying to make a matching bruise on the inside.

Oh shit.

"The balls *were* travelling at thirty miles per hour. They will now travel at fifty. Do try and stay aware of what you are doing, Carver. This can stop just as soon as you tell me how you are doing it."

I should have called out. I should have said something; begged or pleaded with him. Instead I lay against the frame like an idiot, and watched him as he left.

The first ball launched before I really knew it was coming. The impact left me gasping as it slammed into the swollen and bloody welt on my chest. I blinked back the tears as my eyes watered at the pain, looked at the clock still hanging from the wall, and swore.

"Johnson?" I called. I don't know that I was really expecting an answer. I'd never called any of the visitors before and even as I did it, I didn't expect it to be this simple. The result was about what I'd expected—nothing.

I tried again, calling out inside my head. If the visitors were aspects of my own fractured mind, this was probably a good place to start.

Johnson! I need your help.

There was no response. But then I hadn't really expected one. I closed my eyes, concentrating on calling out to the man I'd watched bleed to death. The darkness seemed to help, and I almost felt like I was getting somewhere until the machine rumbled into life again and the next tennis ball slammed into me.

I'm not sure if I passed out. If I didn't, I certainly got close. My vision narrowed until it was just a hazy image at the end of a dark tunnel that seemed to get smaller and smaller. And then I was blinking at the light, looking around and trying to make sense of what I saw.

Everything seemed at once too crisp, sharp, and bright. I stared at the launcher, feeling time pass as I called out to the visitors.

Johnson? Turner? Fuck it, answer me!

The answer was more an emotion than anything I could call a verbal response. It wasn't anger, or even animosity, but it was pretty clear Johnson was telling me to piss off.

The rumble of the machine brought me back to myself and my vision snapped into focus as I glared at the hateful thing. My anger uncurled from a quiet place inside me, and all rational thought left me as I raged at the contraption.

My thoughts were already dark, and my anger snatched at them, gathering up all of the resentment and physical pain, using them all as fuel for its own fire. I screamed out as the ball launched, throwing my hatred and anger against it as I willed it to stop.

The ball stopped dead, but only for the merest second before it flew backwards, slamming into the glass wall and splitting into pieces. I didn't give myself time to wonder at that, but instead turned my gaze back to the launcher, letting my anger rule me as I lashed out again.

I could feel the impacts as the thing toppled over, and then I was smashing at it, tearing it as my rage ran free, unfettered as it gloried in an orgy of violence. Somewhere a small part of me was horrified at the spectacle as my anger became a force unchecked, a law unto itself; but the rest of me revelled in this, and my grim smile grew until a maniacal laugh escaped my lips.

I sank back against the frame, sagging down against the wrist restraints, and just hung there like a puppet on its strings. I wasn't breathing hard, though my pulse was racing—I was just done in.

The technicians rushed in, fussing over the electrodes on my head and taking photos of the wrecked launcher before they swept up the pieces.

I was only dimly aware of them. The exhaustion I felt was almost overwhelming. There is a march during selection for Special Forces called the Fan Dance. Don't get excited, there's nothing sexy about it. It's named after the mountain on the course, *Pen Y Fan*. It's a fifteen-mile *TAB*, or *Tactical Advance to Battle*, which is a load bearing march, over rough terrain, in the Brecon Beacons mountains in Wales. The rough translation of all that is that it's a bloody miserable hike, carrying sixty-five pounds of kit, which has to be finished in under four hours. It sounds bad but, despite the fact that it's actually worse than it sounds, it's far more about mental strength than physical fitness. The course is designed to knacker anyone out, no matter how fit they are. The test is whether you have the mental strength to ignore your body's bitching and whining, and just push through to get the damned thing finished in time. You need to concentrate on your pace. Too fast and you'll burn out. Too slow and you won't have the strength to finish. It's easy to let things slip, like drinking often enough. A few people have died over the years. Most people cross the finish and just drop. There are worse exercises, but it's the Fan Dance that stays with me.

Until I destroyed the ball launcher, that *TAB* was the most wiped out I've ever felt. The fatigue that hit me made that hike feel like a gentle stroll. I ignored the techs as they poked at me. Part of it was exhaustion; but something far more powerful was calling, drawing all the attention I had left to me. I could feel the power, curled up in my mind like a poked bear slowly going back to sleep. I was done. Fatigue reached out and took me. I couldn't care less what they did to me right now. I slept.

CHAPTER TWENTY-SEVEN

Mackenzie's head jerked back as she lurched awake, rattling the metal in her restraints, and blinking her eyes open to the blackness of the cell. Her neck felt strange. The thought fought its way through the fog inside her head until she really took note of it. She twisted, tilting and turning her head as she felt at the thing encircling her throat.

How had they even got this thing onto her? Somehow, they'd drugged her again, she realised.

She reached for the feeding tube without thinking and took a mouthful of the grainy, hummus-like substance before the fact of its existence registered with her.

When had they connected that back up?

She sipped at the water and stiffened. Of course, she realised; they'd simply drugged the water. It wasn't as if she had any choice but to drink it. They could drug her any time they liked. It would be easier to simply inject her, but maybe they didn't want to risk getting too close. At least, not now she had harnessed her power.

As if they were somehow connected to the food tube, the lights flickered into life and Mackenzie blinked at the brightness as she squinted around at the room. Nothing else had changed other than the feeding tube, so far as she could see. She looked herself over as best she could. The IV board had gone from her arm, along with the needle in the back of her hand. The wrist restraints had been removed as well, the leather cuff replaced with steel bands. An ugly bruise spread from the back of her hand, mute testament to the sloppy work of the technicians.

She curled her lip at the state they'd left her in. Any nurse worth the title would never have made a mess like that, though she'd known a few doctors that she wouldn't dream of letting near an IV kit.

The food was helping already, though she only dared to take small amounts. She sipped at the water again and looked across the room at the glass wall. They'd replaced the panel she'd melted, if she'd ever melted it at all. The worry that this was all some kind of delusion or hallucination was still with her. It clung to her, ever present.

For a moment, the fear gripped her fiercely and she searched the featureless wall in panic until her eyes caught on a tiny reflection at its base. A tiny globule of glass that must have run down the panel, only to cool and set hard on the cold floor.

Mackenzie drew in a deep breath and let out a heartfelt sigh. In a way she could cope with the pain, the endless aching of her back and shoulders as her muscles protested at being bound to the frame. She could even cope with the cycle of food deprivation, and Janan's strange attempt at befriending her, and winning her cooperation. It was the fear of her sanity ultimately breaking, and her descent into madness, that haunted her.

Her sanity was all she had left to her. They had taken her body away from her. If they took her sanity as well, then they would have finally won. She would be broken.

She ate as much as she could stomach and then dozed, taking the opportunity to recuperate where she could, until the door woke her. She let her head loll back to one side, keeping her eyes as slits as she watched it slide open.

"There is no point in pretending, Mackenzie. I know you are awake," Janan said with a faint curve to his lips as he made his way over to the frame.

Mackenzie shrugged, barely hearing him as her gaze followed the second figure. Elias walked close to Janan, almost hiding behind him, as he avoided Mackenzie's gaze.

"You can't hide, you bastard!" she shouted out at him.

"Now, Mackenzie, that's not fair," the big man began.

"Fair?" she cut him off. "How fair does this fucking look? Look at me, get a good look, everyone else has."

"This is all very interesting, but we do have some more important things to discuss," Janan said, cutting her off in mid-flow. "By now, I am sure you have noticed the collar around your throat," he said, waving a small, black, plastic device at her. "After your assault on the window and observation suite, we have been forced to take steps. The collar will prevent any more unfortunate incidents."

"It's a shock collar, Mackenzie," Elias explained, responding to her confused look.

Janan shook his head with a pained expression. "I do wish this wasn't necessary. I had hoped you'd moved beyond all of this. For a time, it looked like you were ready to cooperate, and even participate in this programme; but you're not the person I thought you were. You've gained some control over your power, but you've become violent, even dangerous…" he fell silent, looking at her as horror mingled with the sorrow on his features.

A shock collar. They'd tied her up like a violent bloody dog. Maybe they were right. Maybe she was dangerous. She turned her face away, closing her eyes for a moment as she sought to shut out the world.

"There has been some good come from this debacle," Janan continued. "Elias, tell her."

"Erm… Really? Now?" He shrugged in response to Janan's look. "Okay, well we did manage to collect some interesting data from the sensors in the room as you melted the glass. The temperature in here dropped four degrees." He grinned at her, his enthusiasm crashing against the cliffs of her blank expression and retreating, as undeterred as the waves.

"The room should have heated, not cooled," Elias explained, as if this were somehow not obvious. "This implies that you somehow draw some of the heat energy from the air around you."

204

"Do you feel it?" Janan demanded, stepping in front of Elias. "I need to understand the process if we are to replicate it. Did you feel yourself drawing in the heat?"

Mackenzie shook her head in silence as she glared at him. There wasn't a process to this. On one level she understood that the heat and the fire had to come from somewhere, but he was asking for things she didn't have, and she wouldn't give them to him if she could. They had bound her up like a wild animal, strapping this shock collar to her as if she were a danger to others. And she was. She made a silent promise to herself then as she stared into his eyes. She would be that danger. Just as soon as the opportunity arose, she would burn him down to his fucking shoes.

Janan stalked away, slamming a fist into his palm.

"We cannot find *any* biological component to this!" he said, spinning around to face her. "I've had your DNA analysed—no mutations, no abnormalities; you are as human and normal as any of us."

"Unlike Armond," she said then, her eyes flashing as she looked back and forth between the two of them.

"Exactly!" Elias said, his smile spreading across his face, oblivious to her rising anger. "Armond's abilities were genetic. Some manner of defect or mutation at the cellular level that impacted upon his natural healing ability. We were never able to replicate it."

"Do you realise what that means?" Janan cut in. "It means that either this ability of yours is a skill—something that could be learnt by almost anyone, or that there is some biological element that we cannot detect. And if it is a skill, then it could be taught. I just need you to understand how you are doing it. I need you to *teach* me."

"Unlike Armond," she said again. "Which is why you tested him to death."

"We had to know what his limitations might be," Elias chided her.

"Oh my God, you *knew*!" She had him. The words had slipped from him without a thought and she had him caught in his lie.

Elias glanced at Janan for a second.

"You knew about the fire, didn't you?" Mackenzie pressed. "About using Armond to goad me?"

Elias flinched back from her anger as if she'd tried to hit him. "It was in the interests of—"

"You son of a bitch! You fucking burned him to death in front of me just to see if I could put it out! Then you lied and tried to convince me I'd dreamt it all up when on your fucking drugs. I bet the whole thing was your damned idea."

He grimaced and looked away as her eyes bored into him.

"You bastards. You sick, fucking, *bastards*!" The rage was familiar to her now and she didn't fight it. Instead she slipped into it like a warm bath, reaching out to embrace the power that surged within her.

The fire came easily, bursting to life in the air before her and she welcomed it. She took a single moment to relish in the heat of it against her skin and then, with a scream of rage, sent it rushing at Elias.

The cry was agonised as it tore from her throat. Pain wracked through her and she shook and convulsed as the electric current ripped through her flesh. The fire was gone, winking out in an instant. Any attempt at concentration died almost before it began, and she hung limp from the restraints as the smell of her own scorched hair filled her nostrils.

"Now, Mackenzie," Janan chided her. "That was just a bit rude, don't you think? There really is no need for all this unpleasantness."

She bit off the words, spitting them out like broken teeth. "You have me chained up, like a fucking animal. What the hell do you expect?"

"And why do you think that is?" he snarled at her, lunging in at her face as his own temper snapped. "You have behaved like a rabid dog, and so you are chained up like one. You had every chance, Mackenzie. We brought this power out of you. We showed you what you could become, took you out of your cell and into a place of support and comfort, when we could easily have left you in here. And how do you repay this kindness? By attempting to flee, and by butchering anyone who stood in your way."

His words cut into her, leaving her reeling, and she stopped really listening as he went on. Dear God, he was right. She was like a wild animal, locked away from the world in case she bit someone.

"What do you want from me?" Her words were soft, barely more than a whisper as his rant faded.

Janan looked to Elias and nodded.

"We need you to talk us through the process of it, Mackenzie." The big doctor's voice was soft, gentle. The voice you'd use with a trauma victim, or a frightened animal. "We know a large part of the process lies in believing you can do it, we may have bypassed that by means of hypnosis, but there is another component, another step that we're missing somehow."

"If I do this, will you let me go?"

Janan exchanged a long look with Elias and sighed. "Yes, Mackenzie. If you give us what we need then you will have your release."

She looked at him then, holding his gaze for a moment as she considered it. Was this a real offer, or just another game? And then that word. *Release.* It could mean any number of things. It didn't matter, she decided. It wasn't like she had many options. She was drowning, anything she snatched at to save herself would be better than simply slipping under the waves.

"I don't know how it works, not really," she sighed. "I've told you this a thousand times. It's like… it's like breathing."

She looked at them both expectantly but received nothing but frowns.

"How do you breathe? I mean you could take a breath for me now but most of the time you don't even think about it, you just do it. How do you make a fist? Lift your arm? Nobody thinks about these things, about the mechanics of making your muscles work, you just do it."

"Are you saying that your abilities are more like a reflex?"

"Yes… no, I don't know," she admitted. "It's easier when I'm angry, and there is a feel to it, but I don't know if I can explain it."

Janan had faded into the background as they spoke, leaving the questions to Elias. He stepped forward now, whispering something into the big man's ear and handing him the trigger to the shock collar. Elias grimaced and took the thing, turning it over in his hands like it was a live snake.

Elias came alone the next day, bringing in a stool and sitting close to her as he made notes whilst she summoned the flame, breaking down the process as much as possible. It was frustrating and exhausting, but by the end of the session she felt that some progress had been made.

The technicians came alone on the third day, running fresh tests as she produced the floating flame over and over. They barely spoke to her unless asking her to summon the fire, but pored over the EEG results as the paper spewed from the side of the machine.

She woke early the next day, ready for the blast of cold water from the sprinklers around her frame, and eating early. She shivered as she dripped dry and then wondered at her own stupidity.

She could create fire at will, why was she suffering through the cold and shivering? Could she do it without being angry? The power seemed to feed on her rage, but was it actually necessary?

It felt different. Always before she'd reacted, her anger providing a fuel for the fire. Without it she felt like she was snatching at moonbeams, there was nothing tangible to grab hold of.

The sweat beaded on her forehead as she strained. She became aware of every sound as she worked in the silence. Her own breathing seemed suddenly impossibly loud, overlaying a periodic muted thud somewhere in the distance.

A spark blinked into existence and vanished just as quickly as she stared at it in shock.

Mackenzie swore and tried again, closing her eyes. She could feel the flame, a raging fire just out of reach. She bore down, clenching her teeth. Fire bloomed into life in front of her face, she could feel the heat of it even before she opened her eyes. Then a scream came through the wall—a muted howl of pain and anger followed by a distant crashing as something mechanical was beaten to pieces.

CHAPTER TWENTY-EIGHT

"Mr Carver!" The man beamed as he came through the doorway. His grin was pure excitement that had bubbled up into his big face. There was nothing small about this man. Everything about him was large, from his ham-like hands to the exuberant smile on his bearded face. That said, there was something about him; before I'd even drawn breath to reply, I'd decided I didn't like him.

"He's stepped out," I said sourly from where I was still chained to the wooden frame. "You can leave a message with me if you like?"

The man chuckled. "Very droll. They told me you had a good sense of humour. I'm Dr Toby Elias, and I cannot tell you how much of a pleasure it is to finally meet you. You have quite the collection of stories circulating around you."

"Yeah, I'm a regular fucking legend. What do you want?"

His smile wavered for a moment before it rallied. "I'd have thought that was obvious, John. We want to study your ability with a view to replicating it. You've shown remarkable progress in such a short space of time. With other subjects we've had to resort to mild sedation, or a cocktail of consciousness expanding drugs, to really see their abilities manifest, but with you…"

He waved at the wreckage of the tennis ball launcher laying in the corner of the room as if that was all the explanation I needed. I wasn't really listening, my attention caught on that one word. Others. He'd said there were others.

What in the hell had I fallen into here?

"So, you want me to be your volunteer guinea pig?" I shook my head. "Sorry, Doc, I'm not really up for that."

The smile slipped, taking on a false, used-car salesman quality before it gave up entirely.

"Mr Carver, we can gather the data we require with or without your cooperation. It will just be easier for everyone involved, including you, if you're a willing participant."

"Who's this prick then?" I didn't need to turn my head to know it was Turner. Even without the accent, he's the only man I've ever known who can squeeze that much contempt into words of one syllable.

"Or what?" I snorted at Elias. "You're going to strap me down and shoot me in the leg again? Make a mess of my chest? Short of killing me, I can't see that there's much more you can do to me; and I can't see you bumping me off just yet, not while you still want something from me."

Elias sighed, giving me a look that told me a lot of what he thought of me. "No, you're right, we won't kill you. Given your recent advances, I would like to see what you can do against a bullet again though."

"Fuck that," Turner spat. "He's having a bloody laugh!"

I gave Elias a look. He had to be joking. "You can't be serious."

"I'm completely serious." Elias said without a hint of a smile. "You've done it before, in Kabul in 2013, I believe. There are a whole host of tales about it, even aside from the first-hand accounts, that's the reason you were acquired. Plus, look what you managed to do with the launcher here."

I paused, letting the silence fall before I spoke again. "It's a bit risky though, isn't it?" I asked him. "What if you nick an artery or chip a bone? All it takes is one tiny bone fragment making its way through my arteries and you're looking at a stroke. That happens and you can kiss goodbye to your data."

"Oh, I don't think that's too likely, Mr Carver. We can be quite precise." He made his way to the door and turned back as he reached it.

"I'll have some people set up the weapon experiment. Please think on this as a learning experience. I had hoped to speak a bit more with you, I have a great number of questions. Perhaps when you're feeling a little more cooperative."

I watched him go as Turner made a slow circuit of the room, squatting down to inspect the wreckage of the tennis ball launcher as blood dripped from the bullet hole in his forehead.

"Don't look so miserable, Carver," Turner said. "If you don't manage to pull this off then we'll have matching holes." He grinned, pointing to his forehead. "We can be bullet buddies!"

I shook my head, lying to myself that it was the situation I was shaking it at, and not Turner. Rule Three again, it was going to the dogs lately.

The techs came in a few hours later. Thanks to the clock on the wall, I could enjoy every second of my captivity and know just how long I'd been in here. The apparatus they set up wasn't much more than a broad-based bracket with some kind of remote trigger mechanism.

To be honest, I was more concerned with the gun. It was a small-calibre, which was the one thing I had going for me. If and when the damned thing shot me, at least it wouldn't be blasting a tunnel through my flesh.

The laser sight wobbled as they adjusted the gun until it was aimed at my upper thigh. The opposite leg to the one they'd already shot.

"At least it'll match the other side, Roasties," Turner said with a grin.

"Fuck off," I muttered. The techs working on the gun gave me an odd look and exchanged glances. "Yeah, and you lot can do one as well."

This was bad.

I almost laughed at the thought. 'Bad' was an understatement. This wasn't a stupid action film where the hero gets shot in the leg and five minutes later is climbing stairs and doing bad kung fu moves. I'd been lucky the last time, and this time they'd chosen the best place to shoot me; but taking another bullet, even from a small-calibre handgun like this one, carried a high chance of something going wrong. All guns are basically miniaturised, and slightly modified, canons. Causing minor, and non-lethal, wounds just wasn't what was in mind when they dreamt them up.

I had the good grace to wait until the techs had gone before I started to really panic. I'd managed to stop the tennis ball on my own. The problem was, I still didn't have the first bloody clue how I'd done it. Rage had definitely been a part of it, but I wasn't angry right now, I was shitting myself.

"Turner!" I called out. Rule Three be damned. "Turner can you get Johnson for me?"

The Scot gave me a look. "What am I now, your bloody PA? Shall I fetch some teas and coffees in too, Mr Carver?"

"Jesus, Turner," I said, looking down the barrel of the gun. "Now really isn't the time."

"What are you worried about?" he asked, looking genuinely curious. "Just stop the bullet like you did with the tennis ball."

"I don't know *how*, you dick! What am I going to do?"

"Get shot, I imagine."

"Thanks a bunch, arsehole. Will you just fetch Johnson?"

He vanished, leaving behind a filthy laugh.

"What do you want, Carver?" Johnson said from somewhere behind me. "I thought you had your rule about not talking to us?"

I twisted on the frame until I could see him, realising as I did it that this was a stupid idea. The gun had been aimed at a very specific point on my thigh, twisting like that had just shifted all of that.

"Fuck, I'm an idiot."

Johnson barked out an ugly laugh. "Finally, something we can agree on."

"This thing's going to fire soon, Johnson. Can you stop it?"

Johnson shrugged. "Why don't you do it yourself?"

"Because I don't fucking know how!" My voice rose to a frantic shout, echoing off the bare walls.

Johnson moved around me to squat down in front of the gun, peering into the barrel. "What makes you think I do?"

"You did it before!" I burst out.

"So did you!" Johnson said with a laugh.

"Are we about ready, Mr Carver?" the voice came from the speakers in the ceiling.

"No, I'm bloody not!" I yelled back. I looked down at Johnson. "Johnson, will you stop pissing about?"

He sighed. "Fine, I'll do what I can to help you."

"Thank you!" I broke off as the gun shifted slightly and the laser sight painted a red dot on my thigh. "Wait, do you mean you'll stop it, or that you'll help me stop it?"

"Is there a difference?" Johnson laughed.

"Johnson!"

"Please try and focus, Mr Carver. The only person in that room is you." Elias' voice sounded almost as tense as I was.

I focused on the gun. Maybe Johnson was doing this too, maybe he wasn't, but I couldn't take the chance. I used my frantic state, scraping up every last ounce of fear, anger, and frustration at the whole crazy situation, and hurled it at the gun. A moment later it fired.

The gunshot was loud. They're always loud, but this was a small, enclosed room with stone floors. The sound was enough to make me flinch but I'll admit I'd already looked away at that point.

My next thought was that I wasn't in pain. Either the damned thing had missed somehow, or Johnson or I had stopped it.

I've never seen a gun backfire. It's a misleading term since guns don't really backfire in any real sense, but it was the best thing I could think of to describe what had happened.

It tends to happen with faulty ammunition—either too much powder in a cartridge, or not enough, which eventually leads to a blocked barrel. The second situation is usually worse than the first. A gun works by way of a controlled explosion, forcing the bullet itself out of the cartridge and down the barrel, propelled by superheated expanding gases as the powder explodes. If the barrel is blocked somehow, then all of that force has to go somewhere. If you're lucky, it's not into your hand.

The gun was in ruins. Pieces of the barrel and slide were scattered against the glass wall and a spiderweb of cracks surrounded one of the larger impacts.

"Looks like you've made a bloody mess again, Carver." Johnson made his way over to the gun, crouching down to examine the remains before he went over to the glass wall, and then carried on smoothly into the corner as the door hissed open.

Elias pushed his way through the gap before the door had reached even halfway, rushing first to the gun and then the cracked window. He ran his fingertips over the glass and shook his head.

"Remarkable. Just remarkable. You realise what you've done here, don't you?" he asked, looking over one shoulder at me.

"Managed not to get shot?" I muttered.

"Ha! Yes," Elias snorted. "More than that though, you've somehow not only stopped the bullet but destroyed the weapon. I wonder if you didn't somehow stop the bullet in the barrel itself?"

"Yeah, well, I'd like to say I'm sorry about that..."

"That's not important," Elias cut in, waving away the non-apology. "There is something vitally important that we need to talk about though, if you're prepared to listen?"

I jiggled the wrist restraints enough to make the metal clink. "It's not like I have much of a choice, is it?"

Elias nodded, letting the accusation pass. "You're aware there is a microphone system in here? Of course you are, you've spoken to us over it. We've heard you talking to other people in here. Turner? Johnson? These are names that several of us have heard. Would you like to talk about that?"

I'd heard these types of lines before. Therapy wasn't anything I'd ever really put much stock into. I don't have unresolved issues with my mother, I'm not angry at my father, my issues are a bit more specific: I see dead people who, as it turns out, can stop bullets. Somehow, I doubted a group hug was going to help with that.

"Not especially," I told him.

214

Elias nodded as he began to pace.

"You were a soldier, or so I've been told. I assume you've seen your share of grisly things, leading that kind of life one would tend to expect that. I'd imagine you've heard the term 'PTSD' a few times as well?" He looked at me waiting for a nod that he wasn't going to get. He nodded anyway as if I'd answered him. "PTSD isn't anything new. '*Post-Vietnam Syndrome*', '*Shell Shock*', '*Soldier's Heart*'? They're all more or less the same thing. As a species we've come so far in terms of our technological advancement, yet we still seem to resort to hacking each other to bits with sharp pieces of metal. All modern technology has done is give us the ability to do it from slightly further away from each other."

He was still warming to his subject, but I wasn't really up for a lecture, not when I was literally a captive audience. A night's sleep would normally have left me rested and ready for most things, no matter what I'd done the day before. Of course, that would be a night's sleep in a bed, or even on the ground. My sleep when chained up to the wooden frame tended to be fitful and broken, and I was too tired still to put up with much more of the man's crap. "What's your point, Doc?"

"My point is that war does things to the human mind. Combat and battle aren't anything new. What *is* new is our advanced level of medical knowledge, and more specifically, our trauma care. Those who witnessed the true horrors of warfare in the past didn't generally survive to tell of it. It's only in the last few decades that we've come to accept PTSD for what it really is. The mind can be wounded just as easily as the flesh; some wounds are harder to heal."

I sighed. I didn't want to hear this. "Why are you telling me this? I've read the pamphlets."

"Because of what we're doing here, John," Elias said, stopping his pacing and spinning around to face me. "You don't mind if I call you John, do you?"

I laughed at that. They had abducted me, chained me up naked in a room whilst they shot things at me, but he was suddenly worried about being overly familiar?

"No, by all means," I managed, still laughing.

"Your abilities, and the abilities of everyone we have discovered, have one thing in common. They all come from someone who is psychologically damaged in some way. Some are worse than others, there are one or two I would go so far as to call broken. It was this that first led me to the hypothesis that these abilities are rooted, or dependent, on our notion of reality.

"Essentially, that they rely upon an ability to reject or bypass our beliefs of what we know to be possible or not. From there it was an easy step to experiment with sedation, hypnosis, even consciousness expanding drugs." He stopped to glance at me, probably checking I was still awake. "Are you following this?"

"Yeah, you're saying that this thing comes from the fact I'm a little bit crazy. I'm a soldier, Doc. I'm not an idiot."

Elias grimaced. "Crazy isn't a term I'd use but, yes, the ability to break with reality, to effect a 'disconnect' if you will, seems to be central to bringing out these abilities."

"You're obviously building up to something here, Elias," I said. "Why don't you just spit it out?"

"This break comes at a cost, John. It seems to be that as much as the power of a given ability is increased by the depths and profoundness of the break, the break itself is intensified the more the ability is used."

I sucked on my lip, digesting that as he watched me. "So, your little experiment here, shooting tennis balls and bullets at me until I found a way to stop them? That has the side effect of possibly driving me nuts?"

"No, nothing quite as dramatic as that," Elias said with a smile, waving away the accusation. "I think you misunderstand in any event. You seem to be remarkably resistant to the negative effects, despite your 'visitors.'"

"So, it's the *other* poor bastards you have locked up in here you're talking about?"

He winced. "There have been a number of minor incidents, yes."

"And what happens when they finally lose the plot and start chewing on the furniture?"

"I don't think that's really the point here," Elias said, clasping his hands behind his back. "What's more important is how you are managing to maintain the plateau you've reached, so to speak. Tell me about this 'Johnson' you've been talking to."

"Tell him to get fucked," muttered Johnson from the corner. I hadn't even noticed he was there.

"Go fuck yourself," I said, looking back at the doctor with a smile.

"I'm sorry?" Elias sputtered. "Mr Carver, I don't think you're really understanding the situation."

I shook my head, still smiling. "No, Doc. I think for the first time in weeks I understand perfectly. It's *you* that's got it wrong. You need something from me. You've been picking away at the others you've got chained up in this place, and now that the rubber bands inside their heads are starting to snap, you've found you can't cope with the mess. You want me to help you with that? Get fucked, mate."

Elias grimaced. "Carver, it's a little worse than I said. Just think for a minute, imagine someone with enhanced abilities like your own, but with only the most tenuous grip on reality. Someone who has achieved these abilities through hypnosis and a Cocktail of consciousness expanding drugs and sedation, focusing on their anger to bring them to the fore."

I nodded. "They don't sound like they'd be much fun to play with, mate. Good thing we're all chained up, isn't it?"

"If only, Mr Carver. If only."

I shrugged and flashed him a quick grin.

CHAPTER TWENTY-NINE

Mackenzie stared at the wall. The crashing had been muffled, but clear enough that she didn't doubt her own senses.

"Hello?" She didn't wait for the answer, calling out again, louder this time. "Is somebody there?"

She listened hard, straining her ears into the silence that followed until she called out again. And then again. A cycle of calls and listening that faded into a stillness broken by her own tears of frustration.

The feeling came over her all at once and she remembered that somewhere, somebody was watching a screen with her on it. She felt exposed in a way she hadn't in months, her nakedness rushing back to the forefront of her mind as she felt the unseen eyes crawling over her.

The sensation was like a bucket of cold water. What was she doing? She'd been cooperating with Elias and Janan, helping them with the research as if it would somehow help her. They were never going to let her go. They'd already given her a taste of freedom and she'd used it to try and escape. If she did somehow manage to get out, then the risk that anyone she told might actually believe her story was minuscule; but even that risk was large enough that they couldn't take the chance on it. They would never let her leave this cell again. She was destined to become just another Armond. They would test and examine her until they decided they couldn't replicate her ability, and then they would test her limits until it killed her.

She shook her head at the thought. Just how many Armonds had there been? Was the crashing she had heard caused by Janan's latest plaything? Some other specimen for him to test to death? Or was it someone recently captured, and was she now the one waiting for Janan to grow frustrated with her, and begin experimenting with just how far her powers could be pushed?

The idea didn't worry her as much as she thought it would, and she pondered the notion of dying. It would mean an end to all of this, at least. A release from it all. Suicide had never been an option before now. Other than starving herself, she hadn't had the means even if she'd had the desire. Was it possible now? Could she concentrate long enough to actually kill herself?

"Stupid," she muttered. Summoning the flame needed her to focus. Even in a blind rage she would still feel the pain. If, by some miracle, she could maintain the power long enough, there was always the danger that she might live. That was the real worry. She might survive and be forced to live out her days as a maimed and charred mess, driven half-mad by the constant agony.

She glanced at the metal cuffs. That was why they'd replaced them of course, in case she attempted to burn through them. She looked to the smoked-glass wall, running her gaze over it as she searched for the red light of the camera. It didn't take her long to give up. With the glare from the lights it would be harder to spot anyway, and who was to say the new camera even had a red light, or that they hadn't covered it up? The only thing she could really be certain of was that they would be watching.

"It's time," she murmured to herself. Whoever it was that had made the crashing noise, if it actually had been another captive or not, didn't matter. Sooner or later they would bring in another one like her. Another victim to be tortured and twisted as they ran their tests. And what if they did eventually succeed? What kind of monster would Janan become if he gained a power like hers?

She bit down on her lip as she took a deep breath. It was time to get out of here; the only question was how. The door wouldn't be a problem.

She'd melted through the glass to destroy the camera, she could handle the door. It might take some time, but she was confident she could burn a way out. No, the issue was the metal cuff binding her to the frame, and the collar around her throat. She was going to need help, and that help wouldn't come willingly.

The thought came from nowhere and she burst out laughing at the simplicity. The problem would be how to practice without the camera watching. Her eyes rose to the ceiling. The smoked glass wall didn't reach from floor to ceiling and there was a section of maybe a foot and a half between the top of the glass and the ceiling. The smile that curved her lips was cruel and born of vengeance.

She had no visitors that day. No technicians, no tests, and rather than bothering her, she revelled in the time alone. Where before it would have just led her to worry and then despair, now she had a plan. She tilted her head back enough that she could focus on a white tile just above the edge of the smoked glass, but not so far that anyone watching would be curious what she was staring at. She didn't need this to be big. If anything, smaller would be better.

She concentrated, bearing down as she forced the flame to her will. It was harder than before, her excitement seemed to work against her in the same way that the rage had worked for her, but eventually she succeeded. The flame was tiny, not much larger than the head of a match, and she concentrated as she blinked it in and out of existence, the flame turning from orange, to blue, to incandescent white, until she was too exhausted to raise a spark.

They left her the next day, and then again on the next; ignored and forgotten. The days she had been without food as Janan punished her for her escape attempt had left her weak, and so she ate and slept whenever she could. Practise with the tiny flame was building her endurance up, but this would only be half the struggle. She deliberately did not think about the ordeal she might face if she actually made it out of the complex.

The muffled crashes and screams continued intermittently. She tried calling out, shouting until she was screaming herself hoarse, but there was never a reply. Whoever was making the noise either couldn't hear her or was unwilling, or perhaps unable, to answer.

It was another three days before Elias returned. Mackenzie tensed as the door hissed, swinging to one side on the metal struts as it opened. She forced herself to relax as Elias burst into the room. There was a risk in this. If this plan failed, she wouldn't simply be punished, she'd be killed.

"He did it!" The big man blurted. "Janan, he did it. He made the disconnect."

"He made a flame?" she did her best to sound pleased, but doubted it was convincing. It was time to get out of here. If she died trying, then so be it.

"No, not a flame." Elias shook his head, still grinning. "Something else, but that's not the point. He's made the first steps, the process *works*. It's possible that we could harness almost any power from here."

She glanced past him at the doorway, but he looked to have come alone. "Can you take me to him?" she asked.

Elias stopped in mid-flow, glancing down at the control device in his hand. "I suppose…" he said, giving her an odd look.

Mackenzie smiled, trying to look eager. Acting had never been anything she'd been good at. If he fell for this, it would be a miracle. "You've got the keys to these, don't you?" she nodded at her wrist.

"No," Elias said, still frowning. "They don't have a lock, it's just a bolt on the back."

"Let me out, Elias." The smile fell, dead, from her lips.

He looked genuinely regretful as he spoke. "I can't do that, Mackenzie. Not yet, you know that."

She took a deep breath. This was it. This was the moment. "Let me out, Elias. Or I'll burn you right down to your fucking toes."

He shook his head with a sad smile, waving the shock collar's remote trigger at her. "I don't think so, Mackenzie."

"Do you really think that little toy can stop me?" she said, using the words to cover her frown as she concentrated. The fire was tiny, little more than the size of a ball-bearing, but within the confines of the trigger's housing it bloomed like a miniature sun. The fragile circuitry melted in less time than it took to take a breath.

Elias dropped the smouldering device as it burst into flames and looked at her in shock.

Mackenzie focused again and summoned a ball of flame, letting her anger grow. This man had lied. He had feigned ignorance of Armond's death when he had known full well that it was exactly what Janan had planned. He'd probably had a hand in the whole thing.

Elias fumbled with the bolts as she watched. The fat man was sweating. She'd never thought of him as fat before, just big, but then she'd never been ready to burn him to death before either. She'd lost any kindly thoughts towards him the moment she realised he'd been a part of Armond's death.

"You'll never get out of here like this, Mackenzie," he sputtered. "The guards will stop you the moment they see you dragging me along."

The first of the restraints came loose and clattered to the ground as she pulled an arm free. He was right. She hadn't thought this through. She couldn't afford to take him with her. She climbed free of the frame, working the clasp open on the shock collar and glaring at Elias as he shrank back against the wall.

"Give me the key-card."

He looked at her blankly until she pointed at his pocket, snapping her fingers.

"They'll kill you," Elias told her as he handed the card over.

She smiled at that, shaking her head in disbelief. "Wouldn't you have killed me anyway? Come on, Elias, admit it. You were never going to let me go."

He had no answer to that, but his silence said everything she needed to hear.

She looked him over, considering.

"Give me your shirt," she snapped.

"My shirt?"

"I've been naked long enough."

It didn't take long. Within minutes she was dressed in his shirt and was tightening the bolts on the steel cuffs as she tied him into the frame. Somewhere a camera was watching her. She'd known this from the moment she decided to escape. There was nothing she could do short of burning the lens out, and without the red light she couldn't see the camera right now anyway. She just hoped it was set to record, rather than being monitored.

She shoved the sleeve of Elias' jacket into his mouth, binding it around his head in a make-shift gag that should take him a while to work free. The hours she'd spent screaming in this place made it unlikely he'd be heard, but it was better not to take risks.

"I should burn you, Elias," she told him. "But that would be too quick. I know someone will find you in here, sooner or later. I just hope it's later."

The observation room was empty, and she passed through quickly, pressing an ear to the door she knew led out into the hallway.

Silence.

She grimaced, and glanced back at Elias, just visible as the glass-fronted door pivoted back into place. She'd made her choices, it was time to go.

The hallway was silent and empty; Mackenzie scurried along it, keeping close to the wall. She'd made the trip from her rooms to Elias' office, or to the dining hall, a hundred times or more, but she'd only made the journey out of this place once.

She passed two doors before she paused. Were there others like her behind those doors? Did she have the time to find out? Indecision gripped her and she froze beside the door until she realised what she was doing. Time was her enemy right now. She needed to move.

The door opened easily at the touch of Elias' key-card on the reader. She threw it open and lunged inside. The observation room was identical to the one outside her own cell, and just as empty.

Mackenzie pressed her fingers to the window. From this side, the glass didn't even look tinted and the man strapped into his frame was clearly visible. He looked broken. Even at this distance she could see the expression on his face, despair etched so deep it had become his face at rest.

She paused at the door. A keypad sat next to the card reader on the wall. She stared at it until she shook her head at herself. Either the card alone would work or it wouldn't. The reader beeped as the card made contact and the low hiss of the pneumatics began easing the door open. Mackenzie reached over to the video camera, positioned on its tripod before the glass, and lowered the lens until it pointed at the floor. With luck, anyone seeing it would think the tripod had just slipped.

The man didn't look up as she made her way into the room. The stone floor felt cold under her feet and she walked in silence, as if afraid to wake him.

"Hello?" she spoke gently, as if waking a sleeping child.

His head came up with a start, eyes wide and fearful.

"Please?" a desperate plea forced into that one word. He looked at her before she could answer, his eyes first narrowing and then growing wide in shock. "You shouldn't be here."

"I'm Mackenzie, I'm trying to get out. Will you help me?"

He shook his head violently. "No, I can't get out."

"I could let you out. I can undo the restraints."

"No!" His response was a pitiful wail as he shook his head. "No, I can't. You can't let me out of here."

"I…" Mackenzie broke off, frowning. This was the one thing she hadn't expected.

"Please?"

"Fine," she grimaced and glanced behind her at the open door. This was already taking too long. He was making too much noise.

"Please?"

"Please, what?" Mackenzie snapped. "I already said I'd leave you."

"Please, kill me? Won't you, please kill me?"

She gaped. She'd thought about suicide in her lowest moments, but this man was literally begging for death.

"I can't do that." The words spilled out on their own.

His face fractured, reforming into a picture of agony. "Please kill me, I'm begging you."

She backed away as his voice rose, but her eyes were on the exposed flesh of his torso. Dark lines ran along his veins, and they bulged and throbbed in time with his pulse.

"Please!"

Her back hit the wall and she turned to look for the door as he began to scream. The skin on his chest and at his shoulders seemed to split as black

tendrils pushed their way out through his flesh, lashing at the air around him.

She edged along the glass wall. His scream choked off as a thick rope of the black substance burst from his mouth, slamming into the glass beside her hard enough to crack it. She found the door, slamming a hand down on the switch inside to close it. She didn't look back, though she could hear the black tendrils thrashing at the ground around him.

She ran.

CHAPTER THIRTY

Her feet slapped on the cold, tiled floor, making more noise than she would have liked; but it was a choice of either fast and loud, or quiet and slow right now. Fast was never going to lose that fight in this place.

Doorways flashed past her as she ran, marked with meaningless combinations of numbers, or signs written in Pashto that she didn't have the time to stop and translate. Some would be cells, she knew. Doors that led through to observation rooms, and maybe more people like her. After the last attempt she wasn't in any hurry to try again.

He had begged her to kill him. He had *pleaded* with her. Just how many people had this place broken?

The corridor ended abruptly at a plain doorway and she stared at it stupidly for a moment before pressing her ear to it. A distant sound from behind her somewhere pulled her ear away and she tapped the card to the reader, pulling the door open. The hallway turned to the right but, other than that, it was identical to the one she'd just left. She pushed at the door until it clicked shut, and set off.

Already she was tired. Her muscles had been wasted, rehabilitated, and then starved for days. They were unused to this treatment, and her legs were swearing at her as loudly as possible.

The pain in her thighs and calves was nothing compared to the bone-deep fatigue that clawed at her. Using the fire had weakened her more than she wanted to admit, and already she had to fight to keep going. More than once she'd caught herself dropping back from her jog into a walk, and each time she had to force herself to start running again, it grew harder.

She had no idea where she was going. The thought began as a quiet whisper and her panic grew, until the notion of being lost and running in circles claimed her utterly. She hadn't been paying attention when Janan had led her out of her cell. She'd been overwhelmed at the sudden taste of freedom and her hazy memory of it was of no help to her now.

Where was the lift? There should be a set of stairs beside it. At least, there had been in the hallway leading from Elias' office. All she had to do now was find it.

"Shit, shit, shit!" she muttered as she ran.

The door was less than twenty feet away when it opened. Mackenzie skidded to a halt, almost falling over herself as she scrambled to a stop. She looked around frantically for somewhere to hide, but knew what she'd see before she even turned her head—the corridor was empty aside from the doors. There was no chance of concealment.

She pressed herself to the wall, knowing it was futile, as a man emerged. The technician froze as he looked up from the small trolley he was pushing. They looked at each other for a long moment before either moved. His hand broke the stillness, reaching for the radio at his belt, and then she ran.

She charged at the cart, shoving it back into him as she burst past. The fatigue, and the aching in her legs, were less than a memory as she sprinted along the hallway.

She stopped as she rounded a corner, chest heaving, her throat burning as she sucked in air. He wasn't following her. She held her breath for a moment to listen.

No, he wasn't following her. Help would be on its way to him though, and whatever time she might have had was done. She ran to the first door and tapped the key-card to the reader, pulling it open. Another observation room lay inside and she moved on quickly, rushing along the hallway to the next door. Time was her enemy now, and the fact that guards with tasers would be coming for her far out-weighed her fear of encountering more lab techs.

She made her way along the corridor quickly, moving from door to door as her panic rose. Distant voices had her moving faster, until she was tripping over herself and dropping the key-card.

A flash of movement turned her head and she glared at the lone guard staring at her in shock. He was young, barely in his twenties if she was any judge.

"Stop," she called out as his hand reached for the radio clipped to his shoulder. He paused for a second, clearly not understanding, and she tried again in Pashto. "Don't do it."

He wasn't stopping and she reached for the break, for the disconnect inside her mind. The tendrils of her thoughts wormed their way into the narrow crack, forcing it wider as she reached for the power that lurked within it. Her vision shifted as the hallway slipped out of focus for a moment and then the fire surged.

"Stop!" she cried out again in Pashto, as the flames rose from her hands. She wasn't even sure he understood, but fear was clear on his face as he backed away from her. "Don't make me do this!" Her voice fell to a whisper, almost lost in the tears that ran unchecked down her cheeks. "Don't make me do this…"

His eyes were wide with fear or horror, she couldn't tell which, but his hand never left the radio. His finger depressed the button and he managed a single word before she turned his speech to screams.

The fire raged, a beast uncaged that ran amok as the young man staggered and flailed within the column of flame that engulfed him, embracing him within its fury, and holding him close.

Mackenzie wept, sinking down into herself and pressing her face to one knee, even as a single hand still reached out towards the fire. She wouldn't stop, it didn't matter that this thing was turning her into a monster.

She had no choice. They were giving her no choice.

The smoke had set off an alarm, and sirens blared, an endless cycling *whoop-whoop* noise that was just high enough to be piercing. The man's screaming had stopped, and the only other sound was the crackle of the flames as they ate away at the corpse. Mackenzie shifted on the floor, bare feet crunching into the frost that encrusted the tiles surrounding them.

"Enough," she whispered, a barely audible command as she strained at the break in her mind. The wound had grown, tearing at the fabric of her sanity until it had become a fissure. She could feel the power in it, but beyond it there was something more, something she shrank back from.

She forced the break, pushing the edges together, her mind recoiling from the alien sensation of the disconnect. She had to get moving, she knew that, but on a deeper level she found herself questioning.

Should she even be fleeing? She was becoming another version of the man in the cell, that twisted wreckage of a person with the black tendrils bursting from his arms. As much as she wanted to be free of this place, what right did she have to inflict the horror she was becoming upon the world?

Her hand pressed down against the ground, slipping on the melting frost as she pushed her way up. She moved like a drunk; staggering past the charred ruin of the young guard. She was so tired. All she wanted to do was sink back down, sleep, and let the darkness take her.

"Mackenzie." The voice came over speakers set in the ceiling as the sirens drifted into silence. "Mackenzie, there is nowhere for you to run to. Please do not force us to hurt you."

"Fuck you!" she muttered. There was no way for Janan to hear her, but that didn't matter—it felt good to say it anyway.

She carried on along the hallway, checking the doors as she passed. Voices that had once been a distant murmur were closer now, more distinct. She tapped the key-card to the reader as she looked back over her shoulder.

Christ, they were close.

The observation room was dark and she eased the door closed behind her, wincing at the noise the locks made as they engaged. There was nowhere to hide in here, either. The long desk that ran in front of the camera on its tripod was facing the door. If she hid there, she'd be spotted in seconds.

A door slammed shut out in the hall and she tapped the reader.

"Come on, come on!" she hissed at the pneumatic door as it slowly pivoted open on its struts. She eased her way through the gap before it was even half-way open, tapping the card on the reader inside in the hopes that it wouldn't have to finish opening before she could close it.

"Well, it's an interesting outfit, but then, who am I to criticise?"

She spun around to the amused grin of the man strapped to the frame. He was tall, though growing lean enough that he might be called thin. His dark hair looked like it needed a trim, and he had the beginnings of a beard—all signs that he had been here too long. Other than that, he was completely naked.

"Just be quiet," she hissed, and ran around behind him, ducking down behind what meagre cover the frame provided, trying to ignore the fact that she was less than a foot from his bare arse.

"Not the greatest hiding spot," the man noted in a low voice.

"Shut up," Mackenzie hissed. "They'll hear you."

The man snorted. "There's a camera in the next room, love. There are mics in the ceiling. Somebody somewhere is seeing and hearing every word of this."

He was getting on her nerves.

"I know that, you fucking peanut. I'm talking about the guards out—" She broke off at the muffled sound of the door opening inside the observation room.

"Have you come with that steak I ordered?" the man on the frame called out to towards the glass wall. "It's going to be a bit of a bastard cutting it, what with me being all tied up like this, but I'll give it a good go."

"Are you out of your mind?" Mackenzie hissed.

"You know," the man whispered. "Normally I'd say no, but it's getting to be hard to tell lately."

She shook her head, crouching deeper into a ball as she tried to make herself as small as possible. She couldn't be caught now. She wouldn't let them take her. Could she summon the flame again? Would it be enough to make a difference? Enough to end it all if it came to it?

"They're gone," the man in the frame muttered. "Now, how about you tell me what the fuck is going on?"

She made her way out from behind him and crossed the room to stand in the corner, against the glass wall and out of shot of the camera. Whoever he was, he was a mess. A mass of purple and blue bruises covered his chest, with the skin at the centre split and scabbed. A bandage was bound tight around one leg, and an empty IV bag hung on a stand beside him. She peered at the bag for a moment and turned to examine the wreckage in the corner. Was that some kind of hopper?

"Hello? If you're quite done inspecting the place, do you mind telling me what's happening here?"

"I'd have thought that was obvious," she told him. "I'm trying to escape."

He nodded, running his tongue around inside his lip. "Sounds like a bloody good idea. Fancy some company?"

She ran a critical eye over him, pausing at the fresh dressing on his thigh. "I don't know. Can you walk?"

"I can give it a damned good try. Just let me out of this thing. We're on borrowed time as it is."

She nodded and went behind the frame, working the bolts loose on the torso restraint. Thankfully they were the same type of wingnut used on her wrist cuffs. It was easier than having keys for each prisoner, she supposed. "What's your name?"

"Carver," he told her. "You?"

"Mackenzie," she said as the first of the bolts came free. "How long have you been here?"

"Look, love, do you think we could leave the chat for later? I really don't know how long we have here."

Mackenzie sniffed. He was probably right, but she didn't need to admit it. Besides, there was something about him she found incredibly irritating.

231

"What happened to your leg?" she asked, straining on a stubborn bolt.

"They shot me," Carver told her, letting out a low groan of relief as one side of the torso restraint came free.

"You were trying to escape? They tasered me."

"No, they thought I could stop bullets."

Mackenzie snorted a laugh until she realised he was serious, and nodded at his leg. "It doesn't look like you're very good at it."

Carver turned his head to give her a grin. "You might be right. Listen, we're going to need to find me some clothes too. I don't fancy escaping from here in the buff, and this is already the least fun I've ever had naked with a woman."

PART
III

CHAPTER THIRTY-ONE

I couldn't tell you how good it felt to be out of the frame. I've never been very eloquent and this sensation deserved more than the heartfelt groan I let out as I clambered free of the thing. If you've ever spent a full day and night in a car, or a plane, without being able to get up, that first stretch—the back-popping, grinding one that you simply don't want to end-that comes close to brushing near to how good this felt.

The Aussie woman, Mackenzie, watched me with a wry grin and I glanced away, fighting down the embarrassed look on my face.

She was shorter than me, but not by much, and her dark hair had been pulled back into some sort of bird's nest pony tail. The bones in her face stuck out a little more than they ought to, and the muscles in her calves were barely even there. She'd been starved at some point in the not-too-distant past, and I wondered how she had the energy to stand up, let alone move as quickly as she did.

"Looks like you've pulled, mate," Johnson whispered as he leant in close to my ear. I gave him a puzzled look until I caught myself. It was bad enough to be breaking Rule Three without actually being *seen* talking to the visitors. The look said enough on its own.

"Well, she's in just a shirt, you're in the buff. Have I interrupted something?"

"Jesus Christ," I muttered.

"What now?" Mackenzie demanded, glaring at me whilst somehow completely ignoring my naked state. "Let's just get going, yeah?"

I followed as she tapped the card to the reader, and then eased past her into the dark room beyond.

"It's an observation room," Mackenzie muttered, nodding me onward to the other door. "There's a corridor beyond that one. I was making my way along it from the right, when I had to duck in here because of the guards."

"How many were there?"

She shrugged. "I don't know. I never saw them, but at least two or three. Enough to hold a conversation."

I grunted, leaning in to listen at the door. This wasn't going to be much fun. Escape and evasion, I can do. You don't get far in the forces, and certainly not into any of the special units, if you can't master it. Escape and evasion whilst half crippled and stark-bollock naked— that's a new one on me, and doing it with a bloody civvy wasn't going to make it any easier.

The handle turned smoothly, and I cracked the door just wide enough to let through any faint sounds it might have muffled. The hallway was silent, and a wider crack didn't reveal much more. I eased my way out, motioning for the woman to follow me.

Mackenzie. Her name was Mackenzie. I needed to remember that.

I made my way ahead of her, motioning for her to wait a moment while I listened for any sign of the guards. She seemed quiet enough, padding along on bare feet, but I needed to be sure.

She glared at me again as I waved her on and she caught up, clearly not happy about being ordered about. "What are you doing?"

"What?" I frowned at the question.

"Are you some kind of soldier? You look like you're playing commandos."

I snorted at that. "Yeah, something like that. What about you?"

She winced. "I was a nurse. Before, you know..." she waved an arm about her.

"Yeah," I nodded. "Before."

The hallways were plain and floored with white tiles. The kind that would turn to a gore-spattered ice-rink when the blood started flowing.

I spotted three cameras before we made it to the end of the hallway and passed through another windowless door. Either they weren't being monitored at all, or someone was playing silly games here.

The first set of guards looked almost as surprised to see us as we were to see them, and they froze as we came through the doors. There tends to be three types of people in a fight; the freezers, the runners, and those that just pile in. Piling in, given that I was still completely naked, was probably a bad idea. So I did it anyway.

The guards weren't much more than amateurs. The same kind of gung-ho morons you'll find guarding gates the world over. These are the people who think wearing a crumpled uniform and a gun somehow makes them tougher than the donut-chomping fuck-wit that looked back at them out of the bathroom mirror that morning.

The first one went down hard, taking a jab to the nose that I hadn't actually expected to make contact, and a stamping kick down on the side of his knee. I heard, and felt, the crack as he went down, but his scream almost covered the approach of the second man. I turned just in time to watch Mackenzie's arm snake around his neck as she locked him into a choke-hold. It wasn't the quickest way to take a man down, but I couldn't fault her technique.

I kicked the screaming guard just hard enough to send him off to sleep and looked to Mackenzie as she disentangled herself from the now unconscious guard.

"What the hell was that?"

"Brazilian Jiu-Jitsu," she smiled up at me. "What? You think just because I'm a woman I should be cowering behind you? I rescued *you*, remember?"

I gave her a nodding shrug and looked down the hall. The closest side door led into another observation room. I scowled at it for ten seconds before Mackenzie said what I was already thinking, and we dragged the guards another hundred feet or so to what turned out to be a storage cupboard.

Neither one of the men were close to my height, but any clothes are better than none. My bare legs stuck out of the bottom of the stolen uniform like I was wearing a karate gi. Add into the mix that his shoes were far too small for me to bother with, and I both looked, and felt, like an idiot. Mackenzie, had none of these problems, shoving on a pair of stolen boots to go with her uniform; and the grin she wore as she looked me up and down made this more than apparent.

I snorted a laugh and then got to work. The guards weren't carrying guns, but both had a taser clipped to their belts. I stiffened in remembered pain and then took them both. I'd rather have had a decent Glock, but beggars can't be choosers.

"Do you know how to use those?" Mackenzie whispered, glancing up at me as she wound tape around the wrists of the second guard. Her confidence had left with her smile as she bound and gagged the guards. The tape was some kind of electrical tape that had been left on a shelf in the cupboard. The rest of the shelves were filled with cleaning supplies, so it had no business being in here. Maybe someone up there had finally decided they owed me some luck.

"Yes," I told Mackenzie in a low voice. "They're not much good past thirty feet or so, but something's going to be better than nothing."

I paused, looking her over. "We're going to get out of here, Mackenzie. We just need to be smart."

She nodded, glancing at the door. "Well, if we're going to be smart, we better figure out where we're going."

"Up," I said with a shrug. "From there we'll work it out. Do you know anything about this place?"

"Not much, only what they told me about the project, and then what I saw myself later on. I didn't have much access, only a couple of hallways, my own rooms, and the cafeteria."

"Anything you know might help. How many people are in here, any idea?"

"Janan told me they had almost a hundred, not counting the guards and support staff."

"Janan?" I asked her with a confused frown. "Afridi?"

She nodded and I grunted, busying myself with the belt as I clipped the tasers to it and chewed on what she'd said. She'd had her own level of access at some point, and she spoke of Afridi on first name terms. If she'd cooperated with them once then…

"Yeah, like you didn't beg when it came to it," I murmured.

"What?"

I gave her a look that was probably as guilty as I felt. "Nothing. Let's get going."

The hallway was clear which was both good and confusing.

"Didn't you say there were guards looking for you?" I asked.

"At least two or three, yes." Mackenzie sounded as confused as I was. "I don't think these are the same ones. They would have been behind us."

"Not that I'm complaining, but where are they then?"

Her shrug didn't do anything to reassure me.

The corridor was silent as we made our way along, moving as quietly as we could, slowing only when the passage turned.

The lift stood at the end of a small corridor; an aluminium and steel cage that was next to useless to us, with a CCTV camera on the ceiling to keep it company. I was under no illusions as to our chances of getting out of this place in one piece, regardless of what I'd told Mackenzie, but I wasn't about to gift-wrap and deliver myself to Afridi's goons in that thing.

Mackenzie carried on as I paused, dashing to a door close to the lift and tapping her key-card to the reader. It beeped, and she cracked the door wide enough to peer through, then glanced back at me with a grin.

"Stairs," she called in a hoarse whisper.

"Well that's a plus," said Turner, peering past me to the doorway. "Beats getting filled full of holes in that metal box, doesn't it?"

I ignored him while he laughed at himself. Turner never had a problem with finding his own jokes funny. Death hadn't changed him, apparently.

The staircase ran both up and down further than I could see and we'd barely started moving before our heads shot round at the sound of running from below.

"Go!" I said, but Mackenzie was already moving, running up the stairs faster than I could have managed with or without a bullet hole in my leg.

The steps were rough and cold on my bare feet but that was the least of my concerns. Whoever was coming up the stairs wasn't taking a leisurely stroll, and the pounding of the boots on the concrete made it clear these weren't lab-techs who were late for a meeting.

"Mr Carver," the voice was calm as it came over the speakers. "I see you've met Ms. Cartwright. I really would hate to have to hurt either of you. Please hand yourselves in. There really is no need for any unpleasantness."

"He's out of his goddamned gourd!" I muttered as we passed another floor.

Mackenzie said nothing, her head was low as she hauled herself up the stairs, relying on the rail as much as her legs to force herself up each step. We were both slowing, the weeks I'd spent chained to the frame had ruined most of the muscle I'd had, and the half-healed bullet wound throbbed with each step.

"This isn't going to work," I gasped, pulling a taser from my belt.

Mackenzie gasped beside me, bent double as she sucked the breaths in. "How many shots do those things have?"

"One each," I admitted. I didn't need her to reply. The odds weren't great and I knew it.

The guards were still coming and I crouched low as I readied the taser. Mackenzie shot me a look from where she knelt, her face creased in concentration.

"Don't freak out," she muttered between clenched teeth.

Flames erupted from the steps, roaring upwards until they met the bottom of the next flight. Even at this distance I staggered back from the heat. I couldn't see the guards, but I heard their cries of panic. I've said before my Pashto isn't that great. It's one of the childish things about us, or maybe it's just men, that we tend to learn the swear words in other languages before anything else. I couldn't be sure but I'm reasonably certain that the sudden burst of Pashto from the guards translated to, "Fuck that!"

I looked from the flames, to Mackenzie, to the thick frost that had coated the stairs beneath us. "What the hell was that?" I asked, but she was already running before I finished the sentence.

The fire guttered and died behind us before we made it up another two flights. The guards were still down there, following, but definitely not rushing about it.

"Seriously, what the fuck was that?" I demanded.

Mackenzie shrugged. "You stop bullets," she glanced at my thigh where the bulge of the bandage was visible through the stolen uniform. "Badly, apparently. I do fire."

There was no time for questions, the sound of boots on steps carried well in a concrete stairwell, and this time they were coming down to us from above. Mackenzie had long enough to give me a startled look as I grabbed at her with one hand, tapped the card to a reader, and dragged her through the door.

CHAPTER THIRTY-TWO

The hallway was dark as I pushed the door closed behind us but fluorescent lights in the ceiling were already flickering to life. The darkness was both good and bad, I knew. On the one hand, it meant this floor was quiet enough for the lights to turn off on their own; on the other, it meant that we would literally be leaving a blazing trail behind us. The one bit of good news was that there were no cameras in this corridor.

"Come on," I muttered, reaching for Mackenzie again.

"Don't grab at me," she snarled, snatching her hand away. "I'm not a bloody child."

I ignored that and started running. Of course, when I say running, I mean a lurching hobble. My leg had not appreciated the run up the stairs. The pain was sharp, stabbed with each step, and the bandage felt too warm and wet for my liking. I'd probably ripped the stitches.

I didn't have the patience for dealing with a civvy right then. I'd always hated it. It's one of the major reasons I didn't go into security, or close protection work, after the army. A life in the forces rewires your brain to a certain extent, you learn to put your emotions on a shelf whilst you get the job done. It doesn't matter if someone is being a prick, if the job doesn't get done then people die. You can bawl them out later. Civilians are unpredictable and emotional, two things that can get you killed in a heartbeat.

I slapped at the light-switch just before we passed through a set of double doors, plunging the hallway back into darkness. We hadn't been fast enough though, and before we'd gone ten feet, I saw the lights flicker back to life through the small windows in the doors.

"Shit!" Another minute or two and there might have been some question over which way we'd gone. As it was, the light from our hallway had shone through the small rectangles of glass towards the guards like a beacon, pointing out the way we'd fled.

"There is nowhere to run to, Mr Carver," Afridi's voice came over the speakers, echoing what I was thinking. It didn't help my mood that the bastard was right.

Fuck it. I dropped to a crouch, pulling both tasers and training them at the doors as I shuffled closer.

"Carver, what the—"

"Shut up!" I hissed back at her, not bothering to turn.

The doors parted as the guards wrenched them open and I was firing as soon as the figures emerged. Two needles erupted from the ends of the taser and flew the ten feet it took to bury themselves in the flesh of the first guard. I was already focusing on the second and firing before the distinctive *click-click-click* came from the first taser. The guards didn't have time to scream. The most either of them managed was a low moan from between clenched teeth as the electric pulses over-rode their nervous systems.

They were still writhing on the ground when Mackenzie gripped my arm.

"Carver, that's enough!" she ordered.

I blinked and took a deep breath, shaking myself. It had been a long time since I'd locked up like that. I moved quickly; searching the guards produced both cuffs and a gift from God—a pair of guns. They were nothing special, Glock 17s, or clones of it. I didn't have the time to inspect either of them, beyond checking that they were loaded, and the safeties were on.

It took the work of moments to have them both bound. I glanced once at Mackenzie. It would be better to kill them both—dead men don't tell tales—but she'd probably throw a fit. Another good reason not to work with civvies, they have odd ideas about what's important. Don't get me wrong, I'm no bloodthirsty murderer, but I'll do it if the occasion demands it. Right now, it would be easier, faster, and smarter, to kill both these guys than to tie them up.

I worked quickly, cuffing both men behind their backs, overlapping the cuffs so they were bound together. I tossed the keys along the hallway and debated gagging them but there was no time.

"Here," I handed the gun from the second guard to Mackenzie. "Do you know how to use one of these?"

She looked at it like it was a live snake, which more or less answered my question before she spoke.

"Look," I told her as she shook her head. "You'll only need it if things go tits up. Hold it like this." I showed her. "This is the safety, just hold it firmly and squeeze the trigger. You don't need to be a great shot, just point the noisy end at them and fire."

She took it without comment, I'll give her that much. She was no damsel in distress. This woman was made of barbed wire and rusted nails. Any other place or time and I'd be looking at her with different eyes. Unfortunately, we were probably going to get shot, so I needed my eyes elsewhere.

The second guard also had boots which fit me, and I pulled them on quickly before silencing them both with a quick kick. Tasers might shut your body down, but they don't do a lot to keep you quiet for long.

The hallway led through the complex in a winding mess lined with storerooms and what might have been empty living quarters. There was no time to really inspect them and, at this point, all we really needed was another set of stairs heading up.

I stopped dead as the lift came into sight and Mackenzie raced past me before lurching to a stop and looking back at me. "What?"

I shook my head. "This is no good."

She cuffed at her nose and sniffed between snatched breaths. "What are you talking about?"

"We're being herded. Afridi isn't an idiot and there have been cameras everywhere but this level. Even if we weren't being watched to start with, they sure as hell ought to have tracked us since we reached the stairs. They know exactly where we are."

"So… what?"

"So, they know where we're going and, sooner or later, we're going to run right into a full squad of Afridi's men."

"So, what are you suggesting? We hide? I can't see that working."

I shook my head. "No, you're right. Hiding in a closed complex like this won't help us at all. The only way out of here is up, and that's exactly where Afridi will be expecting us to go."

She frowned at me. "But we have to go up to get out of here."

"We do," I nodded. "But that doesn't mean we have to do it on our own."

"I don't understand," she admitted.

"Not here." I tapped the card to a reader and motioned her into a storeroom.

"Nice…" Johnson sniggered as she followed me in. I gave him the finger behind her back and pulled the door close to the frame, but didn't close it.

"You were let out of the cells, weren't you?" I asked. "I mean, you had some level of freedom, right?"

She nodded, giving me a guarded look.

"Did you see any others, down in the cells? We can't have been the only ones still down there."

"No," she said in a quiet voice. "We weren't but, Carver, you need to understand what this place does to people. It breaks them. That's the whole point. Janan and Elias, that's what they built this place to do—to drive people mad."

"What the hell would be the point of that?"

"That's where they think these powers come from. Didn't Elias ever talk to you?"

I nodded, chewing on a lip as I thought. "Okay, so how many others are down there?"

"I have no idea," she admitted. "I only ever met two others aside from you. The first one, Janan burned to death in front of me."

247

"Why?" The question crept out before I could stop it.

"To see if I would be able to put the fire out," she muttered through clenched teeth. She looked away for a moment and I inwardly kicked myself for asking.

"Well that was smooth, John," Johnson told me from the corner. "No wonder you're so good with the ladies."

He grinned back at me as I glared at him, silently telling him to go fuck himself. If he was just a hallucination, I hoped maybe he could hear me.

"And the other?" I prompted Mackenzie.

She shuddered as she looked back at me. "He was broken, completely gone. All he wanted was to die."

"Was he…?" I trailed off, not having the words.

"Like me?" she finished for me. "Yes, sort of. He had these things that came out of his skin, like smoke but somehow solid at the same time."

"Well then, let's go and pay him a visit and see if he has any friends." I reached for the door.

Mackenzie stared at me. "Are you out of your fucking mind?"

"Probably," I admitted. "That's what Afridi wanted, after all. Let's go and give it to him."

"*What?*"

"The other prisoners. Let's let them out."

She looked at me like I had lost it. "Carver, we can't do that. I mean, if even one of them has powers like me… We can't let that loose on the world."

"I'm not letting them loose on the world, Mackenzie," I told her with a cold smile. "I'm letting them loose on Afridi. As for the world, well the world can look after itself."

The lift was made for cargo, built to hold fork-lifts and pallets. A camera looked down on us as I punched a button and then smiled up into its lens. Mackenzie shook her head in mock despair for a moment, and then reached up to slam the butt of the gun into the lens, showering us both in glass and plastic.

"You know, Roasties," Turner said, leaning against the wall of the lift. "I could grow to like this girl. Try not to fuck it up, eh? You've got a bit of a history and it's the little disappointments that can really stay with a person. Forgetting birthdays, showing up late, letting them get shot in the head…"

The lift motors whined as we descended, and I fingered the gun, flexing my hand around the grip. There had to be a real response to us at some point. So far, we'd blundered into a handful of guards who offered no real resistance to us. The real danger here would be growing complacent.

Mackenzie pressed herself back against the side of the lift as it shuddered to a halt and the doors parted. The hallway beyond was empty, but then I'd expected it to be. We were going in the opposite direction to where Afridi thought we should be going, or at least, that was the hope.

I leaned out of the lift doors just far enough to spot the camera mounted above it. It was an older model and a quick yank ripped it and the cables free of the wall. I shot Mackenzie a smirk as I stepped back into the cargo-lift and stabbed another button, this one a couple of floors above us.

"What are you doing?" she asked, narrowing her eyes.

"I want to just throw them off the scent a little," I explained. "They'd have to be idiots not to be trying to track us with the cameras by now."

Three floors later and after a spate of minor vandalism, we were back on the bottom level. I had only the roughest of guesses that this was where we would find the cells, and we weren't disappointed.

Our footsteps thumped along the hallway as we ran, the sound of our boots echoing in the silence. There was no time for stealth. Moving silently in boots requires you to move incredibly slowly, and Afridi already knew we were loose. We had a horde to unleash.

CHAPTER THIRTY-THREE

We found the stairs first. What I had planned was balanced right on the line between dangerous, and just plain stupid. Working our way through the maze of hallways to the emergency stairway, and propping the door open, worked to bring the plan back from the brink of complete insanity, but only by half an inch or so. All in all, there were close to twenty occupied cells on this level and the floor below. There seemed no order to the placement, some spread out, others clustered together in groups of four or five. It probably came down to nothing more scientific than dumb luck, and how long Afridi's little experiments survived.

Mackenzie stood in the doorway and waved me closer. I didn't need to cover the distance to see the horror on her face.

"There's one in here," she nodded at the doorway. "Are you sure about this? I'm still not sure this is a good idea, Carver."

I looked past her into the observation room. "Well we'll just have to see, won't we?"

She shook her head. "I can't go in there, Carver. I just can't do it."

I've seen the look that was on her face before, on the faces of more people than I can count over the years. It was a broken expression, the look someone gets when they are forced into situations the mind was never meant to cope with.

I saw it last on a demolitions expert in Helmand Province. We'd located an IED near a major checkpoint just outside Camp Bastion. God only knows how it got placed without us spotting the bastards when they set it up. It was a fluke that we saw it at all really. We were on the way back from a recce and just happened to be looking the right way at the right time.

Explosive Ordnance Disposal had shown up pretty quick, but the first guy out of the Mastiff looked like he'd been pulled from a sick-bed. He didn't just look ill; his skin was like ashes. I watched his hands shake as his team talked to him, trying to bring him down. Eventually they got him to sit inside the truck whilst they dealt with the IED without him. I only found out later on what the problem was. He'd lost half his team because of a bad call. They'd been working on a massive IED on the Helmand-Kandahar highway, the kind that will rip even a Mastiff in half. Against all the odds, they'd made the damned thing safe for collection—no small task considering how these things are thrown together. IEDs might be built from a junk and chemical cocktail, but they're solid gold as far as the intel guys are concerned. He'd gone to water the desert when the blast hit. Three men killed in an instant, gone before they even knew what had gone wrong. And the only reason he'd survived was because he was taking a piss.

That EOD guy hadn't been scared for himself. In a way I don't think he'd even been scared of actually making another mistake. He'd been scared of the situation, of standing face to face with possibility itself, and looking into its dark eyes.

That fear was dripping from Mackenzie. Whatever was in this cell it was something she was truly terrified of. Probably not the poor bastard locked up in there, but maybe the level to which he'd been taken. Afridi was in the business of breaking minds and, by the look on her face, I knew it was *that* she couldn't bear to face. Maybe it reminded her how close she'd come, how far she might have fallen. Or maybe she was scared she hadn't finished falling yet.

I gave her arm a quick squeeze, and slipped through the door to find an observation room identical to the others I'd already seen, right down to the camera filming through the glass. I paused next to the tripod and shifted the lens down until it was filming the desk.

I leaned in towards the glass, trying to make sense of what I was seeing. The man was strapped into the same kind of frame I had been, though without the torso restraint I'd had for some reason. He looked to be about thirty or so; sallow skin sporting a tattoo that ran the length of an arm too wasted to show it properly.

The guy had been in here for a while, the facial hair alone showed that. Blood ran down over his lip and dripped down his beard until it met the congealed mess on his chest. It took me a moment to realise he'd gnawed through his own lip.

His hair was cropped short but was growing untidy, and I wondered if he'd had a shaven head when they took him. I watched him in silence for a good two minutes before I made a move for the door.

He let out a soul-searing howl that sounded loud to me even through the glass and I pulled my hand back from the card reader set next to the door. He thrashed in the restraints, throwing himself left and right and then... he *phased*.

I can't think of a better way to describe it. It was like he shuddered and split, until there were three of him occupying the same space, but somehow almost transparent as he threw himself against the straps. I shook my head at the sight him, rubbing my eyes as I watched.

"Well, shit. That's a new one on me!"

I glanced over at Johnson as he peered through the glass. He ignored me, watching the captive with interest. Pearson looked up at me from where he was curled into a ball by Johnson's feet, staring at me with the same terrified, accusing, expression he always wore. I hated Pearson. He creeped me the fuck out.

The door thunked as the locks released, a sound I'd never heard when I was on the other side of the glass. It hissed as it swung open and I slipped through the gap.

The howling cut off as I entered and the man froze, watching me in silence through narrowed eyes.

"Easy," I said, holding out my hands the same way you would with a spooked horse.

He licked at his bloody lips, cocking his head like a curious bird. "What do you want?"

I stepped further into the room as he watched me.

"You're not one of them, are you?" he asked after a moment.

I glanced down at the uniform. "No, mate. I'm like you, just trying to get out of here."

"Nobody gets out. Nobody." He laughed, but his voice cracked as the pain leaked through. His laughter was suddenly too high, too broken, and it drifted off into something I couldn't put a name to. Something jagged and splintered that held the ruins of his sanity.

"Let me go, please?" he asked then, his voice low and plaintive.

"What would you do if I did?"

"Die."

I blinked. His admission was so raw and heartfelt that, for a moment, I had no words.

"What about Afridi, or Elias? The people that kept you here?"

He pulled his torn and bloody lips away from his teeth. The smile was close to a snarl and grew more feral the longer I looked. "They can come with me. I'll take them with me."

I nodded, watching his eyes track me as I made my way around the frame. The truth of it was he was barely human, the animal in him so close to the surface that he was almost lost under it completely. His mind was broken, and I knew for damned sure I didn't want him loose with us anywhere nearby. His restraints were simple Velcro cuffs, but wrapped around each wrist and ankle three times or more, so he had no chance of working himself free. With even one loose, it wouldn't take him long to escape.

He held still while I pulled the cuff apart; at least until I stopped. His wrist was still bound but I doubted it would take him more than a couple of minutes to pull it open. He gave me a look as I stepped back, then he frowned at his wrist.

"You said you'd let me out!" He gave a tug on the cuff and his cry of frustration became a howl of rage as he wrenched at it.

The Velcro gave slightly, making that tearing paper sound, and then he was thrashing about again, breaking into that split, shuddering image that made my eyes hurt just to look at. Not that I was looking. I ran. Bullet wound be damned, I was out of there.

I couldn't tell you how long it took to let them out. We went down to the lower level first—I didn't want to run the risk of bumping into the crazy bastard I'd just set free, and chances were he'd be heading upwards. I left the cuffs a little tighter on the rest of them, they could work themselves free, but each of their minds were as broken as the last. They wore their abilities as openly as their madness, things that would have made me question my own sanity if I'd been anywhere else. It's a strange day when the guy who talks to dead people begins to think he's the normal one, but after what I'd seen I just wanted to run. We didn't need much time to get to a safe distance, but I wasn't about to risk it.

We huddled down in the darkness just inside the door of an observation room. The door wasn't as secure as the one into the cell itself, but neither of us made the move to seek shelter in there. Having the key to get out didn't make a difference, it was still a cell and neither of us wanted to be locked in again.

The noises started within minutes. Cackling, moans, and a high-pitched laughter that turned to screams far too quickly. I couldn't tell if they were killing each other, or just howling at the walls. If all went well, they'd find the stairs and head upwards soon enough. Afridi had spent millions on this place, Christ, maybe it was billions. He'd invested the wealth of nations into finding a way to break these people and set their power free. Now all of those broken shards were coming to find him, seeking retribution in his flesh.

I almost pitied him.

Almost.

Mackenzie was a mess. The sounds from the hall pushed her over the edge and she curled up against the wall behind balled fists. I sat there like a useless idiot, watching her silently sob until the awkwardness, and Johnson's whispered urging, forced me to move.

My touch on her shoulder might as well have burned her from the way she flinched, but I didn't let go.

"We're going to get out, Mackenzie," I whispered. "We will. We'll get out."

She didn't pull away. She didn't move at all, other than to stiffen. I kept repeating the promise like a mantra, until the words lost their meaning and just became as soothing a sound as I could manage in the murky observation room. Eventually the tension bled from her and she leaned into me, taking comfort where it could be found. I held her, staring into the blackness of the room until it shifted and Johnson leaned in close to my face.

"Don't fuck this up, Carver."

CHAPTER THIRTY-FOUR

We found the first body before we heard any gunshots. The stairway looked like an abattoir; the blood and gore almost enough to make me gag. Mackenzie didn't seem overly bothered as she picked her way through the mess, but maybe she'd already gone numb to it. More than likely, I reasoned, she'd seen worse. If she'd been nursing for any period in Afghanistan, she'd definitely seen worse.

While she was stitching people back together, I'd been killing them. I've killed a fair number of people. When you get right down to it, it's part of the job, but there's a level of unreality to it when you're at a distance with a rifle. Even when you kill up close there's a way to hide what you're doing from yourself. A way to justify it all. It's for the mission, or it's protecting civilians, or more often—it's protecting the boys. We'll do almost anything to look after the idiot stood beside us, sweating their balls off in the desert for some stupid reason, usually involving suits in London.

There's a damned good reason for all the rules, regulations, and ritual in the forces. A lot of it is so we hide what we're actually doing from ourselves. It's the same reason for basic training. You break a man down to their base parts and refashion them into a soldier, into a person who can go where they're sent, jump when they're told, and kill on command. It's like a muscle-memory that bypasses thought and speaks directly to the finger on the trigger. The uniforms, the ranks, rituals, regulations and all the rest of the bullshit are just that—bullshit, but it's a necessary bullshit needed to convince us that we're doing a job, that we're protecting, that we're not just butchers.

Whoever had done this to the poor bastard of a technician wasn't even a butcher, they were an animal. I could see how the tech had tried to run. How he'd been chased down and torn apart. He'd been shredded, like wet paper.

The mess stuck to our boots, there was no way to avoid it. Our footprints joined those left by the others who'd already gone through, forming a lurid red streak that wound up the stairwell. The tracks of madness, a parade of insanity that we'd sent charging through the gore to paddle in the blood.

The gunshots were distant, muffled, echoes that carried down the stairwell. I glanced at Mackenzie, but she seemed oblivious to it, blocking it out, I hoped. It probably didn't make me the nicest of people I suppose, but I needed her. I didn't know what she'd been through in here, but I could guess based on the little she had told me, and what they'd thrown at me. I knew they'd broken her to some extent, but I needed her help. If she cracked on me now, I was probably fucked.

"What are you playing at, Roasties?" asked Johnson as he appeared in front of me. I've never seen him appear before, usually he would speak and I'd to turn my head to find him standing beside me, or something similar. This time he emerged from a swirling black mist and crouched down into a defensive position with his weapon. I stepped past him. Now really wasn't the time for conversations with dead people.

"Roasties, this is a bad idea."

"How do you mean?" I asked, looking back at him.

Shit, I swore silently to myself, glancing back at Mackenzie. I'd answered him and there was no way she hadn't heard it.

"You're wasting a tactical advantage, mate. You should be in the lifts already."

I paused on a landing, biting on the inside of my cheek for a moment as I thought about it. He was right, the stairs gave us time to hear anyone coming, but really nowhere to hide. If a real response came at us, we'd had it. The lifts all had cameras around them, probably in them too, but this game came down to speed, surprise, and control.

Combat becomes a hot mess faster than most people might think. For all the training and planning, all it takes is someone to do something unexpected, for someone else not to react in time, and you're up to your neck in trouble. It can happen in moments.

Letting the captives out to cause chaos had taken a lot of the control out of Afridi's hands. I doubted anyone was still sitting back, calmly watching the CCTV monitors, and tracking our movements. By now they were dealing with twenty howling maniacs with abilities that made stopping bullets look like a party trick. They would be stretched to their limits, and maybe even close to panic, but it wouldn't last long. While we were creeping up the stairs, Afridi was probably restoring order. A howling maniac is intimidating, but they usually lose in a fight against a bullet.

"We're going to have to make a move for the lifts," I told Mackenzie. She gave me a startled look and frowned.

"We need to take advantage of the time we've got," I explained.

She nodded, and then glanced around the stairwell, her eyes narrowing. "Who were you talking to?"

Shit, this was not what we needed. She had to trust me, and there aren't many who will trust someone who takes advice from their imaginary friends. "No one, just thinking out loud, I guess."

"You're lying." It wasn't a question. She folded her arms.

I sighed, pinching at the bridge of my nose. "Look, Mackenzie. Now really isn't the time for this."

"I saw you, Carver," she began, her voice too loud on the concrete stairway. She fell silent, glancing around us with guilty expression.

"I saw you," she hissed in a hoarse whisper. "You looked at something, or someone. You listened, and then you spoke. Don't treat me like a child, and don't lie to me. I've been lied to enough in my life to spot it."

"You said it yourself, Mackenzie," I said with another sigh. "This place breaks people. I was broken when I got here, they just smashed the pieces up a bit more. I was in the army. I lost some good friends. Sometimes I still see the boys from the squad, is all."

I had no idea what the expression on her face meant. She looked at me for a few moments, in a silence that dragged on as her gaze held me. Finally, she nodded with a shrug. "The lifts?"

I nodded stiffly and followed her, completely certain that was not the response I'd expected.

The next floor led out onto a level that looked to hold laboratories and offices. A red light spun on the ceiling in a silent alarm as we made our way across the tiled floor. I saw movement once, a woman in a lab coat ducking out of sight from behind the windows that lined the hallway. Her face had told me enough to know she was no threat. The look of terror had been etched deep. If this was *Jurassic Park*, then we were the velociraptors.

"Some kind of PTSD?" Mackenzie asked suddenly. Her voice sounded too loud in the silence, and I grimaced as much at the noise as I did the question.

"Something like that," I grunted. "They died, I didn't. They blame me."

"Too bloody right," Turner spat. I didn't need to look around for him—half the squad were making their way along the hallway with us.

"What happened?" she asked, her voice quieter this time.

I sighed, giving her a long look that didn't seem to have any effect. "We were cornered. Well, captured, really."

"Bloody disaster is what it was," Johnson muttered from behind her.

I bit my lip at the interruption she wouldn't have heard. "They were working their way through us, shooting them one by one in front of me."

"Oh my God!" her eyes went wide. "What happened to you?"

"The bullet stopped," I admitted. It felt good to talk about it with someone who didn't instantly think I was crazy. "In mid-air, right in front of me."

"Oh, it was a neat trick, don't get me wrong," Turner put in. He poked at the bullet-hole in his forehead. "Your timing was well shit though, Roasties. I mean, it wouldnae have hurt you to decide you were Harry bloody Potter a wee bit sooner, would it?"

She fell silent at that, though she watched me as we walked, making our way past the labs and offices. She was probably trying to decide if I was going to snap. If I was an asset or a liability. To be honest, I was probably both.

A haunted expression slowly grew on her face as we walked. She glanced at the windows often. She knew this place, that much was obvious. Something had happened here and by her expression I suspected it was more something she'd done, rather than something that had been done to her. I didn't ask about it. We didn't have time, it was none of my business, and some things are best left buried—it's keeping the bastards in the ground that seems to be where my trouble is.

We moved quickly, there was no point in being subtle now that at least one person had seen us. I heard doors slamming twice, but we didn't see anyone until we reached the lift. The smell of the blood and gunshots reached us before we even saw the bodies. Half a dozen guards lay strewn across the hallway, broken and twisted next to the splintered remnants of the door leading out to a stairwell, but it was the figure in the wall that stopped me cold.

The body was half-encased in the substance of the wall itself, as if he'd been thrown against the surface and he'd somehow sunk into wet cement. One leg hung almost fully free of the wall's embrace, with his pelvis and lower torso completely encased. An arm reached, clawing at the air in a desperate, silent plea, beside a face that spoke of a pain I could only imagine.

"Christ," Mackenzie whispered. "Elias!"

I leapt back, snapping the gun up as his eyes opened, which was better than letting out the girly scream I'd kept locked behind clenched teeth. His pained gasp was followed by a bloody, hacking, cough as his eyes locked on Mackenzie and he sucked in another ragged breath.

"I'm sorry, Mackenzie," he managed. "About everything. I can't tell you how sorry."

"Shhh…" She stepped in, reaching for his cheek but stopped herself, biting her lip and glancing down at her feet for a moment as her face grew hard. She ran her gaze along the length of him, taking in the blood on his lips, and the bruises on his face until she sighed and her eyes softened. "It doesn't matter now," she said, shaking her head.

I don't have that level of compassion. Sometimes I wonder if I ever did. She turned and gave me a hard look, glancing down at the gun. Her meaning was clear enough. We couldn't spare the ammunition really, but even I'm not that cold.

He looked at the gun for a moment before he met my gaze. The smile was small, but it said enough.

"Get out if you can, Mr Carver," he wheezed. "Janan deserves to keep the things we created to himself."

I nodded. I'm not above granting a man's dying wish when I can.

There are a few ways to muffle a gunshot if you really need to. A pillow works reasonably well, so does firing through water. I didn't have either of those to hand, but a gun pressed hard into flesh will do the same job to an extent. It wasn't perfect by any means, but it was the best I could do.

Mackenzie didn't look away as I did it. I suppose I'd expected her to, but she watched, holding his gaze until the end.

"I want to kill him," she said then.

I frowned for a moment before I spoke. "Afridi?"

She nodded, pulling her gaze from Elias's body. "He needs to die, Carver. I've spent my life learning how to help the wounded and the sick, but some things you simply can't cure. He's a cancer on the world, and I'm going to burn him out."

"Now this," Turner said, grinning at me. "This, I can get on board with."

I sighed as I pressed the button for the lift. Between Mackenzie and the visitors, I was completely outnumbered.

CHAPTER THIRTY-FIVE

I crouched low in the lift, pressed close to the wall by the doors. It wasn't much cover, but it was the best I had. Mackenzie huddled down in her corner, eyes fixed on the lights of the lift buttons. It was only the broadest of assumptions that the lift would even take us all the way to the top floor and deliver us to a way out. This was a passenger lift, but there was nothing that said it had to go all the way up. I already regretted not taking the cargo lift, but that would have meant going back down to the lowest levels to find it, and I wasn't about to risk that.

"You ready, Roasties?" Johnson stood in the centre of the lift, tooled up with an FN Minimi machine gun. He looked ridiculous, with the ammunition belt draped over one arm and hanging down to the floor, like an actor from a bad 80s action film.

I shook my head with a tight grin and focused on the door as the lift slowed. This was probably going to go one of two ways. I didn't move until the door had opened fully. If I'm honest I'd expected the bullets to start flying long before then. Crouching low was the only thing that would have saved us; people tend to shoot at chest height.

As it was, the door opened onto an empty hallway leading off to the right, and silence. Not what I'd expected, and everything I'd hoped for. I leaned far enough to make sure the hallway was truly empty, and that there were no surprises on the left, and then dove out in a low roll, ignoring the pain in my thigh, gun trained and ready.

Mackenzie watched me until I relaxed and then let out a snort.

I gave her a black look as she stepped past me. "What?"

"Nothing," she said, still laughing. "Come on, Rambo. Let's get out of here."

Johnson let out a snigger as he stepped past me. "Rambo!"

It took me until we were almost at the end of the hallway to notice that the red emergency lights were no longer flashing. I frowned up at one as we passed. Did that mean that the escape we'd engineered had been dealt with? Or was Afridi just controlling the flow of information, averting a panic on this floor? Or maybe, the damned lights had just got on his nerves and he'd turned them off.

Mackenzie followed close behind me, moving when I moved, seeking cover where I indicated. I doubt she'd thank me for this, the nurses I've met have tended to have a low opinion of military types, or maybe just a low opinion of me, but she had a real knack for it. If you'd have given me six weeks I could have made a decent soldier out of her.

The first resistance we encountered was panicked and ugly, a lone guard that blundered through a set of doors and found my bullet before he knew what was going on. I didn't feel bad about it; he only had a taser, no gun, but his radio was more dangerous than any weapon he could wield.

I ignored the look Mackenzie gave me and went to check the body. I needn't have bothered, I knew I'd hit him in the head, but the amount of people who still manage to reach for a radio after they've been shot might surprise you. Some people just don't have the decency to die quietly.

"Did you absolutely have to do that?" Mackenzie hissed at me.

"Yes," I shrugged. "I did."

She opened her mouth to argue but I cut her off with a look. "We're not going to be able to sneak out of here, Mackenzie. You know that. If shooting a poor bastard like this means we don't have to cope with another fifteen chasing us down then I'll do it, every time. You can hate me for it later."

Her mouth might have closed but her eyes told me that she'd do just that.

The doors were good and thick, which I suppose was one thing to be thankful for, but I would have given a lot for a silenced weapon. The gunshot had probably been muffled but we were already on borrowed time.

We moved as quickly as we dared, shifting into a run when the hallway was straight and clear. The place felt like a hospital—sterile, white, walls that all looked the bloody same. The rooms we passed seemed to have no sense of order. Store-rooms sat next to medical bays that smacked of triage and intake, which then sat next to empty rooms with no discernible purpose. Either this place was designed to be busier than it was, or it had gone operational in a hurry, and they'd never really caught up with themselves.

I glanced back at Mackenzie, meeting her gaze as we slowed.

"What is it?" she whispered.

"I don't have a clue where we're going," I admitted. "We could be heading out as easily as we could be heading further in."

A set of doors crashed open further along the hallway, and I yanked Mackenzie through a side door as gunfire tore the wall to shreds. I'm normally critical of poor shooting but, right now, I wasn't about to complain.

"Jesus wept!" Johnson shouted over the gunfire. "Would you look at the state of this?"

He had a point. The guards had some kind of fully-automatic weapon and were firing in long bursts. This is usually a complete waste of time; your aim goes to hell after the first two or three shots. The only thing they were really accomplishing was keeping us trapped in the room.

I peered out long enough to snap off a couple of shots, more to stop them moving in closer than any real attempt to hit them.

"You stay there and you're dead, mate," Johnson advised as he stood in the hall.

"You think I don't bloody know that?" I snapped.

"Carver?" Mackenzie's voice was level, but too controlled to be anything other than terrified. "Carver, talk to the real people here for a minute. What do we do?"

Shit, Rule Three was in bloody pieces by now, and she'd seen me twice!

"I'm open to ideas!" I snapped back at her.

"I thought you said you stopped a bullet?"

"Yes! I stopped one!" I stabbed a finger in the direction of the guards. "Does that sound like one bullet to you?"

"Sometimes, mate," Johnson muttered, suddenly crouched beside my ear. "You're just so bloody negative."

"Sexual frustration," Turner put in, picking at something in his teeth. "I'll bet that's what it is. How long's it been, Carver?"

"Jesus Christ," I risked another glance out into the hallway. "Just kill me."

"Come on, Johnson," Turner said, glancing down at me in disgust. "We can take 'em."

"Best idea I've heard all week," Johnson grinned.

There have been two or three times in the last few years when I've genuinely wondered if I'm losing my mind. Watching the hallucination of two dead people standing in that hallway, with improbably large guns, and blasting imaginary bullets at the guards as I burst out laughing probably tops that list.

"Carver!" Mackenzie screamed.

I huddled down inside the doorway, as bullets ripped holes in the concrete wall, and put my head in my hands. My body started to shake, tiny shivers at first, rising to full shudders just shy of a convulsion.

I was lost.

I was done.

The stress of being taken, of the torture, and then finally getting bloody free of that cell only to end up pinned down in here was suddenly all too much. I balled my fists and ground them against my eyes, acutely aware of how much like Pearson I must look. I'd failed her.

I'd failed them all.

We were going to die. Just as soon as they got tired of shooting holes in the walls and came down here to get us, we were dead.

The pressure grew, and I felt a searing pain as the stress found the crack in my sanity and ripped it wide. Voices poured out—my squad, my visitors, friends I'd pushed away, people at home with their sad eyes and pity—it all came roaring out and engulfed me.

I snapped.

"Will you all just *shut* the *fuck up!*"

The force of my fury flew out of me in a wave, throwing Mackenzie back across the floor, ripping the door from its hinges, and hurling it out into the hall.

I didn't stop to think. Thinking leads to doubts, and this really wasn't the time for doubts. Legs that seemed intent on ignoring the small sensible voice screaming at the back of my mind, carried me out into the hallway—and then my hands shot forward again.

This time the force was no wave, it was a battering ram. It blasted into the press of Afridi's guards, a visible distortion to the air as it hit, and tore through them like leaves before a hurricane.

Johnson lowered the FN Minimi, smoke still pouring from the muzzle as he surveyed the mess of guards scattered across the hallway. "Damn it, Roasties. Why didn't you just do that in the first place?"

I grabbed at Mackenzie and ran.

Somewhere behind me I could hear Turner as he made his way through the tangle of fallen guards. "Take that ya feckers! Yer just lucky I didnae get to you first!"

*

I crashed through another set of doors, leaving the mad bastard behind me. The fact that Turner was just another part of me, and that I might actually be the one who was insane, wasn't important right now.

The corridor widened as we turned a corner and joined another hallway. I threw a grin back at Mackenzie and pointed at the floor.

"What?" she frowned as we ran, looking at me with a curious mix of confusion and concern. I didn't have the time or the breath to explain, but the twin lines of rubber and dirt were as good as any signpost.

Pain throbbed through my leg, working in concert with the ache in my chest, to create a symphony of hurt that ran in time to my footsteps. My leg was the worst, what had once been a dull ache had been abused until it had grown to a fiery agony. I ran in a lurching hobble, one hand pressed to the wound. The fabric of the uniform felt hot and wet, even through the bandage. I needed time to look at my leg, but time was something we simply didn't have.

"Carver!" a voice roared down the hallway behind us and I twisted, almost falling as my thigh gave way.

A figure stood just inside a distant set of double doors. Even at this distance I could sense the fury that emanated from him, rolling off him in waves. The doors burst open behind him as a black mass of guards rushed to catch up with him.

"Carver, you bastard. I'm going to kill you slowly!" his voice rose from a shout to a hoarse scream as he launched into a sprint.

I levelled the gun slowly, taking my time with it.

It wasn't even that hard of a shot, though I'd much rather have had a rifle for this range. Afridi was less than two hundred feet away and closing fast. I squeezed off a round and swore as it buried itself into the wall. Even allowing for the drop it should have easily taken him in the chest.

I fired again, and again. With every shot Afridi staggered, jerking a hand forward with a grunt, and every shot was taking chunks out of the wall or the floor.

Somehow the bastard was deflecting the bullets.

I saw the snarl on his face as he grew closer, watched him throw his hands down towards the ground as his fists burst into flame. His eyes were savage. This was never going to end peacefully, but there are fights and then there is carnage. This wasn't going to be a normal fight.

The cry came from behind me. A scream that was more feral than anything I've ever heard, made all the more terrible by the fact I knew it came from human lips. The kind of sound that bypasses the ears and speaks directly to the legs, urging them to get you the hell out of there. I turned but I already knew what I would see.

267

Mackenzie had cracked.

Elias and Afridi had forced open the cracks in our minds, burrowing down into our grip on reality to draw power to our gifts. But Mackenzie had let go. She had torn the fissure wide and power surged through her as her mind shattered.

She glared at Afridi with utter contempt for the length of a snatched breath, and then she ripped the flames from him. That's the only way I could describe it. She made a savage clawing motion in the air before her, and the flames blazing around his fists guttered and died.

"You wanted me to find my fire, Janan!" she shrieked as flames curled up through her fingers, wrapping around her arms like ivy embracing a house.

It wasn't a scream, or even a shout. There was no control in this woman. She wasn't furious, she *was* the fury. She was rage incarnate, and the flames writhed and clung to her as they revelled in her power. I backed up until I hit the wall, watching wide-eyed as she faced Afridi. I wasn't scared. I was shitting myself.

"You made me into this… *thing!*" she spat. "You wanted me to burn. You wanted me to call the fire? Then taste it, Janan. Feast on it, and fucking choke!"

Flames rose around her, leaving her clothes, her hair and her skin untouched. I could feel the heat on my face, but clearly it didn't touch her. Afridi snapped something over his shoulder at the guards as panic swept over his face. I saw the rifles level at her as I reached for my own power, but I already knew it was useless. I was spent. The force I'd thrown earlier had taken all I had.

This was how it would all end. In a hail of bullets in some forgotten corner of Afghanistan, or Pakistan, or wherever the hell they'd taken us.

I missed the first click, but I heard the others. Firing pins striking unresponsive bullets as Afridi's men pulled triggers on guns that now did nothing. The sound of their panic was lost in her laughter. It rose, cold and terrible, like the broken laughter at a funeral, as hysteria carves a channel for tears.

"Bullets need a spark, Janan," she whispered, in a voice that somehow still managed to carry. "I *own* the fire!"

The guards broke.

First one man, and then the others, turned and bolted back through the doors. There was no thought to their flight—this was a primal terror and I shared it as I watched on in horror. She was broken. She was what I would become, unless there was a way back. Unless there was something to cling to.

Johnson and Turner stood with Pearson as they watched me, eyes soft as I finally understood it all. We are each of us insane. Maybe there is no true sanity. All any of us have is the control we cling to, and any one of us can be swept away.

She took two steps before Afridi fled, running as if the hounds of hell themselves were chasing him. Perhaps one hound was, but all it would take was one lucky shot and she would be finished.

I don't know what I was thinking. She was on a precipice. If she wasn't brought back, even just half a step, she was lost. And right then, right there in the middle of this nightmare, I realised I couldn't let her fall. I couldn't face this alone.

I grabbed at her arm as she made to follow. She snapped around, her face terrible as she glared back at me, twin flames rising up from her eyes and cheeks. I reached out and pulled her close, ignoring the heat as I sought her lips. Her fire burned, but I didn't care. For the length of three frantic heartbeats I kissed her. Until she staggered back and looked at me with wild, darting eyes.

"What the fuck was that?" she demanded.

"I had to do something. You were losing it. Besides," I shrugged, "it seemed to work."

She glared at me, anger showing all the more clearly in her eyes now that her flames had gone.

"I can't just let him go, Carver," she admitted, glancing back along the hallway. "Not after all of this. Not after Armond, and everyone else he's done this to."

I reached for her shoulders, ignoring her as she flinched. "We can't go after him, Mackenzie. Not now. He's probably got more guards around him already. Then there's the others we let free. Who knows where they are by now? There are just too many unknowns, and neither of us is in any condition for a fight."

She glanced down at my leg, at the fabric of the uniform clinging to the wound it covered, and sank down into herself.

"Fine," she sighed. "So how the hell do we get out of here?"

I grinned. "That, at least, I think I can do." I pointed down at the floor.

She frowned me, and then peered down at the dark lines of dirt on the tiles.

"Rubber?" she guessed, after a moment. "From a trolley or something, bringing in supplies?"

I grinned as her smile grew. "And so?"

"So, they'll lead to a loading dock, and a way out!" She grabbed for my hand, almost dragging me along.

The hallways were silent, a stillness made somehow more pronounced by the noise we made as we crashed through doors and hurtled along the passageways. Our pace wasn't just fuelled by a desire to be out of here. Afridi would be back, and he wouldn't come alone. Twice I paused at some half-heard sound, both times Mackenzie tugged at me until we were running again.

It hadn't escaped me that the dark marks and scuffs could just as easily lead to where the supplies were going as they could to the loading dock. Even odds weren't the best, but I've leapt at a lot worse before now.

A burst of gunfire in the distance pulled us both to a stop and we froze, ears straining against the silence that followed. I fought against Mackenzie's tug as she urged me on, and turned towards the faint glow of a computer screen shining through a window into the hallway.

The glass was smoked, almost tinted, and the glow was slight. I'd never have seen it if we hadn't stopped to listen to the gunfire. I pressed an ear against the door for a minute and then tapped the card to the reader.

The security room was empty. A bank of monitors sat against one wall, with a half-eaten meal abandoned on the desk. I stepped around an open cabinet door and the Kevlar vests that had spilled out onto the floor, and touched one finger to the food. It was still warm, but only barely.

"Someone left in a hurry," Mackenzie muttered.

I grunted and examined the monitors. The CCTV footage ran throughout the complex, and scenes of carnage filled two of the screens before I even began fiddling with the controls. The captives had made it further up than I could have hoped. The mag-locked doors simply weren't designed to hold back that kind of force. By cycling through the cameras, I could trace their progress upwards through the facility.

"Found them," I muttered. I watched three guards working their way backwards along a corridor. For all my mockery of their skills, they looked to have had some military training, effecting a fighting retreat as they leapfrogged each other's positions.

Their bullets were having little effect, and the frantic waving of the guards combined with their soundless shouts as they scrambled back towards the camera. The figure was a blur at the farthest limits of the screen, charging against the retreating men. The image blurred as he moved, distorting as his form seemed to shudder and fracture, multiple images occupying the same place at once as he ran through a storm of bullets that didn't touch him.

He shifted again, his image shuddering as he covered thirty feet in an instant. The guards stumbled back, falling over themselves as he laid about him with arms and fists that passed through flesh, sending gore spattering over the walls.

The footage was silent, but the panicked cries of the guards were written on their features. I couldn't make out what was being said, not by the guards anyway.

The words were clear on the lips of the man who tore them to pieces. Two words, screamed and sobbed over and over from a face I'd looked into as I undid his restraints.

"Kill me!"

"Kill me!"

"Kill me!"

"Jesus Christ!" Mackenzie breathed over my shoulder. "Where is that? Where is he?"

I glanced at the numbers in the corner of the screen. "Close enough for us to worry about it. Let's go."

CHAPTER THIRTY-SIX

Distant machine gun fire began again as soon as we left the security room. I couldn't be sure, but it sounded closer than before. I didn't really need more of an incentive to get out of this place, but it was good to know Afridi's guards were occupied.

I've never been one to pass up an opportunity, and we raided the security room as thoroughly as we could. The Kevlar vests weren't built to fit anyone as small as Mackenzie, but even an ill-fitting vest would give her more protection than the stolen uniform on its own.

There was no time to look for a map. All the folders that looked to hold procedures and manuals were locked into a metal cage on the wall.

As it turned out, the marks on the floor proved more useful that I'd expected. There was still a 50/50 chance we were going the wrong way but as the marks became darker and more pronounced, I took it as a good sign.

Gunfire echoed loudly behind us again as we ran, and when I say ran, I mean a pained, lurching, jog.

Mackenzie glanced behind often but the looks she gave me were as confused as they were worried.

"This isn't right," she muttered as we slowed.

"How do you mean?"

"Look around, Carver," she said, waving an arm. "Where is everyone?"

Empty hallways weren't at the top of my list of worries at the moment, but she had a point.

"Probably caught up in that mess," I jerked a thumb back over my shoulder.

"What, all of them? Even if every single person they have in security is busy, what about the science staff?"

I grimaced. She was right. Most people will run once the bullets start flying. The fight or flight reflex isn't an equal split. People run, it's built into the very fabric of what we are. That's why the human race is still around.

"How many? A hundred or so? Is that what you said?"

She nodded. "Something like that. Janan said close to a hundred, and that was only the scientific staff."

Shit, there could be upwards of two, or three, hundred people down here. Even if half of them were stuck in the lower levels, that still left more than enough to cause us problems. Being faced with a panicking mob was not going to help our situation.

I suppose that makes me sound callous? Maybe I am, but you reach a point when you have to just look out for you and the squad. In this case, Mackenzie was my squad. I couldn't save everyone in this place. Half of them had been complicit in keeping us here, and I wouldn't save them, even if I could. They could fucking rot.

Mackenzie saw the blood before I did and jerked to a halt. Drips and spatters that painted a trail along the floor and grew until it was a lurid streak leading to a body slumped in the hall. I wasn't bothered by the body, or the blood. It was the footprints I was worried about. Someone had chased this man down. Someone wearing heavy combat boots.

The lab-coat only made the blood more pronounced. He'd crawled the last hundred feet or so, dragging himself along before whoever it was hunting him had finally cut him down. Like I said, the body didn't bother me, neither did the way he'd dragged himself. Maybe it's part of the life I've led that I'm desensitised to these things. Maybe I'm just an arsehole. In any event, it was the fact that he had died from gunshot wounds that was more important to me than anything else.

I pulled Mackenzie on. There wasn't anything to be gained from examining the body and time was something we couldn't afford to waste.

The hall widened as we rounded the corner and faced the cargo lift and a set of large double doors leading into the loading dock. I would have sworn at how much time we could have saved by just taking that route, but the scene in front of us took the words from my mouth.

I didn't count the bodies. More than twenty lay in the hall in front of the lift, but I stopped taking it in after that. Most of them had been shot in the back as they ran. A few must have turned and tried to fight, but fists have never been much good against bullets. They'd been massacred; gunned down as they tried to flee the chaos that was rushing up from the lower levels. I suppose some might find a sick kind of justice in all of it, but that wasn't a sentiment I wanted anything to do with.

I almost missed her. If it hadn't been for the business suit she wore, I probably would have. The majority of the bodies were dressed in lab coats and her dark suit stuck out, the blonde hair lending a contrast. I moved closer, crouching to roll her over, ignoring Mackenzie's whispered calls.

Artemis looked up at me in shock as she sucked in a pained breath through pale lips.

"Hello, Jo," I said softly.

"Carver?" she gasped, her eyes showing how much it hurt her to speak.

I swore to myself under my breath as I looked at her. She had no business being here. Unless, of course, Johnson had been right, and she'd never had anything to do with the CIA or the US Government. I shook my head as the pieces fell into place. The phone in my kit, the moved passport. She'd been involved in my abduction from the very beginning, and I wandered into the trap as trusting as a lamb.

"Son of a bitch!" muttered Turner from somewhere behind me.

I managed to keep my voice level as I spoke, but my fists were clenched hard enough to make my hands ache. "I suppose I should ask what the fuck you're doing here, but it all seems pretty obvious now. One question though?"

"Why should I tell you anything?" she managed. "Get me out of here and maybe we can talk."

I sucked on my lip for a moment, glancing at Mackenzie. She gave me a shrug and looked back down the way we'd come, eyes darting.

Jo had lost a lot of blood, that much was obvious from the state of her suit. It had soaked through the jacket, spreading out from where her hands pressed to the wound. Laying on her hands was probably the only reason she was still alive.

"You'll never make it, Jo. If I move you, you'll bleed out in minutes."

She smiled; a sad, cruel, smile that might have just been the truest reflection of who she actually was. "Then why should I tell you a god-damned thing?"

She had a point, and I didn't have an awful lot to bargain with. Still, I needed answers, and she was the only person who could give them to me. I raised the gun, letting her get a good look.

"You're dying, Jo. Nothing is going to change that. I can end it for you now, or I can leave you with the pain before you eventually slip away."

"Bastard!" The word came out as a whisper but the venom it carried with it more than made up for the lack of volume.

"Carver," Mackenzie hissed. "It's nice that you've made a friend, but do we really have time for this?"

Artemis gave her a cool look, dismissing her with a glance. "What do you want to know, Carver?"

"How far?" I asked. "How far back along the trail does this go? You've been in on this since the beginning. How many others were involved in getting me here?"

She laughed, a pained chuckle that brought blood with it. "Who's the rat? Who set you up? Everyone, Carver. I've been tracking you for months. I had your casino habits, your debts, your friends, and all the people you might go to for a job if things got desperate."

"McCourt?" I spat.

The word brought another pained smile to her lips. "Oh yes, Mr McCourt. His empire isn't nearly as stable as he makes out. It really didn't take much to get him on side. You've been my marionette, Carver. I just had to pull the right strings to get you to dance."

I closed my eyes for a minute, sitting back on my heels.

McCourt? Fuck!

I very nearly threw the whole idea out as bullshit. I've never claimed to be a paragon of virtue. I've done shitty things the same as anyone, and probably worse than most. There's one thing that's always been drilled into me though: you don't shit on your mates, and you *never* shit on the squad. It's a bond that's hard to describe outside of the forces. It's more than simply being friends, most of the time it's closer than family. These are the people that you literally trust with your life, while they trust you with theirs. Shitting on that just didn't even make sense to me. Except it did. In an awful way it made perfect sense.

"Why?" I asked the question before I thought.

Her laugh was harder this time, bringing more pain and more blood. I can't say I was feeling much sympathy at this point. "How innocent *are* you? For the money, Carver. Afridi offered a small fortune for you."

"So why the fuck are you still here?" Mackenzie hissed, spitting the words out as she drew closer. I hadn't seen her hovering; hadn't thought she was paying attention.

"Why do you care?" Jo replied, unruffled in the face of Mackenzie's fury.

"I care, because it makes no sense," I told her.

Mackenzie was right. This was a contract job; locate me and orchestrate my delivery like a sack of meat. Why was she still here? Why had she ever been here in the first place?

"Why are you here, Jo?"

"Because he was working with miracles, Carver." Jo's eyes were wide, her pain forgotten for a moment as the wonder filled her voice. "The things he told me about you and the others... I had to find out more. I had to come here and be part of this. And then the things I've seen here since, Carver... You just wouldn't believe. Or maybe you would."

"And that's what killed you," Mackenzie told her. "That's why you deserve to die. How many others did you set up? How many abductions have you arranged, you bitch? You don't deserve any mercy. I can't think up anything bad enough for you to deserve. At least you can die slow and hard."

I looked at her then, and the thing that looked back at me could never have been a nurse. She was all fury, and spite, and jagged edges.

"She's got a point you know, Roasties," Turner put in, chewing on a thumbnail. "Leave the bitch. She had you delivered here like some kind of big, ugly pizza. You don't owe her shit."

I levelled the gun before I could give myself more time to think. I'd argued with myself enough already, without Turner and the others wading in.

The shot was loud, echoing along the hallway until the silence came back to claim it. Mackenzie gave me a frosty look that I more or less ignored. I've never been great with women. This ability to ignore the danger signs sent my way probably has a lot to do with that.

I should have known Jo was in on this. I should have seen it but I hadn't, and I hated myself for it almost as much as I now hated McCourt. In hindsight, putting a bullet into Jo might not have been the greatest idea in the world. She certainly didn't deserve a quick ending.

We left the pile of bodies to bleed, and followed a passage that sloped down through a set of large double doors and into a loading dock. I slipped through them slowly, almost gasping at the blast of stifling air that washed over me as I ran my eyes over the area, not letting them settle on anything. The human eye is attracted to motion, and I had far more chance of catching somebody moving than simply spotting them. Whoever had killed the people by the lift hadn't left any tracks and they could as easily be in here as anywhere else

I motioned to Mackenzie, and ran for the closest row of pallets. The room was cavernous, lit by fluorescent strips that hung, suspended, from the ceiling. Giant ceiling fans did their best to circulate the air, but it didn't seem to do anything other than add a low rumble that, somehow, didn't truly dispel the silence.

I moved through the heat, making my way to the end of a row of pallets, and resisted the urge to cough as the dust found me. A pair of forklifts were visible as I peered past, parked against one wall with long racks of metal shelves beside them, stacked high with supplies.

The place was well-lit, but it was an ambusher's paradise. I glanced at Mackenzie and pressed my finger to my lips. She nodded, gripping her gun, and we set off towards the next row of pallets, heading for the farthest wall and the rolling door that I hoped would be there.

Mackenzie moved quickly, keeping close enough that I always knew where she was, but not so close as to be in the way. I crouched low against a pallet stacked high with boxes, and bound in plastic sheeting, and listened.

The place felt empty. I can't really explain that, but a building or a house has a different feel to it when there's someone else there. Maybe it's the tiny noises, or minute air currents that have been disturbed, that our subconscious processes as a *feeling*. Maybe I'm just full of shit. Either way, it's true.

I crouched down beside the pallets and gnawed on a knuckle, working to order my thoughts. I hadn't actually expected to get this far, and the lack of any plan bothered me.

"Get out. That's a good first step," I muttered to myself, drawing a raised eyebrow from Mackenzie. Getting out was all well and good, but it would be exceptionally crap to escape and then die of hunger or thirst.

We moved in spurts, darting between rows of pallets towards the farthest wall. The retractable doors were hard to miss; tall, metal structures that would roll up to allow the forklifts out to bring in supplies. It was only as I reached them that I allowed myself to relax. The place *was* empty.

The door beside the roller doors was small and set into the wall to the left of them. Sunlight streamed in through a small window, painting a splash of light on the floor. I pressed myself close to the door and peered out, enjoying the touch of the sunlight on my skin. It felt good, like a warm caress. I didn't let myself dwell on the fact that it was the first natural light I'd seen in months.

The view didn't tell me much, though. I couldn't see any roads or paths. A large, clear area off to my right suggested what might be a landing pad for a helicopter, but the narrow field of vision didn't reveal much more than that. All I could really see was dusty, sun-baked dirt, which didn't tell me much of anything.

"We're going to need some supplies," I said, turning to Mackenzie. "Water especially. Can you go and see what you can find? I'll buy us some time."

She glanced around the loading dock for a moment before nodding. Maybe she needed that minute to convince herself it was safe, at least for now.

I watched her go then made my way back towards the forklifts.

"What are we doing, Roasties?" Johnson asked, falling in beside me as Pearson followed and Turner took point. "We're sneaking around this warehouse like we've broken into fucking IKEA."

I ignored him, but Turner grinned, looking back over his shoulder. "He's looking for the meatballs, mate. It's the only reason to go to IKEA. They put crack in them."

Johnson shook his head. "They do not put crack in the meatballs, Turner."

"No," Turner shook his head, agreeing. "Not crack, but they put something in. My brother met a bloke down the pub who works for them. He reckons there's an additive that makes you crave them."

Johnson gave him a long look. "A bloke in the pub? For fuck's sake, mate. Would you listen to yourself?"

"There's bloody *something* in them. I'd crawl through Helmand in a pink bikini for an IKEA meatball."

"You'd do that for a stale cheese sandwich. I've never seen anyone need food like you."

Turner struck a pose, waving a hand down at himself. "Yeah well, it takes a lot of fuel to run something this gorgeous."

I turned, glaring at them both. "Will you two please, for the love of God, shut the fuck up?"

"I'm telling you," Turner whispered, as I set off again. "Crack."

The forklift looked new, which was one small mercy. The key left in the ignition was another. A brief look showed that it was almost idiot-proof too. Almost any moron can drive a modern forklift. As I pulled myself up into the seat, I hoped I'd fall into that category.

I'd driven some rumbling heaps in my time in the forces. Things that were held together by nothing but rust and pure stubbornness. The forklift was nothing like that. It almost felt like a bloody mobility scooter as I eased it backwards and up the ramp, as close to the doors as I could manage.

The nice thing about these machines is they're not particularly stable on a slope, especially when you park them sideways. It didn't take long for me to drive the other one up and tip the first one over. Shunting it up against the doors was the work of moments and then I was running back to find Mackenzie.

Barricading the door would only help us so much. There was at least one more way in and out of this complex and I wasn't naive enough to believe that there wouldn't be some guards outside too. My efforts weren't going to hurt though, and anything that slowed them down was a bonus.

Mackenzie had been busy. Four large jerry cans stood close to the door, next to a small heap of food and supplies.

"I didn't know how much to get," she said with a shrug, stuffing the supplies into a pair of bags she'd pilfered from somewhere. "I figured too much was better than not enough."

"Yep," Johnson muttered. "She'll do."

"Okay," I said, puffing out a breath as I reached for the door handle. "Stay here for a minute while I have a look around."

I didn't give her time to argue, though I could feel the look she gave me as I eased the door open. I walked calmly along the outer wall of the building, fighting to move without limping and trusting in the boots

281

and uniform to disguise me, rather than trying to hide. Half of conceal-ment is letting people see what they expect to see. A man in a security uniform, even one with paler skin than normal, would raise far less eyebrows than some idiot trying to run for cover.

The area outside the complex was a flat plain that stretched out forever, littered with rock formations and low hills. Dust, sand, and rock, surrounded by more dusty rocks. A large formation facing the complex looked to have been quarried out, and regular shapes in the shadows of the cave hinted at a concealed store. A number of other small caves faced out towards the roller doors. I glanced behind me at the complex as I headed for the largest cave.

The thing was a work of art, nothing that anyone would have looked at twice. It looked to have been concealed beneath the overhang of a large rock formation, and from above it would have been invisible. The roller doors themselves were painted, or tinted, somehow to blend in with the surrounding rocks and dust. Someone could pass within five hundred yards of this place and never see it for what it really was. A plane, or a satellite, would have no chance.

I turned back to the cave just as a man emerged. He waved me over, calling out something, but he was speaking faster than I could ever hope to follow, even if I had known the language. I made some vague gestures, cupping my free hand to my ear as I walked towards him to close the distance. Shooting him wasn't a great idea. There aren't many things that will carry as well as the sound of a gunshot. Surrounded by rock formations like this, the noise would echo on for ages, and I had no idea how many men might be out there.

I nearly made it. The guy was within twenty feet of me when he stopped, eyes narrowing as his hand flew to the gun on his belt.

Mine was already in my hand. He didn't stand a chance.

I grimaced as the gunshot echoed off the rocks, the sound rolling around the hills as blood stained the sand. I stopped long enough to take his gun and then made my way past the body.

"Well that was subtly done, Roasties," Turner said, giving me a slow clap.

I glanced back at him, fully intending to give him the finger. Pearson crouched low over the body, fists balled up against his cheeks as he looked at me in horror. The silent accusation was clear enough.

Another death.

Another killing.

And again, all my fault. I wondered sometimes if Pearson was my conscience, silent but still there, accusing me of all the awful shit I'd done. The rest of the time I just wondered how to make the bastard piss off and leave me alone.

CHAPTER THIRTY-SEVEN

The cave was deeper than I'd thought. I'd hoped to find vehicles and wasn't disappointed as I slipped between the cave wall and what looked to be an old Soviet military transport truck. Beggars can't be choosers and I'd take it if need be. Those things are just about immortal, and will run forever, but they're not the fastest set of wheels on Earth. Right now, I really wanted to put some distance between me and this place.

I was smoke as I drifted along the back of the cave. Shadows have made more noise than I did. The cave was quiet, but someone had to have heard that gunshot, and now was not the time to relax. The line of trucks ended at a small collection of Toyota four-wheel drive pickups, all clearly being worked on. They'd be faster, but not ideal, and I'd rather take the old Soviet beast than something that might conk out after a mile or two.

The helicopter stopped me in my tracks, and I stood gaping at it as I dreamt up new swear words to use. It was an old Soviet bird by the looks of things. It was also easily the single biggest kick in the teeth since Mackenzie had let me out of my cell.

If this were a movie I'd just climb in, flip a switch, and off we'd go. In real life, flying a helicopter isn't that simple. I'd heard that just about anybody could fly a plane once it was in the air. Most people could even struggle through a take-off with some help. Helicopters aren't like planes. Flying through the air with a windmill strapped to your back takes some serious training. I couldn't fly one, and I wasn't about to try now. All of that said, the fact it would have solved all our problems in one fell swoop was not lost on me.

If I'd had the time, I'd have ripped a few choice wires and parts out of the other vehicles, especially the helicopter; but time wasn't something we had much of. I went back to the Soviet truck, threw three large cans of fuel into the back and climbed in. One good thing about military vehicles is they don't generally have key-start ignitions. The bad thing? Dear Christ, the engine was loud.

Mackenzie was already coming out of the door as I pulled up, dragging two jerry cans with her. I ran past her for the rest of the supplies, and we ferried it all into the back of the truck.

"What the hell is this thing?" she demanded as we clambered in.

I gave her a look. "It's all I could find," I muttered and stamped on the accelerator.

It would have been nice if we'd pulled away with a screech of tires and flying dust, but that's just not how these things work. They're like a boulder on a shallow slope; almost impossible to stop once they get going—but it's the getting going. Her silence spoke eloquently of her disdain for the full five seconds she managed to hold it in, but it was never going to last.

"Seriously? This is *it*?" she demanded. "We need to move, Carver. Let's go!" She looked out the window for a moment as we trundled along. "Would it help if I got out and pushed?"

Afridi's complex had no fence or perimeter wall. It didn't need one, and it would have made the place impossible to hide. What it did have was its location, and as we gathered speed, I began to realise just how effective a wall that was. There was nothing as far as the eye could see in any direction. Sun-baked dirt, dust, low hills, and rocks. Anyone escaping the place on foot would be lost in an hour, and dead within days. I tried not to think how long we might last if the truck gave out. It's not often the heat that kills you in the desert, it just feels like it. Normally it's your body being unable to stay hydrated enough to cope with the temperature, and there was no way we could carry enough water with us to make a difference if we ended up on foot.

I heard the impact of the bullet rather than the shot itself. The Soviet truck was loud, and we might have been shot half a dozen times already for all I knew.

"Shit," I muttered as I glanced in the wing-mirror.

"What?" Mackenzie asked. "Carver?" But there was no need to explain, she was already leaning to check the mirror on her side.

The truck looked like an old Toyota Hilux. The damned things are nigh-on indestructible, but the guy driving it seemed determined to test this theory as he threw it over the dust, and patches of rough ground. Whoever was driving the car following looked to be as bad.

I watched a man lean out of the passenger window again, levelling the handgun at us. Being shot at is never a pleasant experience; watching it coming in a mirror didn't improve it any.

The gun jumped as he fired again, and I flinched. I wasn't particularly worried about the odds of actually being shot myself. The Hilux was bouncing around like a thing possessed, and he would have enough trouble just hitting the truck. If he got lucky and hit the tyres, that would be a different matter. I'd rather take the bullet myself, than die of thirst out here.

"Carver?" Mackenzie said again.

I chewed on my lip. We didn't have a whole lot of options. "Do you think you can…?"

She glanced into the mirror and back to me. I was asking her to commit an act of extreme violence at best, cold-blooded murder at worst. Her thoughts were clear enough, and they flickered over her face before she closed her eyes in concentration, and then they were lost in her rage.

Anger was the key. I knew this now. It had always been the key. Whatever powers Afridi had unlocked in the people he'd had chained up in his zoo, they were never going to usher in a golden, magical age. These were powers born of rage and torment. They would only ever bring pain and destruction.

Mackenzie glared into the wing-mirror for long moments before she leaned out of the open window. The flames came out of a clear blue sky. A pillar of fire that drove down into the front of the Hilux, boring through the metal of the bonnet in moments before it tore into the engine. The car that had been following slammed into the side of the Hilux as it slewed sideways and exploded, though I doubt any of the passengers really noticed the collision. Neither one of them were going to be going anywhere.

I gasped as the cold hit, and watched my breath steam in the cab of the truck. Frost coated Mackenzie's clothes, reaching out with icy tendrils to engulf the seat around her, and spread over the dashboard to the steering wheel. Mackenzie squeezed her eyes tight as she sank back in her seat, oblivious to the crunch of the frost.

She was done. Fatigue mingled with pain on her face, painting a portrait too miserable to hang anywhere. A better man might have felt guilty at having to use her like this. I never said I was a good man. I get by, I do what I can, but in the end we all take what we have to.

Mackenzie looked behind us every few seconds, checking for signs of pursuit, until she finally began to relax. She let out an explosive sigh after the second hour and looked over to me as a smile grew broader on her cheeks. "We did it!" she grinned. "We're out. Dear God, Carver, I didn't think we were going to make it."

I didn't say anything. I didn't have to. Johnson and Turner were already yelling abuse at her from the back of the truck. It might be an army thing. Maybe it's just me, but you never celebrate until you're back at base with everyone in one piece, or two pieces in a pinch.

I pointed the truck away from the sun and drove. Right now, I had no idea where we might be, but it felt like afternoon. East was as good a direction as any. The terrain looked like Pakistan, but it could easily have been Afghanistan, with the rocks and scrubland. You can find dust, sand, and rocks in an awful lot of places.

It was rough going. The truck could put up with a lot of abuse but it wasn't like there was a road to follow. For now, the ground

287

was sun-baked earth, and level enough for me to risk some speed, but pushing much past 40mph risked cracking our heads on the ceiling of the cab.

The complex had been built at the far end of a dusty plain which looked like it might be shifting into sand dunes in the distance. That was great as far as it went. The truck managed it easily enough for now, and we made better time than we otherwise might have done if we'd been working our way through a network of valleys, but we weren't exactly inconspicuous.

The landscape was an almost featureless expanse, and we would be visible for miles in any direction. I followed Mackenzie's gaze and glanced behind us often, grimacing at the clear tracks and plume of dust that stretched out behind us as the hours slipped by.

We ate as we drove, sipping at the water sparingly. Mackenzie had grabbed close to sixty litres of water; it sounds a lot but it wouldn't last us long. By my reckoning, we had enough water to last us six days if we were careful with it. Twelve if we rationed it. Water wasn't likely to be an issue unless things went wrong. If something happened and we lost the truck, we were basically fucked. My leg was equally fucked, and I had to switch driving with Mackenzie often, both to give my thigh a break, but also so we could snatch what sleep we could.

Wherever we were was hotter than Satan's balls, and we were sweating out almost as much as we were drinking. If we lost the truck, we simply wouldn't be able to carry enough water with us. Neither of us were going to come right out and say it, but we both knew the chances of things going wrong were higher than things going right.

Night came slowly as the sun sank down behind us, swallowed by the endless dusty expanse. I thought briefly about turning on the headlights but decided against it. Afridi's men, assuming they were still looking for us at all, would be behind us, but it made no sense to advertise our location. We had no friends here, and I wasn't about to try and make new ones in the dark.

For a time, we drove into the gloom as the light failed entirely. The truck shook violently as I drove over something that scratched and clawed at the chassis, probably a patch of dead brush, and I let the truck come slowly to a halt.

Mackenzie stirred after a moment, rousing herself and peering into the darkness. "What was that? Why have we stopped?"

"It's too dark," I said in a low voice. "We could hit something and damage the truck, and I can't see where we're going anyway. We could end up driving in circles."

She mulled that over for a moment before shrugging. "At least it's too dark for anyone to see us." She hugged herself suddenly, rubbing at her arms. "Christ, it's fucking freezing!"

"Yeah, I didn't think about that," I admitted. "It's going to get a lot worse. We'll have to huddle up."

She nodded and then gave me a look in the gloom. "Don't get any ideas, Carver."

"What?" I laughed.

"Well clearly you're not above random kisses."

"Sorry about that. It was all I could think of."

She shrugged. "Don't be. It wasn't bad. You're out of practice though."

"Is that right?" I gave her my best incredulous look.

"We're not practising," she said as she moved closer and pulled my arm over her shoulders.

I leaned forward and killed the engine, plunging the cab into darkness. In the silence, Johnson's whispered voice was clear in my ear. "I think you're in there, Roasties."

I stayed awake longer than she did. For all the strain I'd put on my body escaping from Afridi's complex, I found I couldn't sleep. I watched the wing mirrors, scanning the darkness as Mackenzie leaned on me, breathing softly. Twice I thought I caught pinpricks of light far in the distance behind us. Both times they vanished but they were enough to keep me awake.

Afridi bothered me, more than I really wanted to admit. I've never been particularly civic minded. Selfishness is a natural state and it's not one I fight all that hard against. I joined the army for the career; not from any particular sense of duty to Queen, country, or the world at large. For all that though, the prospect of simply letting Afridi loose on the planet did not sit well with me. I didn't have a clue what I planned to do about him just yet, but I'd be damned if I was simply letting him go back to torturing people into madness.

*

I woke early, before the sky was fully light, easing myself out from underneath Mackenzie and clambering out of the cab. The dusty ground needed watering and I was dying for a piss, so it seemed fair we sort each other out.

I let out a groan as I rolled my neck, working out the kinks and aching muscles. My chest was sore, but it seemed to be on the mend. My leg, however, was throbbing with a hot, angry, ache, and would need some real attention far sooner than we would be able to provide it.

The creak of the other truck door told me Mackenzie was awake. I stayed quiet—nobody really wants company at times like this. It was only as I turned away from the side of the truck and glanced towards the horizon that I saw it. The sun hadn't risen yet, or so I'd assumed, but it was light enough to see the dusty murk that filled the sky. The dust-storm looked like a huge brown wall, reaching up from the parched ground for the heavens.

I walked slowly to the front of the truck, drawing out the word as the sight became clearer with every step. "Fuuuck!"

"What?" Mackenzie came around to my side. She followed my pointing finger to the brown wall of dust and sand that filled the sky ahead of us.

"Shit! How long do you think we have?"

"Not long enough."

I've lived through dust storms before. They hit Afghanistan most months and can last for days at a time. Normally they aren't much more than an inconvenience, but if it wrecked the engine, this one could kill us both.

"What do we do?" Mackenzie asked as she slammed the truck door shut.

I thought for a moment, drumming my fingers on the steering wheel. Driving into it risked ruining the engine as the sand worked its way in and forced it to overheat. Staying put risked getting bogged down, and then there was always the chance of Afridi's men somehow catching up with us.

"We don't have much of a choice," I told her. "We can't stay here. We have to keep moving."

The truck started easily, and I jammed it into gear, pushing it as fast as we could stand as we bounced around inside the cab.

The dust was more of a danger than I wanted to admit. It would be bad enough if we were in a Mastiff, or an American Humvee, but at least those had air filters built for this kind of thing. You can shake them out and just carry on. The KrAZ lorry we were trundling along in was older than I was, and I seriously doubted its engine had any kind of filters that were worth the name.

I kept an eye on the engine temperature as we went. The dust in those storms was fine enough to work its way down into your lungs, so the engine really wasn't going to enjoy it. It was too fine to see to begin with, but within an hour the visibility had dropped to mere feet and the dust was hissing against the windows as the wind drove it on.

"How do you even know where you're going?" Mackenzie asked at one point.

"I don't," I admitted. "I'm just going in as straight a line as I can manage. It's all we can do. We should hit some kind of road, or spot one, eventually."

"And if we don't?"

I gave her a long look. "Then we don't. I don't have a better plan, Mackenzie."

I wasn't about to sugar-coat things. We'd both gone through hell in Afridi's prison. I wasn't about to pretend life was all hearts and flowers now.

The engine fought on until the middle of that afternoon before it gave in. To its credit I don't think many other machines would have lasted that long. I let the truck roll to a stop as Mackenzie and I exchanged glances while steam boiled out from the bonnet, and then there was nothing to do but wait, and listen to the wind as the dust fell.

She watched me for a moment, then pulled her legs up on the bench seat of the truck, facing me with a pair of intent eyes that made the space in the cab feel all that much smaller.

"So, you see the dead men from your squad?" she asked, as calmly as if she was asking me what I wanted for lunch.

I've spent most of the last five years avoiding this conversation. I'd managed to avoid it with Susan, she only saw the barest edges of how fucked up I really am. I'd be damned if I was being dragged through it now. I tore my eyes away and looked at the dust storm. Nope. No help there. Mackenzie waited, eyes holding my gaze whenever I was stupid enough to look her way. "I suppose I do," I replied eventually.

"You said they blame you? Back on the stairs, you told me they say it's your fault?" She looked out at the dust storm, letting the question hang in the silence until I sucked in a deep breath and sighed.

"There was an… incident," I told her. "Back when I was in Kabul. They died. It was my fault. That's about it." My tone had been harsher than I intended. Talking about this stuff makes me need a drink. I hoped that she would take that as enough of an answer. And for a good long minute, I thought she had.

She glanced down at the laces of her boots, playing them idly through her fingers. "I'm sorry, John. That's really shit."

I looked up at her. Had she ever used my first name before now? I haven't met many Aussies, they're an interesting people. Us Brits can be a bit closed off, we hold things in that Aussies just let out. Her voice was careful though. It spoke of someone who had known death. Not just someone who had seen it in hospitals and war zone clinics, but someone who was haunted by the wounds death leaves in the living.

"Did you ever talk about it? Properly, I mean?" she continued, her voice a murmur against the hiss of the wind-driven dust outside.

I shook my head and looked at my hands. "Wasn't something I could really talk about. It's how I ended up in that shithole." I jerked my head back toward the complex and she frowned.

"What do you mean?"

I sighed. In for a penny, in for a pound, I guess. "It was the first time I stopped a bullet. My team were being shot to bits next to me, and when my turn came, I stopped the bullet in mid-air in front of me. Didn't help them though—they were already dead. So, they follow me around, reminding me every day that what happened was my fault, and generally giving me shit."

I don't know what I expected her to say, but when she said nothing, I glanced up and was met with a face full of fury.

"That is the biggest load of bullshit I have ever heard."

"I'm sorry?" I started.

"Your squad! It wasn't your fault. A blind man on a mountainside could see that!"

I shook my head again, anger and pain building in my chest. This is why I didn't tell people. This was why I kept it to myself. "It was my fault. I didn't stop the bullets that—"

Her hand caught my wrist and squeezed. "Just stop. Listen to yourself. Remember what Janan and Elias said. These powers, they come from something broken, a place in us that isn't whole anymore. I can feel mine, inside my mind. It's like a gaping chasm where a part of me has been torn open. Any shreds of what I've been plugging the hole with for years burned out of me when they... when they killed my friend."

She shuffled closer on the seat, spreading her hands and taking a deep, steadying breath. "My family died in a massive fire. Gutted the whole building, killed my birth parents, my sister, and other families too. I was just a kid and they found me huddled in a room, untouched by it all. I stopped the fire that day, not because I somehow knew all along how it was done, but because I watched it kill my family. It murdered them, and I think that was when my mind fractured. I've been clutching at the splinters of it ever since. My point is, you didn't have this ability to stop bullets before your mates were killed. You couldn't have used it to save them, because it didn't exist. You stopped the bullet *because* they died, John, not the other way around. You stopped the bullet, because watching them die, and not being able to do a single thing to stop it, broke you."

Her words washed over me and my hands clenched. "No, that's not—"

"Carver?" Her hand found my wrist again, gentle this time.

I stopped and looked up. Fuck, I'd managed five years without crying about this. I hoped she couldn't see the fucking tears.

"It was never your fault."

I spent what felt like forever staring out the windscreen at the sand. Pearson, Turner and Johnson sat in the back, silent for once, as if the truth they'd been trying to show me had finally been exposed underneath all the lies I'd told myself. Pearson nudged Turner and nodded out the door, and the three of them vanished; leaving me, for once, alone with my thoughts and the woman who'd forced them onto me.

According to the clock on the dash, it was an hour before Mackenzie handed me a water canteen. "Right, sad sack, get your pants off."

I spat my mouthful across the steering wheel and gave her a startled look. "Um, what?"

"Don't get excited, big guy. I just want to look at that leg."

I cleared my throat, flushing as she tugged my trousers down over my knee.

"You could have at least bought me dinner first," I muttered with a grin.

Her eye-roll almost covered her smile, but not quite.

"Christ," she said, picking at the matted bandage somehow still clinging to my leg. "You're a mess."

"I bet you say that to all the boys."

That earned me a real smile but then her gaze drifted to my chest. "We need to replace this bandage, Carver. You're going to get infected."

"We're not exactly surrounded with supplies here, Macca."

"Macca?"

"Mackenzie is a bit of a mouthful," I said with a smile.

"But you haven't even bought me dinner yet," she said with a snort. "I'm going to need some of your shirt, I think."

I gave her a long look. "Do you plan on stripping me entirely?"

She blushed then, looking down so her dark hair fell across her face for a moment before she met my gaze. "If I was stripping you, Carver, you'd be moaning a lot louder."

I flushed at that, glancing away and busying myself with ripping a strip from my shirt as she fell silent.

Then she reached for me, her hand was cool on my face as she lifted my chin, but her lips burned as she found mine. The first kiss was tentative, but the second was full of hunger, and I matched it with my own.

Any shock I'd felt was quickly smothered by far more important thoughts as her hands roamed over me, and my own found her body. Her shirt lifted easily, clothes falling to the seat and draped over the dash as she climbed into my lap. There was no awkwardness now, just the two of us as skin whispered over skin and I moaned against her throat as I pulled her down to meet me.

"Told you I'd make you moan," she gasped.

I didn't speak. There were no words to match the urgency that held me now even if I'd been capable of voicing them. This was no innocent girl. She knew what she wanted and she was taking it—and I was more than willing to let her. The wind hissed dust against the truck, and we were swallowed by the storm as her legs wrapped around me. I was lost. I didn't ever want to be found.

CHAPTER THIRTY-EIGHT

The storm lasted almost two days before we were finally free of it. We took advantage of it while we could. I'm no blushing virgin, and Mackenzie knew exactly what was going on. We were taking what comfort we could, any way we could. Making plans would have been stupid. There's no point in planning your life if you don't know if you'll have one in the morning.

Our water was disappearing faster than I would have liked. The dust had us trapped in the heat of the truck, we weren't making any real progress across the plain, and the fact the radiator might need topping up hadn't escaped me.

We drove through it at a snail's pace, slow enough that we wouldn't wreck the truck on anything we hit. I lost count of the times we had to stop to let the engine cool, and the hours we lost watching the temperature needle slowly drop. The storm didn't help with that either. All of the things you could normally do; lifting the bonnet, or opening the radiator valve, would just have let more dust into the engine and made things worse.

I wasn't overly worried about Afridi and his men finding us—they wouldn't be able to travel any faster than we could, and with any luck the storm should have covered any tracks we left. I was more worried about our supplies.

Storms like this don't end like rain storms; simply stopping. The dust just grows thinner over time until you can't see it anymore. For two days we'd had no choice but to point the truck at the lightest part of the sky in the morning, and hope that we weren't driving in a massive circle.

Naturally the dust storm passed off to our left, rather than out behind us where it might have hidden us from anyone still searching. As it turned out, the dust had done little to hide our tracks. It wasn't a sandstorm or a heavy snowfall, and the truck was simply too heavy. The cracked ruts in the ground we had passed over were still visible to anyone who took the time to look. I checked the mirrors often, and kept my gun close to hand as we drove.

I heard it before I saw it. That heavy bass-line *thwopping* that every soldier the world over has learned to hate. You can hide from a plane— by the time they spot you they're already halfway to being gone. You can see tanks or tracked vehicles coming for miles if you're lucky. Helicopters are just bastards. Without an RPG launcher, or a gun big enough to do the job, there's not much you can do but run, and escaping a helicopter in a stolen Soviet-era rust-bucket was about as likely as the Taliban hosting the next Miss World competition.

I met Mackenzie's wide eyes as the helicopter thundered over us, coming in low and sweeping around to face us as it hung in the air. Even from this distance I could make out the rocket launchers slung low on either side of the cockpit.

"Shit," I breathed and glanced over at Mackenzie. "Do you think you could...?" I left it hanging.

"God, John," Mackenzie shook her head. "I don't know if I can. I don't know if there's anything left in me."

The gunship inched closer, the threat looming, and as obvious as a cliff-edge.

"Fuck!" I slammed on the brakes, and threw myself out of the truck as it slid to a halt on the dusty ground. A handgun is a ridiculous weapon to try and take a helicopter down with, but it was better than hurling rocks and bad language.

I'd gone from fatalistic, to downright fucking furious, in the space of half a breath. I was damned if I was going out like this.

I took my time with the first two or three shots, squinting against the wind as I aimed for the helicopter's glass windows. The rest of the shots went to shit. I might as well have been tossing the bullets at it with my hands. The rotors were kicking up dust and I doubted any of the shots even got close.

"Come on, then!" I screamed into the wind. "Fucking do it!"

Mackenzie grasped my arm. I hadn't even realised she was out of the truck. She was tugging on me, urging me back, or to run, or to do something other than stand there screaming at a helicopter in the desert. "John!"

"Bastard!" I screamed. I hurled the cloned Glock at the gunship, knowing it had no chance of hitting.

I was done. Spent. After all the effort of fighting our way out of Afridi's circus, to end like this seemed especially cruel.

"Roasties," Johnson's voice was a whisper on the wind, drifting to my ear over the sound of the rotors. "Stop the bullets."

I shook my head, shielding my eyes with one hand from the dust that the damned thing was kicking up, as I fought off Mackenzie with the other. "What fucking bullets? They're not even shooting yet."

"No, they're not. But what's out there that's moving almost as fast as a bullet?"

I blinked.

This power, this thing that Afridi had woken in me, was so utterly alien it ran contrary to instinct. It was a thing apart from me, and the very touch of it repulsed me. I didn't seek it; I shied away from it. This was a sorcery that had slipped through the fingers of Prometheus as he fled Olympus. Something never meant for man.

They had strapped me to a wooden frame, to my own personal crucifix, naked and abused as they tortured me. They had shot me just to see if I was able to stop them as they demanded I grasp this magic. They kept pushing until I was a broken animal. Until finally I learned to reach for the power just to stop the hurt. Until the action became like muscle memory, and all I had to do was reach.

298

The magic was waiting for me. That same nausea-inducing strength, lurking on the other side of the fissure in my sanity. I could picture it now, a blazing white line that had been scored through the very fabric of my being. Something unnatural, and better left alone.

But I was beyond all of that.

This one last time I would reach for it, and this time Afridi would bleed.

"There is nowhere left to run to, Mr Carver," Afridi's smug, condescending voice blasted out of a speaker under the helicopter. "I'd like to say I don't want to harm you, but that simply wouldn't be true. I'd love nothing more than to kill you both, right now. Unfortunately, I find that I *need* the pair of you. Thanks to your little distraction, most of the subjects in the Project are no longer viable. You two may well be the most important sources of data left to me. Return to your vehicle and drive back to the complex."

"Fuck that," Johnson called out. "Take him out, Roasties."

"I'll take him, ma'self," Turner snarled. "I'll climb up in his wee chopper and nut the bastard to death."

"Do it, Carver."

I knew that voice. The words rocked me, and my grip on the fissure faltered. I turned to find Pearson beside me, hands by his sides as he looked at me calmly. His eyes were steady, clear of the fear and the horror for the first time since his death.

"Do it," he said, glancing over to Mackenzie. "For the squad."

"For the squad," I muttered, as I reached for the fissure and ripped it wide.

My vision blurred as the power tore through me, overriding my senses, driving all thought from me. This was nothing like the force I'd thrown at the bullets. That was a whisper in the face of a hurricane.

Dimly, somewhere at the base of my consciousness, I felt panic.

This was too much. Too much for my mind to handle, too much for me to come back from… but I was past caring. This one time, in this shithole of my life, there would be justice. This one time, I would do what was right.

The power tore out of me, burrowing a hole out through the tatters of my sanity as I sent it out in a white-hot surge that burnt along my arms, and out of my hands. The helicopter rocked back, and then froze, caught like a fly in amber as I tore at it. The spinning rotors stopped dead, shivering for half a second as they slammed into a force as immovable as mountains, and then exploded into fragments that hung in the air like a cloud of razors.

I smiled then, a grin of savagery as what little remained of me revelled in this power stolen from gods and demons.

And then I closed my fists and turned the force inward. A thousand jagged shards formed from the shattered rotor blades spun in a vengeful swarm around the stricken machine, clawing rents into the fuselage until the gunship exploded, the blast wave and flames held tight within a sphere of pure force.

I felt a touch on my mind and looked up from where I'd sunk down to the dirt. The fiery wreckage dropped hard, crashing into the sun-baked earth as the flames devoured it. I frowned, staring until my eyes caught the movement at its heart.

The door was a twisted mess that should never have been able to open, but Afridi sent it skittering over the rocks with a single kick. Flames clung to him, dancing over his skin, encasing him rather than consuming. He clambered out of the wreckage, body jerking as his torso twisted and spasmed.

"That was a *mistake*," he hissed, flicking flames from his body like water.

I staggered back. How had he survived that? How could anyone?

A blast of fire shot past me and I scrambled away from the heat. Mackenzie stood with one hand outstretched, her face twisted in pain as she grasped at her head with the other.

"This is down to you, Roasties," Johnson murmured, close to my ear. "She has nothing left. She reached her limits getting out of the complex. If she keeps pushing like this there'll be nothing left of her to save."

I looked back to Afridi. Mackenzie's flames had driven him backwards but didn't seem to be doing much else. He stood with both hands raised against the fire surrounding him, warding it off, and already her flames were fading. I watched as she sank down to her knees, and toppled sideways into the dirt.

"Shift yer arse, Roasties!" Turner urged me on.

I didn't stop to argue, or even to think, sprinting forward over the broken ground towards Afridi. I dropped to the dirt as Mackenzie's flames died and Afridi shifted to face me. The slide probably wasn't anywhere near as timely or graceful as I thought it was, but it did the job. Something passed over my head, the air splitting as Afridi sent a ribbon of something dark slashing past me, hissing like a spiteful cat.

My fumbling hand snatched up a rock and I hurled it before I'd even stopped sliding through the dust. Afridi flinched away, shock etched into his features, deep enough that I would have laughed any other time.

Now really was not the time. I snatched up more rocks, hands scrabbling in the dirt, and hurled them at his face; jagged chunks of dusty stone the size of my fist that would have smashed a crater into his skull if any of them hit.

Afridi dodged, twisting and lurching faster and faster, even once the rocks had stopped, until I finally grasped what it was he was doing. His torso thrashed, shuddered, and split as he phased into three blurred images. Afridi hadn't just grasped my ability and Mackenzie's fire, he had others too. I didn't know why I was surprised. Nothing else had gone my way lately.

His laughter was wild and high, as delight flirted with hysteria.

"Really, Carver," he said as his body slowed again and became a single, solid figure. "Are rocks the best you can do?"

"Fuck you!"

He frowned, tutting at me as he wagged a disapproving finger. "There really is no need for all of this. Return to the complex with me, Carver. Mackenzie is in no condition to be running through the heat like this."

301

I glanced back to where Mackenzie had slumped to the ground, surrounded by the figures of Pearson, Turner and Johnson as they watched over her.

Johnson's shout came too late, and I turned back to Afridi just in time to watch the attack coming. The tendrils writhing out of him looked like they were formed of a dense, oily, smoke; but they flew towards me like lightning, and felt like ice-cold spiderwebs. I froze as they settled on me, and then screamed as they sliced through the stolen uniform and the pain began.

I rolled in the dirt, not knowing how I'd gotten down there as I convulsed. The pain was cold, cutting away at me like a thousand frozen knives as the tendrils sought out my nerve endings and laid siege to my nervous system. This was more of an attack on my mind than my body, clawing at my sanity via the pain centres of my brain. I had precious little left to me, and I wouldn't last long.

I fell slack as the pain stopped, and the back of my head crunched down into the rocky ground. The touch was feather-light, just enough for me to register it as a hand shook me.

"For fuck's sake, Roasties. What's the point in having a squad if you don't use it?"

My eyes flickered opened and I squinted against the sun into Johnson's face.

He had touched me. I had felt it.

"What *are* you, Johnson? Are you real?"

"I haven't the first fucking clue, mate," Johnson said with a smile. "Use me anyway."

I took the hand he offered me and clambered to my feet. The smoke-like tendrils thrashed around me like kelp in a sea at storm, but they did not touch me. I was surrounded by a sphere of pure force, safe in the eye of this cyclone.

I walked towards Mackenzie without stopping to worry if the protective bubble would move with me. Afridi screamed, practically raving as he abandoned the black tendrils and hurled fire at me again.

Pearson and Turner turned as I approached, stepping over Mackenzie and forming a circle with me. We stood in silence, we four, and for the first time I met their eyes unflinching—the dead and the living, and at once I realised why Afridi had never understood why my sanity ever truly broke.

I was already fractured. I was a shattered mirror, the shards of glass pushed tight together, close enough to still function, but broken nonetheless.

Turner grinned at me as he offered his hand. "It took you bloody long enough, Roasties. I was beginning to think you were as stupid as you looked."

I snorted and took his hand, reaching to grasp Johnson's with my other hand. Pearson stood facing me, the fear finally gone from his face as he reached to take the hands Johnson and Turner offered.

Power tore through me as doorways opened in my mind, portals to rooms filled with pain, horror, and self-loathing that I had locked away behind barriers formed from my own guilt. The force surging through me was almost more than I could fathom, and still more lay waiting at my fingertips.

"Take it, John." Pearson's whisper cut through the roaring in my ears, and I reached out to grasp it.

Afridi flew backwards at the first blow, tumbling over the cracked earth before he rose into a crouch and pulled a shield of force together around him.

I reached out again, prodding at the shield with a tentative thought and watched him tumble again. I toyed with him for a moment, a cat playing with its prey. And then I destroyed him.

The power I unleashed was a visceral thing, a feral beast uncaged that ripped and clawed at Afridi's shield as if it were nothing. I sent him staggering across the baked dirt as he threw fire and tendrils of smoke at me that I batted away with barely a thought.

The power. Jesus Christ, the power! With this I could do anything, be anyone. There was nothing that could hope to stand against me. I ground Afridi down until he had nothing left to throw at me, then I hefted him into the air before me. He dangled there, thrashing, like a puppet at war with its strings.

"You wanted to find true power, Afridi," I said in a voice that I struggled to recognise as my own. "Did you like what you found?"

I didn't wait for an answer. The power was already talking to me louder than what little conscience I had left, and I'd spent so many years ignoring that small voice that I hardly heard it. I sent the force surging into him, reaching down into every orifice and tiny cut, and then I ripped him to pieces.

The ground came up to catch me as I fell, and then all sensation left me. I felt nothing as Pearson grabbed my hand and helped me to my feet, but by then the world was already fading to white, and I was already gone.

*

The bunkhouse snapped into existence around me between blinks and I stared around me wildly.

"Here, Roasties," Johnson called, stepping past the bunks to bring me a steaming mug. "I reckon you probably need this."

I looked down at the cup and cradled it in my hands, huffing against the steam as I tried to suck the warmth from it and into my flesh. Pearson grinned at me as I took a sip and looked around at the bunk-house. It looked like something out of the fifties, worse than anything I slept in during basic training.

"Where is this? What am I doing here?"

"One last job, matey," Turner said. "Nothing too hard, just a decision you need to make."

"It might just be time to say goodbye, Roasties," Johnson told me as he put a hand on my shoulder. "It all depends on the choices you make."

I looked around at the three of them, friends I'd had for years, and then visitors that I'd had for half a decade. The question was clear in their eyes. Did I end it all now, and push my fractured parts together, going on alone? Or did I accept what I was, maybe what I'd always been meant to be? I glanced over my shoulder, back towards where I sensed I'd left everything else behind, and then back to Johnson. I suppose the answer must have been clear in my eyes as well.

Johnson nodded, a faint smile on his lips. "So be it, mate. Some people were always meant to be broken."

EPILOGUE

I smiled back at the furtive glances of the other people in the lift. To be fair, I wasn't looking my best. The month I'd spent in the hospital in Kabul had helped with the worst of my injuries, and the two I'd spent in Selly Oak Hospital in Birmingham had done the rest. But I still looked like I should be horizontal. At least I was in a suit this time round.

Mackenzie caught my grin and looked down at the floor, shaking her head, her long dark hair almost hiding her own smile. I hadn't wanted her to come along to this little reunion, but she'd dragged me the length of the Registan Desert whilst I raved in the truck next to her. There isn't much I'd say no to if she asked me.

McCourt's offices hadn't changed; the same cold opulence laid out in marble and chrome.

"Good morning, sir," the receptionist smiled up at me. It was more than she'd done the last time I was here. Then again, maybe she didn't recognise me. "Can I help you?"

"I doubt it," I told her, avoiding the kick Mackenzie aimed at my leg for my rudeness. "You might want to tell McCourt that John Carver is here to see him though."

I turned my head to nod at the security guard against the wall. He was a bigger man than the last one I'd met here.

The name must have sparked a memory that my face hadn't, and panic stole through the cracks in the mask of the receptionist's professionalism. Her eyes shot past me to the security guard, but he was already moving.

"I wouldn't bother, love," I told her. "I just want McCourt. Nobody needs to get hurt here."

"I think it's time you left, sir," the security guard rumbled as he took another step towards me.

"Would you?" I asked, turning to glance at Johnson.

"Be a bloody pleasure, mate," Johnson said with a grin. I almost felt sorry for the guard. He couldn't see the thing that held him. All he knew was that, he couldn't move.

Mackenzie mouthed a sarcastic 'sorry' at the receptionist as I watched Turner kick the doors in. I'm not sure she noticed though—she was busy stabbing at the panic button.

McCourt wasn't hard to find. The route to his office wasn't long, but he met us in the hall before we even reached it.

"John?" he blurted, face creased in shock and confusion. "My God, mate. I thought you were—"

McCourt had never been all that small, and I'd lost a lot of muscle mass in Afridi's little holiday camp. I'd never have been able to lift him with my arms alone—so I used my mind instead.

The door to his office probably wasn't designed to withstand the impact of a thirty-five-year-old man hurled through mid-air, and it tore from its hinges with a satisfying crunch. We stepped through the threshold, McCourt staggering to his feet where he'd landed in front of the desk.

"Would you do you something about the door, sweetheart?" I asked, shooting a grin at Mackenzie.

"I can manage that," she said with smile. Fire shot up from the floor, filling the doorway behind us with a sheet of flame that felt like it was scorching my hair even from this distance.

McCourt was on the verge of losing it. He stared back and forth from the fire, to Mackenzie, then to me; eyes bulging as his mouth flapped over the words he couldn't get out.

"How are you, Jim? You're looking well." I said, sinking down into the chair behind his desk. "Business booming?"

He stared at me, gaping. "What?"

"How's work? Looks like you've made some changes round here since I left. Is this a new desk? It's almost like you came into some cash, mate." I eyed him, watching his face contort as he caught my meaning. He swallowed hard but didn't speak. "You look surprised to see me, if I'm honest."

"I..." McCourt stared at me, then at Mackenzie, who was leaning against a bookcase, inspecting her nails. "I just hadn't heard you were back, mate."

"Bullshit," Mackenzie muttered, and I shot her a tight grin.

"No, Jim. I don't think you expected to see me again, at all." When he didn't respond, I leaned forward and laid my arms on the desk. "So, it seems you know a man called Janan Afridi?"

McCourt almost choked on his own breath. "Who?"

"Janan Afridi? Bumped into him while I was away." I nodded at Mackenzie. "You could say he introduced us."

"I don't know—"

I waved his assertion away. "Maybe the name doesn't ring a bell, but he knew you."

"I don't know what you're talking about."

"Bullshit," I said, echoing Mackenzie with a friendly grin.

"You could get your girlfriend to burn his balls off," Turner suggested, circling McCourt like a ginger shark.

"She's not my girlfriend," I muttered, as McCourt frowned at me and Mackenzie shot me a startled look.

"Oh aye?" Turner cocked his head on one side.

"She's my fiancé."

"Um... John?" Mackenzie gave me a wide-eyed look.

"Smooth," Pearson snorted. "Bloody smooth, mate. Most people ask first."

McCourt didn't seem to know where to look first. "Carver, what the hell is going on? Are you out of your fucking mind, mate?"

"Yes," I told him with a grin. "And you have no idea how good it feels to finally admit it. That said, you stitched me up, McCourt. You sold me out to that bitch Joanne, or Artemis, or whatever the hell she called herself, and you sent me off to Afridi. About the only thing you didn't do was gift-wrap me."

McCourt shook his head, gnawing on his lip, but I wasn't about to give him the chance to talk now.

"You fucked over a bloke from your own squad. There are things that just aren't done, Jim. That's one of them."

His eyes flicked past me to Mackenzie. "He's lost it, can't you do something?"

"Nah, mate." She shrugged. "You're fucked."

They make the windows in skyscrapers to withstand high impacts. Paragon's offices were only on the fourth floor, and London doesn't have as many skyscrapers as you might think, but it made a pretty noise when it broke. The glass exploded out over the street as I sent McCourt flying through it. His screams were loud enough to stop the traffic even if the spectacle hadn't been. There aren't many people who've seen an executive piss himself as he dangles fifty feet above the street.

"You don't fuck with the squad, McCourt," I shouted out over his screams. "Say it."

"Fuck you!" he sputtered.

"Ah, just drop the scheming bastard," Turner muttered as he leaned against the window frame.

"I'll drop you right there in the fucking street, Jim," I called out. "Say it!"

"You're fucking crazy!"

All credit to the man, he had a weighty pair. Floating fifty feet above a busy street, with seemingly nothing keeping him in the air, and he still had the guts to yell at me. I dropped him for a split second, grabbing at him with my power before he'd dropped ten feet, but not before he'd managed to let out a girlish scream.

"John?" Mackenzie called, eyes on the flames in the doorway that were now licking merrily away at the ceiling. "Time to go."

"Spoilsport," I grumbled.

"You going to drop him?" Johnson asked, scratching at his cheek as he followed me back towards the desk.

"Not today," I admitted, and turned to Mackenzie. She gave me a knowing look as I hauled McCourt back in through the window and sent him crashing across the floor.

"I'm not done here, McCourt," I told him as he rose to his knees. "Not with you, and not with Paragon. You sold me out, and now you owe me in ways you can't even begin to fathom. When you've had a bit more time to consider your situation, we'll have a proper chat. Right now, I've got shopping to do."

He stared after us both, eyes flicking from one to the other as the flames parted and we made our way through the charred doorway.

Mackenzie looked back over one shoulder at the man I'd once called my friend. "Good luck with the fire," she said with a sweet smile and glanced up at the ceiling as the flames bloomed and spread.

"Let's get out of here." I suggested. "We still need to sort out a ring."

She rolled her eyes but couldn't fight down the grin. "You still haven't bloody asked me!"

The End

ALSO BY GRAHAM AUSTIN-KING

The Riven Wyrde Saga:
Fae - The Wild Hunt
Reaver – A Riven Wyrde Novella
Fae - The Realm of Twilight
Fae – The Sins of the Wyrde

The Riven Wyrde Saga is also available in an omnibus edition

Faithless

ACKNOWLEDGEMENTS

This has been a hard book to write. It has proven far more challenging than I expected, and I've come close to abandoning it more than once. Setting the book in this world, rather than one of my own imagining, required a level of research that often took me by surprise. My internet search history became seriously dodgy for a while.

As always, I owe a debt of gratitude to my family and friends for putting up with me. My heartfelt thanks also go out to Alicia Wanstall-Burke, Bethan Hindmarch, and Sarah Chorn for their efforts with editing, and helping this all to make sense. Thanks, once more, go out to the ever-amazing Pen Astridge, for her incredible cover art, and to Clare Davidson for internal formatting. I simply couldn't have produced this book without the help of Mike Evans. His assistance with my endless questions, and his patience when I didn't understand which end of the gun was which, have both been invaluable.

Finally, my thanks go out to everyone who follows me, and who reads my books. Slowly, but surely, you are making a dream come true.

ABOUT THE AUTHOR

Graham Austin-King was born in the south of England and weaned on broken swords and half-forgotten spells. A shortage of these forced him to consume fantasy novels at an ever-increasing rate, turning to computers and tabletop gaming between meals.

He experimented with writing at the beginning of an education that meandered through journalism, international relations, and law. To this day he is committed to never allowing those first efforts to reach public eyes.

After roaming across England and Canada he settled once again in the north of England surrounded by a seemingly endless horde of children. The Riven Wyrde Saga is his first completed trilogy and draws on a foundation of literary influences ranging from David Eddings to Dean Koontz.

Visit his blog at http://grahamak.blogspot.co.uk where you can sign up for e-mail updates and be the first to hear about new releases.

Find Graham on Facebook at http://on.fb.me/1pMyWmK He loves to chat with readers.

Follow him on Twitter at www.Twitter.com/Grayaustin

www.ingramcontent.com/pod-product-compliance
Lightning Source LLC
Chambersburg PA
CBHW031216120726
47905CB00002B/358

9 780993 003752